"If you like your crime fiction with a special dark twist, I can't recommend the AJ Bugbee series, by Jan Bogue and Bill Keller, highly enough. The stories have enough suspense to keep you reading all night, and the characters are so real they'll be like old friends by the time you're done. You'll be *dying* to read the next book!"

Steve Hamilton,
two-time Edgar Award-winning author of *Let It Burn*

"A perfect recipe for exploring the dark side would be sitting in front of a roaring fire late at night with a warm drink and this book, listening for the things that go bump in the night. A great mood-setter that keeps you guessing."

Frank Hayes,
author of *Death at the Black Bull*

Also by Janis Bogue and William Keller
Mystic Bridge

MYSTIC SIREN

Janis Bogue and
William Keller

This is a work of fiction. The characters, places and organizations are either fictitious or used fictitiously.

To Zoe and Maisy

ACKNOWLEDGMENTS

Thanks to Steve Hamilton and Frank Hayes, for camaraderie, invaluable advice and for setting the bar so high. Thanks to Sara Keller and Lyn Desautel, for your generosity and your keen eyes. And thanks, Lyn, for being such a wonderful sister and friend. To the real-life Dr. Schwartz, Lisa and Scott, for the use of your names. Jarett, maybe we'll see you in the next book. To Bonnie Merchant and Jean Sorensen, for so many years of friendship and a boost to our confidence, and to many other friends old and new, for your encouragement. To Dad and Mom, for everything.

1

Maggie came out of the dollar store fast, like it was a crime to shop there and she was making her getaway. She dropped the bag with the nail polish into her purse. Then, trying not to be too obvious, she checked out the parking lot to be sure that no one she knew happened to be there, watching.

Straight ahead, a gray car was backed into a space. A guy sat in the driver's seat, with the window down and his arm resting on the door, like he was waiting for someone. He looked a little older, maybe already out of high school. Maybe a new Navy recruit. Their eyes met. He wasn't anyone she knew but he fixed on her, squinting a little, like he thought he recognized her. It made her shiver, even with the warm sun.

She veered left, circling around to her car, keeping her head down. She quick did the key and the seat belt, then backed up fast and zoomed out to the light. "Weirdo," she said. In the minute that she was stuck there in the line of cars, he came up behind her. She heard the hum of the engine and looked in the mirror and there he was. It was like the person he'd been waiting for was her.

She was being stupid, she told herself. Stupid and paranoid. Her mom always said that the movies she watched all the time would scare her, make her imagine things. As if anything was going to actually happen in Mystic or Stonington or even in Groton, which was rougher in some spots, but still quiet, still safe. And on the Saturday of Memorial Day weekend, the official start of summer, when the last day of school, not just for this year but *forever*, was just

3

three weeks away. As if anything was going to happen to anyone you knew, let alone to you, yourself. Crazy paranoia, that's all it was. The light changed, and the cars ahead of her made the left turn toward I-95. She took the other way, straight through, staying on Route 1. The gray car did, too.

Still, that was no big deal. Lots of locals took the back way instead of the interstate, especially on a weekend when the tourists from New York City and Hartford made the traffic so bad. Maybe he even lived somewhere between Groton and Mystic – there were plenty of houses along the way. This is what she told herself, checking the rearview mirror constantly, seeing the car there every time.

They went mile after mile like that. He was always there but never too close, a safe distance back that would make any driver's ed teacher proud. It was hard to get a good look at him. There was nothing special about the car. Plain gray. Not especially dirty or clean or old. It had a little rust, like most cars in Connecticut, from the road salt. That didn't exactly mean he was a stalker.

She reached across the seat, pulled her cell phone from her purse and placed it in the cup holder. Just in case. She drove and he followed. Ordinarily, this would have been a nice drive, with the trees full and green, little square clouds in the sky. But all of that was ruined by the gray car in the mirror, glued to her.

He was still there when she reached Mystic. As they came over Baptist Hill, a couple of kids ran across the road right after her. The gray car had to slam on the brakes. There was an opening, then, and a minivan coming out of High Street slipped in behind her. It filled the mirror, making the gray car disappear.

"Thank you," Maggie said.

She thought of the drawbridge, then, just ahead on Main Street. The perfect thing would be to go across it right before the gate went down, trapping him on this side. You'd have to be lucky – there was no way you could time it that well. She checked the clock in the dashboard. It wasn't going to happen.

She was pushier than usual, merging into the Saturday traffic, and a car got between her and the van. It looked like maybe another one snuck between the van and the gray car. As she went past the shops, she saw lots of people out, like everyone was feeling summer coming on. The drawbridge stayed down and the grates buzzed under the tires, making the whole car a massager for a second. She relaxed a little. She swung left toward the Seaport. Another left put her on Greenmanville Avenue. She checked the mirror. Now the van was behind her, a ways back. No sign of the gray car.

The knot between her shoulders loosened and suddenly she was starving, thinking about the McDonalds not far ahead. Her mom was at Aunt Chris's for the evening, so she'd treat herself. She glanced at the mirror again, checking in with her friend the van. The driver was a woman – no doubt a mom, hauling her kids to a game or the grocery store or something. Maggie smiled, feeling a little bit safer. That's when the gray car edged out into the other lane, just far enough to let the guy see around the van, to see her.

"Fuck!" she said. "This isn't happening!"

In that freaked-out moment of extra clear thinking, she had an idea. She turned up the hill and then into a development – all cute ranch houses with green lawns and bushes hiding the foundations. She'd always liked this place, even imagined living here one day. Today especially it seemed like a perfect little peaceful neighborhood. But what really mattered was that the street was a loop, which made it a good test. First of all, if he turned in. Second of all, if he followed her the whole way around and back out again. Then she would know.

She started down the loop, slowly, watching the mirror. For a second there was just the empty pavement and lawns behind her. Then the gray car, making the turn.

"Shit," she said. "Shit, shit, shit."

She gripped the steering wheel so tight that a fingernail dug into her thumb and she had to actually check for blood. She kept going, looking back and forth like maybe there'd just happen to be a policeman standing in a yard. She'd yell to him, he'd take control.

House after house. Green lawns under the blue sky.

If only Bev Warner still lived in the house just around the bend, Maggie would stop there. Bev would be surprised but glad, would invite her in. They'd get sodas and take over the sun room. Maggie would show Bev the nail polish she just bought, wouldn't even lie and say it was from the drug store. The floor tiles would be warm and they'd take off their socks and try the polish on one nail. They'd talk about school. They'd talk about the party on Stonington Point after the last day of finals. There wouldn't be any mention of the gray car. When Maggie came outside again, that creep would be long gone.

She went past Bev's old house, past one after another, shiny black driveways and big picture windows. Maybe any second the gray car would turn into one of these driveways.

But he didn't. She went all the way around the big circle and so did he. She was coming up to the road now, past the very last house, and she looked in the mirror one more time. He was still there.

There was no doubt now. He would turn onto the road when she did. He would make every turn with her. When she eventually took a side road, he would, too. They would wind down the patchy little lane, through the trees, together, all the way home. Maybe not right then, maybe sometime later when he was sure she was alone, he would come after her. He would break the lock on the flimsy front door or smash a window, and then he would be inside, and there would be nothing she could do to stop him, and he would do whatever he wanted to her, whatever crazy thing was in his crazy fucking brain.

When she reached the main road again, instead of slowing down to check the traffic, she stepped on the gas, holding her breath and thinking that this is how she'd die, getting slammed into by a dump truck or something, because she hadn't looked first.

If only a dump truck would hit him. But there was no dump truck, and the gray car pulled out behind her and then, like he knew he owned her, like he was sure she couldn't do anything about it, he closed the gap.

For a second she looked hard in the mirror. She could see short hair, a thin face. She'd wasn't sure she'd recognize him later if he came to her door in some phony uniform, with a fake name stitched on a patch, and said he was with the electric company and he just needed to look at something real quick.

She picked up the phone, called her mom's cell. No answer. Same with her dad's. Jesus Christ, her parents were the most backward people on the planet. Their cell phones were only for emergencies, they said, so they were always leaving them in the car, or in the house, half the time turned off. Wasn't this an emergency?

Maggie hesitated, the phone in her hand, then dialed 911. But the fucking battery. The thing didn't even get to the last number before it died. She'd told her mom a thousand times that she needed a new phone because this piece of crap didn't hold a charge anymore, but her mom said she'd have to make do for now, that she'd just have to keep it plugged in and be careful with her calls. It wasn't like she was asking for an iPhone, just a phone that actually worked. Why did they have to be so goddamn cheap, why did everything have to be so hard? It was going to get her killed. Couldn't they see that?

She threw the phone into her purse.

Now where? She couldn't go home. She couldn't lead him to where she lived. Without really thinking, she was heading back toward Route 1. That's where the police station was. She wouldn't even have to go inside, just sit in the parking lot. He'd give up, then. He'd find some other girl to chase, to hunt like she was a fucking deer.

He'd be her shadow the entire route, and she'd have to drive the whole way normal speed, like it was any other day, like she was just going to the store, like she was showing him where the store was. She couldn't drive fast because – it was like, you don't run if an animal is chasing you. It only makes them want to chase you more.

She actually checked the speedometer to make sure she wasn't going too fast. That's when she saw it – the yellow light shaped like a gas pump. The light that meant you were almost out. The light that said *Fuck you. You are so screwed.*

Maybe she could still make it to the main road, to a gas station, or a store. But if she ran out of gas, it was over. He wouldn't have to bide his time, come back for her. He could have his fun right now. In the car, or in the woods. Wherever he decided to take her.

She was going to have to lose him somehow, make a turn he didn't expect. She looked around for an escape as she went down a hill. There were only a few houses along this narrow road – big ones, back in the woods.

Tiffanee – no, *Taylor* – lived on this road. Not that Maggie had ever actually been to her house. Not that Taylor would ever invite her. Maggie knew where it was, though. In the winter, with the leaves down, you could kind of see through the trees, see how big it was, get a glint of glass from a window. It was just ahead. The one with the mailbox in the brick post.

She looked at the little yellow shape on the dashboard again. Now or never. She turned fast, barely touching the brake, and zoomed up the silky smooth driveway. When she got to the flat open space by the garage, she checked the mirror. He wasn't behind her. She turned the car off and rolled the window down. She could hear a car driving away. Then she couldn't hear it anymore. Everything was quiet. She closed her eyes and a big breath came out of her.

She opened her eyes again and sat there looking at the big white house with the blue shutters, as perfect and clean as something from a bakery, like you didn't want to live in it, you wanted to eat it.

"Jesus," she said.

She wondered if anyone was home. You couldn't tell from the empty driveway because at a house like this, the cars were always put away, even though they were beautiful new Mercedes or Jaguars or something. Those windows on the second floor would be bedrooms. Maybe one was Taylor's. Maybe Taylor was looking at her right now. Maybe they all were.

What should she do? Get out, walk up that long sidewalk, find the doorbell, tell them what had just happened? Tell Taylor the whole long story?

Not in a million years.

What would they even do? They wouldn't believe her. Probably wouldn't let her in. Taylor's mom might call her mom and there'd be a whole mom drama thing that would end with her in trouble. On Monday, Taylor would tell her friends about that psycho Maggie showing up at her house with some lame story about being chased. How it was all about trying to see Ryan, like her friendship with him counted for anything, now that he was with Taylor. So pathetic.

She let another couple of minutes pass. There were no sounds from the house or the road. Her heart slowed down, finally. She started the car again. The little yellow light was off. Maybe she could make it to the gas station, after all. She backed the car around and rolled down to the mailbox. The road was straight and she could see pretty far. There was only one other driveway nearby and he wasn't in it. A couple of cars went past. Just normal, everyday traffic. No one chasing, no one running away.

She looked up the driveway in the rearview mirror. Maybe she should go back, ring the bell, explain to them what had happened. Warn them about the guy she had led to their house. She put the gearshift on R.

But then she thought, it's actually lucky that she'd led the guy here. Sort of lucky smart. She had him all confused, now. Obviously no one driving this shitbox, with the dented doors and the spots of red primer, would live in that house.

Maybe he'd think she was the maid or something. A poor relative.

God, it was a nice house. Big and white and safe. A house like that would definitely have an alarm system. He'd know that. He wouldn't risk it. Even if he did, and he saw Taylor... She didn't look anything like her – too thin, too tall, her hair too straight. If he'd picked out Maggie, then Taylor wasn't his type.

Yeah, right. Taylor was every guy's type.

She put the car in drive and pulled out onto the road. The yellow light didn't even come back on until she was on top of the hill. She went slow and the car kept moving. She made the green light on Route 1 and coasted up to the first pump just as the engine started to sputter.

Then it took forever to get home. When she finally turned in past the faded sign for Dusty's Trailer Park, she was – like for the first time – actually happy to be there. She parked on the little patch of hard dirt that was their driveway and went in.

Her mom was watching TV. "Did you get your nail polish?"

"Yeah." She held up the bag. There was some kind of howling noise on the TV. "What are you watching?"

"Did you hear about this? They've got a bunch of wolf-dogs, some kind of cross-breed, running around Pachaug. They don't know where they're coming from. I hope you kids weren't planning on going up there anytime soon."

Maggie's mom always said *you kids*, even though it was just her and Olivia, since Bev moved and Ryan started going out with Taylor.

There was more howling from the TV.

"I hope they round them up," her mom said.

Maggie thought about telling her mom what had just happened, but since she was already worrying about the wolf-dogs, it probably wasn't a good time. When her mom had too much to worry about, she made life miserable for everyone else. "I'm going to go try the polish," Maggie said.

"Okay. You can do it right here if you're careful." Her mom finally took her eyes off the TV and held out the remote. "You can pick the channel."

"That's okay. I don't want to get any on the couch. I'll show you when I'm done." Maggie grabbed a soda from the fridge and went to her room. She wanted to call Olivia, tell her the whole story, but she knew Olivia was with her dad all weekend. She sat on the bed, opened up a spiral notebook for school and did her nails over it. She focused on applying the shiny color just right, and not thinking about the guy in the gray car. There was another howl from the TV in the living room. Maggie looked up, like the wolf-dog thing, whatever it was, might be coming through the door. "Predators everywhere," she said.

2

A little after two a.m. in a pitch black room, AJ Bugbee sat up suddenly in bed with his eyes wide open. He blinked, breathing fast, waiting for his pupils to adjust. A hand reached out from behind him and grabbed his wrist.

"What is it? Did you hear something?" Claire propped herself up on her elbow.

"No. It's okay. I just had a bad dream."

"Oh." Claire lowered herself again. "Are you all right?"

"Yeah." He stayed sitting up. "I haven't had a dream like that in a long time."

"You mean, about a ghost?"

"You should go back to sleep."

"Did you set the house alarm?" Claire said after a while.

"It's on. I set it before I came upstairs. Don't worry."

She gave his arm a squeeze. AJ lay back into the pillow. Taking measured breaths, he stared up at the ceiling. Claire turned on her side and pushed up against him. She fell asleep. AJ remained on his back, looking up at the ceiling.

When he next checked the dotted blue face of the clock, almost an hour had passed. He edged away from Claire, then slid his legs off the side of the bed. He reached for the end table next to him, found a cell phone. He thumbed a button on the face and it lit up. With his other hand, he reached behind him for his pillow. He tucked it under his arm.

Holding the phone in front of him like a flashlight, he moved to a window. When he pulled the curtains aside, he saw only himself, a gray figure in the glass. He let the phone go dark. Buck, the greyhound, got up from his bed and joined him at the window. AJ patted the dog's head, thin and hard as a cane handle. With the phone shining in front of him again, AJ crossed the room, the dog following. AJ pointed at the dog bed and snapped his fingers softly once. Buck returned to his bed, groaning. AJ went down the long hallway. After hesitating at the top of the stairs, as if studying the turn that made wedges of the treads, he descended cautiously, testing with his toes.

He went to the front door, tried the lock. When he checked the panel for the security system, he saw the pinpoint green light that meant it was armed. He turned toward the back of the house. His shoulder brushed the blueprint that had hung there for almost a year, promising changes – straightening the front stairs, closing the back ones, opening up the attic – that were intended to smooth the knife-like memory of what had happened there. In the doorway to the kitchen, he paused, quieting his breath, listening. A year ago, it had been the soft metallic tapping of a bottle cap bouncing across the tile. That was the sound that had changed everything.

He didn't hear a bottle cap, or anything else.

In the living room, he dropped his pillow on the sofa. He lay down under the big dark window. He didn't try deep breathing, or rhythmic counting, or imagining a peaceful place. He didn't even close his eyes. He just lay there, waiting for the earth to turn and the sun to come up.

From outside, rising and falling as it raced down some distant, winding, country road, came the wail of a siren. AJ sat up and looked out the window. Another siren mixed with the first. Then one more, from another direction. AJ peered into the darkness until the sound was gone.

***

It was a warm morning – full-blown summer on the first day of June – so he took his coffee out to the screened-in porch. He was sitting there, still wearing his boxers and T-shirt, when Claire came downstairs.

"You're up early," he said. "Want some coffee?"

"In a minute." She came over to him, kissed him. She was dressed for bed, too, in soft shorts and a pastel top. Her blonde hair had been brushed only by her fingers. "How are you? Did you have any more bad dreams?"

"No more sleep, so no more bad dreams."

"I'm sorry. You must be exhausted. It's your day off – maybe you can nap later, get caught up."

"I'll be all right."

"What was the dream about? Were you back in Bridgeport?"

"No, I was here in Stonington. The Road Church cemetery, actually – the one on Flanders Road."

"That's different. Where did that come from?"

"Who knows?" AJ took a sip of his coffee. "I hit a deer. In the dream, I mean. Right in front of the cemetery."

Claire sat down across from him, studied him for a moment.

He looked past her toward the trees. "What are you doing today?" he said. "It's going to be a nice one."

"I'll be upstairs writing all morning," she said.

"You're not going to scare yourself again, I hope." His eyes came back to her and he smiled.

"Maybe. But you'll be here, and Buck will keep me company, so... I promise you, my next book will be all about bunnies and butterflies."

"Now *I'm* scared."

In the trees behind the house, a woodpecker drilled a tree, making a sound somewhere between music and Morse code.

"Are you going to the market this afternoon?" Claire said.

"Yeah, probably. I told my dad he really needs to just hire someone, but he's afraid to – doesn't want to have to let them go if the economy goes south again."

"I wish he would. Hire someone, I mean. You're busy enough with the P.D."

AJ's cell phone, which was on the table in front of him, buzzed. He picked it up. "Hey, Chief. Yeah." He turned away. "Yeah. I can be there in a few minutes." He put the phone down.

Claire reached across the table. "What is it?"

"There was a fire last night – one of those new houses on Whitfield Road. Chief says he needs me to take a look."

"Take a look? So it isn't just a fire – it's a crime scene. A murder scene."

"Yes." AJ sat back.

"What are you thinking?"

"We've had a long, quiet stretch." He pushed the hair back from his forehead. "I guess it couldn't last forever."

"I wish it could," Claire said. "I wish that you didn't have to go over there. I know it's your job, and I know Chief Brown is your friend, but I wish he didn't ask this of you."

"I haven't had an experience in a long time. I'm not even sure..."

"What? Are you doubting your ability? Can you lose something like that? It would be like losing your hearing or your sense of smell."

"People lose their hearing, or their sense of smell."

"Not without some cause – an illness, or a brain tumor or something."

"There's a cheery thought."

Claire laughed. "Bad example. Maybe you've just gotten better at blocking it out, or controlling it."

"Maybe."

"I guess the question is, if your ability is blocked, do you really want to unblock it? If it just made you unhappy?"

AJ looked out at the trees again. "It's about the victim, and the victim's family. Helping them."

"Okay. Then maybe you just need to open your mind." Claire spread her arms wide.

"So what are you saying? Magic mushrooms?"

"I just mean relax. Think positive thoughts."

"Uh huh." AJ smiled at her. "I think I can, I think I can," he said, in rhythm.

"There you go."

***

In uniform but driving his Jeep, AJ bounced down Pequot Trail. He passed the Road Church, a good New England place of worship, upright and white on its stone foundation, the front with its modest steeple facing away as if the church were turning its back on the world. Just beyond it, he took the left onto Flanders Road. By the cemetery, he braked suddenly, then pulled onto the shoulder.

In front of him was a large, dead doe. It lay on a narrow strip of bright, neatly clipped grass, looking unharmed, as if it were on display. Broken glass glittered on the asphalt. He got out, picked up the larger pieces. Back in the Jeep, he dropped the glass into the glove compartment. He stared out the window at the cemetery, a rectangle bordered by trees and stone walls. There were maybe two hundred headstones, the oldest mottled and smoothed, only the carved winged skulls still clear.

A few minutes later, he turned into an inky black driveway. Several police cars were parked on the lawn, and beyond them, fire trucks and an ambulance. The big, white house with the blue shutters looked almost unscathed from the outside, except that soot made a dark collar around an empty window frame on the first floor, and the clapboard above it was marbled and deformed, the eaves black.

AJ edged the Jeep into the woods, out of the way. Chief Brown was on the other side of the yellow tape, talking to a firefighter in full turnout gear. He noticed AJ, slipped his large frame under the tape, and met AJ as he was just closing his door.

"Jesus, Chief, what happened?" AJ said.

"It's bad. Looks like somebody killed a teenage girl inside, then set the house on fire."

"What about the parents? Where are they?"

"In Boston for a wedding. They're on the way back right now."

"Who called it in?" AJ said.

"The boyfriend. Claims the house was on fire when he got here, which was around 2:30 a.m. He went inside, anyway, and managed to get to her, but she was already dead. Ended up with some bad burns for his trouble."

"Any chance he did it? Killed the girl and started the fire?"

"He says he was at a party right before he came over here. If we nail the times down, and his story checks out, we can probably take him off the list."

"Anyone else on the list?"

The chief rubbed his smooth scalp. "Not yet."

They were quiet for a while, watching the activity around the house. A fireman retrieved a fat hose that snaked across the lawn into the front door.

"How'd she die, Chief?"

"We'll have to see what the doc says. It looks like you could take your pick. There was a pretty good gash on the back of her head and a scarf around her neck, too. Not to mention the smoke inhalation, if she was still breathing."

"Rape?"

"No sign of it. She was fully clothed. We'll see what the medical examiner has to say. We're still waiting on him."

AJ watched another fireman enter the house. "Now may not be the best time for me to be looking around, Chief. There's a crowd here."

"I know. But at least stick your head in. I just want to know if there's something here. You can come back later for the conversation."

"Okay, but what's my reason for going inside? In case anyone asks? Who's in there, Mike?"

"Mike and the EMTs, probably a few firefighters. Just say that I asked you to help the firefighters clear out with a minimum of damage."

"All right." AJ didn't move. "Where was she?"

"Bedroom, upstairs."

AJ started toward the house.

"Taylor," the chief said. "Taylor Fraser. That's the girl's name."

AJ looked toward the missing window. "I'll see what there is to see. For her sake, I hope she's long gone."

3

Inside, the smell of burned wood and wet drywall was overpowering. The smoke-blackened ceiling was like a low cloud overhead. A charred bannister led up the stairs. Where she would be.

Putting off that meeting, AJ followed a slack fire hose across the tile, over a pile of ash, to a doorway. This was where it had started, the source of the fire and smoke. It was still recognizable as a living room, spacious and well appointed. But the color scheme was surreal – black. Black everywhere. The sofa looked as if it had been burned, turned inside out, then burned again. At one end of it was a pile of chunky ash that had been a table and a lamp. A skewed rectangle – picture frame? flat screen television? – leaned across a wall.

A fireman came in the front door, his heavy boots thudding on the tile. "Jesus, what a mess," he said.

"Sure is."

The fireman was thin and very young. The yellow jacket hung off of him like a hand-me-down Halloween costume. "Would have been a lot worse if the trailer worked."

"What do you mean?"

"See that line of ash going back across the hallway?" He pointed behind him. "Something was laid out there to set the bannister on fire, then carry the fire upstairs. We got here before it made it all the way."

AJ nodded.

"You been up there yet?" the fireman said.

"No."

"You ever seen a dead body before?"

AJ really looked at the fireman's eyes this time. There was am emptiness in them, as if he had fled this scene a long time ago.

"I was the first one up there," the fireman said. "I wanted to be a hero. This is only my third fire, but I've had extra training, more than some of the old guys. I thought I was ready, but..." He reached down for the hose. "They're just waiting for the medical examiner, then they'll take her. If you want to see her, you'd better go."

AJ headed up the stairs. He stayed close to the wall, away from the blackened wood. As he climbed, he heard voices. Subdued, somber. He followed the sound to a teenage girl's room. He paused in the doorway, took a deep breath. Then he stepped inside.

The room was neat and decorated – a fuchsia bedspread matched by a pillow and the jacket on a stuffed bear – but the smoke had found this place, too, smeared the walls with gray, tainted the lacy curtains, collected on the dresser. The girl was on the floor in the center of the room, her skin like wax, her eyes pointed toward the ceiling and her hair fanned out around her head, fixed in a pool of blood.

An officer and two EMTs stood beside the body. AJ's gaze traveled to each corner of the room. One of the men turned and seemed to watch him, as if wondering what he was searching for, but no other eyes looked back at him. AJ let the breath he'd been holding in escape between his teeth. He retreated into the hall, made a quick tour. The bedroom above the living room had been lightly scorched, but otherwise, there was no sign that anything unusual had happened in this house – except for the thick, charred smell, which was everywhere. He went downstairs, looped around into the dining room, then the kitchen, a sitting room with a stone fireplace, and an office with a huge, modern desk on which sat a pair of large computer monitors. Everything was still and solid.

He went out the front door. The chief left a conversation with someone from the fire department and led AJ back to the driveway.

"Well?" the chief said.

"Sorry. Nothing."

"It could be just too early. She could still show."

"Maybe," AJ said. "I can't be sure."

"Okay. Well, if there's a chance... I'd like you to try again when you have the place to yourself. Tonight. By then, everyone else will have cleared out."

AJ looked over the chief's shoulder without saying anything. Detective Wheeler was crossing the lawn toward them.

"Hey, AJ," Wheeler said. He was a tall, angular man, middle-aged, his pale cheeks dry despite the damp ocean air. "The door around back's still locked. Whoever did this just walked in the front door. Or was let in."

"I'm going to talk to the girl's parents in a little bit," the chief said. He checked his watch.

"Do you want me to cover that, Chief?" Wheeler said.

"Mr. Fraser was pretty insistent that he speak to me. Don't worry, Sam, I still remember what questions need to be asked."

"Okay. I'll start with the boyfriend." Wheeler looked at AJ. "You were on the high school detail when Janson was out. You know the kids."

"I was on campus a couple times. I wouldn't say I know them."

"Well, you're a familiar face and you're closer to their age. That and the uniform..."

"Wheeler's right," the chief said. "Why don't you go with him."

"Good." Wheeler dropped a notepad into the pocket of his sport coat. "I'll meet you back at the station, AJ. We'll go from there." He walked back up the driveway.

The chief watched Wheeler climb into his car. "The truth is, teenagers terrify him. He couldn't deal with his own, let alone the general population. It is a good idea, you going along with him. The more you know about the girl, the easier it will be for you to make contact with her."

AJ went around his Jeep and opened the door, then looked over the roof. "I passed the scene of an accident on the way here. Someone hit a deer. There was glass on the road, looks like from a headlight."

"They'll send a town truck around."

"I had this weird feeling about it... I don't know."

"Weird how?"

"Like it was more than just another dead deer," AJ said. "I mean, it could be related to what happened here. Someone fleeing the scene."

"Okay. See if anyone called it in. Pick up that glass if you can. We might want to match it to a headlight."

"I have the glass."

"Okay. When you get to the station, give it to Wheeler."

AJ climbed into the Jeep.

The chief moved close and motioned for AJ to roll down the passenger window. "You're okay with coming here tonight, right?"

"Sure, yeah."

"Do you need a partner?"

"What?"

"Tonight. Do you need someone with you? Maybe I should come along."

"Thanks, but no, it's probably better if I go alone." AJ dragged his seat belt across. He waved and the chief pulled back.

"And I have a feeling that's what I'll be," AJ said. "Alone."

4

AJ leaned across the counter. "Hey, Dee."

On the other side, the dispatcher, a heavyset woman with a bad dye job and a bright scarf, tapped on a keyboard. "Hi, AJ. Didn't think you were coming in today. The chief called you in?"

"Yeah. Did anyone report hitting a deer this morning? Flanders Road? It would have been sometime after midnight, I think."

"I came on at six, so I'll have to check the log. I can tell you Annie Davis called about that deer. By the Road Church cemetery, right? That was how my day started. Said she's got a group coming down from Pomfret to tour the cemetery and if we don't get someone out there to clean it up, she'll drag it into the middle of the road."

"I wouldn't doubt it. Did you call for the clean-up?"

"Oh, yeah." She watched the computer screen. "I don't see anything about a deer getting hit before that. That time of night, whoever it was may have had a few drinks. They might have been afraid to report it."

"You're right."

Wheeler was in the doorway behind him. "Hey, you ready to go?"

"Sure. Thanks, Dee."

AJ and Wheeler went out into the parking lot.

"What were you talking to Dee about?" Wheeler said.

"Nothing, probably." AJ explained about the dead deer by the cemetery and his idea that Taylor's killer might have run into it fleeing the scene. "I have some glass, probably from the headlight, in my Jeep. The chief said to give it to you."

"Okay, let's get it." Wheeler changed course. He put his hand on AJ's shoulder. "You're wasting your talents on patrol, my friend."

"You have no idea."

***

They drove past the Civil War monument, a granite soldier in a tight traffic circle, into the neighborhood that bordered on the seaport museum. The place they were looking for had one of the plaques used for historic houses, with a date in the 1800s and a blue anchor, next to the front door. The cruiser just fit between the hedges that lined the driveway.

"I could never live in one of those old places," Wheeler said, as he squeezed past the leafy wall.

"Because it might be haunted," AJ said, shaking his head.

"What? No. They're way too much work."

The door swung open. The woman on the other side wore a crisp, yellow top, but there were circles under her eyes. After the introductions, she led them up a narrow staircase, made more narrow by framed family photos hanging on the wall.

"Ryan's very upset," she said, when they were at the top.

The ceiling was just above the men's heads, and the walls seemed just far enough apart for their shoulders.

"We just want to ask a few questions," Wheeler said.

She looked doubtful but led them to a door, knocked, then opened it.

Ryan was in bed, watching something on his laptop. There were bandages all up and down one arm.

"Ryan, can you talk to these policemen?" the woman said. "Are you up to it?"

"Yes, Mom," he said.

She moved out of the way. When Wheeler and AJ stepped inside, the room was full.

"Hi. I'm Detective Wheeler. This is Officer Bugbee."

The boy closed the computer. "Hi." He had a boy's version of his mother's features. He had recently been crying.

"How are you doing?" Wheeler said. "Looks like you have some burns."

"I just got back from the emergency room. Second degree, they said. Not too bad."

Wheeler stood there stiffly for a moment while the boy and AJ waited for him to continue. There was a buzzing sound. The boy plucked a phone from the bedcovers.

"So is the news already out?" AJ said.

Ryan looked at the phone. "Yeah. A couple of kids know people on the fire department. But I haven't actually talked to anyone."

"We just need to ask you a few questions," Wheeler said.

From behind them, Ryan's mom said, "Are you sure you feel up to this, Ryan?"

"I'm fine, Mom."

"We'll try to keep it short," Wheeler said. "Taylor was your girlfriend?"

"Yes. We've been going out for – since Christmas break." The boy looked back and forth between the two men. It was as if each time he refocused his eyes, his resolve got weaker. His blank expression slowly collapsed.

"Oh, honey." The mother pushed her way between the cops and sat on the bed.

"Mom, God," Ryan said.

She turned to Wheeler. "Do you really need to do this now? He's just so upset."

She reached for her son's hand.

He pulled away. "Can you just go downstairs, please?"

The woman sighed, stood up and left the room.

"Why don't you tell us about last night?" Wheeler said. "You were at a party?"

"Yeah," Ryan said. "At Jake Reynold's house. Then I went to Taylor's."

"What time did you arrive at Taylor's house?"

"Two-thirty, maybe three."

"Why so late?"

"The party was for the soccer team. I had to be there. Then I just lost track of time."

"Was Taylor upset that you stayed at the party so long?" AJ said.

Ryan nodded. "Yeah, kind of."

"Did you talk to her while you were there?" AJ said. "Maybe you texted?"

"We talked a couple of times."

"Can you tell us when that was?" Wheeler said.

23

Ryan checked his phone. "10:12 and 12:30."

"Okay." Wheeler made a couple of notes on his pad. "Was she alone?"

"Yeah," Ryan said.

"Her parents were out of town?"

"Yes," Ryan said. His face suddenly flushed.

"Why don't you tell us about what happened when you arrived at the Fraser house," Wheeler said.

"I turned in the driveway. I could already see the fire. These flames were coming right out of the living room window. I called 911 right away, while I was running to the door. They told me not to go in, but Taylor was in there. I couldn't just stand outside and watch the house burn down with her in it, so I went inside."

"What did you do next?"

"It was really smoky. I yelled for Taylor but she didn't answer. The 911 operator said she was sure Taylor had already gotten out of the house and that I should, too."

"Did you?"

"No. I went upstairs to look for her."

"That's how you got those burns?"

"Maybe. The railing was on fire, but I think I avoided it. It was crazy."

"So you made it upstairs. Then what happened?"

"I went to her room." The boy pressed his eyes closed for a second but the tears came, anyway.

"What did you see?"

"Taylor. I saw Taylor on the floor."

"What did you do after you saw her?"

"I left."

"You didn't try to help her?" Wheeler said.

"She was dead." Ryan was crying openly now.

"You didn't touch her? You didn't try to revive her? How did you know she was dead?"

"Did you see her? The blood, her eyes and that thing around her neck." He held his fists to his throat. "I mean, Jesus, she was dead! Wasn't she? I left her there because I thought she was dead!" A look of horror came over his face. "Oh, God!"

"Ryan." AJ held up his hand. "She was gone. You couldn't have helped her."

Wheeler gave the boy a moment, then asked, "So you went back downstairs?"

"I don't really remember. I was completely freaked out. I must have run out of there. I think that's when I got the burns."

"Were you on the phone with 911 the whole time?" AJ said.

"No," Ryan said. "I hung up before I went upstairs, when they told me to just wait outside. Does it matter?"

Wheeler made another note on his pad. "Can you think of anyone who would have wanted to harm Taylor? Anyone at school, or anyone at all?"

"No. No."

Wheeler tapped his notepad, then flipped a page. "That party you were at, for the soccer team – can you give me some names of the people you were with?"

"Sure. I was with Sean Moye, Dick Mazza, Sandy Grenier – "

"Here," Wheeler said, handing the pad and pencil to Ryan.

For a while the only sound was the scratching of Ryan writing the names.

"Okay, that's fine," Wheeler said, taking the pad again. "I think we're done for now." He handed Ryan his card. "In case you remember anything more."

"Thanks, Ryan," AJ said. He stepped into the hall.

"One last thing," Wheeler said. "When you went into the house – how did you get in?"

Ryan looked confused. "The front door."

"Do you have a key?"

"No. It was unlocked. She left it unlocked for me."

"A teenage girl alone at night in a secluded house and she leaves the door unlocked?"

"Taylor wasn't afraid of anything."

"Okay."

Ryan's mom was standing in the hallway.

"He did fine, Mrs. Hardy," AJ said.

She didn't respond, other than to lead them downstairs.

"I gave Ryan my card," Wheeler said when they were at the bottom. "Make sure and have him call if he remembers anything that he feels is important."

"I will."

AJ and Wheeler went outside, then worked their way past the

hedge again and into the car.

"You think I was too hard on him," Wheeler said as they headed toward Route 1.

"No."

"I know the kids here aren't gang bangers like you had in Bridgeport, but they're not all innocent angels, either."

"I know. Don't forget I graduated with the Button brothers."

"Oh, Christ, those two. The twin terrors."

"Yeah."

They crossed a narrow inlet, and to their right, the train tracks crossed it, too. Beyond the tracks there was a marina, white boats blurred by lingering fog.

"So what do you think about Ryan?" Wheeler said.

"He doesn't seem like a murderer, if that's what you mean. But I don't think he was totally straight with us, either."

"Okay. What in particular?"

"The part about waiting until 2:30 to go to Taylor's."

"Yeah," Wheeler said. "When I was his age, if my girlfriend's parents were away – hell, it wouldn't have mattered if I was team captain, class president, or king of the whole damn school. I would have been up that driveway before the parents were across the town line. Why'd he leave her there alone until almost dawn?"

AJ glanced left as they passed the Bay Market, where his parents would be hard at work getting ready for the lunch rush, expecting him to show up before too long.

"We need to find out what really went on before he finally showed up at Taylor's," Wheeler said.

"You know the kids are all talking, right? It'll be hard to get to any of them before they've had a chance to compare notes."

"I know," Wheeler said. "I want to stop at the high school and get a list of all the kids on the soccer team. Maybe take a look at a team photo if they've got one."

"I think there's a picture outside the office. Are you planning to talk to the whole team?"

"No, but I would like to know who wasn't part of the captain's crowd. The odd man out may be more inclined to give us the straight scoop on Ryan."

"You'll be able to find the odd man out by looking at the picture?"

"And talking to the coach."

"But would those kids – the ones not tight with Ryan – have been at the party?"

Wheeler shifted in his seat. "I always went to the parties. I was usually the only one who stayed sober, the only one who could remember who did what, and with who."

"Soccer?"

"Football. Defensive end." Wheeler paused. "I know I don't look like it now. Actually, I didn't then, either."

"I bet you were all about speed."

"Exactly."

They continued on to the station. When they went through the locked inner door, there was a sudden quiet.

"Who died?" Wheeler said. He noticed the eyes turning toward him. "Jesus, did someone die?"

The chief came out of his office. "AJ, Claire's fine."

"What do you mean, Claire's fine?"

Dee approached from the other direction. "She called a little while ago. There were a couple of guys banging on the doors."

"What guys?" AJ punched buttons on his cell phone.

"She's fine, AJ," the chief said. "Embarrassed, but fine. I got on the line and talked to her until Janson got there. He was at the Fraser house, so it was maybe five minutes."

"Who the hell were they?"

"Just someone pushing religious pamphlets, I guess."

AJ swore under his breath. "They can't read? They didn't see the signs -- *No Trespassing, Private Drive, No Solicitation*?"

"Did Janson cite them?" Wheeler said.

"AJ, you should just head home," the chief said.

"What about the interviews?" He looked at Wheeler.

"We'll sort that out," the chief said.

AJ stood for a moment without saying anything. "Okay. Thanks." He headed toward the door.

"AJ," the chief said, "make sure she knows she did the right thing."

When AJ arrived, the big, brown face of the house, and the spent daffodils along the foundation, were in shadow. "Claire?" he said as soon as he was inside. He went toward the kitchen.

She was there, at the microwave. "Hey," she said, an apology in her voice.

"Are you okay?"

"I guess you talked to the chief."

"Yeah. Damn. Do those people read?"

She backed up to the counter. "I don't want to be a wimp. But they just wouldn't stop. They rang the doorbell, then they banged on the door. When I didn't answer, one of them came back here and banged on this door." She gestured toward the porch.

"They actually came into the porch?"

"Yes! I guess I was stupid to panic. I'm so sorry, AJ."

"You don't need to feel stupid. With all of the signs we have up, they shouldn't have even come down the driveway. You did the right thing. The chief said to be sure to tell you that."

"Dee put me through to him. He was so nice. They don't think I'm crazy down there?"

"No. Absolutely not."

The microwave beeped and went dark. Claire opened the door and took out a mug. She dunked a tea bag a couple of times.

"You know you could have called me," AJ said.

"You're in the middle of a murder investigation. I didn't want you to feel like you had to leave," Claire said. "Of course, that's the way it turned out, anyway."

"I just feel bad that, once again, I wasn't around. It's good that you called the station. I was in Mystic. Janson was much closer. But I'm here now."

"I don't want you to feel like you have to baby sit me."

"I don't feel that way at all. Between the police department and the fish market, I've left you alone a lot. You've been doing great here on your own – better than anyone should expect. Now that we've had another murder, the whole town's going to be on edge, not just you."

She put the mug down and AJ wrapped his arms around her.

"You know what would probably help?" AJ said.

"If we did this for a few hours?"

"Actually, I was thinking food."

Claire shook her head, smiling. "So, that's what you really came home for."

"I am hungry."

From outside, there was the thud of a car door.

"That must be Melody," Claire said, looking sheepish. "I called her, too."

"Good. She always cheers you up."

AJ opened the front door for Melody, a woman a few years older than AJ, with big, honest eyes and chop sticks that held up her dark hair.

"Hi, AJ," she said. "How's she doing?"

"Okay. Better, now that you're here."

"Melody to the rescue, again," Claire said, coming out of the kitchen. "You've been my guardian angel since the day I moved here."

"Before that. That first morning you showed up at the Honey B, I stopped you from ordering the eggs Benedict."

"That was my first day of real house hunting. I was about to come to see this place."

"Yep, that's right."

It was quiet then, and the idea that a true guardian angel might have warned Claire against buying the big, empty house with the violent past, might have saved her from all that followed, seemed to hang in the air.

"Thanks so much for coming over," Claire said.

"Well, I'm sorry it happened, but it's good to see you. I've been wanting to do a girls' night. In fact, Jack just called me and said he's staying in Manhattan tonight. So I was wondering if I could talk you into staying at my house. We can go over the research I did for you, you can help me pick some colors... What do you say?"

Claire looked at AJ.

"You should go," he said. "The chief wants me to work tonight."

"You're going back over there," Melody said. "To the crime scene."

AJ nodded.

"The chief has you on special duty, huh?" Melody said. "You should take the Daves. They could bring their gear, help you out. But then, you don't need any gear, do you?"

AJ's lips made a flat smile. "I guess I'm about to find out."

29

5

The phone in the kitchen woke her up. *Ring!* Her mother kept the volume on max, like they had a huge house, when really even if you got as far away as you could, the phone was still practically in your ear. *Ring!* Usually she would have slept for another couple of hours at least. Sleeping in was one of her talents. *Ring!* The sleep of the innocent, her mother always said, sarcastically.

She was on the floor, wedged between the wall and the bed, because Olivia had slept over. Olivia's hand was hanging off the mattress, just above her face. Even after the third ring, Olivia didn't budge, like she was dead up there.

The ringing stopped. Her mom had picked up. At first Maggie couldn't make out the words, but there was something in her mom's voice...

"Oh, my God!" her mom said, loud.

There was a long pause.

"She was here, all night."

Was she talking to Olivia's mom?

"Yes, I'm sure. What are you implying?"

Olivia was in trouble for something. But they hadn't gone anywhere or done anything last night.

"How dare you, Helena."

Helena? Taylor's mom? Why was she talking to Taylor's mom? Maggie felt something clench inside her.

The front door slapped closed – the thing was too flimsy to really slam – and that was enough to finally wake Olivia up. She swung her feet off the mattress. Maggie had to dodge out of the way.

"Sorry!" Olivia said.

"Not your fault. This room's bullshit." Maggie got up and opened the window a crack.

"What are you doing?"

"Wait."

Maggie's mom was outside, pacing in the little strip of lawn out front. She pulled the phone away from her ear and jabbed at it.

"What's going on?" Olivia said. Just then, her phone buzzed on the end table. She grabbed it. "Holy shit!"

"What?" Maggie kept watching her mom.

"Taylor Fraser's dead."

"What?" Maggie turned around. The thing inside her squeezed tight.

"She's dead." Olivia was reading another text.

"What do you mean?"

"Jesus, murdered," Olivia said.

"Murdered? What the hell? Are you sure?"

She didn't really have to pretend to be shocked, even though she'd thought about this. More like fantasized. She'd tell the cops her story about the gray car, and they'd arrest the psycho serial killer who was on a multi-state spree. Or Taylor was the hero, facing the guy down, bullying him like she did, coming at him and at him until he was huddled up on the floor, bawling. Or *he* was the hero. He found his way back to Taylor's house, did his work, and then there was one less heinous bitch in the world. Maggie had thought about all those things. But they weren't really going to happen.

There was the front door again. Maggie's mom came thumping down the hall. She didn't knock, just pushed the door open and stood there for a second, thin as a cigarette in her favorite leggings, her face twitching. "You've heard about Tiffanee," she said, mixing up the name, a mistake they never made anymore, especially in front of people. She was rattled, too.

"You mean Taylor?" Maggie said. "Yeah, Olivia got a text. What happened?"

"There was a fire."

Olivia held up her cell phone. "My cousin said she was murdered. My uncle is an EMT. He was there."

"She was murdered," her mom said. " And the house was set on fire."

Maggie stood there looking at her mom. It was a fight just to get a normal breath.

Olivia's phone chirped – a call this time. "Hi," she said. "Yeah. I know. No. I haven't even had breakfast yet. Mom! Okay. Okay. Jesus Christ." She let the phone drop. "My mom's freaking out. She wants me home."

"I'll take you," Maggie said. She and Olivia got dressed. When they went outside, Maggie's mom was sitting on the front step, looking down the road between the trailers.

"Maggie?" her mom called after them, when they were already at the car.

"What?" Maggie jangled her keys, looking at her mom's boney face, terrified for that second at what her mom might say.

"Nothing. Just come straight home."

"I will."

Maggie turned the car around and went down the lane.

"Pretty damn scary, huh?" Olivia said. "Right here in Stonington. And someone we know."

"Did your cousin say if they caught the guy?"

"No. Let me text her."

Maggie stopped at the paved road. She couldn't help looking for that gray car. She had mostly stopped doing that the last couple of days, but now...

Olivia was busy with her phone while Maggie drove. Finally she looked up. "Where are you going?"

"I want to drive by Taylor's."

"That's kind of creepy, isn't it?"

"I just want to see it. Don't you?"

"I guess, maybe. Is the house even still there, after the fire?" Olivia's phone buzzed again. She opened the message. "Oh wow, guess who found her."

"I don't know, her mom?"

"No, her parents were gone. It was Ryan."

Maggie almost swerved off the road. *Ryan?*

"You know," Olivia said, when the car was back under control, "the killer is usually a guy the girl knows. A lot of times it's the boyfriend."

Maggie gave her a look. "No way it was Ryan. He couldn't do that to anybody, not even Taylor."

"I know, it wasn't Ryan," Olivia said. "Whoever it was, they'll catch him eventually. Fingerprints or hair or fibers from his clothes or something."

Maggie shook her head. "Maybe on television, but I don't think it's like that in real life," she said. What she wanted to say was, *I think it might have been a creep in a gray car who hangs out in the parking lot of the dollar store in Groton.* But she couldn't say that, even to Olivia.

The last part of the route was the same as the one she'd taken the week before – the turn, then down the little hill. Taylor's house on the right, behind the trees. She tapped the brakes. "It's hard to see," she said, ducking down to get a better view.

"There's a cop in the driveway," Olivia said.

"Looks like some black, but that's all. The fireman must have gotten there right away."

Then they were past it.

Olivia turned around. "So weird. Taylor was murdered right up there. She was in her house, feeling totally safe, and then... Who could do that?" Olivia faced front again. She checked her phone. "I still think it was someone she knew," she said. Like she was reminding herself.

Maggie didn't say anything this time. Maybe Olivia was right. Which would mean that there was no point in telling anyone about the creep in the gray car. But she had something new to worry about. When the cops started looking at kids that Taylor knew, how long would it be before they connected the dots from Taylor Fraser all the way back to Tiffanee Burns and her tubby little friend named Magda?

6

Over the phone, the chief told AJ to come in at the end of the day, when Wheeler was due back. In the meantime, he should rest up for a long night. Instead, AJ went to the Bay Market, the small seafood place that his parents had run for most of their adult lives, doing a steady business in lobster rolls and fried clams and french fries, which customers took home or ate outside on picnic tables. AJ had been slated to put in a half day there, but that was before the early morning summons from the chief, the burned-out living room and the girl lying on her bedroom floor in a pool of her own blood.

His father, George, was behind the counter, his ample chest and belly swelling a stained apron. "Hey, there you are," he said, the *r*s soft and slow.

"Hi, Dad."

"You just missed your buddies."

"I think I'm going to see them later."

"Good, good."

"How's it been? Busy?"

"We had a good lunch rush, yeah."

"I don't have to be back to the station for a while," AJ said, "You have something for me to do? What were the Daves doing?"

"Okay, c'mon," George said. "Since you're here, you can shuck a few clams."

His mother, June, in a cap and apron, pushed her way through the plastic strips that served as a door to the back of the place. "Hi, AJ," she said, without looking at him, the lenses of her glasses fogged. She edged slowly toward her husband, hands out in front of her. "Could you help?"

He tugged a napkin from a dispenser, removed her glasses, wiped the thick lenses and then slid the temples under her fine, pale hair.

"Thanks." Now she faced her son. "I just heard something on the radio." She continued to hold her hands up – the gloves were wet with some undefinable marine slime. "Someone was killed over on Whitfield Road?"

"Jesus," George said.

"You're going to catch the guy, I hope?" June said.

AJ grabbed an apron from a peg. "We're going to try."

"All you can do," George said.

* * *

AJ found the chief at his desk, staring at the little combination TV-VCR against the far wall. On the screen, a reporter in a flak jacket was pointing across a dry wasteland. The chief picked up the remote and silenced the voice. "How's Claire?"

"She's okay." AJ sat down in a molded plastic chair. "Thanks for helping her. I've got to thank Janson, too."

"I don't mean to pry, but with what she's been through – has she had any counseling?"

"She was going in to the city to see someone, but after a while she said it was more trouble than it was worth."

"How about I ask my wife, see if she knows anyone local who's good?"

AJ nodded half-heartedly.

"You sure you're up to this tonight? You look tired. Even for you."

"I'm fine," AJ said. "How did it go with the Frasers?"

"They're taking it pretty hard – especially the mom."

Just then Detective Wheeler came through the door and dropped into the chair next to AJ. He tipped his head back against the wall. "You were talking about the mom and dad? Did you learn anything useful from them?"

"I don't think they were the most involved parents," the chief said. "They seemed to have a general idea of what Taylor's been up to, but were a little short on the details."

"Well, they were out of town," Wheeler said, "so they're off the

35

list. How about the rest of the family?"

"One stepbrother away at school. No one else they are in contact with."

"You said the father worked at the casino?" Wheeler said. "How about those connections?"

"He is going to provide us with the names of current employees, but he claims to be on good terms with everyone there. He said they're pretty careful about who they hire." The chief passed a sheet of paper across the desk to Wheeler. "For now, I think we concentrate on Taylor's peers. The parents gave me the names of a couple of her friends."

Wheeler scanned the list. "Any enemies?"

"Well, if you ask the dad, she was a really popular girl."

"What did the mom say?"

"She didn't say much of anything. Maybe if we go back to her, when she's recovered a little bit..."

"Yeah," AJ said. "If Taylor was so popular – one of the cool kids – then I guarantee there were kids who hated her."

"I don't doubt that," the chief said. "But what was done to her was way beyond your typical teenage animosity."

"Yeah."

The chief rubbed his bald head, as if to massage a thought out of it. "So you think the boyfriend was straight with you, or was he holding something back?"

AJ glanced at Wheeler. "I'm not sure the evening went exactly the way he said it did."

The chief nodded. "Sam, what did you find out from Ryan's friends?"

"Most of the boys Ryan said we should talk to have gone camping for the weekend. It's been planned for a while – an Eagle scout thing. I did speak with one of the moms. She said she's known Ryan for years and that he's a good kid. She said that Taylor was a beautiful girl and that the boys couldn't keep their eyes off of her."

"Maybe we're looking for someone who wanted her but couldn't have her," AJ said.

"When are the campers due back?" the chief said.

"Tomorrow afternoon."

"Did you talk to any of the boys from the soccer team?"

"Yeah, I found some guys who weren't part of the inner circle,"

Wheeler said. "They're the ones I really wanted to talk to, anyway. And this is where it gets interesting." He took out his little rectangular notepad. "Nick King and Carlo Ruggeri, both teammates and both at the party. King said Ryan left the party at about one o'clock."

"That doesn't match the story Ryan gave us," AJ said. "Was this kid sure of the time?"

"Yeah, he's sure. He saw Ryan drive away, and thought it was odd, with the party still going strong. Before he left, Ryan had a serious conversation with a girl named Jessi Wade. Now another boy, Carlo Ruggeri, swears he saw Ryan at the party a whole hour later, around two a.m. This time, Ryan was having an argument with Ms. Wade. And Ruggeri saw Sean Moye – one of the kids who's camping – give Ryan some money. He thinks Ryan left soon after that. At least he didn't see him again."

"So Ryan left the party, then came back to conduct some kind of business," AJ said.

"Yeah. Could be drugs."

"Could be anything," the chief said. "Did you talk to that girl he was seen with?"

"Not yet."

"Do we have time of death?" AJ said.

"Between one and three."

"Nick King said Taylor wasn't at the party," Wheeler said. "He was surprised. She was making it a habit to be wherever Ryan was. He said she was a snob, and she was turning Ryan into a snob. When I asked Ruggeri if he was a friend of Taylor's, he laughed and said Taylor never spoke to him. He said if you weren't considered one of the cool guys, Taylor didn't think you existed. If you were an uncool girl, she was just mean."

"I wonder how mean," AJ said. "Did you talk to Taylor's friends?"

"Two of them, yeah. I tried, anyway. Their parents are being very protective, and they were both upset. All I got was what a good friend she was. No real enemies. A couple of ex-boyfriends, but everyone's moved on, they said, no problems. Both girls said that there were lots of girls who were jealous of Taylor." Wheeler closed the notepad. "That's it. That's my day's work."

"It's a start, Sam," the chief said. "We need to nail down what

Ryan did that night, when he left the party. Both times. But I think the answers may just be typical teenage drama."

"I can get those boys back from the camping trip," Wheeler said.

"No," the chief said. "Most teenagers have something they want to hide. Some of it's big stuff, but mostly it's little stuff that they make big. Either way, getting the complete story is tricky. If we haul those boys home, we'll probably just scare them silent. Let them come home as scheduled. Talk to them then, like it's no big deal. Which, I'm afraid, is probably the truth."

"We need to go back to Ryan," Wheeler said.

"I'd see what you can get out of his friends first. Talk to that girl from the party, see what she and Ryan were discussing."

"Right," Wheeler said, tapping AJ on the shoulder. "Tomorrow. You're coming with me, right?"

"Maybe," the chief said. "I need to talk to him for a second."

Wheeler stood up. "I have two words for you, AJ."

"Yeah?"

"Detective exam." He went out.

The chief splayed his thick fingers on the desk. "You going to be all right?"

AJ gave him a quizzical look.

"I should tell you, the power's off. Exposed wires, I guess."

"That's okay," AJ said. "The pros like to work in the dark. That's what the Daves tell me, anyway."

"We've got some good lanterns. Take one of those."

"Yeah."

"If you see anything, call my cell right away."

"You'll be up?"

"Yeah. Until we get this guy, I'll be up."

***

When AJ arrived at the Honey B Dairy, an inconspicuous restaurant on the main street in Mystic, his two longtime friends, Dave DaSilva and Dave Sela, referred to as *the Daves* by everyone who knew them, had already taken their usual table near the window.

"Did you order yet?" AJ slid across the varnished bench.

"Nope," Sela said. "We were waiting for you. As usual."

AJ checked the pink sheet that explained the specials.

"I don't know why you're looking at that," DaSilva said. He was the thinner of the two, with a prominent, active Adam's apple. "We know you're having the burger and onion rings."

"Yeah, and you're having the clams," Sela said.

"God," DaSilva said. "If I see another clam today I think I'll hurl."

"I think I heard him gag a hundred times today," Sela said, lifting and then lowering his Red Sox cap. "That's just what you want to hear as you order your seafood."

"Other places have background music," AJ said. "My parents opted for barfing."

"Gives the market its special ambiance."

"Screw you guys," DaSilva said. "I never gag in front of customers."

AJ put the menu down. "I saw Melody today. She said Jack was in New York City. Which made me wonder – was he there for you guys, for the show? Is *Mystic Afterlife* about to make a comeback, on a real channel this time?"

"Who knows," Sela said. "Melody keeps saying to be patient, trust Jack."

"He's had our demo tapes for six months," DaSilva said. "And we never see the guy."

"He's either away on business or out on the boat."

"Or tagging along with Melody on her research. I guess he helps, I don't know."

"Some of that research is actually for Claire," AJ said. "Claire's with her right now. You want me to text her, see if there's any news from Jack?"

Sela just waved his hand.

A waitress stopped at the table and took their orders.

"So how's Claire doing?" DaSilva said. "Better, right?"

AJ let out a breath. "She had a scare today. A couple of hardcore religious types looking for converts were at the house, kind of freaked her out. They were very persistent. Came right onto the screened-in porch."

"Even with all the signs you put up?" Sela said.

"Yeah. It really spooked her. And I have to work tonight. That's why she's staying with Melody."

"Damn," DaSilva said. "She seemed to be doing so good. I thought maybe she was over it all."

"Are you kidding?" Sela said. "After what she went through? You don't get over that." He glanced at AJ. "I mean, it takes more than a year."

The waitress brought the drinks in tall, dripping glasses.

DaSilva slurped some ice out of his. He cracked it between his teeth. "I thought we might see you at the market today."

AJ raised his dinged-up hands. "I was there right after you left. Dad really needs to hire another person."

"Yes, he does."

"So you're on patrol tonight?" Sela said. "Do we even need a nighttime patrol in this town? What are you going to see – someone boosting a dolphin from the aquarium?"

"Penguins," DaSilva said. "They're worth a fortune on the black market."

"That would be the black and white market."

"Uh huh."

AJ sat back and crossed his arms.

"What?" Sela said.

"You didn't hear the news?"

The Daves looked at each other.

"No," Sela said. "What's going on?"

AJ reached for his glass, gave it a spin in its puddle.

"Come on, AJ."

"There was a fire on Whitfield Road. One of the family members, a teenage girl, was found dead."

"You mean, she died in the fire?" Sela said.

AJ shook his head.

"So, foul play?" DaSilva said. "Wow. Murder and arson. No wonder Claire was on edge."

AJ's phone buzzed. He pulled it from his pocket. "That's her. I'm going to step out for a minute."

As soon as AJ left, Sela leaned across the table. "If it was a murder, then you know what the chief has AJ doing tonight."

AJ had taken up a position just outside the window. The Daves watched him.

"Do you think he'd let us come with him?" DaSilva said. "He has no gear, nothing."

"I guess if you ask him, he doesn't need gear. His is built in."

"Yeah, I guess. Anyway, it's a crime scene. No way he'd bring us."

AJ gestured as he spoke.

"Why's he so calm?" DaSilva said. "That stuff used to freak him out."

"Yeah." Sela watched AJ for a moment more. "I know why. Because he doesn't expect to see anything. Because he hasn't seen a single thing since Ben."

***

AJ ducked under the yellow tape that ran between trees. As he went up the sidewalk toward the front door, the smoke-blackened clapboard loomed over him in the fading light – all the windows dark now, not just the one that had been a chimney for the fire. He paused there, as if remembering the night from the previous summer, coming up on another house. The unlocked door with the *No Trespassing* sign. Inside, DaSilva asking him to kill the light despite the pitch blackness. Sela taking off toward the stairs. And then, disaster.

He switched on his flashlight and illuminated the little pointed shrubs, perfectly trimmed, perfectly spaced. With his other hand, he carried a lantern, not yet lit. At the entrance, he put the lantern down, unlocked the door, then ducked under more crime scene tape. He reached back to retrieve the lantern. As soon as he closed the door behind him, the smell hit him again – the heavy tang of a blaze extinguished by a deluge. He could feel the residue, bitter and damp in the air and in his throat. He let his eyes and his nose adjust, then went down the hallway, stepped over what the fireman had called a trailer – the line of ash running across the tile toward the bannister – and continued on to the living room.

The big window along the front wall, its curtains gone, was faintly lit from the outside, but the light vanished inside the room. Even his police-issue flashlight was no match for that space. He aimed the beam up one wall and down the next, the light swallowed up by the sodden surfaces it found, revealing only a relentless black. He stepped into the middle of the room, killed the flashlight, and turned slowly in undisturbed darkness.

He pressed the button on the flashlight again. Moving carefully, quietly, he tried the rest of the first floor. Dining room, each stiff-backed chair in place. Kitchen, spotless except for a few dishes in the sink. The back room with the rustic fireplace, then the office. In each, he was alone.

He came around to the stairs again, and went up, staying clear of the charred bannister. Bypassing Taylor's room, he did the tour of the others – large bedrooms, gleaming bathrooms. He stood outside Taylor's room, taking deep, deliberate breaths. He switched on the lantern. He went in.

His eyes and his light moved from the blood-stained carpet to the bed to the dark corners. Earrings glinted on the dresser, and then, from a chair, a stuffed bear's glass eyes. There was no other glow or shimmer. She was not there.

"Hello," he said. "My name is AJ. You might have seen me at your school. Maybe you don't recognize me out of uniform." He touched the hem of his T-shirt. "I'm a police officer, but I'm also a..." He paused. "I don't know what. A medium? A ghost whisperer?" He rolled his eyes and said, "That's stupid," under his breath. He made a half turn. "If you're here, I'll be able to see you. And you can talk to me. I know you've been through something awful. I can help you."

A creak came from the hallway. He darted out of the room, pointed the flashlight one way, then the other. He tried all of the bedrooms again, the bathrooms with their big gray mirrors that showed a crazy man with a light in each hand. Nothing.

Back in Taylor's room, he went to her mirror. There were pictures taped to the frame – high school girls mugging for the camera, too close to the lens. He faced the room again. "What happened to you? Don't be scared. Whatever it was, it's over. No one can hurt you anymore."

The room, the entire house, was silent.

The stuffed bear stared at him from its spot in the corner. AJ went over to it. "What about you?" He lifted it from the chair. "I've probably got a better chance of talking to you than to Taylor's ghost. You saw the whole thing. What happened?"

The bear hung from one arm, its eternally round eyes pointed to some indefinite spot over AJ's shoulder. AJ sat down where the bear had been, holding it in his lap. He let the beam of the flashlight wander around the room for a while, searching the desk, the short bookshelf, paperbacks mixed with stuffed animals. The chair was soft and comfortable. He settled back into the cushions, keeping just his neck taut, his head upright. "I can do this," he said. "My mind is open."

He sat there, listening. Nothing. He checked his watch. "The chief's going to be disappointed," he said, barely above a whisper. He rolled his head, getting a couple of quick cracks. They were the only sounds in the house. As the minutes passed, he sank deeper into the chair. His shoulders sagged. The still silence settled on him.

"Jesus."

A voice, over his shoulder.

He was asleep. That was him, sleeping in the chair. Ben was with him, watching him sleep.

"You are one lame-ass ghost hunter," Ben said.

AJ's head was tipped back, his mouth slack. The flashlight had slipped and the beam lit the floor.

Ben came closer and shook him by the shoulder. "Wake up, AJ. Hey! Wake up!"

AJ's head snapped back. He gasped, opened his eyes. The lantern was off and the darkness had closed in. He gripped his flashlight and swung it back and forth. "Ben?" he said.

Downstairs, a metallic click. AJ stood, holding his breath. A hiss and another click. A door closing. The faintest glow in the doorway to the room.

"Hello?" A man's voice, from below.

AJ bolted into the hall. "Police!" he said from the top of the stairs. "Stay where you are."

A young man stood by the front door, his hands raised, the flashlight in his right hand making a hollow circle on the ceiling. As his arm wavered, the circle wandered like a jellyfish in the tide.

"Who are you?" AJ said, as he descended. "What are you doing here?"

"I'm Jonathan Fraser. This is my house. My father's house."

AJ continued down the stairs. "Can I see some ID?"

Squinting in the glare, the man reached into his back pocket and produced a wallet. He held it open in front of him.

"So you're Taylor's brother?" AJ said.

"Stepbrother."

AJ took the wallet and held it under the light. "This address is on your license. You live here?"

"On paper, yeah, so I can get in-state tuition. But really I live in Massachusetts with my girlfriend." He studied the badge on AJ's belt.

"What are you doing here?"

"I just came to get a few things from my room."

"At two a.m.?"

"I was at my girlfriend's. I got here as soon as I could. Mind if I ask what you were doing in my sister's room?"

"You didn't see the crime scene tape? Two lines of it?"

"I saw it. But I also saw a Jeep parked in our driveway. So I wondered what the hell was going on."

AJ kept the flashlight aimed just below the man's face, where his shirt was stretched taut over a muscular chest.

"Can't we turn the lights on?" Jonathan said.

"The power's off. Which room is yours?"

"The end of the hall."

"I'll take you. You can get what you need. But don't make a habit of dropping by here, until you get the okay from the police department. All right?"

Jonathan nodded.

AJ directed the beam ahead of them and followed Jonathan upstairs, past Taylor's room, to the end of the hall. Jonathan's room was plain – nothing on the walls, a little unremarkable clutter on the dresser, no photos anywhere.

Jonathan went to the closet and slid the door open. He grabbed a couple of shirts that were hanging there. He held them to his nose. "Shit. They smell like smoke."

"Is that it? Is that all you wanted?"

"Yeah, that's it." Jonathan yanked the shirts off the hangers and folded them loosely. "Can I get something from the kitchen?"

They went back down the hall. This time, Jonathan hesitated as they went by Taylor's room, though he didn't look in. He went slowly down the stairs, looking around him, studying the smoke stains. At the bottom, AJ directed the beam to the left, away from the living room, but Jonathan went right. AJ followed. Stepping over the ash, Jonathan sped up.

"Holy shit," he said, looking into the burned-out room. "I heard it wasn't that bad."

"Only in this room. They were able to keep it to this room."

Jonathan stood there, his jaw grinding on some distasteful thought.

"What do you need from the kitchen?" AJ said.

Jonathan started moving again. They went around to the kitchen.

AJ positioned himself so that he could watch Jonathan and still look back through the dining room toward the front door. Jonathan went to the refrigerator. AJ watched him, then glanced the other way. Beyond the long dinner table, past the dark pointed backs of the chairs, something moved – a faint glow that flashed across the open space.

"What are you looking at?" Jonathan said. He was holding a bottle of wine to his cheek. He came over to AJ and stood next to him.

"Let's go." AJ gave Jonathan's arm a tug, then went through the dining room, quickly. He turned into the front hall.

"Jesus, what's the hurry?"

"Can I have your number," AJ said, his eyes scanning the darkness, "in case we need to reach you?"

Jonathan rattled off the ten digits.

AJ took it down on a notepad. "Are you staying in town for a while?"

"My dad and stepmom are at the Hilton. You know, across from the aquarium. I'll stop and see them, if they're still up. Why?" Jonathan tried to follow AJ's eyes, which were pointed past him. "What are you looking at? What do you see?"

It happened quickly, while Jonathan spoke – a glimmer in the dark end of the hall became a shape, approaching. A woman, young, beautiful. Her face, her bare arms and legs, even her straight, dark hair, her shorts and her lacy top, all shone with a cool and empty light. There was no sign of injury. No scarf around her neck and no bruises there. No blood. She stopped just out of reach and glared at Jonathan. When AJ looked back at her, she turned to him and her gleaming eyes widened. She tried to speak but made no sound. She put her hands to her throat. Her chest heaved, like she was gasping for air.

Jonathan watched AJ. "Are you all right?"

Taylor's mouth opened wide. Nothing came out, but she was screaming.

"Officer?" Jonathan matched the direction of AJ's gaze, peered into the dark.

With one last soundless shriek, Taylor flew toward the front door, racing headlong, unafraid of the collision. Just before she hit, she vanished.

For a moment, AJ stared at the door. A line of sweat striped his cheek.

Jonathan shook his head. "I think I'd like to leave now."

AJ let Jonathan pass. From the window beside the door, AJ watched the car go down the driveway. Then he faced the room.

"He's gone, Taylor. He can't hurt you. Nobody can hurt you."

He stood there for a while, alone. Finally, he climbed the stairs back to her room. She wasn't there, either. He picked the lantern up from the floor, flicked the switch a couple of times. It didn't come on. He went downstairs again.

He went out, locking the door behind him. He got in his Jeep. With the key in the ignition, he sat there counting deep, even breaths. Finally, he punched a number into his cell phone. He got the chief's voicemail.

"Chief, it's AJ. It's about three a.m. I saw her. She didn't tell me anything. Didn't seem like she could talk. Call me back when you get this."

He ended the call and dropped the phone on the seat. He swiped his damp forehead, looked toward the house one last time. Then he turned the key, backed up quickly and drove away.

7

When she found him, he was asleep on the couch, under the big window, with a pillow over his face. It was a little after eight a.m.

"AJ?" she said, softly.

He moved the pillow and tried to focus his eyes. "Claire? What are you doing here?"

"Well, I live here."

AJ sat up suddenly and snatched his phone from the coffee table. He pressed buttons without saying anything. "The chief hasn't called?"

"No." Claire touched his leg and he made room for her. "Rough night?"

"Yeah." AJ set the phone down again. "I thought he'd call." He brushed Claire's hair away from her temple, revealing a straight white scar. He kissed her there. "Sorry. I'm a little out of it."

"What time did you get home?"

"After four."

"You were in that house until four? I thought you were going to just scope it out and then leave."

"I left the house at three. I had something to do in Mystic."

Claire waited to see if more would come. AJ leaned back into the cushion.

"Can I get you some breakfast?" Claire said after a while. "Eggs, coffee? Or do you want to try to sleep some more?"

"Coffee would be good."

"Okay." Claire started toward the kitchen.

47

"I saw her," AJ said.

Claire turned around. "You did?"

"Yeah, for a few seconds."

Claire came back and sat down on the arm of the couch. "I don't know if I should say congratulations or sorry." She watched him. "The chief will be glad, right?"

AJ said nothing.

"Did you communicate?" Claire said after a while.

"No. No. I don't think I'm going to get anything out of her. She didn't even seem able to make a sound."

The greyhound came into the room from the direction of the kitchen. He went straight to AJ and pressed his nose into his hands, dividing them.

"Hey, boy." AJ worked a spot behind the dog's ears. "I'm sorry I'm not cured," he said, without looking up.

"Who said anything about wanting you to be cured?"

"Wouldn't it be better for you, too?"

"You mean, would I be less afraid to be in my house? No. My little problem has nothing to do with your thing. The ghosts were on my side, remember?"

"Okay."

Buck let out a satisfied groan and lowered himself to the floor, covering AJ's feet.

"What happens next?" Claire said.

"I'm not sure. I guess I go back there, when it's empty, try to talk to her. And Wheeler and I have regular police work to do, live people to talk to."

"Any chance you'll figure this out quickly? Do you have a suspect?"

"No, not really. All we have is a dead girl and a devastated family, devastated boyfriend."

"That's awful. Do you know much about her?"

"She was popular, and kind of mean. You know the type."

"Yeah. It's still awful."

"Yes, it is." AJ put his hand in the middle of Claire's back and made a slow circle.

"So she was popular, but there were probably a lot of kids she antagonized, kids who didn't like her."

"Maybe they didn't like her, but they were too intimidated to come near her."

"Individually, maybe, but in a pack..." Claire's voice trailed off.

"A pack?"

"If this were a book that I was writing, that's how it would happen."

AJ seemed to be considering the idea. He rubbed his eyes.

"I'll go start the coffee." Claire stood up.

AJ checked his phone again. "Don't hurry."

A while later, his phone woke him. He had a quick conversation, then went into the kitchen.

"Was that the chief?" Claire said. *The Day* was open on the table in front of her.

"Yeah. How much coffee did you make?"

"A full pot. I thought I'd have some iced later. Why?"

AJ went to the cupboard and grabbed two mugs. "The chief and Wheeler are coming over."

"Here? How come?"

"I'm not sure. He has something he wants to talk about. He said he didn't want to do it at the station."

"Oh, well. I can go upstairs. I need to get some writing done today, since I lost most of yesterday. It would be good to get started early."

"No, I think he's bringing pastry for you. He called from Happy Pastry Shop and he asked if you were home. Is that all right?"

"Absolutely. Happy Pastry, happy Claire."

"Good." AJ put the mugs down. "I'm going to take a quick shower."

When AJ was gone, Claire went out the door to the screened-in porch. The air was warm. Sunlight hung golden in the space between the house and the woods, where hidden birds sang. Claire took it all in, then went back through the door. She collected utensils and napkins and carried everything out to the table on the porch. She made one more trip to fix herself a mug of coffee with milk and sweetener, then sat down at the table with the paper. After a while, Buck joined her. He lay down with his back against the screen. In seconds, he was sound asleep.

Claire had already finished the three stories about the events on Whitfield Road when the doorbell rang. She hurried back through the kitchen to the front door.

"Hi, Chief," she said, letting him in.

Chief Brown wore a nylon jacket with a big Stonington Police emblem – an anchor crossed by a rope and a spyglass. Underneath the jacket was a Bay Market T-shirt. "Good morning," he said.

"If that's a new look for the SPD, I like it."

He smiled weakly and held out a pastry box. "I brought a little something. I hope you like these."

"I'm sure I will, thanks," she said, taking it.

"Where's AJ?"

"He's getting dressed. Come on in, I'll get you some coffee." She went toward the back of the house.

The chief paused by the stairs. "I really want to talk to AJ before Wheeler gets here."

"Oh," Claire said, turning around.

Just then there were footsteps above. The chief looked up to where the stairs disappeared around a narrow turn.

"Hey." AJ came into view. "Chief, you look like I feel."

"AJ, I want to let Wheeler in on our secret. I wanted to tell you that before he got here."

"What?" AJ stopped on the landing.

"No," Claire said.

The chief put one hand on his smooth, pink scalp. "He likes you, AJ. You can trust him. And you may be working more with him for a while."

AJ came down the last steps but didn't say anything.

"Chief," Claire said, "you promised AJ that you'd keep his ability private."

"I did." The chief fell silent, his head down. When he looked up again, his eyes were brimming.

"Roland?" AJ said. "What is it?"

"It's my granddaughter. Tara. She has cancer. We just found out last night."

"Oh, God," AJ said.

"C'mon, Chief." Claire took him by the elbow. "Let's not stand here in the hall. I set up out back."

They went through the kitchen to the porch, took places at the picnic table. The chief gave them the details. The cancer was a rare kind called Wilms' tumor, found in the kidney. The doctor said they knew how to fight it and that gave them hope. There would be surgery and chemotherapy. They'd been referred to a woman at Yale, supposed to be one of the best in the world. Their doctor had said, "To beat this, Tara's going to need the Yale team's help, and she's going to need yours."

Claire put her hand on his arm. "You know I make my own schedule, so, whatever you need..."

"That goes for me, too," AJ said. "Anything I can do."

"Thanks. I'm worried about being away from the job. For your sake, AJ. If I'm not around, you're going to need someone else who knows what's going on. That's why I want to bring Wheeler in on it."

"I get that," AJ said. "If it becomes necessary – I promise I will tell him. For now, I'd like to continue to keep it between us."

The chief let out a long breath. "Okay. For now. You'd better tell me quick what you saw last night, before Wheeler gets here."

Just then the doorbell rang.

"I guess it's going to have to be later," the chief said.

AJ left to answer the door. He came back to the porch with Wheeler behind him. Claire said hello, then ducked into the kitchen.

"You okay, Chief?" Wheeler said. He was dressed for church in a sport coat and tie. "What's this all about?"

"Thanks for coming, Sam," the chief said. "I wanted you to know that I may be a little preoccupied." He swallowed hard, then filled Wheeler in about his granddaughter.

"I'm so sorry, Chief," Wheeler said. "If she's half as tough as you..."

"Thanks." Chief Brown scraped his fingers against the stubble on his chin. "Now, let's get back to the case. While I was at the hospital last night, our Ryan Hardy was brought in by ambulance. Apparent drug interaction."

"Was it suicide?" Wheeler said. "Is this some kind of admission of guilt?"

"He's alive," the chief said. "And it was accidental."

AJ took a seat on the bench next to the chief. Wheeler sat down across the table.

"How did it happen?" AJ said. "Is he all right?"

"He's stable. He'll be okay. I guess he was refusing to take some anti-anxiety medicine that his doctor had prescribed. His mother thought he was just being stubborn and decided to slip it to him in some ice cream. A while later she found him passed out and couldn't wake him up."

"So he was refusing for a reason," AJ said.

The chief nodded. "They found oxycodone in his blood. Apparently he'd taken some earlier that night. I guess he knew better than to mix it with whatever his mom was trying to give him."

"So he was a user," Wheeler said.

"Looks like it."

"That money he took from his friend at the party," AJ said, "it was probably a drug sale. He was either selling or he was getting money for a buy."

"Drugs could explain a lot of what went on Friday night," Wheeler said.

The chief nodded. "Including Taylor's murder."

"I haven't had a chance to tell you," AJ said, "when I was at the house last night, Jonathan Fraser showed up."

"You were at the Fraser house last night?" Wheeler said.

"Yeah. I couldn't sleep, so I drove over there."

"When I can't sleep, I turn on the television."

AJ shrugged. "I wanted to take another look around."

"So Jonathan, Taylor's stepbrother," the chief said. "A couple of years older than Taylor."

"Right. He has the Whitfield Road address on his license," AJ said, "but said he's been staying at his girlfriend's, in Massachusetts."

"His mother has a house up there, too," the chief said. "Mr. Fraser gave me her address for Jonathan. Though he also said she pretty much goes from cruise to cruise these days. She's a week into a Mediterranean trip right now."

Wheeler shook his head. "So if Jonathan was living with his mother or his girlfriend, what did he come to the house on Whitfield Road for?"

"He said he wanted to pick up a few things," AJ said. "I stayed with him. He grabbed a couple shirts from a closet and a bottle of wine from the fridge."

"Not much to justify a trip to a murder scene in the middle of the night," Wheeler said. "Unless he's very particular about his outfits."

"That's what I thought."

"So maybe he was really there for something else," Wheeler said. "Something that he couldn't get because you were there. Like drugs."

"Yeah. He said he was going to stop to see his dad and stepmon at the Hilton. I went over there after I left the house. His car was in the lot."

There was silence at the table for a while.

"So, we know that the boyfriend was a drug user," the chief said. "It looks like he may have been buying, or selling, that night. We know that the stepbrother made a night-time trip to his house that looked very suspicious. Could be drug-related." The chief's cell phone buzzed. "I've got to take this." He went out the side door to the backyard. With the phone to his ear, he walked away down the long, grassy slope toward the end of the house.

Wheeler eyed the unopened pastry box. "Is that for us?"

"Help yourself. The chief brought it."

Wheeler broke the tape and flipped the lid back, revealing three rows of fat donuts. "Sure. Someone's got to keep the stereotype alive."

***

AJ was rinsing a mug in the sink when Claire came into the kitchen. The donuts had been moved inside. She plucked one from the box. "I was hoping you'd leave me some."

"The chief made sure we did."

She took a bite. "Yum. Thank him for me." She leaned back against the counter. "I feel so bad for him. How old is his granddaughter?"

"She must be about eight. Eight or nine."

"I just read a little about that cancer, Wilms'. It looks like they can beat it."

"God, I hope so."

"So, you're working today?"

"Yeah," AJ said. "Wheeler and I are going to go out a little later. Will you be all right?"

"I'll be fine."

"You can call me anytime. You know that."

"I'll be fine. Really."

AJ put the last mug on the wooden rack, then dried his hands. He stepped in front of Claire, took her elbow. He kissed her. "You taste like a donut."

"I'm just sweet, that's all." She ran her hand down his arm. "What will you be doing today? Are you going back to try to talk to Taylor's ghost?"

"Later, probably. I guess we caught a break there. The chief said the family is in no hurry to get back into that place, after what happened. Even after we release the scene, I'll probably be able to find some time alone there. So for now..." AJ started out of the kitchen, Claire following. He flopped onto the couch.

"When should I wake you up?"

AJ's eyes were already closed. "Two hours."

"Okay. Sweet dreams." Claire kissed him again, then dropped a pillow on his face.

***

They walked up the drive toward the hospital under a bleary afternoon sun. A big, freestanding ceiling with pillars and peaked skylights had been added to the entrance, as if to convey to the industrial brick rectangle behind it, and everything that went on inside, a sense of efficiency and ease.

Wheeler wiped sweat from his flushed forehead. "How long has it been since Ben Shortman died?"

"Almost a year." AJ looked off to the left, where, on the other side of the building, he and the Daves had followed the ambulance carrying Ben that night.

"He did all those investigations of hauntings, right? What was the name of that group? Mystic something."

"Mystic Afterlife."

"Yeah. Do you ever wonder..."

"What?"

"If he came back? As a ghost, I mean?"

"No, can't say that I did."

They reached the shade of the portico. The glass doors opened with a swish. Wheeler stopped at the information desk to ask directions.

"Do you think we'll have trouble getting past the mother?" AJ said, once they were in the elevator.

"We'll see."

The doors opened to a nurse's station and, beyond it, a long hallway with many doors. Wheeler had just introduced himself to a nurse behind the counter when Ryan's mom approached him.

"Detective Wheeler?" There were leaden folds of skin under her eyes.

"Hello, Mrs. Hardy. How is your son?"

"He'll be all right. Are you here to talk to him?"

"Yes ma'am."

"Good." She rooted around in her purse and pulled out a plastic sandwich bag. Inside it was a handful of round pills. "Here. I found these in Ryan's room."

"Oh." Wheeler produced his own plastic bag from his sport coat and held it open. "You can put them in here." He studied the pills through the plastic, then sealed the bag and tucked it away again.

"The doctor said that's what Ryan took."

"Did anyone in your house have a prescription?" AJ said.

"No. I don't know where he got them. I found them in a soccer trophy." Ryan's mom turned away. "He's a captain of the team, you know. He's never done anything like this. He's never been in any kind of trouble."

Wheeler glanced at AJ but didn't say anything.

"He's in room 319. It's that way." She pointed.

"Would you like to come with us?"

"No. He won't talk to me, so I don't think he'll talk in front of me, either. Find out who got him involved in this."

AJ and Wheeler went down the hall.

"That wasn't the reaction I expected," AJ said, under his breath. "Does she realize how much trouble he could be in?"

"No, she doesn't. This is all new territory for her."

They found Ryan sitting up, with the back of the adjustable bed raised. He was watching the TV that hung from the ceiling. His cheeks were pale and his hair lay dark and flat on his head. He had gauze on one arm and a shiny bandage on the other.

"Hi, Ryan," Wheeler said. "How are you feeling?

Ryan didn't respond.

"We spoke to your mom on the way in. She's just outside."

"Whatever."

Wheeler took another step into the room. He dropped the plastic evidence bag onto the swivel-armed tray by the bed. "These came from your room at home. Do you want to tell us about them?"

Ryan stared at the plastic bag. His lips trembled. "I didn't buy them."

AJ picked up the bag and studied it for a second. "There aren't many pills there, but you'd be surprised at the street value for Oxycontin. Or maybe you wouldn't."

"Were you selling the pills, Ryan?" Wheeler said.

"What? No."

"So you didn't buy them and you weren't selling them."

Ryan shook his head without saying anything.

"The night of the party," Wheeler said, "you were seen leaving that party at one o'clock. Then you were seen back at the party taking money from someone."

Ryan said nothing.

"You know what that looks like, Ryan, when you put that together with this bag of pills? It looks like a drug deal."

"No! That's not what was going on at all."

"Okay," Wheeler said. "If you want to get out of this mess, you'd better tell us what was going on."

Ryan turned toward the door, as if wondering if his mom might suddenly appear there. "I left the party to go to Taylor's. I was going to break up with her. I'd been thinking about it for a long time, and I was finally going to do it. But, I just drove around instead. I ended up back at the party. I borrowed some money from a friend because I needed to get gas before I went to Taylor's."

"To break up with her."

Ryan nodded.

"Where'd you go, then?"

Ryan named a convenience store. "I put a couple of gallons in the tank. I got some chips, too."

"What time was that?" Wheeler had his notepad out.

"I don't know. Two, two-thirty?"

"Then what did you do?"

"I went to Taylor's. That's when I saw the fire, and..."

"So where did you get the pills?" AJ said.

"From Taylor. She gave them to me."

"That doesn't make sense. If the house was already on fire – "

"Not then. Before. A couple of months ago she found out that I'd never tried anything. Not even pot." He glanced nervously toward the open door. "She said I should before I went to college. She said it would be fun and help me fit in."

"How did Taylor get the pills?"

"I don't know."

"Did she have anything else besides the Oxy?" AJ said.

"She had some pot."

"Did you smoke it with her?" Wheeler said.

"Once. I didn't like it. And I was afraid my mom would smell it, you know, on my clothes or something."

"But you liked the pills?"

"Yeah." Ryan teared up for a second.

"Were you taking them every day?" AJ said.

"No. Not every day. Just once in a while, with Taylor."

"Why did you have these pills in your room, if you were only using with Taylor?"

"She gave me some extra the last time. She wanted me to give them to the guys on the team. I was supposed to take them to the party."

"Did you?"

"No. Some of the guys are really straight. I was afraid they'd see me doing it and word would get around."

"You must have some idea where Taylor was getting this stuff," AJ said. "Maybe someone at school?"

"Honestly, I don't know." Ryan looked suddenly even more tired, as if it was all he could do to keep himself upright in the propped-up bed. "I don't think it was anybody at school."

"Why not?"

Ryan was quiet for a moment. "I guess because I never saw her talk to any of the druggies. Or even anyone outside her group."

"You don't think any of Taylor's friends would sell drugs?"

Ryan made a dismissive sound. "No, I don't think so."

"Why?"

"They're too lazy."

Wheeler turned to AJ, his eyebrows raised. "That's a convenient story, Ryan," he said. "Puts the whole thing on Taylor, who isn't here to defend herself."

Fear flashed across Ryan's face. "Are you going to arrest me?"

"How old are you, Ryan?" Wheeler said.

"Seventeen. My birthday's in September."

"Well, you're in luck. A few years ago you would have been an adult for, what, nine months already? At sixteen. Since they changed the law, you're still a juvenile."

Ryan looked like he was trying unsuccessfully to digest that.

"We'll work through this," Wheeler said. "You get some rest."

When AJ and Wheeler left the room, Ryan's mom was just outside, positioned to hear everything. "What's going to happen now?" she said.

Wheeler led her a few feet down the hall. "If he's been using with any regularity for a few weeks, he probably has an addiction. He's going to go through withdrawal."

"That's what the doctor said. But I mean... I talked to someone, a friend who knows about this kind of thing. He said he'd probably get probation."

Wheeler gave her a curt nod. "You're going to want to talk to your lawyer. But he's a minor, no prior problems – "

"Will the lawyer tell me I shouldn't have given you those pills?"

Wheeler thought about that for a moment. "We knew he took Oxy. If you hadn't given those pills to us, we would have come looking for them. I think your lawyer will tell you you did the right thing. The main thing is, he keeps talking to us, being cooperative."

"Okay." The woman pressed her lips hard together.

The two cops were silent in the elevator, and silent as they crossed the lobby and followed the sidewalk down to the parking lot.

"I want to believe that kid, but I don't know," Wheeler said, as they approached the patrol car.

"Yeah. If he is telling the truth about Taylor wanting him to pass out Oxy to the team, then she was trying to start up a business."

"Or expand somebody else's," Wheeler said. "Seems just as likely that she raided her parent's medicine cabinet and Ryan was the beneficiary."

"Then why would he make up a story about Taylor telling him to give the stuff away?"

"Because he doesn't want to admit how much he's been taking. Maybe he has his own business. Actually, we don't know yet if Taylor had anything to do with the Oxy. Ryan saw a chance to close off a line of questioning by pinning the whole thing on her."

Wheeler went around to the passenger's side. "Let's go see Ms. Wade, the girl he was seen having a long conversation with at the party." He pulled the notepad from his pocket and flipped through it. "She's on William Street."

AJ paused with his door open. "I like it. Sources who can actually talk."

"What?"

AJ looked across the top of the car. "I just mean, it feels like we're getting somewhere."

Wheeler grinned back at him. "Maybe. We'll see."

8

"Donuts! I've got donuts!"

Maggie rolled into her pillow and kept her eyes closed, but it was no use. Her mom was making as much noise as possible, clacking dishes together, banging cabinet doors. She actually started singing. Maggie got out of bed and went into the kitchen.

"Good morning, sweetie!" her mom said.

Maggie found the tape on the bottom edge of the pastry box and slit it with her fingernail. She lifted the lid. Out came a warm, sweet smell.

"Dad's coming home today," her mom said.

So that explained why she was acting like a crazy person. "Isn't he like a whole week early?"

Her mom opened the refrigerator and stared into it. "Guess it's take-out for dinner." She was trying to change the subject.

"Wait – because of Taylor?"

Her mom kept looking into the fridge. "Yes, but don't worry. He just thinks we should be together right now. I'm not gonna complain." She finally closed the door. "We need to get this place ship-shape before he gets here. After breakfast you can mow the grass."

Maggie finished one donut at the counter without saying another word, then took a second one back to her room. She ate staring out the window. She thought about what her dad had supposedly said – *we should be together right now*. Like they had to mourn their loss. But the family being together was really about something else, from a long time ago – the whole mess with Tiffanee and the trailer fire. That's what both her mom and dad were thinking about. That's why, after she first found out about Taylor, her mom mixed up the names. *You heard about Tiffanee,* she'd said.

When they moved here, after the trailer fire, her parents kept saying it was a better environment. Right. Out of one trailer park and into another. The only improvement in the environment was that they were away from her grandmother. But no one would ever say that out loud.

What would her parents think if they knew that Taylor's death might be her fault? The idea made Maggie feel like she was falling, like there was a wind rushing in her ears. She took another bite of the donut, tried to concentrate on the taste of the sweet dough. Instead she found herself wondering what *Taylor* would think, if she knew it might be Maggie's fault. But that didn't even make any sense. Taylor was dead – she couldn't think anything.

Maggie finished the donut and licked the glaze off her fingers. She picked through some clothes in a drawer, but decided that, since she was going to mow first, she'd just grab yesterday's clothes from the floor. Dressed, she unplugged her cell phone. She thought about texting Ryan. What could she say? How r you? R you ok? Sorry about Taylor? Lame. She dropped the phone in her pocket.

She put her feet into flip flops and went toward the front door. Her mom was on the couch, bending down.

"You caught me," her mom said. She made a pale rose stripe across a toenail. "Don't worry, I'll go back to getting the place ready in a second."

"Is that my new nail polish?"

"No. This is mine." She wiggled her toes and grinned like a little girl.

Maggie hated that smile. There was something flirty about it, which was just wrong. It always made her think about her mom as an eighth-grader, with a boyfriend and a baby.

"Let me see." Maggie swiped the bottle and saw that it wasn't hers. "Okay," she said, handing it back.

Her mom gave her a hurt look. "Move the grill, okay? Don't just mow around it." She dipped the brush into the polish again. She didn't say anything about wearing flip flops to mow the lawn.

Maggie went outside. The charcoal grill belonged in the back yard, but it had been parked out front since last fall, when her dad had brought it around to the hose. She grabbed the handle through the plastic cover and dragged the thing to the side of the trailer. Walking to get the mower, she saw something in the brown spot where the grill had been. She picked it up. A propane lighter, with the little trigger and the long tip for the flame. She'd seen her father use it a hundred times. Today, though, it wasn't just a lighter, it was a sign, a message. Tiffanee had used one just like it on that other night, for that other fire. Maggie turned it over and it seemed to get heavier in her hand.

What if the fires *were* connected? What if the guy who followed her to Taylor's house wasn't just some random psycho, but someone with a reason for revenge, someone who knew what they'd gotten away with? He didn't find Taylor's house because she led him there – he already knew where Taylor's house was. Knew all about Tiffanee and Magda. About the trailer fire. Everything.

She wanted to smash the lighter into a hundred pieces. Her father would miss it, though. She could imagine him coming home and going straight to the grill, like he'd been thinking of nothing else the whole time he was gone. She went back and slipped the lighter under the plastic cover, finding the wire shelf with her hands.

A car was coming up the lane between the trailers. As Maggie watched, it passed the first turnoff. It was going slow and careful, like the driver was looking for something. It kept coming up the slope, heading toward her. It went past the second turnoff. For some reason, Maggie's heart began to beat faster. The car reached the third turnoff, the last. It stopped. Maggie's breath caught in her throat.

It was the gray car.

The car turned left. Once it was sideways to her, she could see that it was obviously blue, not gray. It didn't even look much like the gray car. Then it was gone.

"Hey!"

Maggie jumped at the voice. Her mom was leaning out a window.

"Is there gas in the mower?"

"I don't know," Maggie said.

"Check, okay? Don't let it run out with the lawn half cut. That looks worse than not cutting it at all."

Maggie didn't answer.

"You all right?" Her mom gave her a concerned look.

"I'm fine."

Her mom pulled her head back inside.

Maggie stood there looking down the lane. She had to get control of herself or she was going to go crazy.

She walked to the little shed where the mower was. The shed was made to look like a barn – a toy barn from some toy world. She hauled the machine into the sun and pointed it toward the grass. As she gripped the handle, she tried to forget about the gray car, the lighter and the fire, tried to stay right there, in her yard, in the sun. She even closed her eyes. Bad move. Instantly, she was back in that other trailer park, on that night six years ago. She and Tiffanee were whispering in the dark, serious but almost giggling over what they were going to do. The propane lighter didn't want to go at first, but Tiffanee kept pulling the trigger and then there was a quiet little blue-orange tongue.

"You think that will light the plywood skirt, Tiff?" she said. "Because it's not much of a flame."

"No. But I know what it will light."

"What?"

"You wait here."

"I want to come with you."

"I need you to keep watch." Tiffanee went to the front door of her trailer and opened it, not even worrying about making noise, because her mom was at work.

"Keep watch for what?"

"For anyone. Don't let anyone inside."

Tiffanee went through the door and Maggie was alone in the dark. It seemed like forever. She noticed the sounds from the nearby trailers – a television, an argument. Everyone just going on about their lives. No one suspecting anything. Nothing even the slightest bit different than every other night.

Only she and Tiffanee knew that everything was different. That this night would change everything forever. Tiffanee had seen it work before. Burn down the trailer and there would be no choice but to move to someplace else. And the crazy thing was that everyone, neighbors and friends and people they didn't even know, would want to help the poor homeless family, would chip in to give them someplace *better*.

"Maggie! You going to mow that grass or just stare it down?"

Her mom was leaning out the window again.

Maggie didn't answer. It was still night where she was standing. Tiffanee was with her again. The flame, which had been hiding inside for a long while, long enough that she had asked Tiffanee a couple of times if she was sure it had really caught, if the lighter had really worked, finally showed itself in the window of Tiffanee's mom's room.

Maggie – Magda, back then – felt Tiffanee's hand take hers and squeeze. As the fire burst out into the open like some kind of escaped tiger, hungry and bright, Maggie stood there holding Tiffanee's hand, thinking that they were bonded forever, thinking that in their long future as best friends they would share everything.

She couldn't have been more clueless. Clueless about the real plan, about Tiffanee, about their futures. She didn't know anything, starting with this basic fact – that inside that room being eaten up by flames, a man was passed out on the bed.

9

It was an hour before the Bay Market opened, and the Daves were shucking their second tub of long necks, when George Bugbee came into the back room with a young man in tow. He was tall, slight, with longish hair.

George nodded toward Sela and DaSilva. "This is Dave and Dave," he said. "A couple of knuckleheads, but they're friends of my son's, so I'm stuck with 'em." He gestured in the other direction. "This is Pahka," he said, with no hint of an *r* anywhere.

The guy extended his hand. "Parker," he said, enunciating clearly.

Sela pulled off his gloves, returned the handshake and repeated the name, rolling his *r*s like a Spaniard.

Grinning, DaSilva waved. "Hey."

"He's going to help you two with the prep work for a while," George said. "Then we'll train him up front, so he can cover up there, too."

There was a chime from that direction as the outer door swung open.

"You're about to meet the brains of the operation," George said.

His wife, June, pushed through the plastic curtain. "Ah, here's our crew."

George made the introductions, sticking with his version of the man's name.

"I made a fresh pot of coffee if you want some, Mrs. B.," DaSilva said.

"No thanks. I just came to collect my husband. We'll be gone for a bit. Beth's picking up onions, but she'll be here shortly. Come on, George."

He sighed wearily. "Parker, I'm sorry. Your first day and I'm leaving you in their hands. I'll be back in an hour."

"We'll teach him everything we know, boss," Sela said.

"Yeah? What are you going to do with the other fifty-nine minutes?" George followed his wife toward the door.

The Daves and Parker stood there, silent, listening to the Bugbees make their exit.

"Here, I brought this shirt to put on over," June was saying.

"I don't need that. I haven't had a chance to get dirty."

"Well, you are going to take your apron off, right?"

George mumbled something, the bell over the front door chimed, and it was quiet.

"Okay, chowda time," Sela said. "Can you peel potatoes, Parker?"

"Sure."

Sela led him to a sink with a short counter on which there was a big, white sack. "I can get you a hair net," he said, as Parker slipped the apron over his head.

"I'm good." Parker made a quick ponytail that he tied with an elastic he'd kept in his pocket.

"The man comes prepared," Sela said.

Parker washed a spud under the faucet and then tore into it with a peeler.

"That's some serious skill," Sela said. "You've had KP duty before."

"I worked in a place just like this in Virginia and before that, Hawaii."

"So you're a Navy brat?"

"How'd you guess? Just got here."

"You're in school, or —"

"Yeah. For a few more weeks. I'm a senior."

"Oh, man. You couldn't finish out the year in Virginia?"

"Nah. It's a thing with my dad. We stick together."

"But I mean, the last month of your senior year. You couldn't get him to make an exception?"

Parker started in on his third potato. "My dad doesn't make exceptions."

"Okay. You going to enlist after you graduate?"

"No way. I'm going to college."

"Yeah? Where? UConn's a great school."

"My dad's retiring in a year and moving back to Hawaii. If I wait that year, I can go to the University of Hawaii with in-state tuition."

"Nice."

"In the meantime, I'll pick up a few courses here at Avery Point."

DaSilva, who had been listening from across the room, joined them at the sink. "Which side of the river are you on?"

"Uh, Groton side? Not too far from the base."

"With gas prices, how come you didn't look for work over there?"

Parker took another potato out of the bag. "I heard the girls were prettier on this side."

"Might be," Sela said.

"Speaking of pretty girls, Beth will be here soon." DaSilva checked his watch. "She works the counter."

Parker glanced toward the plastic curtain.

"Don't get any ideas," Sela said. "She's engaged."

"I'll keep that in mind."

Parker peeled another potato. The front door opened again and a young woman came into the back room, lugging a mesh bag. She flipped her red hair away from her freckled face. "Oh, hello," she said, noticing Parker.

Parker wiped his hands on the apron. "Hi. I'm Parker."

"Hi, Pahka."

Sela laughed.

Beth turned to him. "What?"

He only shook his head.

Beth swung the bag onto the counter. "There's more in my car. It's right out front."

"I got it," Sela said.

A minute later, he dropped a bag of onions next to the first bag. "I didn't see your car outside, Parker. How'd you get here?"

"My brother brought me. We're sharing a car right now."

"He drove you all the way over here from Groton?"

"Yeah," Parker said, without looking up. "We're going to have to work something out."

"Maybe we could use him here. Is he like you, a demon with a potato peeler?"

"No," Parker said, turning a potato in his hand and flicking the brown skin free, leaving a smooth, white facet of flesh. "He's not like me at all."

10

"That's the place," Wheeler said, pointing toward a boxy, two-story house with a pot of geraniums by the door. "I want you to interview the girl."

"What?" AJ pulled the key from the ignition.

"You're closer to her age. Remember, that's why you're here – to relate to the kids." Wheeler undid his seat belt. "Anyway, my wife says you should be the one talking to the girls."

"Yeah? Why's that?"

"She says you're cuter. Must be the uniform."

They got out of the car and climbed the front steps. Wheeler rang the bell. When the door swung open, a stout, unshaven man squinted through the screen.

"Mr. Wade?" Wheeler said. "I'm Detective Wheeler and this is Officer Bugbee. We're hoping to speak with Jessi."

A woman with a neat perm and a sweater draped over her shoulders joined her husband in the doorway. "Is this about the Fraser girl?"

"We need to ask your daughter a few questions about a party that she attended Friday night," Wheeler said.

"She's upstairs," Mrs. Wade said. "I'll get her."

Mr. Wade opened the screen door. "Come on in. You want some coffee?"

"No thanks," Wheeler said. "This shouldn't take long."

They went into a tidy room and sat down in high-backed chairs. After a minute, Mrs. Wade came in with a teenage girl. She was wearing sweats, the words *University of Rhode Island* running down one leg.

"This is Jessi," her mom said.

Wheeler stood up. "Hi, Jessi. I'm Detective Wheeler and this is Officer Bugbee. You're not in any trouble. We just need to ask you a few questions."

"It's okay, honey." Mrs. Wade steered her daughter to a chair in front of a spinet piano with wood-framed family photos across the top.

Wheeler opened his notepad.

"Hi," AJ said. He tried a warm smile. "You were at the party Friday night? The one at the Reynolds'?"

"Yes."

"We're good friends with the Reynolds," Mrs. Wade volunteered. "The kids have known each other since they were toddlers."

"Mmm," AJ said. "Jessi, how long were you at the party?"

"I guess from eight-thirty to about two." She had assumed a sort of restless slouch, her arms crossed, one leg bouncing up and down.

"Some of the kids stayed overnight," Mrs. Wade said. "But we don't allow that. No co-ed sleepovers."

Mr. Wade cleared his throat but didn't speak.

"Was Taylor Fraser there?" AJ said.

"Jessi didn't hang around with her," Mrs. Wade said.

"No," Jessi said. "Usually, she was wherever Ryan was. But not that night."

"Ryan Hardy is a nice boy," Mrs. Wade said. "He's been to our house many times. So polite."

Mr. Wade joined in. "His father's in Afghanistan. Connecticut National Guard. Civil engineering unit. Been there, what, six or seven months now, right?"

"Yes," his wife said. "It's a shame. He won't be here for graduation."

"Are you friends with the Hardys?" AJ said.

"No, acquaintances," Mrs. Wade said. "Friendly acquaintances. I work at the pharmacy in Mystic. They've been coming there for their prescriptions for years."

"Jessi, you're good friends with Ryan, right?" AJ said.

"Yeah."

"How long have you known him?"

"I met him freshman year. We were in math together. Then we both joined yearbook staff. Ryan and Kathy and me are the only ones who have been on yearbook all four years."

"Did you spend much time with Ryan at the party?" AJ said.

"We hung out some, but he was mostly with the guys from the team."

"We heard that you and Ryan had a serious conversation."

"Who said that?" Mrs. Wade leaned forward. The sweater came loose from around her shoulders.

Jessi answered with a shrug. The leg advertising the nearby university kept working an invisible pedal.

"Can you tell us what you were talking about?" AJ said.

Jessi looked away. "I don't want to get Ryan in trouble. And I don't want to say bad things about someone who's dead...murdered." She faced AJ again, her eyes suddenly teary.

AJ checked Wheeler, who tipped his pencil as if to say, *go on.*

"Actually, Jessi, what you tell us could help Ryan and may even help us figure out what happened to Taylor. She deserves that, don't you think?"

"Go ahead, Jess," Mr. Wade said. "Tell them what you know."

The girl hesitated, her lips pressed together.

"Was your conversation about drugs?" AJ said.

Jessi's eyes darted to him, then away. She didn't say anything.

"We know Ryan was using Oxycontin," AJ said. "He's in the hospital right now because of it."

"Is he okay?" Jessi sat upright.

"Oh, my," Mrs. Wade said.

"He's fine. He'll be fine."

Jessi's leg was still, now. "That's her fault. Taylor's fault. He never did any drugs before her. She pushed him into it."

"So he talked to you about the drugs?"

"Only a little. I knew it was bad. I didn't think it would put him in the hospital."

"You never saw him with drugs, taking drugs?"

"No, never."

"Ever see him selling drugs?"

"No."

"Did he ever try to give drugs to you or any of your friends?"

"No! God! I don't do anything like that. My friends don't do anything like that."

"Jessi and her friends are good kids," Mrs. Wade said.

"And as far as you know, Ryan didn't have drugs at the party that night?"

"No. He didn't."

"Okay," AJ said. "But is that what you and Ryan were talking about at the party – drugs?"

Jessi tugged at the ends of her long, straight hair but didn't respond.

"Was there something else, Jessi?" AJ said.

"Taylor was pushing him to do other things, too."

"What other things?"

Jessi was silent. Mrs. Wade and her husband looked at each other, concern on their faces.

Wheeler stood up. "Do you still have that coffee?"

"Sure," Mr. Wade said. "I could use a cup." He led the way out of the room. "I'm warning you, I make it strong."

When the two men were gone, Mrs. Wade said, "Go ahead, Jessi."

"Taylor was pushing him to sleep with her." Her cheeks reddened.

"But he wasn't interested in that," AJ said.

"No. I mean, at first he was. A lot of guys thought she was really hot, including Ryan. It was a big deal to go out with her. She was like queen of the school."

"You didn't think much of her."

"I mean, she had her clique and wannabies. But everyone I know pretty much hated her."

"Except Ryan?"

"He didn't really like her, either, before they started going out. They had to do this project together, and she went after him. She could be really nice if she wanted something."

"And she wanted Ryan."

"Yeah."

"Did that surprise you? I never met her, but from what you said, it doesn't seem like he'd be her type."

"A lot of girls noticed Ryan this year because of soccer. He was captain of the team and the best player. I think Taylor just wanted to make the other girls jealous – especially this one girl."

"Can you tell me about her?"

"I don't know." Jessi shook her head, but then continued, "That's what's really great about Ryan – he has all different kinds of friends. She's from that old trailer park, the one that's almost in North Stonington? She's pretty, but she's quiet and kind of weird. He was friends with her anyway." She paused. "I think actually she really liked him."

"You're talking about that Strang girl," Mrs. Wade said. "Maggie Strang." She turned to AJ. "Her mother can't be much older than thirty. Can you imagine?"

AJ kept his eyes on Jessi. "Why did Taylor want to make Maggie jealous?"

"I don't know. Taylor just hates her. Hated her. She hated all of the trailer park kids, but that girl, especially. She picked on Maggie so much that she actually got in trouble for it at school."

"You said Ryan *was* Maggie's friend. They're not still friends?"

"I don't know. I didn't see him talking to her after he got together with Taylor."

"Did he drop his other friends?"

"Yeah, pretty much. Especially if Taylor thought they were uncool. But he told me that he missed everybody. He was hanging out with them again at the party, and he realized how much he missed them. He was sick of Taylor, and the drugs and everything."

"Sounds like he was unhappy with Taylor. Why didn't he break up with her?"

"He wanted to, but he was scared."

"Scared of what?" AJ said.

"Of what she'd do. She could be so vicious. Once she'd get started on somebody, she just wouldn't stop."

"What did he think she would do to him?"

"He thought she had pictures on her phone of him doing drugs. She'd put them online. And she'd tell people that he was gay or something."

"Why would she say that? Why would anyone believe it?"

"Because they hadn't had sex."

"And the only reason a guy would turn her down was if he was gay."

"Yeah." Jessi crossed her arms again. "I mean, he'd already let it slip to one of his friends that he hadn't slept with Taylor, and the guy starting teasing him, calling him Limpy, and Softie – you know, instead of Hardy. So stupid."

Mrs. Wade let out a sigh.

"When Ryan left the party," AJ said, "did you think he was going to break up with her?"

"I hoped he was."

"What time was that? When he left?"

"It was around one, I think. Taylor kept texting him, so he finally went."

"Was that the last time you saw Ryan that night?"

"No, he came back like an hour later. I thought maybe he had broken up with Taylor, and that was why he was back so soon, but he hadn't. He didn't stay that long. He asked Sean for some money. He said Taylor wanted him to buy her some snacks." She shook her head.

"You didn't believe him?"

"I don't know."

"What do you think Ryan wanted the money for?"

She shrugged.

AJ let a couple of seconds tick by. "After he got the money, then what did he do?"

"He left. Then I left."

"Have you talked to him since?"

"No. I texted him when I heard about Taylor. He texted back and said he was okay, but that was it. I think he's mad at me. I'm trying to just leave him alone for now." She began to cry, suddenly and loudly, her hands on her face, tears leaking between them.

Her mother jumped to her side and put an arm around her, whispering, "Honey, honey."

The voices of the men in the kitchen, which had been a steady, rumbling background to the interview, stopped.

AJ shifted his hat on his lap and waited.

"I'm sorry," Jessi said after a while, her breathing under control again.

"It's been a long couple of days, right?" AJ said.

She nodded. "You're sure Ryan's okay?"

"He's fine."

Mrs. Wade gave her daughter another squeeze, then went back to her chair. She had left Jessi with a tissue, and Jessi dabbed her cheeks with it.

"Just a few more questions, okay?" AJ said.

"Okay."

"Ryan was concerned that Taylor would tell people he's gay. Is there any chance he is?"

"No." Jessi frowned. "No, he likes girls."

"You sure?"

"We talk sometimes. About who we like. Who we think is, you know, hot. He would have told me. We're honest with each other about that stuff."

"Okay." AJ picked up his hat, like he was getting ready to leave. "Is there anyone who hated Taylor enough to want to do something to her? This Maggie, maybe?"

"You mean hurt her – kill her? Jesus. No."

The doorbell rang. When Mr. Wade didn't come out from the kitchen, Mrs. Wade got up and went to the door.

AJ tapped the band of his hat. "You said Ryan had the attention of a lot of girls. Besides Maggie, are there any other girls who wanted to go out with Ryan?"

"Probably any of his girl friends would go out with him if they had the chance."

"Does that include you?"

Jessi glanced toward the hallway where her mother was. "He's not my type."

"So there's really no chance?"

"There is *no* chance." Her eyes narrowed. "I really don't want to talk about that, okay?"

Mrs. Wade came back into the room holding a paper plate. "Mrs. Desautel sent over your favorite muffins, Jessi." She looked back and forth between her daughter and AJ. "What did I miss?"

"Nothing," Jessi said.

"I think we're done here," AJ said. "Thanks so much, Jessi. You've been a big help. And you, too, Mrs. Wade."

"You're very welcome." Mrs. Wade turned toward the back of the house. "Carl!"

Wheeler and Mr. Wade emerged from the kitchen. As he handed her a card, Wheeler asked Jessi to call if she remembered anything, even if it didn't seem important. Then he and AJ went back outside.

When they were in the car again, Wheeler said, "So, did you learn anything?"

"Well, for starters," AJ said, "the pool of people who hated Taylor just keeps getting bigger."

11

"Don't kids usually keep lots of pictures on their phones?" Wheeler said. They were driving back down Route 1.

"Yeah, pictures, movies, text messages."

"So you'd expect Taylor's phone to have pictures of her boyfriend."

"Sure."

"I checked Taylor's phone myself," Wheeler said. "There were no pictures of Ryan."

"Seems unlikely," AJ said.

"I guess she could have erased them. Maybe I missed something. You should take a look."

They passed the VFW hall and the big, brick police station came into view. AJ pulled around back.

"I don't see the chief's car," Wheeler said. "I was kind of hoping... Right about now, I'd usually run through everything I have with him."

AJ took the last spot for patrol cars.

"That's tough about his granddaughter," Wheeler said.

"Yeah. Claire looked up that type of cancer. Sounds like there's a good chance the girl can beat it. But it's not going to be fun."

"Poor kid."

They got out of the car and went into the station. AJ was at the coffee pot when Wheeler approached with an evidence bag. He produced a small phone from the bag, slid the keyboard out, then in again, like a salesman demonstrating the features. He handed the phone to AJ.

"See if you have any luck."

AJ tapped the keypad. "There are no pictures of Ryan," he said after a while. "You didn't miss anything." He passed the phone back to Wheeler.

Sealing the evidence bag again, Wheeler said, "I'm starving. I think I'll go home and get something to eat."

"Claire's out," AJ said, "so I'm heading over to the market. Want to come? I'll treat you to a late lunch. Or my parents will."

"Tempting. I'd better go home, though. It's Sunday, after all. Can we meet back here in a couple hours? How about five?"

"Sounds good."

Wheeler started to walk away, then turned. "Can I have a raincheck on that lunch? A plate of fried clams sounds awfully good."

"Absolutely."

***

AJ parked in the hard-packed dirt behind the market and went in the back door. DaSilva was standing over a fryer while June Bugbee rinsed out a steel sink.

"Hey, Dave. Hey mom." He kissed her on the cheek.

She chuckled and shut off the water.

"Hey, detective," DaSilva said. "How's the case going?"

AJ didn't answer.

"Have you eaten?" June said. "I'll get you something."

"Thanks, that would be great. Been busy here?"

She lifted a tray from a stack. "We had a decent lunch rush."

"Where's Dad?"

"Out for his afternoon walk."

"That's good. He's sticking with the program."

"So far."

"What about Sela?"

"He's at a birthday party, for an aunt," DaSilva said. He lifted a basket of fries from the oil. "Here, you can have some of these. I was just making 'em for myself."

"Thanks."

"You'll have to meet the new guy," DaSilva said.

"Oh yeah?" AJ looked at his mother.

"Yes, your dad finally bit the bullet and hired someone. He started today. He seems nice. Picked everything up really quick."

Having packed a roll to bursting with lobster, she added the steaming hot fries to the tray.

AJ took the tray and went toward a stool in the corner.

June gripped his elbow. "You look pale. Go sit in the sunshine. Here – " She handed him a bottled water. "The doctor says to stay hydrated."

AJ backed out the door, then carried his meal around the building. Picnic tables were scattered across a grassy patch between Route 1 and a side road. A few were occupied by people nursing their sodas and their last wilting fries. AJ took the table nearest the building and dug in.

After a few minutes, Parker came out the front door. He took a quick look around, then headed toward AJ. "How you doing? I'm Parker."

"Ah, the new guy. I'm AJ."

"Yeah, I knew when I saw the uniform. Stonington P.D. Your mom talks about you a little."

"Just a little?" They shook hands. "How's it going so far? Hope the Daves aren't giving you too hard a time."

"No, everybody's been great. I know I'm going to like it here."

"That's good news. You'll take some of the pressure off me." Parker undid his ponytail but his hair stayed back from his face.

"Are you done for the day?" AJ said.

"Yep. Just waiting for my ride. Don't let me interrupt your meal."

"You want to sit down? You've probably been on your feet all day."

Parker grinned. "Sure, thanks." He began playing with his phone, which was large and black.

"Is that new?" AJ said.

Parker tilted the screen toward AJ. "Kinda new. I got it right before we moved here. My dad was trying to make up for yanking me out of my school just before graduation."

"Did that work?"

"It definitely helped."

AJ dunked a fry in the milky sauce that had escaped from the lobster roll. "Does it take good pictures?" he said after a while.

"Great pictures. Here." Parker aimed the phone at AJ, then came around the table. "Check it out."

AJ saw a crisp image of himself. "Oh, yeah. Could have picked a better subject." He pulled a cell phone from his pocket. It was like the one he had examined at the police station – small, with a slide-out keyboard. "Do any of your friends still have this kind?"

"Sure, some kids do. But this is what everyone wants."

"So if they can afford it, they trade up to one of those."

"Pretty much." Parker tapped the glass a few times. "It takes great videos, too." He aimed it toward the seagulls searching for scraps in the grass.

A few seconds later, Parker handed AJ the phone. AJ watched the video. "Beats the home movies my parents used to take."

"Right? And it's really easy to put them up on Facebook."

"Facebook. You all use that, right?"

"Sure. Unless you have super controlling parents, I guess."

AJ finished off his fries, then stood up. "It was great to meet you, Parker. Oh, and about your hourly wage."

"Yeah?"

"Make sure they pay you better than they pay me."

Parker smiled. "Got it."

AJ went back inside with his tray. DaSilva was there, wiping down the big front window. "I see you met Parker."

"Seems like a good guy."

They both looked out for a second. Parker, still playing with his phone, was walking toward the road.

Beth spoke up from behind the counter. "Hey, AJ, I didn't even know you were here until I saw you out there with a plateful of food. How about saying hello?"

"I was afraid you'd put me to work," AJ said.

"Don't worry about that. You've been replaced."

"I hope so." AJ crossed the room.

"So you're on the murder case?" Beth said, as AJ passed behind her.

AJ pretended not to hear. "I've got to say bye to Mom." He disappeared through the plastic door just as the rattling industrial air conditioner kicked in, swallowing him in sound.

At the window, DaSilva stood with his cloth pressed against the glass. "Geez. Parker's brother barely stopped long enough for him to jump in."

"I wonder if he's going to get sick of driving Parker all the way over here."

"Probably," DaSilva said, starting in with the cloth again. "I know one thing. If he's going to come here when AJ's around, he'd better take care of that busted headlight."

***

His cell phone to his ear, AJ leaned back against his car.

"Hey, AJ," Wheeler said. "What's up?"

"I just had an interesting conversation."

"Yeah?"

"I was talking to this high school kid my parents just hired. He has a smartphone – big thing, just fits in your hand. He said everyone who can afford one has one. Wouldn't Taylor have the latest technology, the coolest thing, whatever it was? Everything in that house looked new."

"Yes, it did." Wheeler was quiet for a second. "We picked up the wrong phone."

"That's what I'm thinking. It would explain why we didn't find any pictures of Ryan. They're all on her new phone."

"Okay. So where's the new phone?"

"Good question." The speaker beeped in AJ's ear. "One sec." He checked the screen, punched some keys, then raised the phone again. "Sorry, that was Claire. I guess I'll see you at the station in a bit?"

"Don't bother. I got a call from one of our camper's moms. The boys are stuck at the campground. Car trouble. She was on her way up there."

"Great. I was hoping we'd get to talk to them before they go to school tomorrow."

"I know. They're supposed to call me when they're back."

"We could head up there ourselves and try to catch them."

"Yeah, but we'd probably end up crossing paths on the road. I think I'll just wait for the call. If it's late, I may run over and do the interview myself."

"Okay, sure. Keep it low key."

"Right. And give you your evening back."

"Well, thanks."

"I'm sure you'll have a chance to repay me."

"Okay," AJ said. "So if you do talk to them, don't forget to ask –
"

"Right. What kind of phone did Taylor have."

***

As he stepped into the front hall, he could hear Claire and Sela in the kitchen. "Hey!" he called back to them. "I smell pizza!"

Claire appeared, wearing a sleeveless shirt, a big smile on her face. They met there by the blueprint for the attic remodel. She put her bare arms around him, pulling him close. "I'm so glad you made it home for dinner."

He slid a hand into the back pocket of her jeans. "Me, too."

They kissed, then remained there for a while, their foreheads touching.

"You think Sela will notice if we slip upstairs for an hour?"

"He might," Claire said.

"Mmm."

"You'll just have to hold that thought," she said. "I know I will."

"All right."

"You hungry?"

"Honestly, I didn't think I'd get home, so I had a quick meal at the market."

"More for Sela, then."

They kissed again and then went into the kitchen. Buck got up from a nap at Sela's feet. AJ scratched him behind the ears. The dog lay down again, yawning.

"Hey, Sela," AJ said. "I thought you were at a birthday party."

"I was, I was."

"I can vouch for him," Claire said. "When I ran into him at the drug store, he was buying a birthday card."

"Claire said I could use her as an excuse to leave the party early."

"What exactly did you tell them?" Claire said.

"I pretended to get a call. Then I said you had a rabid raccoon in the garage."

"They believed that?"

"Yeah. And I said that AJ was off solving the murder, so it was up to me to come to the rescue. With my family, the more dramatic the story, the more likely they are to believe it."

"I've met them," AJ said. "It's true." He turned back toward the hall. "I'm going to go change."

"Make it quick!" Sela called after him. "I'm hungry."

82

A few minutes later they were all at the table on the porch.

"I met Parker," AJ said. "He seems like he'll work out."

Sela put a second slice of pizza on his plate. "Yeah. He's a hardworking kid."

"You may be out of a job, AJ," Claire said.

"Wouldn't that be tough? Down to just one."

"So how's the big murder case going?" Sela said. "I understand you're working with Wheeler."

Claire winced. "Is it okay that I told him?"

"It's fine," AJ said. "Wheeler and I work well together. He let me do an interview today."

"How'd it go?" Sela said.

"All right, I think."

"To Detective Bugbee, then," Sela said, raising his beer.

The two bottles and AJ's glass of iced tea clinked over the table.

"You need to make contact with the ghost and use those mad interview skills on her," Sela said.

Claire glanced at AJ, then looked away.

"What?" Sela said. "Have you already made contact? There is a ghost? And don't give me that I-can't-talk-about-an-ongoing-investigation crap."

"Yeah, I saw her," AJ said.

"No shit." Sela said. "When were you going to tell me? What was she like? Glowing, like Ben? Or full of holes, like some of the others?"

"I don't want to say she looked like Ben, but yeah. More like that. Glowing."

"Did you communicate with her? What did she say?

"There was no communication, really. She appeared, tried to scream, couldn't, then disappeared. That was pretty much it."

"Damn," Sela said. "Well, that's still huge. It proves you've still got your ability. And if she's stuck, like Ben was, then eventually – "

"What?"

"Ben was trapped here because he died here. I'm sure it's like that with her – she's trapped in that house. So, you'll always know where to find her. You're going back, right?"

AJ nodded.

"When?"

"Tonight."

"DaSilva and I should come with you."

"It's still a crime scene, Dave."

"Ask the chief. He'll say it's okay."

Claire shook her head. "You can't bother him with that right now."

"Why, what's going on?"

Claire told him about the granddaughter.

"Shit," Sela said. "You think they're going to need help? You could talk to your parents about putting a collection jar on the counter, AJ. They've done that before."

"I hadn't even thought about that part of it. Let me talk to the chief first."

The three of them were quiet for a moment.

Sela stood up. "You ready for another slice?"

"I'm good," AJ said. "I had a late lunch."

Claire held her hand over her plate.

Sela went to the end of the table and opened the box.

AJ had his phone in his hand. "Guess Wheeler's not going to call."

"What's going on?" Sela said.

AJ put his phone away. "How long's it take you to catch a rabid raccoon?"

"I'd say until about nine o'clock," Sela said.

"What time's the party over?"

"About nine o'clock."

They all laughed.

"Hang out here as long as you want," Claire said. "I don't have any plans."

"Okay, cool," Sela said. "Thanks. You heading over to that house soon, AJ?"

"Yeah. I'd like to get started before it's pitch black."

"I'm going to have another beer," Claire said. "How about you, Dave?"

"Sure, that'd be good."

Claire went into the kitchen.

"You'll stay here until I get back, right?" AJ said, in a soft voice. "I'm sure she'd be fine, but, with this murder, and another ghost... I think it brings everything back."

"I'm happy to stay. It's no problem."

"Good. Thanks. I won't be long."

"Take your time. Really try to get through to that ghost."

AJ grunted. "I'm going because I know the chief wants me to. But I don't expect to get anything from this girl. Ben didn't remember anything at first. I doubt she will, either. Anyway, how much can she tell me if she can't even make a sound?"

"Maybe she'll be different tonight. Maybe she'll talk your ear off."

"Yeah." AJ picked up his glass and rattled the ice. "Maybe she'll surprise me."

12

The door of the Jeep squawked as AJ swung it open. He got out, the long metal police flashlight in his hand. He ducked under the tape and went down the walk. Someone had covered the big burned-out window in plastic. It looked, next to the sharply glinting glass of the others, like one afflicted eye, the soot like bruises around it.

He unlocked the front door. Holding the tape up with the flashlight, he slid into the house. The soggy, charred smell was still strong. He tried the light switch in the hall. Still no power. He turned on the flashlight and pointed the beam up the stairs. He stood there, listening. "Taylor? Are you here? I'm Officer Bugbee. I want to help you."

Nothing.

He stepped over the arsonist's trailer and peered into the living room. It was as scorched and black as the inside of any furnace. He kept going, to the office, with its blank computer screens. No sign of any change. No sign of Taylor.

In the kitchen, he aimed the flashlight across the counter. The beam reflected off the polished stone and the silver of the appliances and the arched faucet. Everything was clean, silent, calm. But wrong. The geometry was off – the lines were broken. The cabinet doors didn't make an even plane. They were open, some of them just a crack, others a few inches. AJ moved closer and saw that the drawers beneath the counter were open, too.

He turned to face the room. "Taylor, did you do this?"

From above, there was a creak – maybe a floorboard bending

under weight, or maybe the house shifting. AJ listened for a moment, then started up the stairs. His cell phone buzzed. He pulled it from his pocket. "Hey, Detective."

"AJ," Wheeler said. "I'm just leaving Sandy Grenier's house – one of the campers. That phone we've got – it definitely isn't the one Taylor was using. Sandy said she had a new phone. I guess she was always taking pictures and videos with it. I want to find that phone before someone in the family does, and messes with it. Can you meet me at the Fraser house?"

"How close are you?"

"Be there in ten minutes."

"All right," AJ said, taking the last step into the second floor hallway. "I'll head right over." After tucking his phone away, AJ was still, as if absorbing the silence. He aimed his light into Taylor's room, went inside. His eyes went from corner to corner. Nothing. He went back downstairs and out the front door, locking it behind him. He waited there on the front step.

"Thanks for meeting me here," Wheeler said, as he came up the walk a few minutes later. "You were quick."

"So how'd it go with the campers?"

Wheeler shook his head. "They didn't know anything about the drugs. They didn't know much of anything about anything. Except that Taylor Fraser was a really attractive girl. *Hot*, they said. Several times."

"And that she had the latest phone."

"Yeah. They thought her phone was hot, too." Wheeler aimed his flashlight at the house, though he didn't switch it on. "Let's go see if we can find that hot little phone."

AJ unlocked the door one more time.

"You want to look upstairs while I try down here?" Wheeler said.

"Okay."

Wheeler took a few steps toward the dining room, then stopped. "Check the bathrooms, too. These kids take their phones everywhere."

"All right." AJ paused by the blackened bannister, still looking toward Wheeler.

As if sensing the eyes on his back, Wheeler turned around. "You okay?"

"Yeah, sure." AJ climbed slowly, hewing to the wall, his head cocked as if all of his focus were downstairs. He hadn't reached the top when he heard Wheeler's voice.

"AJ! Come here!"

AJ hurried down. He found Wheeler in the doorway to the kitchen, sweeping the beam of his flashlight across the open cabinets.

"It wasn't like this Saturday morning. You were in here, too, right? Do you remember? Was everything open?"

"No."

"Great." Wheeler crossed the room. He went from drawer to drawer with his light. "Somebody was looking for something."

"Could have been whoever put the plastic up on the window," AJ said. "I don't know if that was family or one of our guys."

"We might end up having to fingerprint this whole place again. Make sure you don't touch anything. Here." He produced two pairs of disposable gloves from his coat pocket. When he'd put his on, he went to a cupboard, craning his neck to peer past the open door. He went to the next door, then the next. "Weird. It doesn't look like anything's been disturbed. They were rushed enough to leave the cabinets and the drawers open, but careful enough to put everything inside back in place." He nudged a drawer with his fingertips. It slid in without a sound. "These things work pretty easily."

AJ watched him but stayed quiet.

"We'd better look upstairs."

Wheeler led, his windbreaker whispering in rhythm. At the top, they went straight to Taylor's room. They examined, one more time, the photos around the mirror, the coordinated bed set, the glass-eyed bear, the dark stain on the carpet.

They moved on to a bathroom. The drawers in the vanity were closed. So was the medicine cabinet. Next was a bedroom. It was plain and spare, a place used only for visits. The walls were bare except for a mirror, mounted over the bureau. The glass was broken. It caught the beams of the flashlights and fractured them, sending them down jagged tracks.

Wheeler circled his light around the starburst shape. "This looks like a punch."

"Yeah."

Below the mirror, the bureau top was bare. Wheeler swept the beam of his flashlight across it, then down to the floor. There was a pile of debris – sunglasses, a capless ballpoint pen, a small spray bottle, earbuds.

"This wasn't a search," Wheeler said. "They just wanted to mess things up."

"Luckily there wasn't much to break," AJ said.

"This must be the stepbrother's room, right? What's his name – Jonathan?"

"Right."

After that was the master bedroom. AJ continued to the bathroom. It seemed undisturbed. The marbled counter by the sink, the ledge behind the whirlpool tub, the shelf in the ceramaic-tiled shower, all held jars and bottles in neat rows. AJ picked one up from the counter and held it under his light. The rounded base, which fit comfortably in his palm, was glass. Inside it was a red rose, fixed in clear liquid. It took him a moment to recognize the worn gold lever on the top, with the flat plate for a thumb, and at the other end, a striker. The thing was a lighter – old, maybe an antique. He put it down beside the sink and returned to the bedroom.

Wheeler stood in front of a chest of drawers. There were more of the lighters, some sleek and modern, their function clear only from the little ridged wheel that adjusted the height of the flame, others ornate, with outsized mechanisms.

"Quite a collection," Wheeler said.

"Yeah."

"Nothing's been touched in here."

"Right. Same in the bathroom."

They went out. The flashlights scrambled their shadows on the walls.

"I've seen vandalism before," Wheeler said, "and a real ransacking, when someone was tearing a place apart looking for something. This doesn't look like either."

AJ said nothing.

"Maybe it was related to the drugs. Or just some kids, screwing around in the scary house." Wheeler held his breath for a second, puffing out his cheeks. "The chief's not going to like it. It might mean putting someone on guard duty."

AJ said nothing.

"All right," Wheeler said. "I still want that phone. You want to take the last room up here? I'll go downstairs."

With Wheeler gone, AJ went back into Jonathan's room, stood in front of the shattered mirror. "Taylor, was this you?"

No answer. He moved back into the hall. He waited at to the top of the stairs with his head cocked, listening.

From below, there was a loud bang. Then another. AJ raced down and around the corner. "Sam? What's going on?"

Wheeler stood near the counter, his back to the room. His flashlight pointed at the cabinets just in front of him. Both were closed.

"They slammed shut," he said. "I didn't touch them."

Something glowed, on the other side of Wheeler. It brightened, took shape. First a tapered blouse, then long hair, a shimmering black. Taylor. She was facing the counter, too.

"Sam," AJ said, "maybe – "

"I saw something back there." Wheeler turned his flashlight on a row of canisters lined up against the backsplash. He reached toward them.

AJ could just make out, through the illuminated haze of Taylor's middle, that she was working with something on the counter. Another vintage lighter, heavy, painted, a gold lever on top. Her fingers failed, tried again. This time, they got traction. A flame leapt into the darkness. She slid the lighter across the counter, directly under Wheeler's arm.

"Sam! Watch out!" AJ said.

The fire found Wheeler's windbreaker. It seemed to disappear for a second, then a slit opened in the fabric. Flame shot out of it. As Wheeler jerked back with a yell, AJ snatched a dishtowel from the counter. He threw it on Wheeler's arm and wrapped it tight.

"Shit," Wheeler said. "Shit." He lurched to the sink and pushed the handle. Water sputtered from the faucet. He reached for the flow just as it dwindled and died.

"You all right?" AJ said.

"What the hell?"

AJ tried to get a read from Wheeler's face, but saw only shadows. Both men had dropped their flashlights. They pointed off in useless directions. Wheeler pulled the cloth away, held his arm close to his face. AJ watched him.

There was movement, then, by the counter. AJ turned just in time to see Taylor charge. Her jaw was clenched, her teeth bare. She crashed into him. Her shining form made contact, pushed him back.

He stumbled and fell.

"AJ?" Wheeler looked down at the floor.

Sucking in a deep breath, AJ got to his feet. Taylor was gone. The lighter had been extinguished. "Come on, Sam. Let's go."

They each picked up a flashlight. AJ went toward the dining room. Wheeler hesitated. "The phone."

"What?"

"Behind those jars."

AJ returned to where Wheeler had been. He moved the middle canisters to the side. A slim cell phone fell down onto the granite. AJ picked it up.

They went out the front door and down the walk to Wheeler's patrol car. AJ took the passenger side and switched on the dome light.

"Jesus," Wheeler said, holding his arm, looking back toward the house. "What the hell happened in there?"

"Let me take a look at that."

Wheeler swung his arm toward AJ. The end of the sleeve was just a few twisted shreds of blackened fabric. Red patches of skin showed through.

"That's going to blister," AJ said. "I should take you to the hospital."

Wheeler continued to look back toward the house.

"Sam – your arm – we should go to the hospital."

"It's not that bad." Wheeler let his hand drop. "What the hell happened, AJ?"

"I don't know. That antique lighter – it must have malfunctioned."

Wheeler didn't say anything for a while. He watched the house. "What made those doors slam?" He turned to AJ. "And why did you fall? You just keeled over."

"I tripped on my own feet. I don't know about the doors. Some kind of air current, I guess. A draft. Probably because of that blown-out window."

"Yeah, I guess." Wheeler moved his sleeve into the light. "I bet it was that damn spray that I put on there."

"What?"

"I used this weatherproofing spray. Supposed to make the fabric shed the rain. Maybe that's why it went up like that."

"Yeah, probably."

"Good thing you moved fast or it would have been a lot worse. I told you you'd pay me back for not dragging you out to talk to the campers. I didn't think it would be so soon." He faced the house again. "I think we'd better get a car up here. I want eyes on this place overnight." He reached for the mic.

AJ sat silent while Wheeler talked to Dispatch.

"Romano will be here in a few minutes," Wheeler said, when he was done with the call.

"If you're okay to drive, you should head over to the hospital. I'll stay."

"It's not that bad." Wheeler's eyes were on the house again.

"With a burn, the sooner you get to it, the better. You really should get going."

"It'll only be a minute."

"Yeah, but speed makes a difference. You need ice, or cold water, right away."

"Jesus, AJ."

AJ watched Wheeler for a second. He looked back at the house. "Well, if you're going to wait..." He held the cell phone that they'd found in the kitchen. "Let's see what we got." He tapped the screen. With a couple more taps, he found pictures. "Here we go."

He began flipping through them. Close-ups of teenage girls – making faces, hamming it up – like the photos taped to Taylor's mirror. A more composed shot of Taylor, framed by blue sky.

"That's her," Wheeler said.

"Yeah." AJ watched Wheeler's face, but it showed nothing, no recognition that a ghostly version of that girl had just set him on fire.

Next, a group photo – boys and girls at a table in a restaurant. Then a blurry shot of a soccer game. Another of Ryan in his jersey, a ball under one arm. Then Ryan in a cloud of smoke, glassy-eyed.

"This is what Jessi was talking about," Wheeler said.

"Looks like it." AJ rotated the phone and the picture adjusted to fit the longer shape. He advanced to the next photo – a sleepy-looking Ryan with a lit joint in his hand. Behind him, the curtains of Taylor's bedroom, the window dark. Then, Ryan, in the same spot, his eyes half closed.

"Who's that behind him?" Wheeler said.

AJ zoomed in. "That's Jonathan Fraser. The stepbrother."

Behind them, a car climbed up the driveway.

"Romano," AJ said.

"You want to do me a favor and pull a bag out of the glove compartment?"

When the phone was sealed up, AJ and Wheeler got out of the car. Romano was walking toward them.

"You guys all right?" Romano said. His hair glistened even in the dim light.

"We're fine," Wheeler said. "We just need you to watch this place. Someone's been inside, did some damage."

"They take anything?"

"Doesn't look like it."

"What happened to you?" Romano aimed his flashlight at Wheeler's arm.

"I had a little accident."

"That looks nasty. You ought to have someone check that out."

"Yeah. You just worry about the house. Call me immediately if you see anything."

"Okay, boss."

"You can just watch it from out here," AJ said. "We don't want to disturb anything inside."

Wheeler opened his car door again. "See you at the station bright and early, AJ. I'd really like to talk to the chief. I hope he comes in."

"Me, too," AJ said. "Take care of that arm."

"I will."

"I'll check the phone into evidence."

"Okay."

All three returned to their cars. AJ and Wheeler backed up and pulled away, leaving Romano in his cruiser, staring at the house, which was growing bigger and blacker in the failing light.

**

As he cut across the grass toward the front door, AJ saw the cool flicker of a television in the living room window. He looked left, to where the big lawn sloped away into the night, an opening for stars. From somewhere in that darkness, there was a jingling sound. It came toward him, gaining speed.

"Buck?"

The greyhound hurtled out of the shadows. He pressed his sharp nose against AJ's leg.

"Hey, boy. Let's go inside."

Claire and Sela were in the living room, watching a movie. Claire took AJ's hand as he leaned in to kiss her.

"So, how'd it go?" Sela said.

Claire made room and AJ sat down heavily. He stood up again and went toward the kitchen. "Be right back."

Returning with a beer, he dropped next to Claire and took a long pull. Claire switched off the television.

"Sorry," AJ said. "I didn't ask if anyone else wanted anything. Do you?"

"I'm set," Sela said. There were a couple of empties at his feet.

"You okay?" Claire said.

AJ drank from the bottle again. "I have a question for you, Dave. Have any of you guys ever been hit by a ghost?"

"Ben thought a ghost had touched him a couple of times, but we can't see anything, so it's tough to be sure. Did she touch you?"

"She shoved me. Hard."

"Like, she pushed you with her hands."

"She ran directly into me."

"She body-slammed you?"

"Yeah. Ben had to concentrate just to move a bottle cap. Taylor knocked me down."

"Remember," Sela said, "Ben moved some things, too. Like that vase."

"He saved my life," Claire said. "That was a pretty big move."

AJ squeezed her hand.

"Ben seemed to be able to affect physical objects when he was working off instinct, off emotion," Sela said. "He couldn't be precise, like moving bottle caps. But he could shove something. Maybe it's like that with her."

"She set Wheeler's coat on fire," AJ said. "She had to work a lighter to do that."

"Jesus," Claire said. "Wait, Wheeler was there?"

"Yeah. He called and asked me to meet him. He wanted to look for something."

"She used a lighter?" Sela said. "She set Wheeler's coat on fire?"

"Is he okay?" Claire said.

"Yeah, I think so. There was some kind of vintage lighter on the counter. She had to press the lever with her thumb. The thing made a flame this high." AJ stretched his finger and thumb as far apart as they would go. "Wheeler was leaning across the counter and it caught his coat."

"Damn," Sela said.

"All of the drawers and cabinets in the kitchen were open. Upstairs, a mirror was broken and stuff had been knocked on the floor. I'm guessing that was her, too."

"What did Wheeler think of all of this?" Claire said.

"I really don't know. I'm not sure how much of it registered."

"Did Taylor say anything?" Sela said. "Did you talk to her?"

"No. With Wheeler there, I couldn't. I'm not sure I can talk to her, anyway." AJ drained his bottle and stood up. "I need another one. Either of you want something?" He barely waited for a response.

"I have to tell DaSilva about this," Sela said, when AJ came back into the room.

"Yeah, I know."

"The chief is going to push you to talk to Wheeler," Claire said. "Explain what happened."

"I know." AJ twisted the top off the bottle. He remained standing in front of the couch. "I'm not sure how I'm going to handle it. When Wheeler saw the open cabinets in the kitchen, and the broken mirror, he thought somebody had been in the house. He's got Romano up there now, watching the place. He wants to check for prints again."

"Do you have to go back?" Claire said.

"Yeah. But not tonight."

"If there are cops watching the place..." Sela said.

"The chief will just put me in the rotation." AJ rubbed his eyes.

"What did it feel like, when she ran into you?" Sela said.

"It was... You've had someone run into you before, right?"

"Sure."

"It was like that, but..."

"Electric, like a shock?" Sela said. "That's what I would expect. Spirits can use electricity to manifest. Remember how Ben was always draining batteries?"

"No," AJ said, sounding irritated. "It was cold. But more than that, it was like I felt the force of the blow *inside*. Like she didn't hit here – " He touched his chest with is palm. "She hit me in there, on my ribs – inside my ribs. Imagine someone knocking the breath out of you by pressing directly on your lungs. Kind of like that."

"Shit, AJ," Sela said. "Maybe she wasn't trying to push you. Maybe she was trying to – " He hesitated. "Maybe she was trying to possess you."

"What?" AJ said.

"Possession? Is that stuff real?" Claire said. "Have you ever seen it?"

"Not personally," Sela said. "I've only read about it."

"Oh, come on," AJ said.

"Why are you so quick to dismiss it?" Claire said.

"I thought you were the one who had a hard time with all of this paranormal stuff. Possession? What, now you believe in everything?"

Claire sat back, looking hurt.

AJ inhaled sharply between his teeth. "I'm sorry. I'm exhausted. I should get some sleep." He took a last drink from the bottle. "I'll talk to you tomorrow, Dave."

"Yep." Sela stood up.

"I'm not trying to kick you out," AJ said.

"No, I should go. Thanks for letting me hang here, Claire."

"Thank you for taking care of that raccoon."

"Glad I could help."

AJ and Claire saw Sela out the front door. Then AJ took his bottle back to the kitchen. He rinsed it in the sink.

"You okay?" Claire had followed him after locking the door.

"Yeah. Tired."

"That's scary, what happened tonight."

"The ghosts," AJ said, "the things that I see – they always scare me. But that – that was a whole new level. I've never experienced anything like that."

Claire put a hand on his hip. "Let's go up to bed."

He didn't respond right away. "I'm not sure I can sleep right now."

"So you really were trying to get rid of Sela."

AJ smiled. "I don't know. I just didn't want to talk about it anymore. Not right now, anyway."

There were two bottle caps on the counter. AJ nudged one with his finger. It slid off the edge, then clattered across the floor, finally coming to rest by the table.

Claire took AJ's hand, pulled him toward her. "Come on," she said. "Let's go up. No talking, I promise."

***

"You okay?" she said, sleepily.

The bedroom was dark, the light from the window still feeble and cold.

"Crazy dream," he said.

"What was it?"

AJ sat up with his pillow against the headboard but didn't say anything.

"Do you remember it?" She moved close, her head against his hip.

"Yeah."

"Tell me."

"You should go back to sleep."

"Tell me."

He did. He talked into the darkness, telling the dream, taking himself back into it.

He was at the Fraser house, he said. It was still, quiet, the shadows settled and deep. He went from room to room. There were too many rooms and there was no order. Living room, bedroom, dining room. Empty rooms. Rooms with heavy curtains. All in darkness. Ashes on the floor – he left footprints. Rooms without windows. Drafty rooms, the windows gone.

One more corner, and he was in the kitchen. For the first time, there was light enough to see. The light was a flame, coming from something on the counter – a big-bellied lighter like the one that had burned Wheeler. There was another source, giving off a soft, pinkish glow. The ghost of Ben Shortman. He sat at the counter, facing away. AJ came up to Ben, circled around, trying to see his face. Trying to be seen by him. Ben was looking at something on the counter, something shining in the yellow flame of the lighter. It was a glass jar with the lid on tight. AJ moved close. Inside the jar was a spider – its jointed limbs rough with hair. A hunting spider. As big as a child's hand.

Ben tapped the glass and the spider scrambled. Not away from the sound, but toward it.

Ben finally turned. "This is a nasty one, AJ," he said. "Got to keep it bottled up."

The flame went out, Ben disappeared and the room went black.

13

AJ rapped on the metal doorjamb outside Chief Brown's office. Wheeler was already sitting in one of the molded chairs across from the chief's desk.

"Hey," Wheeler said. "I think I just about got the chief up to speed."

The chief motioned for AJ to come in. "So you had some excitement at the Fraser house last night?"

"Yeah." AJ stepped into the room. "How's the arm, Sam?"

"It's really not bad." Wheeler held it up in front of him. A bandage poked out from the sleeve of his sport coat. "They went a little crazy with the gauze."

"So Wheeler tells me the kitchen looked like it had been searched," the chief said. "Or, sort of. They opened things up but didn't touch anything inside? And there was vandalism, but just in the one bedroom. It sounds kind of odd. What was your impression, AJ?"

"I'd say odd just about covers it." AJ went around Wheeler and sat down in the empty seat. He stared past the chief toward the window.

The other two men watched him, still waiting for an answer.

"I keep coming back to that broken mirror in Jonathan's room," Wheeler said. "Somebody was pissed."

"All right. Who would be pissed at Jonathan?" the chief said.

"Maybe Jonathan was pissed at himself," Wheeler said. "For what he did to Taylor." "You think the stepbrother killed her?" The chief tapped a paper that lay on his desk. "Because it seems to me like you're building a case for Ryan Hardy. He had opportunity and motive. He was afraid of what Taylor would do to him if he broke up with her."

"Yeah, but chief," Wheeler said. "From everything we know about Ryan, up until he met Taylor, he had a pretty clean sheet. This stepbrother is an unknown. We found pictures of him on Taylor's cell."

"And?"

"I'm just saying, we need to take a deeper look at him."

"There might be more on that phone," AJ said. "We need to see how much and what kind of communication Taylor had with Jonathan."

Wheeler put up one hand. "Already done."

"Really?" AJ said.

"Don't look so surprised. Actually, I got help. But, I found no incriminating texts between those two, and only a couple of calls. Still, like you said, I think the photos are enough to warrant suspicion. Maybe Jonathan was afraid there was something on that phone that would link him to Taylor's involvement with drugs. He could have been looking for the phone when you ran into him."

"Okay," Chief Brown said, "Jonathan is of interest. Just keep one eye on Ryan." For a moment, he looked at at the television against the wall, which showed a news anchor, her mouth moving silently. "Sam, you mentioned a Maggie Strang."

"Yeah," Wheeler said. "I guess Taylor bullied her, to the point that she got in trouble at school."

"And this Maggie had a thing for Ryan?"

"That's what Ms. Wade said."

"Maggie Strang." The chief laid a hand on his shaved scalp. "That name rings a bell, but I can't quite place it. Sounds like you need to talk to her."

"Right," Wheeler said. "What about fingerprinting again at the Fraser house? And setting up surveillance, in case whoever was messing around over there comes back?"

"Surveillance would be tough to cover," the chief said. "Why don't you see if Jonathan has any kind of record. I'll talk to AJ about what we can do at the house."

Wheeler got up, wincing as his injured hand pushed against the chair. When he was gone, the chief motioned for AJ to close the door.

"So what the hell actually happened last night? Did any of it have to do with Taylor? Was she there?"

"Yeah, she was there." AJ sat down again. "She set Wheeler's jacket on fire with some kind of antique lighter. And she gave me a hell of a shove."

"She did all that? I thought they were – what is it – ethereal? Not solid. Not physical. Am I wrong about that? Have you seen this kind of thing before?"

"No. She surprised me, too."

"Do we need to worry about this? Can you handle her?"

"I'll be all right."

The chief gave AJ a long look. "That had to be her messing with the kitchen and breaking that mirror."

"I can't be sure, but I'd be surprised if it wasn't."

"If she broke that mirror, then she's the one who's pissed at Jonathan."

"Maybe."

"What do you mean, maybe?"

"She may have broken the mirror, but as far as proving that she was pissed at him? I don't know."

"Because she attacked you and Wheeler, too."

"Yeah. She may just be angry, period," AJ said. "That I have seen before."

"All right. For all we know, Jonathan has a rock solid alibi, anyway."

AJ tipped his head back against the wall. He stared up at the ceiling.

"You seem beat," the chief said. "Wheeler is the one with the burn, but something tells me he got off easy."

AJ straightened up in the rounded chair. "I'm okay."

The chief studied AJ's face.

"How about you?" AJ said. "How's your family holding up?"

"We're doing all right, so far. My daughter's strong. She's a fantastic mom to that little girl."

"I'm sure she is."

The chief cleared his throat. "So, the surveillance..."

"Yeah. What do you want to do?"

"I'm in kind of a bind. As far as parking someone outside – I don't want to pay overtime for guys to watch for an intruder that's never going to show up. And setting up inside – after last night, I'm not sure I want anyone in there unless you're with them."

"So how do you want to handle it?"

"I'm thinking we call Sela and DaSilva in again, like we did at Claire's house when we were trying to figure out what was going on there. They can set up their video equipment. Do you think the guys would be interested?"

AJ closed his eyes for a second. "Of course they'd be interested," he said. "They live for this stuff."

"You have a problem with the idea? Because I don't think it's half bad. It doesn't cost me anything. It keeps Wheeler happy. Who knows, the cameras may actually catch something useful."

"What they catch might be pretty strange. What do we do then? Wheeler's going to want to see the video."

"That's one more reason to let him in on your secret. You had the perfect opportunity last night. It would have been easy to tell him the truth about something he'd just experienced himself."

"No. He was more than happy to accept the explanation I gave him – a lighter malfunction, me being clumsy, drafts moving doors. If he'd been ready for the truth, he would have known that was bullshit."

The chief rapped his knuckles on the desk. "You may be right. So we'll let you and your friends review the video before anyone else. What Wheeler sees will be up to you."

There was a knock at the door. When the chief answered, Wheeler stuck his head in. "Jonathan doesn't have a record. I did find out that he starred in a high school production of *Grease*, and he organized a fundraiser for a classmate with cancer."

"Another good boy," AJ said.

The chief raised his hand. "Yeah, well, one of these good boys may have committed murder. Let's just see if we can figure out which one."

14

"That was too weird," Olivia said. "Mr. Gerber with that speech and then Ms. Addison ranting on and on."

They had just come from an assembly about Taylor. Now they were going to spend their free period in the library. Not because it was such a great place to hang out, but because the cafeteria wasn't open yet. The library was the only place with halfway comfortable chairs and any chance of having a private conversation. They took a table in a corner.

"All these girls crying," Olivia said. "Half of them hardly even knew Taylor. It's so fake. They're just showing off for the police. It's like they see the cop car out front and they think they're on TV."

"Has anyone said anything about Ryan?" Maggie said. "Is he still in the hospital?"

"Why don't you text him?"

"Yeah," Maggie said. She didn't move to get her phone out of her purse.

Olivia checked her own phone. "Oh, God. Mallory said that Ryan and Taylor had a fight the night she died. She said he was so upset that he tried to kill himself. Is that right? Is that why he's in the hospital?"

"Don't listen to her, Olivia! Ryan would never do that. Especially not for Taylor."

"Yeah, Mallory's an idiot." Olivia looked toward the entrance. "Here comes Miss Goody Goody. Looking for you, no doubt."

"Why do you say that?"

"Because she thinks she's your personal guidance counselor."

Maggie opened her notebook and put a finger on a page. "I think Ms. Goodwin is nice."

"Of course you do," Olivia said. "I'll give her two seconds to be at this table."

A woman maybe six or seven years older than Maggie and Olivia, but wearing a skirt and kitten heels, came toward them.

"Hello, girls," she said. "Olivia, could I speak with Maggie for a minute?"

Olivia scooped up her notebook, making sure Maggie saw her overdone smile. "I'll see you in biology."

"Yeah, see you."

Ms. Goodwin took Olivia's chair. "How are you doing, Maggie?"

Maggie shrugged. "Okay."

"It's a lot to deal with, isn't it?"

"I'm fine." Maggie flipped a page in the notebook. Ms. Goodwin was always asking these kinds of questions. Trying to get you to confess to something, like she thought she was Oprah. But you could wait her out.

"All right," Ms. Goodwin said. "Considering how nasty Taylor was to you, it's perfectly normal for you not to mourn her passing. That's really okay."

Maggie kept looking down at her notebook. She wanted to say that no one was really mourning Taylor. Or, almost no one.

"I understand that Ryan is going to be just fine. He's home from the hospital. Have you talked to him? Or gone to see him?"

"He's probably busy with Taylor's friends."

"I bet he'd be glad to see you. In situations like this, people like to be with their oldest friends, friends they can trust."

"Yeah, I guess," Maggie said.

Ms. Goodwin pushed her chair back. "If you need me, Maggie, my door is always open." She got to her feet.

Maggie closed her notebook.

Ms. Goodwin started toward the door, then turned. "Your next class is biology?"

"Yeah. Ms. Addison."

"Why don't I let her know that you're excused today?"

"That would be great." For one quick second, Maggie's smile was wide and bright.

"Okay. I'll take care of that. Talk to you later?"

"Sure." Maggie sat down again. She watched Ms. Goodwin leave. It was turning out, once they got past the assembly, to be a pretty good day.

***

"Where were you?" Olivia said, as she came up to Maggie.

Maggie pulled a book from her locker. "In the library. Ms. Goodwin let me skip."

"Are you kidding? God, lucky you."

"I know. How was biology?"

"Crazier than ever. Logan was up at Addison's desk, sobbing, and Addison was hugging her, patting her hair." She demonstrated with her hands. "It was gross. I heard Addison say something to her about the police."

"What? What about the police?"

"She was going to talk to them or something."

"You mean about Taylor? What for? She doesn't know anything."

"Right. But I guess she has this list of kids she wants to give to them."

"Seriously? A list of what kids?"

"I don't know. It was supposedly right on the desk. Logan saw it. She stopped me after class. She said you're the first name."

"What? Why?"

"I don't know. You hated Taylor, but so did a lot of kids. I guess with you two it was a little more... I mean, you did have that fight."

"It wasn't a fight. I was just standing up for myself, for once. Taylor was the one who ended up in the vice principal's office, not me."

"I know. It's just bullshit. Addison is such a bitch."

Maggie stared into her locker.

"Whatever," Olivia said. "Nobody's going to listen to Addlebrain. Actually, I've been thinking, this whole mess could end up being her fault."

"What do you mean?"

"She's the one who made Taylor and Ryan work together. She assigned partners for that stupid project, right? That's what started it between Taylor and Ryan. If they hadn't worked together, Taylor wouldn't have gotten killed and Ryan wouldn't have ended up in the hospital."

"What are you talking about? Are you saying that Ryan killed Taylor?"

"No. Jesus. I heard that Taylor was alone Friday night because she was waiting for Ryan."

"So?"

"Taylor's parents were gone for the weekend. She was waiting for Ryan to come over. That's why she was alone. That's how she got killed."

"I don't get it. If Taylor wasn't waiting for Ryan, she would have been waiting for some other guy."

"No, see, because any other guy wouldn't have kept her waiting. She wouldn't have been alone. I heard Ryan wanted to break up with her. That's why he didn't go over there until really late."

"I don't know," Maggie said.

"If Addison had stayed out of it and let Ryan work with you, then Taylor might still be alive. Maybe you and Ryan would even be together. She messed with you guys, and that started everything going wrong."

Maggie looked over at Olivia, just thinking about all of that. If she and Ryan were together, maybe she would have been with him that day instead of at the dollar store. The gray car never would have followed her right to Taylor's doorstep. Maggie closed her locker. "It really is Addison's fault."

"Right? She's evil. Come on, let's go to lunch. I'm starving."

Maggie spun the dial on her locker a few times. "I'll be there in a minute."

"Okay."

Olivia headed toward the cafeteria. Maggie went the other way, around the corner into the guidance suite. Usually, there'd be a secretary at the desk, but today the desk was empty. Maggie kept going, toward Ms. Goodwin's office. Someone was talking in there.

"I think it's our responsibility to tell the police what we know."

It was Ms. Addison. Maggie stopped.

"What exactly do you know that you feel compelled to tell the police?" Ms. Goodwin's voice was quiet, but Maggie was close enough that she could still hear. "This looks like a list of students you don't like, to me. What makes you think any one of them could have harmed Taylor?"

"They hated her. Every single one of them hated her."

"I know there are students who disliked Taylor because she was cruel to them. But they're not murderers. They're not capable of that."

"What makes you so sure?"

Maggie stood still, trying not to make a sound. Trying not to breathe, or even blink.

"I'm not saying any one of them did it." Ms. Addison again. "I'm just saying that the police should talk to them. Let the police do their job."

"Nicole, giving this list to the police would be a huge mistake. I asked to talk to you because I've already had complaints about this list. Apparently some students have seen it, or at least know about it. That's not at all appropriate. They've overheard things, remarks you made. Did you really say that you wish what happened to Taylor had happened to a student who wasn't such a good person?"

"I said a person with less promise."

"Oh, Nicole, you really – "

"No, you need to understand something," Ms. Addison said. "Most of these kids you seem determined to invest your time and energy in – your little broken toys – they'll amount to nothing. Best case, they don't end up – well, on a list like this. I'm sorry if it sounds harsh. But when you've worked here a few more years, you'll get it. You'll see things the same way I do."

"No, I'm sure I won't. I'm going to have to talk to Mr. Gerber about this."

"You do what you have to do. And so will I."

Maggie went back into the hall. When she'd gone a little ways and wasn't worried about the noise anymore, she started to run. She wasn't used to running. Her elbows swung wide and her sandals slopped around on her feet. She ran past the closed doors to classrooms and the rows of lockers. She kept running. The long hallway was empty. There was no one at the lockers, no one on their way to class. It was like every single person, except for her, was already where they were supposed to be.

15

The principal, who was showing them the way, got called back to the office. AJ and Wheeler continued toward the main hall. They could hear footsteps receding quickly – soles slapping fast against the floor. Rounding the corner, they saw a girl running away, her curly hair bouncing with each jerky stride. She ducked into a bathroom.

"Must be an emergency," Wheeler said.

"I guess."

"This place has changed so much since I was here. Was it like this in your day?"

"No." AJ looked annoyed. "The renovation happened just a few years ago, Sam."

"Yeah, that's right. Dumb question. I guess it's a sore subject, with you turning thirty this year. I didn't mean to remind you that you're getting so old." Wheeler's cell phone buzzed in a pocket. He raised it to his ear. "Chief?"

A woman, tall and slender and blonde, in a bright, sheath dress, appeared from a classroom and came up the hall, moving quickly.

"Officer," she said, focusing on AJ.

"Yes?"

"I have something I need to give you." She offered a folded piece of paper.

AJ took the paper and glanced at it. There were butterflies around the border. In the center was a list. "What am I looking at?"

Ms. Addison gave him a red-lipped smile. "These are students... I think they – "

Wheeler cut her off. "The chief needs us back at the station."

Ms. Addison crossed her bare arms. "As I was saying, these students all had great animosity for Taylor Fraser."

Wheeler frowned and leaned toward the list, which AJ held between them. "Thank you, Mrs..."

"Addison. Nicole Addison."

"Ms. Addison. If you don't mind, we'll take this with us. We'll have to get the details from you later."

"That's fine."

"I don't know what to make of that," Wheeler said, when they were alone in the hall again.

AJ shook his head. "So what's up with the chief?"

"He didn't tell me. It must be important if he wanted us to drop everything."

"I guess so."

They returned to the office. Wheeler told the principal that they'd been called away but might be back.

"Let me see that list again," Wheeler said, as they stepped out into the bright sun.

AJ handed the paper to him.

"There's a familiar name," Wheeler said. "Right at the top."

***

For a long time, Maggie just looked at herself in the mirror – her green eyes, the little pimple that was trying to come out on her chin, the white scalp that showed at the part of her hair. It was like she had to watch herself, keep an eye on herself every second so that she wouldn't disappear. Besides her, the place was empty. She was sure because she'd checked the stalls. Still, the room was too big to really feel private. When she made any sound at all – a sniffle, a breath or anything – it sounded hard and echoey. So she didn't make any sound.

The bell rang, so loud it made her jump. She started toward the door just as two girls pushed through it and past her, like she wasn't even there. Maggie went into the hall. It was flooded with people, now. She worked her way through the crowd, heading back to guidance.

"Maggie," Ms. Goodwin said, looking up from her desk. "Are you okay?"

"Can I go home?" She didn't try to make her voice sound normal, but she wasn't going to cry, either. She was sure she could hold it somewhere in-between.

Ms. Goodwin stood. "What's going on?"

"I..." She stopped. It was like there was a wet clog in her throat.

"Are Taylor's friends bothering you?"

"No." Maggie said.

Ms. Goodwin studied her, looking for a clue. "Does this have anything to do with Ms. Addison?"

Maggie shook her head. She felt her throat filling again.

Ms. Goodwin seemed for a second like she might come around the desk. Instead, she asked, "Is anyone at home, Maggie?"

"Yeah. My mom and dad."

"Okay. I'll sign you out." Ms. Goodwin tore a hall pass from a stack and wrote on it. Then she took a business card from a desk drawer and wrote on that. She reached across the desk. "The card's for you. It has my cell number. Call me if you need anything."

"Thanks," Maggie said. "Thanks a lot, Ms. Goodwin."

"No problem."

The hall was empty again. Maggie went straight to her locker, then out the front door. The second the warm air and the sun hit her, she felt a little better. She got into her car. She still had the hall pass and the business card in her hand. She held the card up, read the number written in pen. Then she tossed it on the seat next to her and started driving. She wasn't sure where yet. Just somewhere.

***

"So what's going on, Chief?" Wheeler took a chair. AJ sat down next to him.

The chief pressed the *Mute* button on the TV remote, then slid it to the far corner of the desk. "Remember I said that name, Maggie Strang, sounded familiar?"

"Yeah," Wheeler said.

"Well, it finally came to me. I called my buddy at the North Stonington P.D. and he filled in the details."

"Okay. What details?"

"Six years ago, there was a fire at a trailer park out there. A man was killed. Died in his bed. Well, not *his* bed. His girlfriend's bed. The fire marshal concluded it was accidental, that he'd passed out with a lit cigarette. But there was another theory, for a while, at least. A neighbor said there were two girls sneaking around that trailer. One of them lived there. The other was a friend of hers. They were young – middle school. The girls were interviewed, said they were having a sleepover at the friend's trailer and never went outside. A grandmother vouched for them, swore that she'd kept a close eye on them all night. Our guys found her believable."

"One of the girls was Maggie Strang?" Wheeler said.

"That's right. Magda was what her grandmother called her – short for Magdalana. Her friend was a Tiffanee Burns."

"All right," Wheeler said, taking it in. "So the grandmother vouched for them."

AJ sat forward. "Is there more to this, chief?"

Chief Brown locked his hands together on his desk. "The man that died, the boyfriend, was at best a lazy low-life. At his worst, he was an abusive drinker and druggie. He and Tiffanee were known to butt heads."

"So Tiffanee had motive to start that fire," AJ said. "She wanted the boyfriend out of the picture."

"Yeah, but how old were these girls?" Wheeler said. "Eleven, twelve? And the alibi."

"Right," the chief said. "The alibi was solid. Chet was convinced that the grandmother was telling the truth. He said he tried and he couldn't shake her."

"What about the girls?" AJ said. "Did he believe them?"

"Chet said Maggie just seemed scared. Tiffanee – he remembered her as cold. Not scared, not even upset. Calm, almost blank."

"Sounds like a psycho," Wheeler said.

"A psychologist talked to her. His report was that she was in shock."

They were all quiet for a moment.

"Whether or not they set that fire," Wheeler said, "Maggie saw fire solve her friend's problem."

The chief grunted in agreement. "I saved the best for last. This Tiffanee Burns – after the fire she and her mom moved up to Ledyard. The mom got a job at the casino. She became friendly with one of the bigwigs there, had an affair with him, broke up his marriage and ended up marrying him. Then a little while ago, she and

Tiffanee and the new husband moved here, to Stonington. No trailer this time – they've got a nice big house. At least, it was nice, until recently."

"Wait..." AJ said.

"They made one other change, besides moving up the economic ladder. Tiffanee was going by Taylor now."

"Tiffanee is Taylor?" Wheeler said. "Taylor Fraser?"

"That's right. She's our girl."

"Shit," Wheeler said.

"Did you talk to Maggie Strang this morning?" the chief said.

"No. But she's got to be our next stop."

16

Maggie sat at the light by Flanders Road. It would be stupid, she thought, to just go home. Everyone else was still in school. This was her chance. When the light changed, she kept going straight, toward Mystic. She drove along the sound, went around the bend by the train station, then the monument. Made one pass by his house. There was no car in the driveway. Maybe it was parked in the little garage. Ms. Goodwin said he was home from the hospital, but maybe he wasn't actually *at home*. He could be anywhere. She hadn't talked to him, or really even texted him, in a long time. It was crazy to just show up at the door.

But she wasn't going to talk herself out of it.

She parked at the end of the block. Then, so she wouldn't have time to get nervous, she walked fast. She got nervous, anyway. There was a weird whir going on inside her head. Her legs felt like they weren't even hers, like they were twitchy robot legs that she could just barely control. But she kept walking. She went up the sidewalk under the giant trees. She turned in where the big flagstones led to his door. Next to the plaque with the blue anchor, there was the button, glowing, like it was saying *here I am, this is what you are looking for, push me*. She had no idea what she was going to say to him. She had no idea what he was going to say to her. But she put her finger on the button and pushed.

There was still time, before the door swung open, for her to run away, to slip through the hedge and disappear. Then there wasn't. Ryan was standing in the doorway.

He didn't look like he'd been in the hospital, almost dead from a drug overdose. He didn't look like his girlfriend had just been murdered. Or maybe he did. Maggie had never met anyone who'd had those things happen to them before, so she really didn't know. Right now, right in front of her, Ryan looked pretty much the way he always looked. Ridiculously great.

Maybe he looked a little bit surprised and like he didn't know what to do. He stood there holding a can of soda, not drinking it and not saying anything. This went on long enough that she had time to think maybe she would run away after all. But then he said, "Maggie. Wow. Come in."

He closed the door behind her. The light was off in the hall and she couldn't really see his eyes.

"I was out back," he said. "I just came in for a soda. Do you want one?"

"Sure."

They went around a corner to the kitchen and he got a can from the refrigerator.

"Thanks," she said. Her second word. She came all the way over here and now she couldn't talk. She took a sip from the can instead.

They went out a back door into the yard. Ryan sat down at a green plastic table. His laptop was there, and a pad of paper and a couple of citronella candles in little pastel pots. She sat down next to him. He had white bandages all down one arm. Somehow she hadn't noticed them before. There was another long pause while they didn't say anything.

The yard was walled in by shrubs. In one corner there was a dog house that was like a real house, with shingles and trim. There was a worn patch of dirt in front of it, but no dog. In the other corner there was a little wooden shed, with windows and shutters. Then on the other side of the shrubs, there was the garage, with more windows and shutters. It was like those nesting dolls, only with houses.

Maggie watched Ryan out of the corner of her eye. His hair was half combed. He was wearing shorts and he was barefoot.

"So are you okay?" she said.

He nodded. "Are you skipping?"

"No. I got excused."

"Oh," he said. "Sean said it was crazy at the high school today."

"Yeah. It was pretty weird."

On the other side of the hedge, a car pulled in and stopped. A door slammed, and someone walked toward the front of the house.

"Is that your mom?" Maggie said.

"I don't think so. Wait here a sec."

Ryan went into the house. The doorbell rang. Then Ryan came back outside again, closing the door behind him carefully. He motioned for Maggie to be quiet.

"Who is it?" she said, whispering.

"One of Taylor's friends."

He eased into his chair again. They sat there without saying any more. There were footsteps on the other side of the hedge. Then the latch on a wooden gate jiggled.

Maggie watched the gate, waiting for it to swing open. She almost wanted to slide under the table, to hide there. The latch stopped moving. Ryan went toward the hedge, sneaking along in his bare feet. She slipped out of her sandals and followed him. It was ridiculous, the two of them tiptoeing across the yard. They went right up to the gate and put their eyes to a crack between boards.

A girl was standing by a car. Tilda. She was holding a plate and looking like she didn't know what to do with it.

Ryan bumped into the gate and it rattled. Tilda looked toward the sound. Ryan pulled Maggie down and they crouched there, trying not to laugh. He kept his arm over her – his big, warm, bare arm. The next thing they heard was a door closing and the car backing out of the driveway.

"That was close," Ryan said. He sat up. "Frigging Tilda."

"How was she not in school?"

"She has hardly any classes left. She gets done at like, noon."

"Good for her. I wonder if she left her gift."

"Let's check it out."

He slid the bolt and opened the gate. The plate was there, sitting on the cement by the garage door. Cookies, covered with blue plastic wrap. Ryan grabbed them. They went back into the yard and sat down at the table again. Ryan removed the plastic wrap and pushed the plate over to her.

"Snickerdoodles." Maggie took one. "I love those."

"Yeah. Tilda's mom sells them at the Cookie Corner."

"In the Mystic Village. I've been there."

They each had a couple, getting brown and yellow crumbs on

115

their fingers and on the table.

"I'm sorry, Maggie," Ryan said.

"For what?"

"You know for what. For being a total jerk. For not talking to you since..." He turned away.

Since you hooked up with Taylor, Maggie thought. She sat there looking at the crisscrossing curls of his hair. "It's okay," she said.

"No, it's not okay. I screwed up. Big time. My friends, school. Other stuff. My father's gonna kill me when he gets back." He was still facing the other way.

She wanted to touch him. Grab his hand. Just sitting there was impossible.

"I don't know what happened, really," he said. "She had me so turned around. It was like I didn't know what I was doing. Have you ever felt that way?"

"Yeah, I guess so."

"You have?"

"Yeah."

"When was that?" he said. "What happened?"

She didn't say anything.

"Come on, Maggie. It will help me feel better to know that it happened to you, too."

He looked at her, looked right into her. Like he'd understand, whatever she said. Like he already knew. For a second, she let herself think about the one thing she hadn't let herself think before. Taylor was gone. It could be different with Ryan, now. Something totally different could start, right now.

"There's some stuff I haven't told you...stuff about Taylor," she said.

"What stuff?"

"I knew her, a long time ago, when I lived in North Stonington. We were friends."

"You and Taylor were friends?"

"Yeah. Crazy, right? We were, like, twelve." Saying these words felt like going down a slide. She'd let go at the top. She didn't know what was at the bottom.

"Jesus. You and Taylor. I can't see it. Was she the same back then?"

"Yeah, pretty much. She was really good at getting people to do what she wanted."

"So she turned you around, too. Jesus. She get you into trouble?" He was smiling.

"Yeah, she did," Maggie said. "Taylor and I – we did some things. Some pretty bad things."

Ryan cut her off. "But you were twelve. It was kid stuff, right? Nobody ended up dead." He made a sound like he'd been punched in the stomach. "I keep thinking what if."

Maggie waited for him to say more. She was stuck partway down the slide, pressing her feet against the sides, holding tight with her hands.

"What if what?" she finally said.

"I don't know. Pick one. What if I'd stayed at Taylor's that night. What if I'd talked her into going out. What if I'd manned up and ended it with her weeks ago – then she would have been out. What if I'd just said *No*."

"Said *No* to what?"

"All of it." Ryan picked up a cookie. He looked at the cracks in the toasted top. The whistle blew over by the bridge.

Maggie was completely off the slide, now. She was sitting at the table again. Thank God. That was crazy. "It's not your fault," she said.

"Yeah, it really is. If I'd done something different..."

"What about what other people did?" Maggie said. "What if her parents hadn't gone away? What if Addison hadn't made you and Taylor partners on that class project?"

Ryan seemed to think about that for a while. "Addison did sort of start the whole thing. What's up with her? You know she had me and Taylor over to her house for lunch?"

"What?"

"When this all started. When we were supposed to work on that project."

"You're kidding."

"No. Taylor said we had to go if we wanted her to write recommendations for college."

"Is that legal – making you do something for the recommendation?"

Ryan shrugged. "I didn't even need a recommendation. My applications were done."

"So you went to her house?"

"Yeah. She lives down in the Borough, in this tiny, like, cottage behind the old school."

"God. What did you do there?"

"She made us lunch. These gooey ham sandwiches with this white sauce."

"Sounds gross."

"Yeah, and it seemed like it went on forever. She kept talking up Taylor to me, telling me how smart she was, how *on the ball*, I think she said. Then she said she had to make a call and went into her bedroom for like twenty minutes. It was like she was just trying to leave us alone."

"Ew."

"Yeah. The thing is, I guess it worked."

Maggie closed her eyes and tried to let that pass over her, like a wave.

Another car pulled into the driveway on the other side of the hedge.

Ryan checked his watch. "That's my mom."

The car door slammed and there were noisy footsteps on the gravel.

"I should go." Maggie got up. She put her feet into her sandals.

"You don't have to."

"No, I should."

"You can go out the gate," Ryan said.

When they were standing in the driveway, he said, "Thanks for coming over."

"Sure."

They stood facing each other, a couple of feet apart.

"Where's your car?" he said.

"I parked on the street."

He nodded. "Thanks for coming over, Maggie. You really helped me."

"I did?"

"Yeah. I mean, to not think that it was all my fault."

"It wasn't."

"I like the idea of blaming Addison."

"Good," she said. "Me, too."

17

She was still a long way from the trailer park when she saw it, coming from the other direction. A cop car, just like the one that had been at the school. It slowed and the blinker went on. It turned in. She thought about going past, heading back into town or something. But she turned in, too.

The cruiser inched along, ahead of her, like the cops were reading the mailboxes. It took a left. Maggie stepped on the gas. She parked in front of her trailer and ran to the door. Before she went inside, she looked back down the lane, just in time to see the cop car again, coming up the hill. She closed the door behind her. Without thinking, she turned the lock.

Her parents were sitting on the couch. They both stared at her.

"What?" she said.

Maggie's dad got up. He went past her to the window. A car door slammed. Then another one.

"Where were you?" her mom said.

"Ryan's." She twisted around, saw the black and white car in the yard. "Why are they here?"

"They want to talk to us about Taylor."

"What?" By avoiding her parents' eyes she ended up looking at the back door. For a second she thought she should just head out that way and keep on going.

Her dad came over next to her, his hand already on the knob. At the first knock, he turned it.

"Mr. Strang? I'm Detective Wheeler. I spoke to you on the phone.

This is Officer Bugby."

"Come in." Maggie's dad led the cops into the living room.

Only Officer Bugby was in uniform. His big belt was loaded down with weird little pouches. And his gun, right there where he could grab it in a second. The other man, the detective, wore a sport coat, like he was just some friendly guy from the Rotary Club. He definitely had a gun, too. He was just sneaky about it.

"This is my daughter, Maggie. And Cary, my wife."

"Hi," the detective said. "Why don't we all have a seat."

Maggie and her parents sat on the couch, keeping together, not even bothering to move her mom's stuffed animals. Officer Bugby took a wooden chair that was usually in the kitchen. The detective took the recliner, but sat up straight in it like he wished it was a wooden chair.

"Maggie," the detective said, "we're here to ask you and your parents a few questions about this past Friday night, and about Taylor Fraser."

"Okay," Maggie said. She felt her face twitch. She knew that would look so guilty. Which only made her face twitch again, when she tried to smile.

Her mom squeezed her hand.

"Good," the detective said. "To start with, can you tell us where you were that night?"

"I was here. I had a friend stay over."

"They were here all night, with me," Maggie's mom said.

The detective looked at her dad. "Were you here, too?"

"No. I'm a trucker. I was away that night."

"And the friend who stayed over?" the detective said.

"Her name's Olivia. Olivia Parsons," Maggie said.

The detective asked for details – when Olivia had arrived, when she'd left the next morning, what they'd done that night. She knew he was asking the questions because he was trying to see if she could have killed Taylor. It was such a weird conversation to have – this back and forth about how you spent a Friday night, that was really about whether or not you were a murderer. But she was acing it. Of course she was. She hadn't been anywhere near Taylor's house when it happened. That's all the cops cared about. They would never in million years ask about some random day a whole week before.

"Okay," the detective said. "We understand that you had

problems with Taylor. Can you tell us about that?"

Motive. That was about motive. It would probably look like she had that. But it wouldn't even matter, because she couldn't have done it. "She picked on me," Maggie said. "She picked on a lot of kids."

"Taylor was reprimanded for at least one incident that involved you, right?"

"She had to talk to the vice principal. She got detention."

"That sounds like more than the typical teenage girl problems."

Maggie's mom said, "Taylor could be really cruel. She was cruel to a lot of girls. Especially the ones who were..." She looked across Maggie.

"Less affluent?" the detective said.

"Yes."

"Maggie," the detective said, "who else did she pick on, besides you?"

"I don't know, I – "

"You should check with the school," her dad said, interrupting. "They probably have a long list."

The detective reached inside his sport coat and pulled out a sheet of paper. Maggie recognized the butterfly border. It was Ms. Addison's paper. This had to be the famous list. Seeing it made her breath catch in her throat for a second.

"Can you tell us if any of these students had a problem with Taylor?"

The detective read off a bunch of names, but not Maggie's. She knew it was on there, right at the top. He'd skipped over it. He really was sneaky. It was weird how the ones who were supposed to be looking for the truth were such liars.

"I don't know," she said. "Maybe."

"So you never heard of any of these students having a problem with Taylor?"

Her dad sat up straight. "It's not up to her to keep track of Taylor's enemies."

"Of course. We're just looking for information that will help us with the investigation." The detective put the paper away. "Is there anything else that you know about Taylor that could help us?"

She shook her head. They were wrapping up. She only had to get through another minute or two. One of her mom's stuffed dogs was starting to poke her in the back, but it wasn't even worth moving it, now.

"She really wouldn't know anything," her mom said. "We told her to stay away from Taylor and out of her business."

"Was that because of their history?" the detective said.

"What do you mean?" her mom said.

"Did Taylor target Maggie because of what happened six years ago in the trailer park in North Stonington?"

Maggie's whole body twitched this time. Just what she was afraid of – they'd connected the dots. She told herself that it didn't matter. As long as she couldn't have done it.

Her dad looked ready to stand up. "You're not bringing all of that up again. Maggie had nothing to do with that."

The detective raised his hand. A bandage poked out of his sleeve. It seemed like everyone she was talking to today was wounded.

"Okay," the detective said. "I'm not saying she did. I'm just saying, a traumatic event like that, the fire, someone dying, it had to affect them, affect their relationship. Maybe it turned Taylor – or Tiffanee – against Maggie, in some way."

"Well, yeah," her mom said. "Maggie was the only one here who knew about all of that. Knew what she was. That's why Taylor went after her."

"What do you mean, *what she was?*"

Her parents looked over her at each other. She just sat there between them.

"Damaged goods," her dad said. He tipped his head back and let out a big sigh.

"I'm sorry, honey," Maggie's mom said.

Maggie didn't respond. She was trying to breathe. She was trying not to think about walking down the hall at school, with everyone watching her.

"Did any of you stay in contact with Taylor and her mother after that incident?" the detective said.

"No," her mom said. "Not at all. They left the area immediately. A couple years later I heard that Helena had married a wealthy man, but I didn't know any details."

"How about after that, after they moved to Stonington?" Officer Bugby said. "Did you have any contact, then?"

Her mom said, "Helena called me right before they moved here."

"You didn't tell me that," her dad said.

"Me, either," Maggie said.

"Yeah, well...Helena said that Taylor would be going to the private school. So I didn't think we'd ever run into them. I didn't think it would matter to us if they were in the same town, as long as we were running in different circles. Might as well be across the state."

"But Taylor didn't go to the private school, did she?" the detective said. "Do you know why?"

"I have no idea," her mom said.

The detective wrote something down. "Mrs. Strang," he said, "when Taylor started giving Maggie a hard time, did you call Mrs. Fraser?"

Her dad jumped in. "I wanted to, but Maggie said it would just make things worse."

"I called the school," Maggie's mom said. "They did step in, some. Things were a little better there for a while."

"Were things better, Maggie?" Officer Bugby said. "Did Taylor leave you alone?"

He sounded like he really cared. He had a nice face, too, with a shy smile and sort of sad eyes, that made you think he wanted to help you. It was too bad it was all just a trick.

"Maybe Taylor found quieter ways to give you a hard time?" Officer Bugby turned his cap in his hands.

Maggie shrugged. She was surprised to feel tears in her eyes. She was going to cry now? Jesus Christ.

"Like dating Ryan Hardy," Officer Bugby said. "Did she do that to upset you?"

Maggie wiped her eyes quick, but kept looking at the cop. Asshole. Why was he bringing Ryan into this? What was he trying to do to her? "Maybe. Partly. She was like that. If she knew you wanted something, she'd try to get it first. It could be anything. Shoes, a grade, a guy. She was always like that. Even when we were little."

"And now she had money," Officer Bugby said. "So it was even worse. I mean, she had the latest clothes, the newest phone. Even Ryan would notice those things, right?"

"No, he didn't care about that," Maggie said. "He wasn't even interested in Taylor. A teacher matched them up."

"What do you mean?"

"He was supposed to be my partner for a project in biology class. But Ms. Addison made him work with Taylor. That's what started it between them – working together on that project."

"Ms. Addison." Officer Bugby looked at the detective, quickly, almost like he didn't want her to notice.

She wasn't going to let him get away with playing dumb. "That's right, you must have met her." She could hear the edge in her voice, but she couldn't smooth it over. It was like the whole day was boiling up in her – the list, Ryan's story about that lunch with Taylor at Ms. Addison's, and now this. She turned to the detective. "She's the one who gave you that list. You didn't read my name, but I know it's right at the top. She wants to blame everyone else. And most of all me. She's such a bitch."

"Okay, honey." Maggie's father patted her hand.

"It's not okay!" Maggie pulled her hand away and stood up. "She's the reason for all of this. She's the reason Ryan's all screwed up and Taylor's dead. It's all her fault!"

"Listen, detective," Maggie's father said. He was on his feet now, too. He had a firm grip on Maggie's elbow. "I think maybe we've helped you as much as we can."

"I'm sorry," her mom said. "It's been a very difficult end to a very difficult school year."

The cops just stared at Maggie. She was looking at the floor, but she knew they were staring at her. She kept her eyes down. She heard them follow her dad to the door.

"Thanks for your help," the detective said.

Then the door closed and they were gone.

18

"That girl has a temper," Wheeler said, as they went down the hill between the trailers.

"Think it's the kind of temper that leads to violence?"

"You mean murder? I don't know." Wheeler looked out the window at the scraggly yards and the dented aluminum. "This place is looking kinda rough."

"It always has," AJ said. "When I was in high school, I dated a girl who lived here. It was exactly the same, then." He stopped at the paved road. "Mr. Strang was a little on edge."

"Yeah. How old do you think Mrs. Strang is?"

"Jessi Wade's mom said she was just a little over thirty."

"So she had Maggie when she was fifteen, maybe even fourteen."

"Yeah." AJ turned onto the road. "The husband looks quite a bit older."

"When do you and your buddies set up the surveillance cameras at the Fraser house?" Wheeler said.

"After dinner."

"Then why don't you take a break now? Go home for a little bit."

"What are you going to do?"

"I'll go talk to Maggie's friend, see if I get anything else about Friday night. See if their stories line up. Then, I think I'll go up to the Honey B for something to eat." Wheeler touched the edge of his bandage.

"That hand's got to still hurt," AJ said.

"Yeah. I'm due for a couple more pain pills." Wheeler looked across the seat. "Be careful tonight."

"I will."

"I still don't know exactly what happened last night at the Fraser house."

"You'll call me," AJ said, "if you get anything interesting from Maggie's friend, right?"

Wheeler nodded. They were quiet the rest of the way up Route 1 to the station, a square, Georgian building with flagpoles out front, a place designed to project normalcy and calm. Everything under control.

"I'm going to go in for a minute," Wheeler said, when AJ had parked.

"I'll see you later, then."

AJ gave Wheeler the keys and started around the car.

"Hey," Wheeler called after him. "Keep your eyes open."

AJ waved and got into his Jeep. "My problem," he said, "is keeping my eyes shut."

19

Her dad watched the cruiser drive away. "*To Protect and Serve.* Bullshit!" Then he turned back to the living room. He gave her a look. "Jesus, Maggie! You did better with the cops when you were twelve!"

"Don't yell at her," her mom said.

"I'm not yelling! But she can't have a meltdown in front of them."

"You weren't exactly Prince Charming yourself. And you haven't been dealing with this Taylor crap all school year, like we have."

Maggie stood there, not sure what to say, not used to fights – not like Tiffanee.

"Neither of you would have had to deal with anything if you'd let me take that job in Nebraska," her dad said.

"Oh, Christ! Not this again! I couldn't leave my mother. Not when she was so sick."

"She could have come."

"Moving would have killed her and you know it!"

"And staying here made her better?"

"I can't believe you. After what my mother did for Maggie – for all of us. You can be such an jerk!"

Suddenly it was too much. "Shut up!" she yelled. She was surprised to hear how loud her own voice was, how it cut right through the others. "Shut up, both of you!" She couldn't be here another second. Maggie grabbed her purse from the counter and ran out to her car. She flew down the hill, practically spraying gravel. When she hit the paved road, she gunned it.

At first the speed helped. The road twisted and turned and she had to focus to stay with it. After a while, though, that wore off. Another left, another right. More rocks, more trees. She let her foot off the gas. She just drove, not going anywhere.

She ended up on Route 1, heading toward Mystic. When she saw the sign for the Bay Market, she realized that she was starving. She hadn't had anything to eat except for those cookies, at Ryan's. She pulled into the parking lot. When she was opening the door to the market a young guy ran up behind her.

"Excuse me!"

She let him squeeze past and then followed him. He went straight to the counter. He said, "Can I help you?" He was a little out of breath.

"I'll have a hot dog," Maggie said.

The guy put the pencil down. "Really? You come to a seafood shack and order a hot dog?"

"Yeah," she said, pulling back a little.

He grinned, which looked good on his thin face. "Okay, just asking. Do you want bacon on that?"

"No."

"How about cheese?"

There was something about him. He was so comfortable. He made even these simple questions seem like some kind of banter. "No, thanks."

The plastic door to the back split then and Beth came through. She practically pushed the guy aside. "Parker, stop harassing the customers. Would you like the usual, Maggie?"

"I guess it's the usual."

"You got it. Plain hot dog, small fries and a small Coke." She went through the plastic door again.

Parker smiled at Maggie. Somehow it seemed okay to just smile back at him.

When she came out of the kitchen, Beth had an apron in her hand. "Are you going to sit outside, Maggie? Parker can bring your food out to you. Parker, put your apron on." She handed it to him.

"No, it's to go," Maggie said.

"Okay." Beth leaned back against a cabinet. "School must be just about over."

"Yeah." Maggie liked that she had known Beth since she was kid, and Beth was always nice to her, and never in a *poor, weird Maggie* way.

"Then the big graduation."

"Yeah."

Beth didn't ask her what came after that, which was nice, too. Maggie had had enough of that question from Ms. Goodwin.

"Shoot," Parker said, suddenly pulling a couple of dollars out of his jeans. "I gotta bring my brother a soda. He's waiting outside."

"Hurry up," Beth said.

Parker dropped the money by the register, filled a cup, then ran out with it.

Beth rang up Maggie's order. "Be right back," she said, and went into the kitchen.

While she waited, Maggie pretended to check out the fish in the case, even though they were gross, with their half-open mouths and their dead eyes, like someone had snuck up on them when they least expected.... She moved on to the clams, their hard shells all closed up. She heard the door open but she kept looking at the clams until Parker was behind the counter again.

"Coke, right?" he said. He poured it and put it on the counter. "So do you live near here?"

"No, she drove over from Jamestown to buy a hot dog," Beth said, coming back just in time to deliver her line.

"You know, sarcasm won't work with me if you use local references," Parker said. "Not a local, remember?"

Beth looked at Maggie and rolled her eyes, like they were giving him a hard time together. She arranged things in the paper bag she'd brought out from the kitchen. "Here you go, Maggie."

"Thanks." Maggie went out the door. She switched the bag to the Coke hand, squeezing the bunched-up paper with the last two fingers, so the other hand would be free to grab her keys from her purse. Like always, the keys seemed to have burrowed into some deep, secret pocket.

Something moved at the edge of the parking lot and she turned toward it. Her whole body flinched. The cup fell.

A car was sliding slowly up the little access road. Like you would if you were watching, like you would if you wanted to be seen. It was the gray car. The one from the rearview mirror, the one that had followed her from Groton to Mystic, then around the development, all the way to Taylor's house. The guy behind the wheel had turned in his seat. He was looking at her. It was him.

20

At the last second, before he drove away, he smiled. They were across the parking lot from each other, but there was something close about that smile. Like he was saying *I know you. I know what you did. I know what we did together.*

Her feet felt cold, all of a sudden. She looked down.

The Coke. It was all over her, making bubbles on her toes. She hoped he hadn't seen her drop the soda. She didn't want to give him that extra joy. She bent down for the cup. Then she stood there a little while longer.

What should she do now? Should she call the police – ask for the two men who had come to her house? Her dad would hate that. Would the cops even believe her if she told the whole story? That a guy followed her to Taylor's house? If they did believe her, if they found him, if they could prove that he killed Taylor, wouldn't she be in trouble, for leading him to her? Would that make her some kind of accomplice? Never mind that she'd just sat down with the cops in her own living room and hadn't said a word.

"Are you okay?"

It was the guy from the counter. Parker. He had a new cup in his hand.

"Yeah," Maggie said. "I dropped my Coke, that's all."

"We saw that. What were you doing?"

"Doing?"

"Yeah. Standing here."

"Oh. I was just... I was trying to decide if I could ask for another one. I don't have any more money."

He raised the cup. "This one's on me."

She reached for it with the hand that was still holding the bag. He pulled it back.

"That's how you dropped the last one. I'll keep it for you, until you get in the car."

"Okay." Was this guy for real? When she was sitting down, with the bag on the passenger seat, he handed the cup in to her. He gave her a straw, too.

"You sure you're okay?"

"Yup, fine. Thanks for the Coke. That was really nice."

"Least I can do for a regular." He smiled. It was the opposite of the other guy's smile. It was all about wanting you to feel good. "See you soon, I hope."

He shut the door for her. When she didn't do it right away, he made a motion like he was pulling a seat belt across. Then he waited there, seeing her off. Like she was company, like she was a close friend and the visit had gone too fast.

With him hanging around like that, she couldn't sit and take a breath, figure out what the hell to do next. She had to drive like she knew where she was going. Like she was a normal person who was heading home to enjoy her meal. Though of course the one thing she did know was that she couldn't go home.

She backed up, then swung around. She took the access road toward Route 1, thinking the whole time that the gray car might be waiting up there. But it wasn't. At the stop sign, she finally had a break. She looked back and forth, not really seeing the traffic. Suddenly, she was shaking. Jesus.

She stuck the straw through the plastic top, then took a sip of the soda. That seemed to help. She started to feel steady again. She'd just met a cute guy, who actually noticed her. He was cute and he was normal, and he didn't know any different about her. He'd never heard her grandmother say *When you're born from trouble, trouble follows you.* He never heard Taylor and her friends call her *Maggot.* He could like her. Why not?

She put the cup into the holder, then pulled out onto Route 1, heading toward Stonington. Her phone rang. She fished it out of her purse. "Hi. Talk fast, my battery is low."

"A policeman was here," Olivia said. "A detective."

"Yeah, I talked to the police, too. Why are you whispering?"

"My mom. She's freaking out. I guess I am, too. I never had to talk to the police before. Have you?"

"What did they ask you?"

"They wanted to know what we did Friday night," Olivia said. "And the one guy, the detective, asked about you and Addison."

"He did?"

"He had the list. The one I told you about. He asked about any fights you had with Taylor. He wanted to know why Addison put you at the top of the list. He wanted to know if you and Addison didn't get along."

"Jesus Christ, I'm so sick of that woman. Can I come over? I'm on Route 1."

Olivia hesitated. "Not now... My mom – "

Then nothing. Maggie pulled the phone from her ear, saw the blank screen. "Damn battery." She tossed the phone onto the seat next to her. She took another long sip of her soda. When she put the cup down again, she checked the rearview mirror. Just a normal check, just driving.

It was there. The gray car.

She screamed a little, swerving halfway across the center stripe. A car coming the other way swerved, too, to get out of her way.

"Fuck!" she said, smacking the steering wheel. "Where did he come from?"

Her foot had let up on the gas. She was slowing down – the exact opposite of what she wanted to do. She pressed the pedal.

He was still in the mirror, just the right distance back, like he was demonstrating traffic safety. That gray car. It was like a cloud following her, a ghost. What kind of car was it? How would you describe it? What would she say about it, if she talked to the police? She was actually headed toward the police right now. All she had to do was keep going up Route 1. She'd put on her blinker, wait for traffic, turn in. He would never follow her there. The whole place was like poison for him. Like a church to a vampire.

Her dad would have a stroke. She remembered what he said about the cops – *Protect and Serve was bullshit*. Even if she just turned into the lot, they'd have cameras, they'd see her car. Maybe they'd come back to talk to her. Maybe this time they'd figure it all out. That it was her fault that Taylor was dead.

She was coming up to the light at the intersection with Flanders Road. She didn't really think. She turned right, toward the Borough. Of course, he did the same.

The speed limit was thirty-five through here. Houses close to the road, nowhere to turn. But somehow, she was feeling a little different. She could breathe. She'd done this before. Nothing would happen as long as she was in the car, as long as they were two cars on the road. She picked up her drink and took a sip.

She took that left you have to take at the last minute, that goes by the soccer field. Then, over the viaduct. She kept a steady pace and so did he. She didn't look too often, just a quick glance once in a while. He was always there.

She was on Water Street now. Suddenly she knew that she'd made a huge mistake. The Borough was on a little point that stuck out into the sound. Every street was a dead end. Before she could think what to do, she was in the older part. Cute little goddamn shops on either side. Barely room to move. The street got still narrower. It was like a funnel, like a trap designed to catch teenage girls. She was going so slow, she might as well be walking. It felt like he could, any second, show up in the window beside her, tap on the glass. *Hello.* Yank the door open.

Straight ahead was nothing but the little turnaround by the beach. She didn't want any part of that. At the cannons, she went left. She had a second when she thought he hadn't followed. But he came around the corner.

She could feel him. It was like he was in the back seat, like he was breathing on her neck.

She took the left. A long straightaway, now. At the end was the green. Take another left by the post office, then right and she'd be back on the viaduct and out of this trap. In the clear again. Just keep going a couple of blocks, past the big houses behind hedges, and the Portuguese Holy Ghost Society. That was the plan.

But now that she could think again, she knew that was not a plan. She couldn't just keep driving forever. He would keep driving, too. Just like the last time, she needed an end.

Of course.

She took a right, into the neighborhood, toward the old Borough school. It was quiet back here. The houses were all recently painted and the lawns perfectly trimmed, but you didn't see anyone, like it was all done by magic. Before long, the building was just ahead, on the left, big and brick and square. The place was condos, now, but it still looked like an old fashioned school, the kind that you'd see in a black and white movie, with all the grades together, and everyone friends with everyone. The opposite of her own school. She stopped at the corner. The gray car caught up, waited. It was just them. No one else in sight.

Didn't Ryan say *behind the school?* Where was it? Could it be down that short little dead end street, to the left? She didn't like sitting there. She had to decide, fast – turn left or keep going. If she turned left, she'd be trapped with no way out, and him right there, right behind her. That was a whole different thing than moving down a road, two cars in a line. She didn't know what he would do then.

Maggie put on her blinker, some sane part of her thinking how crazy that was, but then, no crazier than turning, then driving herself right into a trap. She turned the wheel, pressed lightly on the gas. Behind her, as she pulled away, he moved up to the stop sign.

This could be a big mistake.

But it wasn't. On a tiny lot that shouldn't even be there, there was a cottage. Ms. Addison's cottage. Just like Ryan said.

She checked her mirror. The gray car had inched a little past the stop sign. The better to see her, to see what she saw. He hadn't followed her, not yet. She went almost to the end, where there were thick bushes that blocked the view of the water. The pavement wasn't any wider there, but the shoulders on both sides made a turn-around. She yanked hard on the wheel and just barely made it. Then she stopped in front of the cottage.

He was still at the intersection. She looked at him, and she knew he was looking at her. She'd gotten used to seeing him in the little rectangle of the rearview mirror. She liked that better. When you looked directly at him, he was so much bigger, so much more *there*.

Maybe she was wrong about everything, and he would come after her. Right now.

But then he was moving again. He swung right, heading back into the village center. He drove off down the street under the big shade trees. He was gone.

She pulled up to the intersection. She didn't want to go the direction he had gone, even though it was the only way out of here. Not yet. She turned right. She drove past the old school again. She took the next right. Unlike the dead end where Ms. Addison lived, this road went right down to the water, then continued as a private drive. She stopped in the little pull-off by the sign. Across the inlet, all by itself on a hill, there was a huge, old house. More like a mansion, really. It looked peaceful and untouchable, and for a few minutes she just stared at it, imagined that she lived there. Her heart gradually went back to a normal beat. The gray car was gone. Everything really was okay.

She picked up the bag from the Bay Market. She unrolled the top. She leaned toward it, took a deep breath, got a good steaming whiff of warm, salty, greasy fries. Then she lifted the hot dog out of the bag. She unwrapped the end. She took a bite.

It tasted amazing.

21

"Hey! I'm home!" AJ closed the door behind him.

Claire came down the stairs in a dress. "Hi."

"You look nice," AJ said. "You sure you and Melody are going to the Historical Society meeting? You look ready for a date."

She stepped off the landing and put her arms around him. "There might be some cute guys there."

"Whoa. Should I be jealous?"

"No, but maybe Jack should."

"Melody does have that thing for older men."

"They'll be older, all right. From the picture in the newsletter, I'd say the average age is about eighty."

"So, not your type?"

"Well, put one in a uniform..." She pinched his crisp, blue sleeve. "Maybe."

"Uh huh." He pulled her in and kissed her.

"Maybe not," Claire said. "Are the Daves coming here, or are you meeting at the Frasers' house?"

"They're coming here."

Claire stepped back and studied AJ's face. "After what that ghost did to Sam, should I be worried?"

"No. She took me by surprise before. She won't, this time. And I'll have the Daves with me."

Claire looked unconvinced. "Text me when you're done, okay?"

"Sure. Don't worry."

"Okay." She went to the table at the end of the hallway and

picked up her purse. "I bought cold cuts in case you guys ended up here."

"Thanks."

"All right. I've got to go. Love you. Be careful."

"You, too. Say hi to Melody for me."

When Claire was gone, AJ went upstairs to change. He flicked the light on in the long hall. He stood there, studying the wall to his right, as if at any moment the smooth surface might be disturbed by a form stepping out of it. Almost a year had passed since that had last happened. He went to the big bedroom at the end. After changing into jeans and a T-shirt, he went back down to the kitchen, made himself a sandwich, then filled a glass with ice and tea from a plastic bottle. He tossed the empty bottle into the sink. He was just finishing his meal at the little kitchen table when the doorbell rang.

AJ joined Buck in the front hall "Hey, Dave," he said, opening the door. "Come on in."

"Hey." Sela patted Buck, who reached forward with his nose. "DaSilva's putting the equipment in your Jeep." He looked out toward the driveway. "I should warn you, he's in a mood."

"What's going on?"

Sela shifted the baseball cap on his head. "Girl problems. And..."

"What?"

"He's been talking about Ben a lot."

"It's just about a year since Ben died. He's been on my mind, too."

"Yeah. I mean, we were all close to Ben, but for DaSilva – "

"Ben was like the big brother he never had."

"That's right. And between the paranormal investigations, our cable TV show, and then living in the Shortmans' basement, he was with Ben all the time. More than any of us." He kept looking out at the driveway. "Really, it was like we lost Ben twice. Once when Ben fell down the stairs, and once when..."

"He moved on."

"Without even saying goodbye. You know that hit DaSilva a lot harder than he let on. It was almost worse than if Ben had never come back."

"I get that."

"It's still hard to believe that he's gone for good."

"Yeah."

"Here he comes," Sela said.

AJ waited with his hand on the doorknob. "Hey, Dave."

"Hi." DaSilva wore a T-shirt with *M.A.* stenciled over a flying skull.

"You guys want to grab a sandwich?" AJ said. "Claire bought cold cuts, in case you wanted something."

"Is she out?" DaSilva said.

"Yeah. She and Melody went to the Mystic Historical Society meeting. Research for a book."

"I don't know if I want a sandwich," Sela said, making way for the other Dave, "but I love that cheese she buys. I could have a slice of that."

"Come on," AJ said, heading toward the back of the house. "You know, they sell that cheese to anybody."

"Yeah? You don't have to be a member of the cheese club or something?"

"No, I'm pretty sure you don't."

"I just can never remember the name of it."

"Fontina."

They reached the kitchen.

"Have you eaten?" AJ said, to DaSilva.

"Sort of." DaSilva puffed his cheeks but said no more.

AJ's cell phone buzzed against the table. "Help yourself, guys." AJ grabbed the phone, saw Wheeler's number. "Hi, Sam."

"Hi. I'm already done with Ms. Parsons – Olivia. She corroborated Maggie's story, down to the last detail."

"Well, either they coordinated or it's actually the truth."

"I'd bet on the truth. We can go over it tomorrow. I'm on my way to the diner. Let me know how it goes tonight."

"Okay. I'll talk to you later." As AJ dropped his phone in a pocket, Sela shook his head at DaSilva, who was leaning against the counter, a bottle in his hand. "Beer, DaSilva? Really? Can you at least pretend to be professional?"

"AJ said I should help myself."

"Do you remember where we're going? A house where we know there's a ghost? AJ's giving us a once-in-a-lifetime opportunity here. You should want to be sharp."

DaSilva shook his head. "Not once in a lifetime. Not even our first." He held the bottle out away from him as if to read the label.

"It's only one beer."

"You had one before we came here."

"God, Sela. Just eat your damn cheese."

"All right, all right," AJ said, from the doorway.

DaSilva took a swig, then looked at Sela defiantly.

"Seriously, guys. Are we good to go?" AJ said.

Sela finished the cheese. "We're good. I just gotta make a pit stop." He left the room.

DaSilva took another swig.

AJ put his plate and glass in the sink. He said, "You know, Dave, in the future, I'd appreciate it if you didn't drink before joining me at a crime scene."

"Okay." DaSilva took a long pull from the bottle. "In the future."

AJ watched him, arms crossed. Then he headed for the front door.

DaSilva turned and stood over the sink, tipping his bottle, stopping just short of spilling the beer. There was a hollow sound from the floor. Buck was there, playing with something. DaSilva bent down. "What'ya got there, boy? Have you been in the garbage? You'll end up in the doghouse." When he stood up, he was holding the empty iced tea bottle that AJ had dropped in the sink. "I'll be right there with you." He put his beer to his mouth and chugged.

AJ shouted from the front hall. "Come on, DaSilva! We're going!"

"Yeah, yeah." DaSilva moved toward the door. "Everyone needs to relax. We're just setting up some cameras. What's the big deal?"

They drove in AJ's Jeep, Sela riding shotgun, DaSilva in the back.

"What's going on with the Frasers?" Sela said. "Are they pushing to get back into the house?"

"No," AJ said. "I guess they have another place just over the Massachusetts border, by Lake Chaubunagungamaug."

"Shauba what?" DaSilva said.

"Yeah, and that's the short version. Anyway, they don't need to get back into this house right away."

"Lucky for them," DaSilva said.

Sela spun around in his seat. "Really?"

DaSilva shrugged.

They were quiet for a while. The sun was going down over trees that were thick and close. AJ passed the Road Church and turned onto Flanders Road.

DaSilva gripped the seats in front of him and slid forward. "Stop! AJ, Stop!"

AJ braked and swerved onto the shoulder. They were by the cemetery, at the place where AJ had stopped on the way to the Fraser house when he'd first been called there. The body of the deer was gone.

DaSilva threw open his door and got out.

"What the hell?" Sela said. "Dave! What is it?"

DaSilva ran up to the stone wall, then turned back to the Jeep. "AJ, do you see anything?"

AJ leaned across Sela to get a better view. "No. What is it?"

"I don't know. A light. A flicker of light. I don't see it, now."

AJ got out and joined him. "I'm not seeing anything."

Sela opened his door. As he moved toward the others, he kept his eyes down and lifted his feet high, like a heron hunting for minnows. "You guys are going to get ticks, for sure."

AJ and DaSilva were staring intently into the graveyard when Sela caught up to them. "Was it an orb, or more like a flashlight?"

"It was weird," DaSilva said. "I'm not sure how to describe it. Like a hologram, maybe. Like a flicker of a hologram."

"It looked like a person?"

"No... Maybe. It was so fast."

AJ kept looking across the lichen-spotted stones. "Did it have color?"

"Yeah, kind of pink. Not pink – more like peach."

"Where was it? Show me."

DaSilva went through the gate, then a couple of rows in. "Right about here, I think."

"I wish I'd seen it," Sela said. "Have you ever seen anything here, AJ?"

"No," AJ said, quickly.

DaSilva came back across the grass. He took another long look. "You don't see anything now, AJ?"

"No. Do you?"

"No."

"We should get going."

They all went back to the Jeep.

"We can come back with the gear," Sela said. "This weekend, if you want."

"Yeah, maybe," DaSilva said.

They climbed in, dragged their seatbelts across and latched them. AJ sat for a moment, looking at the mirror.

Sela watched him. "AJ?"

AJ turned the key and pulled onto the road.

22

As they came around the house, Sela stopped to look at the damage. "I guess the fire was mostly in there?" He pointed at the plastic where there had been a window. "Is that were the body was?"

"No," AJ said, turning around. "She was upstairs."

DaSilva lowered his big duffel bag. "Why set the fire down here if the body is upstairs?"

"The fire was supposed to spread," AJ said.

"Okay." Sela put his bag down, too. "Why not set the fire where the body was? Why not set fire *to* the body – you know, the clothes? Wouldn't that be the best way to get rid of the evidence?"

"Maybe that wasn't the point," AJ said.

"So this guy's like a homicidal pyromaniac," DaSilva said.

"Assuming it was a guy," Sela said.

"It's always a guy, right AJ?"

"Come on. I want to get this done before dark."

The Daves followed AJ under the police tape and into the foyer.

"Wait here a minute," AJ said. "Let me take a quick walk-through."

Sela pushed the door closed. DaSilva switched on a flashlight. He looked from the ash trail that crossed the tile to the charred bannister up to the blackened ceiling. His Adam's apple bobbed in his throat.

"Stay right by the door," AJ said, his flashlight on, too. He looped around the downstairs, seeing nothing unusual. There wasn't even any sign of the confrontation with Taylor in the kitchen. As if her ghost had never worked the lighter and set fire to Wheeler's coat, as if she had never knocked him down. AJ came through the front hall again. The Daves waited there, their impatience visible even in the dim light.

"I'll be down in a minute," AJ said.

"AJ!" Sela complained.

AJ climbed the stairs, following his bright beam. Behind him, he could hear the Daves talking.

"He brings us here, then leaves us standing by the door," DaSilva said. "I mean, let's get started with the ghost hunt."

"We're not really doing a ghost hunt tonight, you know."

"Yeah. It's weird, knowing there's definitely a ghost here. It's weird just knowing, period. That used to be the great mystery, right? Is there life after death? But as of last summer, mystery solved."

AJ stopped at the top of the stairs, but there was no response from Sela. He went into Taylor's room, saw the fuchsia color scheme, the stuffed bear, the stained carpet. He went on to the bathroom. Dark, because there was only one small window. No change. In Jonathan's room, he found the smashed mirror, the pile of bedroom debris on the floor. He bent down, read the warning on the little bottle of body spray – the manufacturer was not responsible for what it made women do.

From the end of the hall, there was a soft thump. AJ held still, listened. He didn't hear any more. He left Jonathan's room and headed toward the sound. When he stepped into the master bedroom, he saw something quick and bright climb the curtains on the big double window. Fire.

He dropped the flashlight, ripped a blanket from the bed, began beating the flame with it. There were quick footsteps on the stairs, and Sela ran into the room. DaSilva was right behind him.

"What the hell?" DaSilva said.

Sela grabbed a bed pillow.

"Jesus," AJ said, when the blaze had been extinguished. He looked the window up and down.

"What happened?" Sela said.

"It had to be Taylor, using that lighter." AJ pointed toward a fat-bellied object, the size of a baseball, on the floor beside the chest of drawers.

"Is she gone?" DaSilva spun around.

"For now," AJ said, scanning the room. "But I want you guys out of here."

"AJ," Sela protested, "we might get some great video."

"No," AJ said. "If she sets fire to the place, you could lose all of your equipment. Or worse."

Sela motioned toward the chest of drawers. "What's with all of the lighters?"

AJ retrieved his flashlight. "Come on," he said, holding his arms wide, herding the Daves out.

As they started toward the door, there was a loud, brittle crash behind them. AJ turned. The mirror hanging there had been smashed. A lighter lay on the floor in the silver rubble. Waiting near the collection of lighters, silent and shimmering, was Taylor.

"Go!" AJ said, giving DaSilva a shove.

The Daves ran to the stairs and down.

AJ stayed back. "Taylor, I know you're scared. We can help you. But..."

She stared at him, or beyond him – maybe beyond anything. She was still dressed in her youthful, summer clothes – the delicate top and short shorts – and she was still lithe and beautiful. Only her stare was ugly. It was a mix of fear and deranged anger.

"If I'm going to help you, you need to talk to me," AJ said.

With a scream, Taylor flew at the chest of drawers. She slammed into it. The lighters crashed into the wall and each other. The smell of lighter fluid leaked into the air.

"Taylor!" AJ said. "Stop!"

Taylor turned and came at him. He jumped to the side and she passed by, out the door. He ran after her. She was at the head of the stairs. She looked at him, her blue eyes burning.

"Taylor, wait," AJ said, keeping his voice low and even. "Talk to me."

From downstairs, he could hear the front door opening, then Sela's voice from outside.

"Come on, DaSilva. AJ will be right behind us."

Taylor turned her head toward the sound. Then she dropped out of sight.

AJ raced after her. "No! Taylor!"

DaSilva paused in the doorway, then looked back up the stairs. He raised his phone, aiming the camera lens. Taylor plunged toward him, her motion as smooth as a bird's. A raptor diving to prey.

"Watch out!" AJ yelled.

DaSilva froze where he stood, confusion on his face. Taylor accelerated. She went straight at him, made contact, merged with him. He staggered backward with a grunt, then toppled off the front step, losing both the phone and the bag as he went.

"DaSilva!" When AJ got to him, he was on the ground, out cold.

"Dave!" Sela said, coming over. "Jesus."

"He's out." AJ had his hand on DaSilva's wrist.

DaSilva stirred. "What the fuck?" He raised a hand as if to push AJ away.

"Are you okay?" Sela leaned closer.

"I don't know." DaSilva lay there, swallowing. He put a hand to the back of his skull.

Sela kneeled next to him. "Did you hit your head?"

DaSilva's hand went to his stomach. "I don't feel so good."

"We'll get you checked out," AJ said.

"The hospital? No way." DaSilva got to his feet, in stages. "See, I'm fine."

"You don't look fine," AJ said.

DaSilva was slightly hunched and trembling.

"We'll go to that urgent care place," AJ said.

DaSilva touched the back of his head again. "Maybe I better."

AJ gathered the equipment, closed and locked the door. He found the phone in the grass and handed it to DaSilva. The Daves went toward the driveway, gingerly, as if across broken glass. DaSilva paused before getting in the Jeep. He looked off into the back yard, toward the trees. He pointed. "AJ, who's that?"

"Who's who?" Sela said. "There's nobody."

"Get in," AJ said.

"What?" Sela looked across the Jeep at AJ.

"Get in."

Sela helped DaSilva into the passenger seat, then climbed in the back. AJ had the Jeep rolling before the doors were closed. He sped down the driveway.

Sela leaned forward. "What did you guys see?"

AJ stopped at the road. He looked behind him, up the rise.

"AJ?"

"It was her."

"Who? Taylor? The dead girl?" Sela practically climbed into the front seat. "Dave? What did you see?"

DaSilva moaned in response. He had tipped his head back. His eyes were closed. "Man," he said. "I really don't feel so good."

AJ looked at Sela. "It was the ghost of Taylor Fraser. Right there in the yard. I saw her. And apparently, so did he."

23

"Okay, Chief. Right." AJ crossed the shiny floor of the waiting room and sat down next to Sela in one of the linked, metal-armed chairs against the wall.

"What did the chief say?"

"He said if the Fraser house burns down tonight, he'll know why."

"Really? That's it?"

"Pretty much, yeah. And he hopes DaSilva is okay."

"Me, too." Sela exhaled.

A boy, maybe fifteen or sixteen, came out through the swinging doors that led to the exam rooms. One arm was in a sling and there was a butterfly bandage on his face. A tiny woman followed him, her angry eyes holding his shoulders as firmly as any hands could do. As they reached the counter, she began to scold him.

"Did you hear the doctor?" she said. Her voice cut cleanly through the noise of wall-mounted televisions and A.C. "You're going to get yourself killed!"

The boy looked toward the ceiling as if he were thinking about crown molding.

Sela watched the pair. "What happened tonight, AJ? To DaSilva?"

AJ didn't answer.

"All I saw was DaSilva flying out the door like he'd been tackled."

AJ took a quick look around the room. The few others waiting there were focused on the mother and son at the counter. "Remember when I told you about Taylor knocking me down?"

"Yeah. You said it was like she actually pushed inside your chest."

"Right. I think it was the same kind of thing. But she was moving fast and she disappeared completely into him. It knocked him right out the door. I guess she went with him."

"Damn."

AJ leaned toward Sela, lowering his voice. "So now *I'm* asking *you*, what happened to DaSilva? In all of your ghost hunting, have you ever heard of anything like this?"

Sela stroked the black stubble on his chin. "The theory is that ghosts are tied to a place by events that happened there. A ghost getting out, on the loose – that's not anything I've read about." He shifted his Red Sox cap. "Before tonight, you've never seen her outside the house, right?"

"Right. The first time I saw her, she ran at the front door. She couldn't even get to it. When she was just short of it, she disappeared."

"And that's what used to happen to Ben when he tried to leave Claire's house."

"Yeah," AJ said. "He'd wake up sometime later, back at the foot of the stairs. So he gave up trying. He said he was trapped."

"Elizabeth – she couldn't get out of Claire's house, either."

"Right."

"What about your other experiences?" Sela said.

"One other time, in Bridgeport, in a convenience store – same kind of thing. He'd fly at the door, it would rattle, but he'd end up back at the far side of the floor. At the exact spot where he died."

"How do you know it's where he – oh. You were on the job." Sela leaned even closer. "So maybe Taylor used DaSilva, somehow. To get out. Maybe that's what she was trying to do this whole time – get out of the house. That's why she set fire to the curtains. Burn the walls down and she'd be free."

"Fire worked for her before," AJ said, barely above a whisper.

"What?"

"Nothing. So she can go anywhere, now?"

"I don't know. Every ghost we ever investigated was attached to a specific place. Even the ones that were outdoors. They were seen in a specific area."

"Like the one in the woods, in Pachaug."

"Exactly."

"So maybe Taylor will be confined to right around the house," AJ said.

"Maybe. Or maybe she's just free."

The boy and his mom finished their paperwork and went toward the exit. She was still lecturing him.

"It's taking a long time," AJ said.

They both checked the doors to the exam rooms.

"Aren't we kind of avoiding the elephant in the room?" Sela said.

"What's that?"

"DaSilva saw a frickin' ghost."

The exam room doors pushed open again.

"Here he comes," AJ said.

DaSilva was wrapped in a light blanket. When AJ and Sela met him at the counter, he was already handing a form to the woman on the other side.

"When you get the bill, I want it," AJ said. "You were helping me."

Sela put his hand on DaSilva's shoulder. "Hey, man, are you okay?"

"Yeah. Let's get out of here." DaSilva tugged the blanket free. He tried folding it but ended up with a misshapen ball, one corner dangling. He pushed it across the counter. Leading the way out, he moved fast, his head down, and quickly opened up a lead.

Sela called after him. "Slow down!" He turned to AJ. "What's he running away from?"

DaSilva was waiting in the back seat when AJ and Sela reached the Jeep.

"Are you all right?" AJ said from behind the wheel. "What did the doctor say?"

"Mild concussion. And some other symptoms that he said are more like hypothermia."

"What kind of symptoms?" Sela peered over the headrest.

"Shivering. Clumsiness."

"Clumsiness? That's just you. That's normal."

"Thanks." DaSilva's whole body quivered for a second. "He asked me if I'd been exposed to cold."

AJ started the engine and turned on the heat. "Can you feel that?"

"I think so."

"Let's switch places," Sela said. "You can be closer to the heater."

"Can we just go?" DaSilva said.

AJ headed out of the lot.

"Do you have to stay awake?" Sela said. "Because of the concussion?"

"No. He said they used to keep people awake after a concussion but not anymore."

"What do you want to do, then? You want something to eat?"

"I want a cup of coffee."

"I thought you said you don't have to stay awake."

"I just don't feel like sleeping, and I want something hot."

"Okay. I'll have some coffee, too. How about you, AJ? We can all stay awake, keep him company."

"Insomnia, remember? No coffee required." AJ glanced back over his shoulder, as if he meant to say more. But then he looked forward again and kept driving.

***

AJ was putting his phone away as Sela came out of the convenience store.

"Were you talking to the Chief again?" Sela slid back into his seat, the ice rattling inside his tall cup.

"I was trying to get a hold of Claire."

The back door slammed. AJ found DaSilva in the rearview mirror. "I'm thinking maybe you should come over to her place."

"Yeah, sure." DaSilva gripped his cup with both hands. A shiver passed through him.

There was little conversation the rest of the way. AJ checked the mirror often. Each time, he saw DaSilva sitting in the same position, clutching his drink. The sun was gone. By the time they reached the long, narrow lane that led to Claire's house, only the nearest trees and stones were visible in the headlights. The rest was darkness.

"You awake back there?" AJ said, checking the mirror again.

DaSilva was staring out the window. "Do you remember coming here – "

"Yeah," Sela said, cutting him off, knowing that he was thinking about the night they'd chased Ben down this same lane. Sela had made the discovery, with his feet. Hurrying blind through the house, he'd tripped on something at the bottom of the stairs – something big and heavy, with a little give. A body.

AJ pulled up to the garage. Claire's car was missing from the driveway.

"She's still not home?" DaSilva said.

"Are you kidding? A bunch of old codgers with Claire and Melody all to themselves? Those old guys will talk their ears off."

The greyhound met them at the door, then followed them into the kitchen. AJ took sandwich makings from the fridge.

"You have those cookies that Claire buys?" DaSilva said.

"There may be some in the cupboard. Not sure where she keeps them."

DaSilva opened a cabinet. He produced a paper bag with a rolled-down top.

"You knew right where they were, didn't you?" AJ said.

"I have a good memory for certain things." DaSilva held up the bag. "You want some?"

"No thanks. Too crunchy."

"How can you not like Chocolatey Chippers," Sela said. "That's un-American."

"You should be glad. There's more for you."

When the sandwiches were made, they all went into the living room. Sela took a seat on the couch. "Can we put the Sox on? They're playing Anaheim. Or L.A., or whatever. The Angels." He picked up the remote.

Boston was batting in the second, up two runs. "I love this TV," Sela said, nodding toward the big screen.

AJ let out a quick, quiet laugh.

"What?" DaSilva said. He was still standing, the bag of cookies in one hand, the coffee in the other.

For a moment, AJ just looked at him without answering. "I was thinking about Ben, doing ghost tricks with this TV. One time, Claire and I were watching your show. Ben was there, trying to distract me. This was before she knew. Anyway, there was a close-up of his face, and he went around the TV and came through the screen from behind. Sort of emerged from his own face, like some kind of amazing 3D effect."

DaSilva grinned. "He was a joker."

AJ patted the empty middle cushion. "Sit down, Dave."

As DaSilva was slipping into his spot, AJ's cell phone rang. "It's Claire," he said, checking the screen. He went out of the room, the phone to his ear. "Hi."

"I got your message," Claire said. "Is Dave okay?"

"Yeah, I think so." AJ kept going into the kitchen. "I guess a mild concussion."

"What happened?"

"Long story. I'll tell you when I see you."

"Uh oh. Did the ghost have something to do with it?"

AJ didn't answer.

"Are you okay?"

"I'm fine. Sela, too."

AJ stood there at the counter, looking down into the sink. "Sorry about landing here. I want to keep an eye him, and I didn't want to leave you alone."

"AJ, don't worry about me. I can be alone. I'm all right."

"I know, but I just feel better..."

"Right now, Dave should come first. If he's okay being at my house, that's fine. But if he wants to go home, take him."

"Okay. See you soon?"

"Yeah, I'm about to leave."

"Okay, bye." AJ went back in to the living room. "She'll be home in a few minutes."

"Did you thank her for letting me come over?" DaSilva said. "And eat her cookies?"

"You can thank her when she gets here."

DaSilva was shivering again, gripping his coffee with both hands.

"Let me get you something warmer to put on," AJ said. "A sweatshirt or something."

"I don't know if it will help. It's like the cold – it's like it's on the inside."

"Still." AJ came back from the front hall with a fleece. "Here, try this."

DaSilva slipped it on. It was a loose fit. "Thanks."

"Drink that coffee," Sela said. "That should warm your insides."

DaSilva took a couple of gulps.

They all watched the baseball game for a while. Buck, who had been lying at AJ's feet, hoisted himself onto his long legs, stretched, then went toward the front door. A few seconds later, the hinges creaked.

"Hello!" Claire came into the living room carrying a canvas tote. She sat down on the arm of the couch next to AJ. "How's your head,

Dave?"

DaSilva put his hand behind one ear. "Not bad. Think I lost a few marbles."

"Really?" Sela said. "I didn't know you had any left."

DaSilva flipped a cookie toward Sela, who caught it and put it on his plate. "Dessert," he said. "Thanks."

"You look nice, Claire," DaSilva said.

"Thank you." She crossed her legs, as if suddenly self-conscious about perching on the sofa in a dress.

"Did you get anything good tonight?" AJ said. "Anything you can use?"

Claire pulled a scrap of paper from her purse. "I got a phone number."

AJ swiped the paper.

"Hey!"

"Who's Bob?" AJ said.

"Oh boy, AJ," Sela said. "Competition."

"He's the sweetest man." Claire took the paper back. "He has a couple of books that I'm going to borrow. Okay?"

"All right," AJ said.

They all fell quiet.

"I'm going to head upstairs," Claire said. "I have a lot of notes to go through." She stood.

AJ did, too. "I'll be right back," he said.

When they were in the front hall, Claire whispered, "What happened?"

AJ pointed up the stairs. Once they were at the top, he said, "We had a run-in with Taylor's ghost." He filled her in, retelling what he'd seen as carefully and evenly as if he were writing a police report.

She watched him anxiously. "And Dave's okay?"

"I think so." AJ let his hand run down her arm, raising goosebumps. "Are you?"

Claire bit her lip. "Just when I think I'm okay with this stuff..."

"Yeah. Taylor – what she's been able to do – it's new territory for me, too."

"Tell them they can stay here as long as they want," Claire said.

"I will."

They kissed, and AJ went back down to the living room. "Claire says to make yourselves at home. Stay as long as you like."

"She's great, AJ," Sela said. "Putting up with us. All of our craziness."

"Yep. I got lucky."

They watched the game, finished their meal. By the ninth, Sela was sound asleep, his head back, snoring. The Angels mounted a comeback and, with two outs, tied things up. The game went into a tenth, then an eleventh, then a twelfth. DaSilva tried nudging Sela a couple of times, but got only a grunt in response. Finally, shortly after two a.m., the Angels went with a whimper on a pop-up. DaSilva motioned to AJ, then looked toward the back of the house. They got up carefully and moved to the kitchen.

"More coffee?" AJ said.

"God, no. I feel like I won't sleep for a week."

"Let's go out to the porch."

AJ switched on a lamp and they took seats at the table. Beyond the screens, the woods were black and quiet.

"How are you feeling?" AJ said.

DaSilva rubbed the back of his head.

"I'm not talking about the bump on your skull."

DaSilva took a deep breath and shuddered. "You saw her, right? When she hit me?"

"Yes."

"I felt it. In here." He laid his hand on his chest. "She was in me, wasn't she?"

"That's what it looked like, yeah."

"It happened so fast. I felt the hit. And I just kept feeling it, in here." He spread a hand on his chest.

"I felt the same thing, when she knocked me down," AJ said. "Her hands hit me and then kept going."

"Yeah."

"Did you feel anything else?"

"Cold," DaSilva said. "This weird cold. It was like all of a sudden every part of my body, inside and out, was cold. Like *my thoughts* were cold."

"I got a taste of that."

"And then I felt angry, AJ. Really, really angry."

AJ's eyes narrowed.

"That anger was her," DaSilva said. "I know it. It's what she feels." He shook his head. "Man. It's no wonder she can't talk."

155

AJ waited without saying anything.

"When she hit you, AJ, was she trying to, you know, get inside you?"

"I don't think so. I think she just wanted to put me on my ass."

"What do you think she was trying to do with me? Was she trying to possess me?"

"Dave, no."

"Well, what, then?"

"Sela thinks she used you as a way out of the house. As a way to break through whatever that barrier is that keeps ghosts in the place where they died."

DaSilva's eyes drifted toward the screen. "Does that mean she's loose now? That she could be anywhere?" He pulled the fleece tighter around him, though it was a warm night, nearly summer. "God, I should have listened to Ben."

"What?" AJ sat forward.

"I've been having these dreams about Ben. He keeps telling me to get out. I thought he meant, like, socially. That's why I had that date with Jovie. I was trying to do what Ben said."

"How long have you been dreaming about Ben?"

"About a week. Not quite a week, I think. Why?"

"Ben's been in my dreams, too."

"Has he been telling you to get out?"

"No. In one dream, he was in the cemetery by the Road Church. Right in the spot where you thought you saw something tonight."

"Really? What was he doing?"

"He pointed to a deer. I found one there, dead, the next morning."

"He's connecting to this world again," DaSilva said, his eyes big. "Maybe he's trying to come back."

"Come back? Isn't that a one-way trip, to wherever he went?"

"I don't know."

"I think he's just on our minds, because we're coming up on the anniversary."

"Maybe," DaSilva said, slumping a little. "But I wish he would come back. I wish I could talk to him about what happened tonight. What I felt. What I saw."

"What did you see, exactly?"

"Taylor's ghost. What do you mean?"

"Can you describe her?"

"Why? You don't believe me all of a sudden?"

"Yes. I just... I've never talked to anyone who's seen.... I want to know if she appeared the same to you as she does to me."

"All right." DaSilva sucked in his cheeks, making his thin face almost gaunt. "She didn't look like a ghost, that's for sure. I thought she was just a person, standing in the yard. I mean, maybe she was a little bright, or something. Lit up."

AJ nodded.

"She's a beautiful girl," DaSilva said. "If you didn't know she was a ghost, that's what you'd notice. Dressed like she knows that she's beautiful, too. Tiny shorts. Some kind of pretty top. Long, black hair." DaSilva spread his hands on the table. "She looked so... human."

"Yeah. Ben did, too. But they don't always. Sometimes they're faded, even torn. Like an old rag. Like a worn-out scrap of a human." AJ stared past DaSilva into the dark woods. "Anyway, it's not so much how they look. It's how they look at you. It's what you see in their eyes."

"She was too far away for me to see her eyes. But I know what I felt, when she was in me."

They were quiet for a moment.

"You were in a hurry to leave the clinic," AJ said. "Did you see something there?"

DaSilva swallowed hard but didn't say anything. He looked past AJ. "Yes," he said, finally. "Will I see them now, everywhere?"

"I don't know. For me, it's once in a great while. Hopefully, it'll be the same for you."

"If Ben comes back, maybe I'll see him."

"Dave, I don't think he's coming back."

DaSilva pushed his chair back and stood up. "Take me someplace."

"What?"

"Take me someplace where there's a ghost."

"I've been telling you guys, I haven't seen anything since Ben left. Not until Taylor."

"Yeah, but you don't want to see them. You never look. Come on. You must know a place. Somewhere you've seen one before."

AJ pushed a hand through his hair. He got to his feet. "All right."

"Really?"

"Let's leave a note for sleeping beauty."

In the kitchen, AJ found a pad and a pen. He handed them to DaSilva, then went upstairs, where he found Claire in bed, asleep, cuddling a notebook. When he kissed her, she stirred. "I'm going out with DaSilva," he said. "We'll be back in a bit. Sela's asleep downstairs."

"Okay," Claire said, her eyes half open, her lips making a half smile.

AJ stayed there as she settled into sleep again.

DaSilva was waiting in the front hall when AJ came down. They slipped out, the door open just wide enough.

"So where are we going?" DaSilva said, as they got into the car.

"Cemetery," AJ said.

"You're kidding me."

"I'm not."

"Okay. Who are we going to see?"

"The caretaker."

DaSilva looked across the seat at AJ. "You know that sounds like the setup of a bad horror movie, right? A couple of guys go to see the caretaker at a cemetery in the middle of the night."

They eased down the lane under a bright moon.

DaSilva watched the woods going by, gray trees and rocks and black shadows. "So tell me about the caretaker."

"When I was a kid, we'd take my grandmother to my great-aunt's grave every week. We'd always see the caretaker. He and my grandmother would talk."

"Wait, she saw ghosts, too?"

"No. He was alive, then. He died when I was fourteen or fifteen. I'd kept seeing him, though, checking the graves. Like he was still trying to keep an eye on things."

"And he's there now?"

"I don't know. I haven't been to the cemetery in a long time."

"Wait – was this guy murdered or something?"

"I think he died mowing the grass. Why?"

"I'm surprised there's a ghost. I thought we figured out that there was a ghost only when the person was murdered. Or at least, died violently."

"Maybe it's any kind of sudden death. I don't know how to

explain it."

"Maybe you have an old murder to investigate."

"No thanks. I have my hands full with the new one."

AJ pulled up to the intersection with Route 1. The light was red, and he waited there, though there was no car anywhere in sight. Straight ahead was North Water Street, the way to Stonington Borough.

"St. Mary's?" DaSilva said, pointing right, toward a cemetery that was just behind some trees, on a grassy slope between the road and the harbor.

"No. Evergreen. Up here on the left."

"Oh, yeah. Man, these old towns – there are cemeteries everywhere, aren't there?"

"I guess there are."

"People just keep dying."

The light changed and soon they were at the gate. It was closed. AJ shut off the engine and killed the headlights. They climbed out of the Jeep.

"Do you have your badge?" DaSilva said.

"In case the caretaker's ghost wants to see it?"

"In case the living caretaker wants to see it."

"I don't think anyone's going to bother us. Come on."

They scrambled over a low wall in the moonlight.

"This way," AJ said.

A paved lane led through the trees. Beyond them, there were grassy grave sites and shrubs huddling in shadow. Now and then, there was an ornamental tree in bloom, the white flowers glowing. A narrow track broke off from the pavement. AJ took it. There was damp grass underfoot, now.

"This is the old part of the cemetery," AJ said.

The headstones were mostly lower here, rounded and stained, the letters eroded, but mixed in were some massive monuments. AJ and DaSilva kept on, their footfalls soft on the soft ground.

"Who were all these people," DaSilva said.

AJ didn't answer.

"Look at that big stone. A whaler, maybe? A ship's captain? One of the founders of this place?"

AJ was moving slower. "My aunt's grave is right over there."

"Is this where you used to see the caretaker?"

AJ nodded. They looked into the uneven dark. The trees and the shrubs and the headstones were black and gray, but they shone, too, as if somehow dusted by moonglow. For a long time, all was quiet.

"Do you see him?" DaSilva said.

"No."

"I guess this was stupid. What are the chances he'd just show up when we want to see him, like he's some sort of ghost on demand?"

AJ didn't answer.

"Should we walk around some more?"

"Shhhh!" AJ reached in front of DaSilva with one hand.

"What? Is he here?" DaSilva looked quickly back and forth.

"Sirens. SPD."

"Yeah, I hear them, now."

"Two cruisers, one from Pawcatuck, and one coming in the other way." AJ tilted his head, as if trying to get a bead on the sound. "They're headed toward the Borough. Come on. Let's go." AJ went back the way they had come, his walk quickly becoming a jog.

DaSilva stayed put, frozen, staring across the grass. "Holy shit."

When AJ reached the pavement, he stopped just long enough to yell, "DaSilva! Come on!" Then he was running again, scaling the wall, searching his pocket for his keys. He got behind the wheel. He tapped the center a few times, making little bleating noises with the horn.

After a minute, DaSilva came over the wall and climbed into the passenger seat. "Jesus Chris, AJ." He was shivering again. "I saw him. The caretaker. The ghost."

AJ looked hard at DaSilva, then turned the key. "Let's hope that's the last ghost you see tonight."

24

She woke up feeling like something was wrong. Something was crowding her. Something rough against her skin. When she opened her eyes, squinted in the dim light, she saw trees, a foggy road, moonlight. A black shape moving in shadows. What the fuck?

She blinked again, let things come into focus. The moonlit road was on the big TV screen. The sound was way down. Which was good, because in a minute, there was going to be screaming. She knew this one. That shitty werewolf movie.

She was in Ryan's house. The den, he called this room. Bookshelves to the ceiling, and Oriental rugs on top of carpets, and comfy furniture. She tipped her head back. Ryan was in a big chair under the window, out cold.

She sat up on the couch and the blanket fell off of her shoulders. Ryan must have put the blanket on her, pulled it up over her legs and her belly and her shoulders. If she hadn't been asleep, she would have felt his hands tucking the blanket around her, could have looked into his eyes as he leaned in close. With him asleep now, she could look straight at him for as long as she wanted. Those eyelashes, those lips. His white skin, all glowing. Or she could go over to him, thank him with a kiss.

She wouldn't go over to him. She definitely wouldn't kiss him. That could be the one false move that ended everything.

The pizza was still on the table, with the lid half open. She could see maybe three slices of an Angelo's pie left. He hadn't taken care of that – put it in the fridge or even closed the box. He'd only taken care of her.

The room was a little chilly. Ryan would be getting the draft from the open window. She tiptoed past him and pushed the window closed, carefully. He didn't wake up. They were taking turns doing little sneaky things for each other.

Upstairs, a toilet flushed. His mom. What the hell time was it? She checked her phone. After three. The witching hour.

Maybe because the running water made her think of it, now she had to pee, too. She went around the corner to the half bath, hurrying, because the house was strange and she felt strange in it. She hadn't done a lot of sleepovers, wasn't used to sleeping in other people's houses. Just Olivia's, and, a long time ago, Taylor's. So it creeped her out a little. She didn't trust the shadows, the mysterious hums and ticks. Then there was the whole second floor, all those rooms you couldn't see. Another thing she wasn't used to. It felt like a big dark secret was hanging over her.

She felt a little better in the bathroom, with the door closed and the light on. When she was washing her hands, she stared into the mirror. Pasty skin, hair a mess. She switched the light off.

Too soon. In the dark, she couldn't find the doorknob. When she reached for the switch, she missed that, too.

There was a loud bang.

What the hell was that? She smacked into the door with her arm, fumbled for the knob, found it.

Another bang.

She stood there, trying to decide whether to go out.

Bang! Not quite as loud, this time. Farther away.

She opened the door a little, saw the hall, the kitchen. Quiet. Nothing moving.

She ran back toward the den. Her bare feet were loud against the wood floor. She turned the corner, stepped back onto the rug. Ryan was still in the chair, but he was awake now. Okay. He would explain. The TV was still on. It was probably just the TV.

Then something hit the window behind him, hard.

Ryan jumped up. "What was that?"

"It sounded like a rock. Is someone out there?" She didn't move. Couldn't move.

Ryan went to the window and looked out. "I don't see anything."

Crack! Another rock, against wood this time.

Ryan backed up. "Jesus."

"Ryan!" It was Mrs. Hardy, from the top of the stairs. "What's that noise? What are you doing?"

"I don't know! It's outside! Something hit the house!"

It was quiet for a while. Maggie had enough time to wish Ryan would back up some more, come to her, put his arms around her.

Then something smashed right through the window into the room.

Maggie screamed and ran. She didn't know where she was until they were all three in the hallway at the bottom of the stairs.

"Are you all right?" Mrs. Hardy said. She had on some kind of summer bathrobe, and slippers. "What's going on?"

"I don't know," Ryan said, heading back toward the den.

He was the only one wearing shoes. He was the only one who was ready for the broken glass. Maggie and Mrs. Hardy stood in the doorway. Ryan bent down in the middle of the floor, stood up with a candle, one of those citronella candles in a little metal pot. From the table on the patio. It was just a little, sweet smelling candle, but right then, when he held it up for them to see, it seemed as weird as a bomb.

"Who's out there?" Mrs. Hardy said.

There was another bang, from somewhere else along the back wall.

"I'm going to find out," Ryan said.

"No!" Mrs. Hardy grabbed his arm.

"Mom. Don't worry."

Rap rap rap rap rap! Quick little sounds, in a burst. Like someone had pelted the house with a handful of stones.

Ryan pulled his arm free and ran into the kitchen. When they caught up to him, he was opening the door to the back yard. He looked out. Then he flipped on the outside light.

"Did you lock the gates?" his mom said. Her hand was on the wall switch but she waited. With the kitchen light off, they could see better outside. See who was out there throwing things at the house and scaring the shit out of them.

"Yes, Mom."

They all moved close to the door. Outside, the floodlight reached halfway across the patio. On the table, where she'd sat with Ryan, eating cookies, there was another citronella candle, like the one that had come through the window. But there was no one to throw it. The light must have chased him off.

"I think they're gone," Ryan said.

Ryan's mom backed away into the room. "Who would do that?"

"Some jerk from school," Ryan said. "Some friend of Taylor's. Hunter, maybe, or Wyatt."

"But why?"

Ryan didn't answer right away. It was because they blamed Ryan for what had happened to Taylor. Which didn't make any sense.

"Because they're assholes," Ryan said. "And they're drunk."

When he and his mom moved away, Maggie stayed by the door, looking out. Maybe the jerks were still out there, waiting for a chance at that second candle. Maybe she'd get a look at them. Besides that, it wouldn't be all bad if they saw her, saw she was here at Ryan's house in the middle of the night. Give them something new to think about.

With the floodlight on, it was almost to see past the table. She turned it off, and now she could easily see the perfect little square yard. The moon was ridiculously bright. She could see the hedges on all sides, shaggy and dark. That empty dog house at the back. She put her face up to the glass, checked closer in. There was no one, but she could make out the gravel path that went between the house and the hedge. Little stones. Perfect for throwing.

"I'm going to call the police," Mrs. Hardy said. "I don't suppose they'll catch them, but still." She picked up the phone.

Maggie took one last look. She almost wanted to run out, grab the citronella candle from the table. Just to be sure it didn't get into their hands. Next to the candle was one of those lighters like Maggie's dad used on the grill. Jesus, it was like those things were following her everywhere. She remembered just the other day, standing in her own yard, holding the lighter and thinking about the old fire... But the lighter didn't weigh anything. Let them go ahead and throw that.

Flame.

A little yellow flame at the tip.

What the fuck?

"Ryan," Maggie said. "Ryan."

He and his mom stopped talking. They came over to her.

The lighter sat on the table, burning.

"What?" Ryan said.

A blur – something moving. Something flying straight at them.

Maggie jumped backward, tripped. The glass crashed over her. Something hard thumped her chest.

Ryan pulled her up. "Come on!"

The thing rolled off of her, spun across the floor.

They were running toward the front of the house. They were in the hall, out the door, running, stones jabbing her bare feet, Ryan still pulling on her hand, his mom in the bathrobe, everything panicked and glowing under the moon, running. She felt a shove from behind and she fell, skinned her hand. Ryan pulled her up again. They made it to a yard when something buckled her knee, like she'd been kicked. She was down again, pulled up again. Then they were on a dark porch, Ryan pounding a door. Lights, shouts from inside.

"It's Ryan Hardy! Please!"

The door swung open. A man keeping his hand on the door, like he might slam it shut any second. Holding a baseball bat in the other hand. But he stepped back and let them in. A woman came down the stairs wearing boyshorts and spaghetti straps, like something from a slasher movie, the dumb hottie who is about to get it. Mrs. Hardy had the phone to her ear. The one she'd picked up in her own kitchen. Like she thought it was a cell phone. She stood there for a second, shaking her head.

"We need a phone," Ryan said. "We need to call 911."

"What's going on?" The man leaned the bat against the wall. "What happened?"

They all looked at Ryan then, like they thought he might have the answer, something to make sense of it. For that second, Maggie thought maybe he could explain it all, even the lighter flame that came out of nowhere and the candle that flew at the house all by itself. He had seen things clearly, he had seen something she'd missed.

They all stared at him, waiting. He took a breath, opened his mouth. But then he didn't say anything. He didn't say anything at all. His mom put an arm around him.

Maggie felt something on her knee, something crawling – a fly or a mosquito. But when she looked, she saw that it was blood – a fat bead of it, making a bright red stripe down her white skin.

25

They raced down North Water Street, the tires ringing against the pavement. Somewhere to the east, a siren wailed, speeding to whatever calamity was out there in the darkness.

"What is that, an ambulance?" DaSilva turned toward the sound.

"It's coming down the other end of 1A," AJ said. "We're going to meet at the viaduct."

AJ skidded around the turn onto Trumbull, rumbled between dark houses, then passed the moonlit soccer field. From behind trees, the siren closed, fast. As AJ reached the stop sign, an ambulance shot in front of them. AJ followed. They hurtled down the narrow streets of the Borough, the ambulance lights bouncing blue and red off of the immaculate, black-shuttered houses.

"I see it," DaSilva said, pointing to their right at a glow behind the trees. It looked harmless, almost soft, like a sunrise. They went toward it. The orange intensified, picked up heat. The neighborhood was stirring. Lights had been switched on – upstairs lights in bedrooms, living room lights, porch lights. There were even a few people moving down the sidewalk.

As they neared the old school, the flame suddenly burst into view. The source, whatever was giving it fuel, was still hidden. A police car was angled across the intersection. AJ parked half on the sidewalk. He and DaSilva got out. Now, looking past the school, they could see the small building that was engulfed in flame.

"Wow, that's a lost cause," DaSilva said.

"Stay by the Jeep, Dave." AJ retrieved his badge from the glove compartment and clipped it on his belt. He walked toward Officer Romano, who was standing in the middle of the street.

"AJ?" Romano said. "What are you doing here?"

"I was nearby, heard the sirens."

"At three o'clock in the morning? You really don't sleep, do you?" AJ looked in the direction of the fire. "Is that a garage, or..."

"It's a residence." Romano motioned for AJ to come closer, then turned his back on the small group of onlookers who had gathered by the stop sign. He had a notebook in his hand. "Belongs to a Nicole Addison."

"Addison?"

"Yeah, do you know her? She's a teacher at the high school."

"I just met her yesterday. We talked to her about the Fraser case." He looked toward the house again, the vague, dark base of the inferno. "Was she inside?"

"None of the neighbors saw her, but one, a Miss Lynn, was out walking her dog around eleven p.m., and remembers seeing lights on."

"So she's in there."

"Most likely, yes."

They both watched the blaze. There was nothing soft about the orange color now. It was sharp and hungry and raw. Two firetrucks were positioned in front of it. One was blasting it with its deck gun.

"They got here right away," the other cop said. "It's what, five, six blocks from the firehouse? But there's not much they can do."

AJ went back to the Jeep. DaSilva had climbed up onto the bumper for a better view. "Was anybody in there?"

"Listen, Dave, I'm going to need to stay here for a while."

DaSilva stepped down. He pulled his cell phone from his jeans. "I'll call Sela, have him pick me up."

AJ reached out and put his hand on DaSilva's phone. "I don't want Claire to wake up with all of us gone." He handed DaSilva his keys. "Take the Jeep back. Just hang out there a little longer, okay?"

"Sure."

"Do you need to be somewhere in the morning?"

"No," DaSilva said. "I'm not going in to the market until later. I'll just crash on your couch if I feel like I need to sleep. I kinda don't think I will, though."

"It's overrated."

"Yeah, so you say."

There were shouts from the direction of the fire.

"I'll see you later," AJ said.

DaSilva got in the front seat and started the engine. AJ moved off. The orange color was gone. Gray arcs of water converged where it had been. As AJ passed the cruiser, the deck gun on the tanker truck shut off. A firefighter approached the charred wreck with a hose. He kicked what was left of the front door aside. A second man followed him in. There was a surge of water, a muffled voice. Then a hush. The firefighters, the paramedics ready with a gurney beside the ambulance, the crowd of neighbors lined up across the little dead-end street, all paused for that moment.

The firemen appeared in the doorway. The crowd groaned, though the men's gestures, in their stiff turnout gear, were impossible to read, and their expressions hidden by faceshields. A third man left the truck and joined the others on the destroyed lawn.

AJ went to them. "I'm Officer Bugbee, SPD. Was there someone inside?"

The firefighter who had entered the house first nodded. He raised his face shield, and there was something startling about his drained, sallow skin, his cheeks sweaty, his mouth slack. "Yes. A woman, I think. We can't even be sure."

"This will be your scene in a minute," the third fireman said. "We just have a little clean-up to do."

"Okay." AJ left the house, walked a few feet up the street, and punched a number on his phone.

"Hello?" Wheeler sounded distant, like he was lying with his face in the pillow, the phone pointing off at a crazy angle from his ear.

"There's been another fire," AJ said. "This time, it took the whole house."

"AJ? Where are you?" Wheeler's voice was clear now, the voice of someone sitting up and wide awake.

"Ms. Addison's house. There was a body inside."

"What, our Ms. Addison? Ms. Addison from the school?"

"Yeah."

"Jesus. Jesus. Tell me where you are."

AJ gave directions.

"I'm on my way."

AJ went back to the cruiser, found the officer there. "Is the woman you mentioned before still around? Lynn, I think you said?"

The officer scanned a crowd that was backed up against a neatly trimmed hedge. He pointed. "There she is."

AJ went toward her. "Miss Lynn?"

"I'm Elaine Lynn," a woman said. Her plentiful white hair was combed in a wave over her forehead. Next to her was a young woman, college-age, in a UCONN sweatshirt.

AJ tilted his badge upward. "I'm Officer Bugbee. Can I talk to you for just a minute?"

The two women stepped forward.

"This is my granddaughter, Deb," the older woman said.

"One of you was out walking your dog last night?" AJ said.

"That was me," Deb said. "It was around eleven. I go to the end of that street. My dog likes to sniff around there by the rocks."

"You noticed lights on in the house?"

"Yeah. So I turned around."

Her grandmother put a hand on Deb's arm. "The woman who lives in that house, Nicole, she's afraid the dog might do her business on her grass. Nicole's come out and scolded Deb a few times."

"I don't walk past her house unless I'm sure she's not home."

"So you saw lights," AJ said. "Did you notice anything else – a car you didn't recognize, or a person, maybe, near the house?"

"No. It was quiet. Just normal."

"What about Ms. Addison's car?" AJ looked toward the house. "Was it parked there?"

"She doesn't have a driveway," Elaine said, "so she parks on one of the upper streets."

"What kind of car does she drive?" AJ said.

"A sports car. Blue. Fairly new. Sorry, I don't know what kind."

"Is she friendly with any of your neighbors?"

"I don't think so. She isn't a very friendly person. But then, neither am I."

"Okay," AJ said. "Well, thank you." He took phone numbers from each of them, said there might be follow-up.

The Lynns turned away. They didn't rejoin the crowd, but went up the sidewalk, holding onto each other.

A few minutes later, Wheeler and the chief found AJ. They both looked like men who had been awakened in the middle of the night. Wheeler's hair was uncombed, the lapel of his sport coat flipped up on one side, showing a strip of brown felt. The chief's pant legs were caught in his boots. There were sagging wrinkles under his eyes.

"Jesus, AJ," Wheeler said. "Was she in there?"

"They found a body."

Wheeler cursed into his upright lapel.

"Just one?" the chief said.

"Yes. We've got to check for a blue sports car – it's hers. The neighbor said she usually parks nearby."

"Okay," the chief said.

The three of them stared down the dead end street, crawling with fireman from the Borough and Pawcatuck firehouses.

The chief shook his head. "Those guys volunteer for this. To get out of a warm bed at three a.m. and walk into a burning building and discover God knows what."

No one spoke for a moment.

"Have you seen the body?" the chief said.

"Not yet. I just had a quick conversation with a fireman who found her."

"Let's go have a look."

They crossed the street and worked their way around the firetrucks, into the thick smell of drenched, burned wood. The chief found his counterpart. "Hey, Bob," the chief said. "I hear we have a body inside."

"Come on." The man led the way to the house.

Inside, every surface was made up of little black, swollen squares. Water dripped from the walls and what was left of the ceiling. Catching the light that came in from every direction, it sparkled like diamonds against black velvet. The sour smell of doused fire didn't just hang in the air, it was the air.

"Watch your step," the man leading the way said.

The floor was uneven, a rut cutting across it.

"See how deep the char is there?" the man said. "Usually that's a sign of an accelerant."

The rut led into a room in the back. They crowded inside. The dresser by the door had been reduced to a pile of black rubble, but there was still something recognizable as a bed, and on it, the least flammable thing in the room, a body. Blackened, too. Clothes just a part of it now, as if they were a sarcophagus, or a cocoon.

Wheeler stepped close and bent down. "There's something

around her neck. If I had to guess, I'd say it was the tie from a bathrobe."

The chief stared at the remains on the bed. "Do you see anything of interest, AJ?"

"Like Wheeler said, looks like maybe a bathrobe tie."

They stood there a moment longer.

"All right, let's get the hell out of here." The chief led the way.

As they emerged onto the soggy, beaten down grass, a uniformed cop pulled the chief aside.

Wheeler turned to AJ. "So, two fires and two murders – both strangulation by ligature. There's no way that's a coincidence."

"Not likely."

"Wheeler, AJ," the chief said. "Get over to the Hardy house. Mrs. Hardy called 911. Says they're being attacked."

"Being attacked?" Wheeler said. "What does that mean?"

The chief looked back at him, all of the life gone from his face. "I don't know, Sam. But you better get the hell over there."

26

When they pulled up in front of the Hardy's house, an SPD car was already parked by the curb. AJ pointed toward a porch across the street. "Seems like the action's over there."

They could see Officer Manfredi talking to someone through an open front door. They started in that direction. Manfredi turned to watch them approach.

"What's going on?" Wheeler said, when they had joined him.

"Disturbance over at the Hardy residence." Manfredi pointed. "A couple of broken windows. I already took a look around. Whoever was there is gone now. The Hardys and a friend are waiting for you inside."

In the front hall was a young couple still dressed for bed. "They're all in the back," the woman said, pointing further into the house.

Wheeler led the way, a straight shot past the kitchen into an eating area with lots of windows. Three people sat at a round table.

"Is that Maggie Strang?" AJ said, softly.

"This just got weirder."

All three looked up as the cops came down the hall.

"Hello, Maggie," Wheeler said. "I didn't expect to see you again so soon."

She only stared back at him.

"Mrs. Hardy, Ryan," Wheeler said.

Mrs. Hardy pulled her bathrobe tighter.

There was only one empty chair at the table. Wheeler and AJ stayed on their feet.

"So, what happened?" Wheeler said.

Ryan described the stones being thrown against the house, the candle breaking the window, then looking out the glass door as something crashed through it. "I think it was another candle," he said.

"So you were standing right there?" Wheeler said. "Did you see who threw it?"

Ryan turned to Maggie. She gave him a blank look.

"No," Ryan said. "I didn't see anyone. I guess it was too dark."

"Maggie?" Wheeler said.

"Yeah, it was too dark."

"You didn't see anyone?"

"No."

"You were staying over at Ryan's house, Maggie?" AJ said.

"I wasn't staying over. We were just watching a movie. Then we fell asleep."

"You were asleep when all of this started?"

"I don't think so," Maggie said. "I mean, I fell asleep, but got up to use the bathroom. I was in the bathroom when I heard the first bang."

"What kind of a bang?" Wheeler said.

"Like something hitting the house. A rock, maybe."

"Did you two, you and Ryan, go anywhere earlier? Did you have any interaction with anyone, any other kids from the high school, maybe?"

"No," Ryan said. "We were just texting, and I asked her if she wanted to come over."

"Maggie came by just before dinner," Mrs. Hardy said, beginning to look like she was getting her bearings. "Ryan asked if she could stay, so they could have pizza and watch movies."

Wheeler produced his notebook and jotted something in it. He asked them to go over the events again, pressing them on what they'd seen in the yard – more like, what they hadn't seen – before the glass shattered. "Okay." He put the notebook away. "We'll go check things out over there."

AJ and Wheeler went back outside, picked up Manfredi, and crossed the street. They went into the Hardy house. Manfredi took the upstairs. Wheeler and AJ went room to room on the first floor. They found the den, glass scattered everywhere. The TV was still playing a B movie. Wheeler turned it off.

The kitchen was next. More glass. Another potted candle, this one on its side, against the cupboard. Wheeler picked his way through the shards to the door. The upper pane was mostly gone. He found the switch for the floodlight.

AJ joined him. They looked out at the plastic table with its matching chairs. On it lay a propane lighter and a plate. Beyond that was the rectangular lawn, walled in by hedges. A dog house at the back. No sign of a dog, except for a patch of dirt. From somewhere beyond, a street or two closer to the river, a dog barked, then another.

Manfredi came up behind AJ.

"Why don't you ride around the block a couple of times," Wheeler said to him. "Maybe we'll get lucky – you'll find whoever did this still knocking around out there."

"Okay," Manfredi said, already moving out.

Wheeler looked out at the yard again. "We could use some luck." He turned quickly. "Hey!" he shouted in the direction Manfredi had gone. "See if you can find where those dogs are barking!"

"Will do," Manfredi answered, from somewhere outside the room. The front door opened, then closed.

The dogs continued to bark. Wheeler and AJ went out onto the patio.

"Well, we know Maggie and Ryan weren't in the Borough tonight," Wheeler said.

"Yeah."

Wheeler went to the table. "Maggie said the candles were right here. So whoever threw them... You'd think you'd be able to see them from the door."

AJ's mouth was clamped shut, the tendons tight in his neck.

The dogs kept barking from somewhere behind the house.

Wheeler tried the wooden gate by the driveway. It rattled a little under his hand but stayed closed. He walked along the hedge, took the gravel path that led to the front yard, ended up at another gate, also locked.

"Those are some serious gates," Wheeler said. "With them locked like that, there's no easy way to get back here. I guess you could climb over, if you were determined enough. Maybe you could force your way through the hedge." Wheeler went to the hedge, then, probed it with one hand. "Seems like a good way to get scratched all to hell." He returned to the step, where AJ was waiting. "Even if you could get back here, somehow, it seems like a lot of work to harass someone. I mean, why not just stay out front? There are windows out there, too."

"Maybe they didn't want to be seen by the neighbors."

"At three in the morning?"

AJ looked toward the barking sounds off in the distance. The dogs got louder, suddenly, almost frantic.

Wheeler turned in the same direction. "Doesn't seem like those dogs are just howling at the moon, does it?"

Then the barking stopped. AJ and Wheeler stood there, staring past the back hedge. All was quiet. Just the occasional whir of traffic on Route 1, and the more distant hum of the interstate.

"Maybe Manfredi followed the barking right to the guy," Wheeler said. "Maybe he's putting the guy in cuffs right now."

"Maybe."

"A man can dream, right?"

AJ said nothing. He kept watching the hedge.

Wheeler went to the table and then turned back toward the door. He motioned for AJ to move out of the way. "How could they not see him?" Wheeler said. "They're standing at the door, and he's right here at the table, picking up a candle." Wheeler looked back and forth from the door to AJ. "You know?"

"Maybe it was the light."

"Yeah, maybe." Wheeler went up the steps, reached through the hole in the glass, killed the floodlight, then looked toward AJ and the table. He stayed there for a minute, as if waiting for his eyes to adjust. Then, leaving the light off, he came back down. "With this moonlight, I could see you pretty well. I just don't get it."

They were quiet for a while.

"I'm going to put the light back on," AJ said. He'd just started toward the house when he heard something behind him – like a chair scraping across the patio stone. He turned toward Wheeler again.

The ghost of Taylor Fraser was right behind the table. She was bright and lithe and beautiful. Every part of her glowed – garish, almost, the only color under the moonlight. She screamed, a wail of endless anger, and threw herself forward. The table tipped up and over.

"Wheeler!" AJ said.

Before the detective could react, Taylor tossed a chair at him and followed right behind it. She slammed into Wheeler, toppling him. AJ got between Wheeler and the ghost just as she threw another chair. AJ slapped it out of the way. He stood his ground, hands out in front of him, ready for the next one. But Taylor was done with the chairs. She picked the lighter up off of the ground. The flame flicked on.

"Enough!" AJ said. "Stop!"

Taylor shrank back, as if startled at being addressed, at having someone look her in the eye. Her mouth closed over her teeth. She was silent. The lighter burned in her hand. The flame flared from the tip, then died back again, then went out. Then she vanished, like she had been switched off, too. The lighter dropped to the patio with a cheap plastic clatter.

Wheeler, on his feet now, looked from AJ to the empty space where Taylor had been.

"You okay?" AJ said.

Wheeler reached around and put his hand just above his waist.

"You got hit hard," AJ said. "How's your back?"

"Who were you talking to? Who were you telling to stop?"

AJ faced away, toward the river and Baptist Hill, where the dogs had been barking.

"What the hell is going on?" Wheeler said.

AJ didn't respond.

"Now we've both been knocked down by something we couldn't see," Wheeler said. "And what is it with the magical lighters all of a sudden? I could have sworn that lighter was just hanging in the air." Wheeler scanned the patio, as if wondering where the thing had ended up. Then he looked at AJ again. "I don't know how, but I think you know something."

In front of the house, a car door slammed.

"That's got to be Manfredi," AJ said. "Let's find out if he saw anything." He went toward the house. Wheeler hesitated, then followed. They met Manfredi at the front door.

"Sorry, I didn't see anyone," Manfredi said. "Whoever it was is long gone."

Wheeler nodded, but peered across the yard, as if giving it one last try.

Manfredi watched him. "Can I tell the Hardys it's all right to come home?"

"Sam," AJ said, "maybe it would be better if they stayed away for a few days."

Wheeler looked at AJ for a long moment. "Okay."

"I'll talk to them," Manfredi said. "And I'll stick around for a while."

The three men headed across the lawn. AJ and Wheeler got into their car, AJ behind the wheel. Wheeler clicked on the mic, told Dispatch they were coming in. Then AJ drove out of the neighborhood. They approached the monument. Left would take them up Route 1 to the station. AJ went right onto Main Street.

"Where are we going?" Wheeler said.

AJ stopped at the curb. He killed the engine and the headlights. He sat there, staring out the windshield. Ahead of them, just visible if you knew where to look, the flagpole marked the bend in the road. Beyond it, hidden, was the drawbridge. The bridge that, a year ago, had gone up at the wrong time, backed up traffic, keeping AJ from going after Ben.

"Are you going to tell me what's going on?" Wheeler said.

AJ let out a breath. "This conversation would go a lot better with a couple of beers."

"Spit it out, AJ. I can take it, whatever it is, as long as it's the truth."

AJ turned to face Wheeler. "Okay, Sam. I'm going to give you the truth. The whole truth and nothing but."

"All right," Wheeler said, sounding doubtful.

"But here's the thing. I swear it's all true, every word. But it's going to sound like the craziest bunch of lies you ever heard in your life."

27

AJ watched the car drive away down the lane. The white metal blinked through the trees, then vanished. He turned and walked across the grass into the broad shadow of the house. When he opened the front door and stepped inside, Buck was there to greet him. The greyhound pushed against AJ's thighs with his nose.

"AJ?" Claire said, from the living room. A laptop and papers were scattered around her.

"I didn't think you'd be up," he said.

"Bright-eyed and bushy-tailed."

AJ shook his head. "I'm sure there's a joke in there somewhere, but I'm too tired to find it." He joined her on the couch. He leaned across her laptop to kiss her, and she moved a folder aside, slid closer.

"Where are the guys?" AJ kicked off his shoes.

"They left a little while ago."

"They were supposed to hang out here until I got back."

"I know they were. When I got up, DaSilva was sitting here like a zombie, staring at the television. I'm sure he hadn't slept at all. Maybe taking him out ghost hunting wasn't the best idea."

AJ didn't defend himself.

"Anyway, I told him they should head home so he could get some sleep."

"I wish they had waited here." As if the mention of sleep had reminded him of how tired he was, AJ tipped back, his hands on his face, his fingertips pressing his eyelids closed.

"It's okay, AJ. I really am all right by myself. With the alarm system..."

"It wasn't on. Anyway, I'm not sure the alarm system is enough." He hesitated. "There's something very bad going on in this town." He stopped again. "Did DaSilva tell you about the fire?"

"He said you ended up at a house fire in the Borough."

"It wasn't just a fire. It was another murder. Same M.O. as the Fraser murder."

"Oh, God. They must be connected somehow."

AJ only pressed his lips together. Claire searched his face.

"And Taylor's ghost really is on the loose," AJ said.

"You saw her?"

"Yeah."

"Where?"

"In Mystic. She pitched some rocks at her boyfriend's house. Then she got more creative and threw some candles. Broke a couple of windows. Wheeler and I went there to check it out, and she flipped a table over next to him. Then she knocked him down."

"Oh my God. How is she doing that? Ben could barely – "

"I don't know how she's doing it. Anger. Craziness. She seems to be able to do a lot of things."

"So, Wheeler – what does he think he saw? What does he think it was that flipped the table and knocked him down? That would be tough to explain."

AJ took a deep breath, as if preparing himself for the conversation with Wheeler all over again. "I told him."

"What?"

AJ nodded.

"How much did you tell him?"

"Everything. Bridgeport, Ben, Elizabeth..." He glanced toward the ceiling. "And now, Taylor. Setting fire to his coat. Using DaSilva to break out of the house."

"Did he believe you?"

"He doesn't know what to believe. I'm sure he thinks I'm crazy. That the whole bunch of us are."

Claire put her hand on AJ's arm, gave him a brief smile. "That sounds familiar. He just needs time."

"Maybe. I don't know." AJ looked down at his feet, where Buck lay with one eye open. He watched the dog's rib cage swell and collapse. "I might be off the case."

"No. The chief wanted you to tell Wheeler. He's been asking you to do it for a long time, right? He'll back you up."

"He will. But it may not matter. I don't know if Wheeler will want to work with me anymore." AJ rubbed his face again.

Claire began gathering up her papers.

"What are you doing?" AJ said.

"You need to sleep. I know you won't go to bed, so I'm making room for you to stretch out here. I'll move to the porch."

"Claire."

"You need to give me your phone, though."

"Why?"

"I'll screen your calls. If Wheeler or the chief calls, I'll wake you."

AJ sat there, considering the idea. Claire put an arm around him, as if to pull him close, but slipped her hand into his pocket and tugged the phone free.

"Nicely done," he said. "If this writing thing doesn't work out, you can always be a pickpocket."

"Lie down," she said. She went back to collecting her papers.

He watched her for a second, then stopped her hand. "Stay with me."

She turned to him. She slid her fingers underneath his shirt, kissed him. She pushed him back onto the cushions. "Okay. I'll be right here."

With her head on his chest, he closed his eyes. "One hour," he said. "No more."

***

"Maybe this isn't a good idea," DaSilva said.

They were heading down North Water Street toward the Borough. Sela was behind the wheel.

"AJ will be mad," DaSilva said.

"He won't be mad. He'll be too busy to even notice us."

"He's a cop. He's trained to notice."

Sela took the left onto Trumbull. "I thought you wanted to test yourself," he said. "If it was me, I would."

"I did. But it's just... I already saw Taylor, and the guy in the cemetery. How many tests do I need to take? I can see ghosts. That's it. That's the way it is."

"You don't seem very happy about it. I'd be happy. It's an amazing thing." Sela looked across the seat at DaSilva. "Are you scared?"

"No, I'm not scared." DaSilva avoided Sela's eyes, instead pretending to watch something on the soccer field, though it was too early for anyone to be out there. He stayed silent as they went right, onto the viaduct that took them above the village.

"Maybe we shouldn't go down there," he said.

"Oh, come on."

"No, I mean park a ways away. Park somewhere and we'll walk."

"Okay."

Sela navigated the narrow street past the little shops and restaurants. He went all the way down to Cannon Square, looped around to Main, then headed the other direction for a couple of blocks. He pulled to the side. They both got out of the car.

"Hey, that's appropriate, don't you think?" Sela nodded at the white building with the high porch. A big green and red sign read *Portuguese Holy Ghost Society*. "Since we're going to see a ghost?"

"That's *Holy* Ghost," DaSilva. "Not exactly the same thing."

"Maybe I should have paid more attention in confirmation class."

DaSilva snatched a baseball cap from the dashboard. "Mind if I borrow this?" He put it on and pulled the brim down over his face.

Sela just looked at him. "What's that, a disguise?"

"Shut up."

"Wait. Dave? Where'd you go?" Sela pretended to look around him for something he couldn't find. "Take off that hat so I can see you."

"Come on, let's go."

They walked down Main for a while, then took a side street into a neighborhood of churches and quiet houses with beautifully landscaped yards. They passed the old firehouse with the three big doors labeled *Steamers*, *Neptunes* and *Pioneers*. A breeze came off the water. The sun found breaks in the big shade trees. It was a perfect place for a stroll, if you weren't going looking for a ghost.

At first the sidewalk was empty, but as they got closer to the scene, there were people going the other way.

"See, we're not the only ones," Sela said.

They passed couples, middle-aged men with heavy cameras, a young mother pushing a stroller.

"Oh shit, here comes a cruiser," DaSilva said. "It might be AJ." He tipped his head down as if he wanted to tuck it into his shoulder. "Just walk normal."

The police car went by. AJ wasn't in it.

At the end of the street there was a small crowd. When they were a little nearer, they could see, beyond saw horses, a single fire company SUV and a couple of police cars. There were no ambulances, now. The scene was oddly peaceful, the emergency responders no longer dealing with an emergency, just the quiet, burned-out wreck of a house.

"I wish we could get closer," Sela said.

"Well, they're not going to let us walk right up to the place."

"There's got to be a way."

"Do you see AJ?"

"No. He must be gone." Sela looked down the cross street. "Maybe we can see better from the other side. Come on."

DaSilva followed Sela by the old school – a tall brick building with a bell tower and a mansard roof. At the end of it, they took a right onto a street that ran along the parking lot, ending at the water. A few people came the other way. They all offered the same greeting – a grim, wordless nod. The two Daves continued until they had cleared the school. The parking lot went on a little further. There, on the other side of it, was the house. Or what was left of it.

It had been remade of black wood, wood that even from this distance looked soft. It was wide open, with new gaps in every wall. The roof was just gone.

"Do you see anything?" Sela said.

"I don't know. What do you see?"

"Just tell me."

"I'm serious," DaSilva said. "What do you see over there?"

Sela let out a sigh. "A fireman doing something with his truck. Another man taking pictures. I don't think he's a cop. Maybe he's from *The Day*. There's a man, some kind of crime scene guy, maybe, poking around inside. Is that enough, or do you want me to tell you what they're wearing?"

"That guy poking around inside – what about the woman with him?"

"Hold on. I can't see anyone right now. They must have gone into another room."

They both stared hard at the house for a while.

"There he is," Sela said.

"She's right next to him. Black hair. Red T-shirt."

Sela moved closer to DaSilva and tried to match his line of sight. "She's right next to him?"

"Yeah. You see her?"

"No. Just the guy. Wearing some kind of official-looking windbreaker."

"That's him. Right beside him. You see her?"

"Still no, Dave."

"Holy shit."

"Holy shit is right." Sela looked at DaSilva. "We have to get closer."

"How are we going to do that?"

Sela turned back toward the house. "Think the chief's over there? He's a *Mystic Afterlife* fan. We could explain that we wanted to do a quick paranormal investigation. He'd be up for it."

"Yeah, that's not going to happen."

"We've got to do something." Sela started moving away. "Let's go."

DaSilva blocked him. "No."

"Come on. We can get closer than this."

"I'm not sure I want to get close."

Sela studied him for a moment. "You are scared, aren't you? I don't blame you, after Taylor. Look, we'll keep a little distance this time. We'll just get a better view."

Sela took another step. DaSilva stayed planted. Sela looked back at him. "This woman with the red shirt that you saw – was she that frightening?"

"It's not seeing her that I'm worried about."

"You don't want her to see you."

DaSilva looked at the house again. "Too late."

"Is she looking at us?"

"Right at us."

For a few seconds, both Daves were silent and still, their eyes locked on the house.

"Maybe you're right," Sela said. "Let's just go."

On the way back to the car, they moved fast, not saying much. Once or twice, DaSilva looked behind him.

"Dave, she's not following us," Sela said.

"I know."

"She can't get out of that house. Not without a little help, anyway."

"She could use one of those cops."

Sela seemed to be thinking about that. "She won't."

"Taylor did it."

"She did. But I think Taylor has some kind of special gift."

"A gift? For what?"

"For being a mean-ass ghost."

They got into the car. DaSilva tossed the cap back onto the dashboard. Sela drove up Main and around the green. "Do you think this is permanent?" he said, when they were back on the viaduct, the Borough behind them. "From now on, you see ghosts?"

"What do you mean?"

"I was thinking maybe it's temporary, like the concussion. When you get over the concussion, this stuff will go away, too."

"Maybe."

"We should look into this kind of thing. You know, second sight brought on by some kind of trauma. See if it's happened to anyone else."

DaSilva only stared out his window. Sela turned onto Trumbull. There was still no one on the soccer field.

"This could put a damper on the ghost hunting," Sela said. "As far as the show goes, anyway."

"How do you figure that one?"

Sela glanced across the seat. "Okay, let's say someone asks us to see if their little B&B is haunted. Good subject for a show, right? Except now, you just walk in go *Yep*, or *Nope*. It takes all of two minutes."

"So they get their answer."

"Kind of takes the drama out of it, doesn't it? Our viewers like a little drama. A little foreplay."

DaSilva didn't say anything.

"I don't have to explain what foreplay is, right?"

"Ha ha."

They were on the long straightaway to Route 1.

"So, you saw a ghost," Sela said. "The woman who died in that house."

DaSilva kept looking out the window. "I have to call AJ. He'll want to try to talk to her. For his investigation."

"You mean, to see how the fire got started? I guess so. But that's more for the fire department to figure out, right?"

DaSilva reached into his pocket for his phone. "In case it wasn't just a fire. In case it was another murder."

***

Claire was on the porch, typing on her laptop, when AJ's phone rang. DaSilva's face appeared on the screen. She touched a button and put the phone to her ear.

"Hi, Dave, it's Claire."

"Hi. Is AJ around? Can I talk to him?"

"He's trying to get a little sleep. Which is what I thought you were doing."

"Yeah, I know. This is kind of important. I saw... It's something he might want to check out."

"If by *something* you mean a ghost, then I think it can wait."

"It's not just any ghost. I mean, it's connected to his job. It's a police thing."

Claire looked out at the trees beyond the screen, where songbirds twittered crazily. She was silent.

"I can call back," DaSilva said. "When will he be up?"

Just then, AJ stepped out onto the porch. "Who's that?"

"It's Dave DaSilva," Claire said.

AJ took the phone from her. "Hey, Dave."

"Sorry, AJ, I didn't mean to wake you."

"It's fine. Where are you?"

"I'm in the car, with Sela. On our way back from the Borough."

"Oh, Jesus."

"I know. But I saw something I thought I should tell you about."

AJ's jaw tightened. "Go ahead."

"We went back down to look at that house that burned."

"Dave."

"I saw her, AJ. The woman that lives – *lived* – there. I saw her."

"Okay." AJ went out through the screen door. He found a spot in the sun, and listened, as Dave told him everything.

"We thought maybe you'd want to try and talk to her, AJ," DaSilva said. "She might be able to tell you something. Maybe she knows how the fire started. If it was an accident, or..."

AJ turned to look back at the porch, where Claire sat with her head down, working. "I don't know if she'll be able to talk, Dave. What kind of shape was she in?"

"She seemed okay. The house is destroyed, but she didn't look like the fire touched her. She wasn't burned."

"This wasn't some previous owner that you saw, was it? I mean, she was from our time, right? She was wearing modern clothes?"

"Definitely. Red T-shirt, kind of tight. Jeans. Black hair, cut short, like my sister's. Modern, for sure."

"Black hair, you said?"

"Yes. Dark, anyway."

"You're sure it was a ghost? Not someone from the ME's office, someone investigating the scene?"

"Jesus, AJ. She was a ghost. I don't have a lot of experience at this, I know. But I'm sure. She had that too-bright look. And Sela couldn't see her at all."

"Okay. What else can you tell me about her?"

"We were kind of far away, so I don't know... Late thirties, maybe early forties, I think. Thin. Short, I guess. Shorter than the cop she was standing next to."

"Anything else?"

"Not that I can remember. Like I said, we were kind of far away."

"All right. Thanks, Dave. I'll talk to you later, okay? Meanwhile, stay away from there."

"Don't worry, I have no desire to go back anytime soon. Anyway, I'm working today."

"Good," AJ said. "I'll tell my dad to keep you busy." AJ pressed End before DaSilva had a chance to say more. He went back into the porch.

"You want something to eat before you go in to the station?" Claire said. "Because I could whip up some eggs while you get dressed."

"That's all right. I'll pick something up on the way."

"Okay."

"Claire, I know you're all right here, but..."

She stopped him. She already had her cell phone in her hand. "I'll call Melody. Again."

He kissed her and went into the house. As he climbed the stairs, he punched another number.

The chief answered.

"Hey, Chief," AJ said. "That body we found in the house in the Borough – I don't think it was Nicole Addison."

28

The chief hung up the phone.

"That was AJ?" Wheeler said.

"Yeah. He thinks the body that was found in Nicole Addison's house isn't Nicole Addison."

"Based on what?"

The chief stared across the desk, his hands clasped in front of him.

"Oh, for Christ's sake," Wheeler said. "I knew some friends of AJ's had that cable show. That supernatural show. I knew that your wife was a fan. But I never would have guessed – in a million years, I never would have guessed – that you all really believed. That you thought any of that stuff was real. Even you." He made eye contact with the chief for an instant.

"Let's see if AJ's information checks out." The chief picked up the phone again and made another call. "Hey, Arthur, it's Roland Brown. Where are you on the ID for that body from the house fire?"

"With the damage done to that body, there's not much to go on. Forget fingerprints. We're going to need dental records. Until we get them, we're nowhere."

"You've got to give me something."

"Like what?"

"How about height, weight? Is it even a woman?"

There was a brief pause and the sound of a drawer opening.

"The body is female. About five foot four, 120 pounds. That's really all I can give you right now."

"That may be enough. Thanks." The chief put the phone down and looked at Wheeler. "You met Ms. Addison. Describe her."

"Late thirties, blonde hair, fair skin, tall, slim."

"How tall?"

"She was almost as tall as AJ with heels. So, maybe five nine."

"The body in the house was only five-foot four."

"He's sure?" Wheeler said.

"Yes."

"So it's not her."

"No, it's not. Just like AJ said." The chief paused, as if waiting for that to sink in. "Look, Sam, we're not all crazy. What we are is a group of people who, because of our experiences, have been forced to accept what other people dismiss. Whether you like it or not, you've had an experience yourself. A definitive experience, if you ask me. AJ has told you the truth. I've told you the truth. Now you need to accept it."

"You make that sound like an order."

"We've got a mess on our hands. I need AJ's special skill on this case. I need your skill as a seasoned detective. I need the two of you working together. And I can't be riding you all the time to be sure that's happening."

"I can't just flip a switch and believe all..." Wheeler hesitated. "Whatever it is."

The chief sat back in his chair, frustration on his face. His gaze went toward the little TV against the wall for a second, tuned as always to CNN.

"Okay," Wheeler said after a while. "I've trusted your judgement for quite a few years, Chief. I still do. I'll keep an open mind."

"Thanks, Sam. Right now, I need some traditional police work. I need you to go over to the high school. Get what you can on Ms. Addison. See if anyone can tell us where she might be."

"School administration is already supposed to be faxing me some information on her family."

"Good. Now, I've got to change that bulletin. We're not just looking for Nicole Addison's car. Now we're looking for Nicole Addison."

***

AJ knocked on the chief's door and poked his head into the

office.

"Come on in," the chief said.

Carrying a tray with three coffees, and a grease-stained bag, AJ looked around, surprised. "Where's Wheeler?"

"Doing some research on Nicole Addison. You stopped for food?"

"Sam's favorite. I thought it might be worth the extra time."

The chief watched AJ put the coffees down on a chair and then pass one to him. "I'm not sure caffeine and cholesterol will win him over, but I'll take it."

AJ sat in the other chair. He pulled a little wrapped package from the bag. "Bacon and egg," he said. He passed it to the chief, who instantly opened the paper, releasing a spicy steam. AJ unwrapped his sandwich and began eating.

The chief seemed completely focused on his first mouthful. "I needed that," he said, putting the sandwich down. "You're right, AJ. That's not Addison at the morgue. How did you know? Did you see something there that you didn't tell me about?"

"Not me. Dave DaSilva. He and Sela went to take a look at the place, early this morning. He saw a ghost in the house, and the description just didn't fit."

"You mean, he saw her with some kind of special gadget?"

"No. He saw her."

"Wait, DaSilva is seeing ghosts now?"

"It's a long story. But yeah."

"All right, save the story. Just tell me what he saw."

"A petite woman with short black hair. She can't be Nicole Addison. The height and the hair color are wrong."

"Okay. That matches what the ME told me. He said maybe five four." The chief sipped his coffee. "That's an old cottage. Maybe the ghost is a previous owner, from a long time ago."

"No. I thought the same thing. But, her clothes were contemporary – jeans and a T-shirt. Her hairstyle, too. DaSilva said it was just like his sister's."

The chief finished his meal with efficient bites.

"Guess you were hungry," AJ said. "You want the other sandwich?"

"No. You'd better save it for Wheeler." For a second, the chief eyed the bag. "Any chance this ghost could tell us who she is?"

AJ leaned his head back against the wall and looked up at the ceiling. "I don't know. Depends on how traumatized she is. How much memory she has. Ben and I had a long talk that first night that I saw him. But Taylor – she hasn't said one word. I'm still not sure she can speak. After what happened to this woman, I'm guessing she'll be more like that. I doubt I'll have much luck with her."

"Well, barring a rational conversation with her ghost, the most important thing is to find Addison. And we have some other things to ask her. Like where she was the night Taylor Fraser was killed."

"You think Addison could be the murderer? What would be the motive?"

"I don't have an answer. For that, we may be back to needing one of our unique sources. Maybe this new woman, maybe Taylor."

AJ looked back across the desk at the chief. "Okay. I can try. But, like I said, I doubt the woman at Addison's house is going to be able to tell me much. And Taylor – first I'd have to find her. She could be anywhere."

"Maybe she's still hanging around Ryan Hardy. I'd go back to that house."

"Manfredi was supposed to advise the Hardys to stay out of there for a while. I got Wheeler to give me that much, at least."

"So, wherever they are, then," the chief said. "If it weren't for this second murder, I'd think maybe we were wrong about Ryan. That maybe he did kill Taylor, and that's why she went to his home. She wanted revenge, or she wanted to point him out to us."

"I don't think she was pointing out anything to us, Roland. She attacked Wheeler, remember?"

"So what was she doing?"

AJ shook his head.

The chief took a couple of hits of his coffee. "I guess there could be any number of things going on. If she is able to reason, maybe she blames Ryan for not being there the night she was killed, because if he had stuck around, she might still be alive."

"Or, she was pissed because he was with Maggie Strang. Maybe Maggie was the target."

The chief paused in mid gulp.

"Shit," AJ said. "I should have thought of that. If Taylor's after her, Maggie could be in danger."

"Think she's at home?"

"After the night she had, I doubt she went to school."

The chief dropped his cup and stepped out of the office. He came back a minute later. "I sent a cruiser to check out the Strang residence. Of course, they won't see Taylor, if she's there, but they can look for anything unusual." The chief went behind his desk again. "I can't have you staked out there twenty-four seven, and I don't have any other officers who can see Taylor."

"You could deputize DaSilva."

Their eyes met. They both shook their heads.

"Should I swing by Maggie's place on the way to the Addison house?" AJ said.

"Unless we hear that something's going on at the Strangs', the Addison house is your first stop."

"Is it too soon, though? There's no point if the place is still crawling with firemen and our own guys."

"If you're looking for privacy – that's only going to get harder to come by." The chief put a hand on his scalp. "We're going to get help from Major Crimes. I haven't gotten the call yet, but I'm sure it's coming. It'll complicate things, for sure. But honestly, maybe now's a good time for them to come in on the case. Tara's having surgery. My family will need me."

"Chief – I'm sorry."

"She'll get through this. We'll all get through it." He was quiet for a moment. "I'm really glad you finally talked to Wheeler. Even if it didn't go so well."

"That's putting it mildly," AJ said. "When he left me at Claire's this morning, I had the distinct impression that he was going to work alone from here on out."

The chief raised his hand. "That's not his call to make. He'll do what I ask him to do. I'm sure he'll come around. Not as fast maybe as I did, because I'd already gone through this with your uncle. And not as quick as Claire because, well, Sam's not falling in love with you."

AJ smiled.

"The best way to speed up Wheeler's process is to have him see you in action."

"What do you mean?"

"I want you to take Wheeler with you to the Addison house."

"And do what?"

"Make him a believer."

29

Wheeler knocked and came in. AJ picked the bag up from the chair next to him, but the detective stayed on his feet, his eyes on the chief.

"What'd you find out?" the chief said.

"Not much. Nicole Addison doesn't seem to be close to anyone at the school. I got the impression she isn't exactly well liked."

"What about the emergency contact?" The chief read from a fax sheet in front of him. "Theresa Fallon?"

"She got married last summer. Moved to Atlanta. The number Addison put down for her is out of service."

"Can't we track her down?"

"Bob's on the computer right now."

"Okay." The chief pointed toward the paper bag that AJ was holding by its rolled-up top. "AJ got you some breakfast. Why don't you have a seat."

Wheeler acknowledged AJ with a blink of eye contact. He took the bag. "Thanks." He sat down.

For a moment, the only sound was the soft crinkling of the sandwich being unwrapped. He worked at it deliberately, flattening the paper on his knees. When he was finally about to take the first bite, the cell phone in his pocket buzzed. He folded the paper back over his sandwich and took the call. "Detective Wheeler." He nodded. "Hold on." Cradling the thin phone awkwardly with his shoulder, he pulled his notepad from another coat pocket. "Okay." He wrote quickly. "Wait," he said, made a face, then put the phone away again.

"What was that?" the chief said.

"Anonymous tip about Addison. Someone from the high school, I think – I heard the class bell in the background." He held the paper closer to AJ, pointing with his pencil. "I've got two addresses. This one is a farmhouse she's supposed to have inherited from her mother. And this is where she keeps her boat."

"Hmmm," the chief said. "A waterfront cottage, a house, a sports car and a boat. That's a lot on a teacher's salary."

"Maybe she inherited money along with the house," AJ said.

"Maybe." The chief took the notebook from Wheeler, scanned the page. "All right. I want you to head over to the farmhouse with a search warrant. Judge Barrett is on notice that we might need him for warrants, so that shouldn't slow you down much. In the meantime, I'll send a couple of units to those addresses, to keep an eye on things until you get there."

"We'll need a warrant for the boat, too," Wheeler said.

"Yeah." The chief passed the notebook back across the desk. "But check in with me after the farmhouse. I might want you to try the cottage next."

Wheeler stood, then turned to AJ. "You coming?"

The chief hid a smile. AJ followed Wheeler to the door.

"You're driving," Wheeler said. "I've got to eat."

***

They pulled up to the cruiser that was parked in front of the old farmhouse. Wheeler talked to the guys through the open window. They hadn't seen anyone or anything. The house was a compact, two-story box with cedar shakes darkened by weather. Topped with flat stones, the stone wall in front of the house was neat and square, but once the lawn ended, the wall reverted to the irregular mounds that were everywhere in Stonington.

AJ and Wheeler cut across the grass. It still showed the back and forth of a mower. The front door was windowless and white. As plain as possible – not even a concrete pad or flag stone in front of it.

Wheeler knocked. No response. "It looks like no one's lived here for a while," Wheeler said.

"It's been kept up," AJ said. "It's tidy."

"That's what I mean. It's too tidy. I don't see a rake, or a flower pot, or muddy shoes by the door." Wheeler looked down by the threshold. "The grass isn't even worn here." He tried the knob. It didn't turn.

A woman was walking a well-groomed collie down the road.

"Excuse me!" Wheeler went toward her.

The woman stepped into the driveway and brought the collie to heel.

"We're looking for a Nicole Addison." Wheeler showed his badge.

The woman adjusted the silk scarf around her neck. "Is she all right?"

"We just need to talk to her."

"I haven't seen her today."

The dog went straight to AJ, as far as the lead would allow.

"Baxter," the woman said, tugging on the lead.

"It's okay." AJ closed the gap and patted the collie's head. "Beautiful dog."

"He belongs to my son and daughter-in-law," the woman said. "They live just down the road."

"Good boy." AJ scratched the dog behind the ears. Baxter sniffed and then licked AJ's hand.

"There were lights on last night," the woman said, nodding toward the farmhouse.

Wheeler got out his pad. "What time was that?"

"It was late. Or early, depending on how you count it."

"Did you notice the actual time?"

"Yes, I have a clock by the bed. It was two something. Closer to two-thirty. I don't sleep well anymore, so I'm often up at odd hours."

"Do you know her well?" AJ said.

"No, not really. She doesn't live here. She stops in just often enough to keep things up. My son actually spoke to her about buying the place, but she doesn't want to sell. I think it's her last connection to her mother."

"Did you know her mother?" Wheeler said.

"She'd come out once in a while as I was walking by, and we'd chat. I think she was more interested in Baxter than in me." She patted the dog's head. "I'm only here for a few weeks in the summer, myself. So, we'd talked perhaps a handful of times. Until I read her obituary, I didn't even know she had a daughter."

"Really? She never mentioned her? You never saw the daughter

196

come by?"

"No. I don't think I saw anyone come by the house."

Wheeler handed her a card. "Thank you, Ms. ..."

"Jones. Mrs. Lena Jones."

"So you wouldn't have any idea how we might get in touch with Ms. Addison?"

"No, I'm sorry."

"If you should see her, could you give me a call?"

"I certainly will. Is she in some kind of trouble?"

"We just need to talk to her."

Mrs. Jones and the collie started off down the road.

"Let's go around back," Wheeler said.

They found another door, centered between sixteen-pane windows. It was locked. Wheeler rapped it with his knuckles. "I'm glad we got that warrant," he said. He produced a slim case from a coat pocket, selected a pick and inserted it in the lock. After a few seconds, the tumblers clicked. Wheeler turned the knob. They went inside.

"Hello? Ms. Addison!"

No answer. They did a walk-through of the first floor. It was cut up into small spaces – a kitchen with white painted cabinets, a sparsely furnished living room, an odd cubby with plastic storage boxes of fabric and a sewing machine on a table. A half bath. The walls were mostly bare.

Wheeler yelled up the stairs. "Police! Is anyone home?"

More silence.

They went back to the kitchen. Wheeler handed AJ a pair of gloves, then began opening drawers. "Still full of utensils."

AJ slid a box of cereal from a cupboard. "This cereal is new. There's pasta, soup. She must stay here part of the time. Maybe Mrs. Jones just didn't notice."

"Let's look upstairs."

Each tread creaked under their feet. On the second floor, there were two bedrooms with low, sloped ceilings. In the first, a cheap dresser sat next to a daybed covered with cardboard boxes. The second room was larger, with a double bed that was neatly made, the quilt squared against the headboard.

Wheeler picked up a framed photograph from the nightstand. "This is the only photo I've seen in the place. That's Nicole, right?"

He held it out for AJ to see.

"I think so. From a while ago. High school, maybe?"

Wheeler studied the picture, the bright eyes, the cheerful smile. "Where are you now, Nicole?" He put the frame down again.

AJ checked the closet. "The clothes look like hers."

Wheeler opened a dresser drawer. "Here, too," he said. "If she's using the house, she wouldn't want the drawers filled with her mother's clothes." He looked around the room. "But you'd think there'd be some memento or picture – something to remember her mother by."

"Not very sentimental, I guess."

Between the two bedrooms was a full bath with a claw-foot tub. AJ pulled back the shower curtain. He opened the medicine cabinet. There was a pill bottle in front. He took it out, read the label, gave it a quick shake. Empty. Pushing aside a bottle of hairspray, he took another pill bottle from the cabinet, identical to the first. Then a third, slightly taller. "Sam," he said.

Wheeler appeared in the doorway. "What?"

"Why would she keep empty pill bottles? Especially her mothers?" AJ took a slim orange bottle from the cabinet, then a squat white one. He dropped them in the sink. The smaller bottle bounced off of the porcelain, fell to the floor, rolled.

"Shit." AJ scanned the dull linoleum. "Where did that go?" He got down on his hands and knees. "There," he said, reaching under the tub. He grunted, grabbed the bottle. Then, he reached back under the clawfoot. He stood up. "Check it out."

"What?"

AJ held out his hand. In the middle of his blue-gloved palm was a round, white pill. "What does that look like to you?"

Wheeler flipped the pill over, revealing the letters OC. "It looks like she missed one."

30

The sun was already shining way too bright when she opened her eyes. She squinted at the clock and saw that it was still early – she'd only missed first period. Right now she'd be in Health class, the lamest of the lame. She reached for her phone, moving super slow, trying not to make a sound. Her parents had let her sleep in, but if they knew she was awake, they might still tell her to get dressed and go. Holding the phone with both hands, she felt the scrapes on her palms, from where they'd hit the pavement. The Band-Aids on her knees pinched, too.

What an insane night.

She typed the message – *Are you awake?* She stared at the screen. The longer she waited for Ryan to respond, the more she wished she'd hadn't sent the text. Normally she thought it all through first – what to say, when to send it. She should have done that this time. But after last night, after what they went through together... It seemed like they would be closer, now. They had a bond, a story. They'd definitely want to hear from each other today.

She shifted onto her back, making the bed creak. For a second, she froze, afraid she'd given herself away. But nothing happened. Her parents didn't yell in to her, or come knocking on her door.

Were they even home? The TV wasn't on. If her mom was here, the TV would be on. Maybe her mom was keeping the volume super low, to be nice. Maybe they were both tiptoeing around, trying to let her rest. Her dad could be in the living room. If he had a couple of fishing magazines or maybe a reel with a tangled line, you could be sitting right next to him and he wouldn't even know you were there.

She checked the phone. No response from Ryan yet.

Probably he was still asleep. Last night, she came home and went right to bed, but Ryan and his mom were going to stay with another family, across the river. They would have had to pack some things, drive, tell their story – which would be partly about her! – figure out who should take what bed. So, he'd been up much later than her. He might not be awake for hours.

She thought about texting Olivia, but instead put the phone down.

She was hungry. Since her parents had let her sleep in, maybe there'd be something special for breakfast. Maybe donuts. Or her dad would make waffles.

She got up. The place was empty. No one in the kitchen or the living room. The TV was black. Apparently her mom had gone to work, and her dad had gone off to do something, like it was just another normal day. Like none of that crazy shit at Ryan's house had actually happened.

Then she heard her mom's voice – quiet, coming through the front door. She was outside, talking to someone on the phone.

Maggie poured herself some apple juice and drank it at the counter, trying to hear what her mother was saying but not really catching it. When her mom's voice stopped, Maggie went out. Her mom was right there on the step, in her bathrobe. Maggie sat down next to her. She stretched her legs out in the sun, feeling the pinch of the Band-Aids again.

"Where's Dad?" she said.

"Fishing."

From that one word, from the voice that was flat and tight, Maggie knew there wouldn't be any donuts or waffles. "Are you mad at him for going?"

"No."

"But you're mad."

"I'm not happy. Neither is he."

"You're mad at me."

"I'm not happy that you were at Ryan's house in the middle of the night."

"You said I could go."

"I never said you could sleep there. When have we ever let you do a sleepover on a school night?"

"It wasn't a sleepover. God, I'm not twelve."

"That's right. You're not. That's exactly why we would never agree to letting you stay over at a boy's house."

"It's just Ryan!"

"Yeah. And he isn't just any boy to you. I'm not blind."

"And I'm not stupid."

"What's that supposed to mean?"

"Nothing."

Her mom finally looked at her, zeroing in on the Band-Aids on her legs. She said, "Look, Ryan is mixed up in something. Can't you see that after last night? If you keep hanging around with him you're going to end up with a lot more than skinned knees."

"Are you saying I can't see Ryan?"

"I guess that would probably be pointless. But please, Maggie, be careful."

Maggie just shook her head. Her mom's dried-up face looked tired, enough almost to make you feel sorry for her.

"I just spoke to that guidance counselor, Ms. Goodwin."

"Why?"

"I explained what happened last night."

"God, Mom? Why did you do that?"

"If some kids from your school are coming after Ryan, I thought she should know about it. I'm worried, Maggie. Who knows what they'll do next? I told Ms. Goodwin that I thought you should stay home for a few days. She agreed."

"What about my school work? I can't get behind. Not if I want to graduate."

"You won't get behind. I'm meeting Ms. Goodwin at two. She'll have all of your books and assignments. Things are winding down, anyway, right?"

They didn't say anything for a while, just stared at the yard and down the hill. The whole trailer park was lit up in yellow light. Everything was quiet – like something big was about to happen.

"I'm supposed to work today," her mom said, "but if you want me to, I can reschedule my appointments."

"No, that will be a hassle. I just want to sleep, anyway."

"Well, if you're sure."

"I'm sure."

"Okay, then. I need to get ready." Her mom stood up. "I could make you some eggs. I think we have eggs... Or are you going right back to bed?"

"Right back to bed," Maggie said. She followed her mom inside.

***

She woke up suddenly, panicked. It took her a minute to realize that it had been a dream. She'd been trapped in the trailer. Loud bangs on all sides. She'd looked out the window and there, crouching down right by the wall, was a girl. Tiffanee. Like she'd been back then. Just a skinny little girl. Holding something up to the trailer skirt. A match. A flame.

Maggie took a couple of deep breaths. She didn't hear anything now. She should have left the TV on, so it wouldn't be so dead quiet.

Bang!

Holy shit! Something had hit the wall. It was all starting again. For a second, she couldn't breathe or move or think. Then she heard whistling, and just as fast, she relaxed. That was the guy down the street. It was garbage day. He was just out banging his cans around and whistling. He was always whistling.

She checked her phone. Nothing. Ryan must still be asleep.

She got up, stopped at the bathroom, then went on into the living room. Just for noise, she turned the TV on. She was starving. She should have taken her mom up on the offer to make eggs. Being super afraid all the time probably sped up your metabolism. She could start a diet, call it Scared Skinny. She'd make a billion.

Her mom was wrong, there were no eggs in the fridge. There was a tube of cinnamon rolls, though. They were for her dad, no doubt, but he wouldn't be home for hours. They could be replaced.

While the rolls were baking, she checked her phone again. Still nothing from Ryan. This time, she was a little pissed off. She'd remembered that the family Ryan had gone to stay with was someone they knew from church, with, like, five little kids. There was no way he was sleeping through that morning routine.

A reporter came on the television, someone local. Before she could hear or see anything, Maggie grabbed the remote and switched to a random cooking show. She pretended to watch for a while.

The timer for the rolls went off. One more thing to make her jump. She took the rolls out of the oven, slathered on the glaze, put two on a plate, then went to the couch. She flipped channels, stopped on a paranormal show. You could tell it was a paranormal show because everyone on it, including the host, looked like a lunatic.

A woman described moving into a big, old house that she'd been able to get for an amazingly low price. Which should have been her first clue. The whole picture went green, like you were seeing in the dark, with some kind of night-vision camera or something. An actress – much better looking than the real woman – was asleep in bed when a loud noise woke her. She lay there for a second, supposedly terrified. There was a bunch of quick tapping sounds. She got out of bed, put on a robe. She went to the front door, then out to the porch. She stepped on something, looked down. It was a small stone. There were stones all over the place.

"What the hell?" Maggie put her roll down.

Bzzzzz!

Maggie jumped. It was her phone. She picked it up, already smiling, so ready to talk to Ryan. But it was Olivia's face on the screen.

"Hey," she said.

"Maggie. There's some weird shit going on. The police were here again. All of the teachers look freaked out. I guess Ms. Addison didn't show up at school today. And she didn't get a sub. No one knows where she is."

Maggie didn't move. It was like she couldn't, like she was frozen solid.

"Are you at home?" Olivia said.

She made herself answer. "Yeah."

"Are you sick or something?"

"No. I just slept in."

"Must be nice. Hey, put the news on. The local station."

Maggie flipped back to the channel with the reporter. It was playing a commercial, now.

"Is there anything on?" Olivia said. "About Ms. Addison?"

"Why are you whispering?"

"They're cracking down on cell phones. A bunch of kids have already had them taken. It's like they're trying to keep this quiet."

"They're not trying to keep anything quiet. They do that every year at some point, with the phones."

"Some kids are saying there was a fire at Ms. Addison's house and she's dead. That's why they don't want anyone using cell phones.

They have to keep it quiet until the police can tell the family."

"Next of kin," Maggie said, quickly. "That's what they call it. They notify next of kin. They would have done that right away."

"Is the news on yet?"

"It's a commercial." Maggie watched a man in a sun costume dance around a breakfast table.

"Just wait. If it's true, it will be the top story."

Maggie could hear Olivia breathing. The news came back on. A reporter talked into her fat microphone. Then, there it was. Black. Half gone. Not a house, just bones, just black bones.

Maggie sat, speechless, empty, no words, only humming, in her head. She heard Olivia calling her name. "What?" she said.

"What do you see?" Olivia said.

"It's true. It really happened."

"What happened?"

"Fire."

"Shit, here comes a teacher. I have to go." Olivia hung up.

Maggie sat there, staring at the television. It seemed impossible, like another bad dream. Only it was real. And it was scarier than any nightmare.

31

"But Chief," Wheeler said, "shouldn't we head to the marina next? We might catch up with her."

"There's already a car at the marina, and no sign of Addison. I want you to stop at her house first. You might learn everything we need to know right there."

Wheeler looked across the seat at AJ. "All right."

"Report in as soon as you're done there."

"Will do." Wheeler seemed like he might crush the mic in his fist. Then he put it back on the dash. For a long time he stared out the window, watching the trees and the stone walls go by.

AJ stayed quiet.

"You don't have to do this after dark?" Wheeler said. "This...whatever it is you do?"

"No."

"So what's going to happen? You're going to walk onto the crime scene and just start talking to thin air?"

"I guess I'll have to figure it out when I get there."

They were silent the rest of the way to the Borough. They crossed the viaduct, looked down at the dry-docked boats. AJ worked his way through the village. He turned onto the street that led to the burned-out house. The saw horses were still blocking the last part of the dead end. A news truck with a dish on the roof had taken up position there. As AJ maneuvered around all of that, a young woman in TV-ready clothes and makeup hurried toward them.

"Excuse me, officer!"

AJ ignored the reporter and kept going. He pulled onto the shoulder behind a cruiser. In front of him was the fire marshal's red SUV. They walked across the street.

The house was black from top to bottom, but there were lights burning inside, making it look like some kind of giant Halloween lantern. A generator hummed at the edge of the yard. From it, an orange extension cord stretched across the muddied lawn, through the front door. Wheeler and AJ followed the cord inside, making the turn into the bedroom, where just a few hours before they had seen the body in its charred cocoon. Two men worked in the glare of caged halogen lamps.

"Hey, Mike," Wheeler said to the uniformed cop.

"Hey, Sam. Did the chief send you back out here?"

"We just need to take a second look."

The other man was the fire marshal. He was big, with round cheeks and a chinstrap beard. The badge on his helmet caught the light. "Just be careful of the floor over there." He pointed. "That's where the fire started. The floor boards are weak."

"Okay, will do," Wheeler said.

From the dark wall behind the men, a woman appeared. Red shirt and designer jeans, black hair cut short. Her eyes met AJ's. Her mouth opened, but she made no sound. She retreated into an open closet, into the shadow cast by the blackened wood. To AJ, though, she remained as visible as ever. Slender, stylish, glowing.

"Sure wish the ME would give us the ID of the woman who died here," AJ said, speaking in a loud and careful voice.

"I bet you do." The fire marshal looked down at his clipboard. "Takes time, like anything else."

The ghost drifted forward, her eyes fixed on AJ. "Helena," she said. "I'm Helena Fraser. Taylor's mom."

AJ nodded.

The fire marshal turned his attention to an exposed wire in the wall.

"You can see me?" Helena said. "You can hear me?"

AJ nodded again. He dug a notepad out of a pocket, opened it and wrote *Helena Fraser*. He held the pad in front of him, as if considering what to write next. Wheeler took a half step toward him and glanced down at the paper. He let out a quick breath.

The fire marshal looked up. "Are you all right?"

"Help me," Helena said.

"Have you figured out how the fire started?" Wheeler said.

"I'll be sending in the full report tomorrow."

"Was it set?"

The fire marshal let go of the wire and turned to Wheeler. "Was the deceased strangled?"

The two men stared at each other.

Helena Fraser put a hand to her neck.

"Fair enough," Wheeler said. "Don't let us get in your way."

"Believe me, I won't." The man traced the wire with his hand. He stood up, then went past Wheeler and AJ toward the front door. The uniformed cop followed, with a shrug.

Wheeler watched them leave. "Now's your chance," he said, in a whisper. "But keep your voice down."

AJ took a step closer to the ghost. She eyed AJ warily.

"Do you remember who did this to you?" AJ said.

"Did what? What happened to me?"

"We think you were murdered."

"Murdered?" Helena's hand trailed down her neck. "Like Taylor. God. Just like Taylor."

"Was it Nicole Addison?" AJ said. "Did she hurt you?"

"Nicole? No. She's a friend. She would never hurt me."

"Do you know what happened to her? Where she is?"

Helena frowned. "She left. I was alone."

Wheeler moved into the doorway and faced the front door. He dug his notebook from a pocket of his sport coat, then opened it to somewhere in the middle.

"Why were you here?" AJ said. "What brought you to Ms. Addison's house?"

Wheeler grunted. "Too loud," he whispered.

Helena shook her head slowly, a lost expression on her face.

"Try to remember," AJ said. "Anything you can recall may help us figure out who hurt you. And your daughter, too."

There were tears in Helena's eyes. She closed them for a moment. "I came to get pills. Prescription pills. Nicole didn't have any here. She said she kept them somewhere else. She wanted me to come back the next day, but I couldn't wait that long. Losing Taylor – it was just so hard. I needed the pills to cope. I told her that I'd pay her double. So she left to get them. I waited for her."

"Well?" Wheeler said.

AJ raised a hand.

Wheeler wrote something in his notepad, then looked straight down the hall to the front door. A third cruiser had stopped at the edge of the yard. "You need to hurry up," he said.

"What happened next?" AJ said.

"I drank some wine. After that... I don't remember..."

"Try."

"I can't!" Helena put a hand on either side of her head.

"You seem sure that Nicole didn't hurt you. I think maybe you saw someone else."

Outside, a cop got out of the cruiser that had just arrived. He opened the trunk and produced a coiled extension cord, then two more of the halogen lamps, each with a little stand and a handle. He went to where the fire marshal and the other officer were talking in the yard. The fire marshal gestured toward the house.

"AJ," Wheeler said.

Helena closed her eyes. She rubbed her temples. "Someone knocked on the door. I thought it was Nicole. I guess that doesn't make sense, since it was her own house. Then, when I opened the door, there was a man."

Wheeler looked toward AJ. "We're about to have company."

"Good!" AJ said. "What did he look like?"

"I can't..." Helena paused. "I can't see his face. But his eyes... They were strange."

"Strange how?"

"Like a dog's eyes."

"What do you mean?"

"I just mean," Wheeler said, a little too loud, "that it's going to be tough to find anything – oh, hey, Joe. What's up?" He took a couple of steps forward, trying to block the man's progress.

Joe, carrying just the end of the extension cord, now, ducked past Wheeler and leaned into the bedroom. "Hey, AJ. I saw your parents a few minutes ago. I had an early lunch at the market. Your dad says he's trying to lose weight."

"Doctor's orders," AJ said.

"Well, good for him."

"Speaking of weight," Wheeler said. "I'm not sure this floor will hold all of us."

Joe patted his stomach. "Not after that lunch I had." He dropped the cord, then turned and went out the way he had come.

"Wrap it up," Wheeler said.

"His eyes?" AJ said. "What about them?"

"They were scary," Helena said. "Glassy, and yellow. Not like a dog. Like a wolf."

"Good. Anything else?"

Her face twisted, as if trying to remember were painful. "No. Nothing. I can't remember." There were tears in her eyes again. "I can't remember anything after that."

"It's okay. That's normal."

"AJ, we better go," Wheeler said. "They're coming."

AJ turned.

"What about me?" Helena moved away from the wall.

"You'll be all right," AJ said. "Once we figure all of this out." He started after Wheeler. Joe was in the hall, carrying the two lamps. The fire marshal was right behind him.

"Wait!" Helena said.

AJ stopped in the doorway. He took his cell phone from his pocket, pressed a couple of buttons, then held it to his ear. He looked back toward Helena. "What is it?"

"My daughter, Taylor. Is she...like me?"

AJ didn't say anything. He just stood there holding the phone, like someone on the other end of the call was telling him something important.

"Is she in our house?" Helena said. "Trapped, like me?"

"No. Not like you. She's not trapped. I've got to go now, but I'll talk to you again." AJ pushed a button on his phone, then dropped it into his pocket.

The fire marshal grumbled impatiently.

"Sorry, guys." AJ squeezed past the two men.

Wheeler was already at the front door. They went out, walked past the noisy generator and across the street to their car. Wheeler took the driver's seat. Before he climbed in, AJ looked back toward the house. Helena was in the doorway, staring out at them, her red shirt like a warning. AJ sat down. He pulled the shoulder strap across, then closed his eyes.

Wheeler watched him for a moment. "You okay?"

"Fine."

"Shit." Wheeler shook his head. "I can't believe I'm saying this, but you look like you saw a ghost."

AJ said nothing. His eyes were still closed.

Wheeler had the key in the ignition but sat without moving, looking at AJ.

AJ sighed. "You want to know what happened in there?"

"No," Wheeler said. "I really don't."

"All right, then, let's go."

"Hold on. I didn't come all the way out here for nothing. Tell me what you..." Wheeler hesitated. "What your instincts tell you."

"My instincts."

"Yeah."

"And you're going to believe me?"

"We'll see." Wheeler tapped the steering wheel. "If it pans out."

AJ said nothing.

"I'm asking you, Officer Bugbee – if you have a hunch about something, you have to let me know what it is."

AJ took off his cap. The hair underneath glistened with sweat. "Okay. My *hunch* is that the woman who died here was Helena Fraser, the first victim's mother."

"Yeah. I saw what you wrote."

"And the guy we're looking for, the guy who killed her, probably killed both of them? He has eyes like a wolf. Like a predator."

32

Maggie got out of the shower and quick dried one hand, so that she could check her cell phone. For nothing. Ryan still hadn't texted her back.

"Jesus, Ryan!"

While she was getting dressed – jeans, because they would hide the damp little bandages on her knees – she heard a car slowing down outside her window. When she peeked out, a cop car was going past the yard. She ducked down. She could still hear the tires on the gravel. They were barely moving. She barely breathed.

Then her phone rang. It still wasn't Ryan. "Hi, Mom."

"How are you doing?"

Maggie peeked out the window again. The police car was pulling away. "Fine."

"Listen, I had a cancellation, so I'll be able to come home early."

The cop car did a slow U-turn, headed back.

"Maggie?"

"Yeah. You said you can come home early. That's nice."

"Your dad called. He had a good day fishing, so he'll be grilling his catch tonight. He knows you won't want any part of that, but he said you could get take out. So think about where you want to get it from."

"I will."

"Okay. I have to go. I'll see you in a little while."

Maggie stood to the side of the window, looking out. The cop car had pulled over onto the grass, just beyond her driveway. They weren't just making some kind of rounds or whatever. They were here because of her. Maybe they were here *for* her.

The idea hit her like a punch. She stumbled back, almost fell onto the bed. *They caught the guy in the gray car. He told them about her. That was why they were here.*

She sat down on the mattress. She gripped the covers, squeezed tight.

No. If they wanted to talk to her, they'd come right in. They wouldn't drive back and forth by her trailer and then park out front like a couple of creepers.

Her phone rang again. Olivia. "Who's Lola?" she said.

"What?"

"Taylor's friends are all pissed off because Ryan put pictures up on Facebook of some girl named Lola. I guess it looks like he spent the night at her house. They're all, like, he's forgotten about Taylor already."

"She's just a family friend," Maggie said. "From church. Lola's family is really into it, the church stuff. Christ, Olivia. She's this nerdy, religious kid. Taylor's friends are just being dramatic."

"Oh."

"Don't sound so disappointed," Maggie said. "What's going on with Ms. Addison? Have they made any announcements or anything?"

"No, everything got quiet. Oh, shit, the bell just rang. Talk to you later."

"Yup. Bye."

Maggie watched the cop car for another minute. She checked her phone, saw the battery was almost dead. She spent twenty minutes looking for the cord, then plugged it in. She sat down on her bed.

Lola. Jesus. As if Ryan would be interested in her.

She turned on the laptop, which took forever to boot up. She killed the time remembering Lola as the chubby little girl with the freakishly long braid. There'd been some kind of picnic, with a bunch of families, maybe at Green Falls? Lola had worn a Camp Wightman T-shit that was too big, and baggy shorts. She'd followed Ryan around like a little puppy. Ryan had finally gotten tired of it and told her her mom was calling. Poor little Lola had been crushed.

Another five minutes to start Facebook. Finally, there they were – Ryan's pictures. Lola at the stove, spatula at the edge of a pancake, ready to flip it. Ryan's face in the shot, too, hovering right above the stove top, all smiles. Then Lola again, holding a plate with the finished pancake.

Lola had lost that extra weight. She had curves now. She knew it, too, because she was wearing a tank top and short short PJ bottoms. Her hair was in a cute pixie cut, with a little highlight. Her smile was all straight teeth and dimples. She was so perfect and so gorgeous it was ridiculous.

Maggie pushed the computer aside, went back to the window. The cop car was in the same place, on the edge of the road. The guy was probably looking right at her. *To Protect and Stare.* Just then her dad's truck came up the hill. He pulled alongside the cop car. They had a conversation through the open windows. Shit, that couldn't be good. Her dad would already be mad about last night, and now he comes home to find a cop practically in his yard.

As her dad rolled into the driveway, the cop drove down the hill and away. Her dad came in carrying a cooler. "Hey, Mags." He gave her a smile. "Don't worry, most of this is going right into the freezer. I know you don't like stinky fish in your fridge."

She got out of the way and let him go past. He began putting taped-up packages in the freezer, plastic bags of cleaned catch in a little saltwater.

"I saw you talking to the cop," she said. Might as well get it over with.

Her dad slid another package into the freezer, then turned to look at her. "Yeah. He might have actually been doing something right for a change."

"What?"

"He said he was watching over you, making sure that nobody came here and tried to smash the windows or something." Her dad slid one last package in with the others, then closed the freezer door. "I'm going to take this cooler out, put it in the shade outside. And I'm going to put myself in the shade, too. Why don't you come out? I can tell you my brand new fish stories. If you're not going to eat the fish, you ought to at least hear about them."

"Uh, sure. Let me grab my phone."

"God forbid we leave that behind." He noticed the rolls on the counter. "Hey, did you make those for me? I thought I smelled something good." He grabbed one.

They sat outside, drinking soda, while her dad described every minute of his day. He was in such a good mood he didn't even care about last night. Maggie half listened, thinking about Lola, and Ms. Addison, checking her phone, getting more pissed at Ryan. Finally her dad leaned back in his chair and closed his eyes. Maggie slipped back inside.

***

When Maggie came out again, her mom was already home, talking to her dad. He was pointing to the road, to where the cop car had parked.

Her dad said, "Maggie, did you hear about Ms. Addison?"

"Yeah. I heard it from Olivia."

"Why didn't you say something?"

"You were all excited about your fishing. I didn't want to ruin it."

Her mom played with an earring. "I guess they haven't said yet whether she died in the fire. But one of the girls in the shop said she heard that Ms. Addison didn't show up at school this morning."

Her dad got up from his chair. "Did Olivia say anything about that?"

"Yeah. I guess Ms. Addison didn't even have a substitute."

"Well, she must have been in that house, then," her mom said. "How awful."

Her dad put an arm around her mom. "So that was the real reason the cops were camped out here. Damn."

Her mom gave him a look. "The police know exactly where Maggie was and what she was doing last night."

"They should. But that doesn't mean they do."

"Jesus. Stop being so paranoid."

"You're the one who cut out of work." Her dad let his hand drop. No one seemed to know what to say then.

Her mom put on a sort of fake smile. "Well, since I am home early, do you want to eat early?"

"Sure," her dad said. "The fresher the catch, the better. And I haven't had a real lunch."

"I'm starving," Maggie said.

"Have you decided where you want take-out from?" her mom said. "Honey B Dairy? Get one of those shakes?"

Maggie bit her lip. "Bay Market."

"What? I thought the whole point was to avoid seafood."

"I like their hot dogs. And their fries."

"Yes!" Her dad rubbed his hands together. "Let's get a boatload of fries."

Her mom had her keys out.

"I'll go," Maggie said.

"You don't have to," her mom said.

"You just got here. Anyway, I need to get out. I've been trapped inside all day."

Her mom smiled for one second, then closed her hand on the keys.

"Mom. I want to go. I'm feeling totally cooped up."

"It's just – " Her mom sighed.

"What?"

"With everything..."

"Geez. Don't go all crazy overprotective on me. Please?" Maggie turned to her dad, who gave her a look like he was going to stay out of it. "The market isn't far, Mom. It's a public place. It's a family place. They're always nice to me there. What can possibly happen?"

She was convincing, and she won the argument, because it was all true. Of course, she'd left out the real reason that she'd picked the Bay Market, the real reason she wanted to go there herself – the new guy behind the counter. Parker. She could picture his smile. But then that picture morphed into the face of the man in the gray car. He'd been at the Bay Market, too. Was it stupid to go back there? Maybe. But he couldn't eat seafood every day. You'd only be there every day if you worked there, like Parker. She'd see Parker, and it would be fine. Everything would be fine.

33

Chief Brown waved AJ and Wheeler into the office. "You've got the pill?"

Wheeler handed the bag across the desk.

The chief reached into a drawer and produced another evidence bag. Inside it was a small aluminum water bottle. He shook it, making a rattling sound. "Oxycontin."

"Where did you find that?" Wheeler said.

"In her car. It was just sitting there in the cup holder, like she'd been drinking from it."

"Hiding in plain sight," AJ said. "That seems to be her M.O."

"What do you mean?" Wheeler said.

"I'm thinking that's what the empty pill bottles at her mother's house were about. She was keeping her stash of Oxy in them. When she stopped there last night, she poured all of the pills into this water bottle. Some fell to the floor – that's how we found one."

"Well, that was a mistake, transferring the pills," the chief said. "We confirmed that she does have a script for Oxycontin. So, right now, the only thing we have on her is carrying a narcotic in the wrong container."

"She was Helena Fraser's source," AJ said. "She had to be Taylor's source, too."

The chief sat forward. "So you saw Helena Fraser at Addison's house? And she was able to talk?"

AJ glanced toward Wheeler. "Yeah."

"All right. What did you find out?"

216

AJ repeated what Helena Fraser had told him – that she'd come to the house for Oxy, that she'd been left alone while Addison went out to get the pills, and that her memories had ended with a man coming to the door.

"That's our killer," the chief said. "Could she describe him?"

"Just one thing. One distinctive thing. He had eyes like a wolf."

The chief looked back and forth between AJ and Wheeler. "Eyes like a wolf? What does that mean?"

Wheeler only frowned.

"Yellow," AJ said. "His eyes were yellow."

"Who has yellow eyes?" the chief said. "Shit. Does this mean we can't trust her memory?"

"I don't know for sure," AJ said. "Ben couldn't remember everything, especially about how he died, at least at first. But what he did remember, he remembered correctly."

"Yellow eyes." The chief shook his head.

Wheeler opened his mouth like he was going to say something, then closed it again.

"What are you thinking, detective?" the chief said.

"If there's any chance this is true, about the yellow eyes, then we could check with the local optometrists, see if they sold yellow contacts to anyone."

"Right," AJ said. "They may even sell those at a costume shop, like that beauty supply place in New London."

"Okay, look into that," the chief said. "Do you think you could get more from her, from Helena?"

"Maybe. But not while there are people crawling all over the place."

"Jesus," Wheeler said, "can we start by talking with Addison?"

"Right," the chief said. "She's in an interview room. She's hasn't asked for a lawyer. I'm hoping we can keep it that way."

"I'll do my best." Wheeler gestured toward the pills. "Do you have something I can put those in? A bigger bag?"

The chief pulled an ordinary plastic shopping bag out of his desk drawer, then put the two evidence bags in it. AJ took the shopping bag and followed Wheeler out. They went around the corner to the interview room. Nicole Addison sat at the table, looking tired but calm. She was dressed for a day on a boat, in slacks and a windbreaker. Pale blue deck shoes.

"Hello, Ms. Addison," Wheeler said. "We met the other day, at the high school. I'm detective Wheeler and this is Officer Bugbee."

"Yes, I remember."

"Can I get you something to drink?" Wheeler said. "A cup of coffee? Water?"

"No. Thanks." Her hands were clasped in front of her. Her blonde hair was pulled back from her face and pinned down with a pair of dark sunglasses.

"Well, if you change your mind..." Wheeler sat down. AJ remained standing just behind him.

"You've been informed about the fire." Wheeler took out his notepad.

"Yes. But I told the officers I wasn't home last night. I don't know what happened. I guess it's a total loss – everything I had."

"They didn't tell you that a body was found in your house?"

"What?"

"Someone died there last night. We have reason to believe it was Helena Fraser."

"Oh my God." Addison put a hand to her mouth.

Wheeler watched her. "Since you weren't at home last night, can you tell us where you were?"

"I stayed at my mother's house. I do that once in a while. Being there...it helps me remember her."

"What time did you go to your mother's house?"

"It was late. Maybe around midnight. I didn't really pay attention to the time."

"What about this morning? You didn't go back to your house?"

"No. I went straight to the marina. I was going to take a personal day, to go out on the boat."

"Aren't you required to notify someone at the school that you're not coming in, so they can arrange for a substitute?"

"I did call for a sub."

"Well, no one at the school seems to have taken that call. Everyone seems to think that you died in the fire."

"The way it works is you leave a message with a service. The service arranges for the sub and notifies the school. The message must have gotten lost."

"I see. Why was Mrs. Fraser at your house? Inside your house?"

"I have no idea. We had had some contact through the school. I know her daughter. Knew her daughter. But that's all."

Wheeler flipped a page in his notepad. "Okay, Ms. Addison. Let's cut the crap."

Addison just looked at him.

Wheeler motioned to AJ, who stepped forward and put the plastic shopping bag on the table. He took out first the evidence bag with the water bottle, then the one with the single pill.

Addison leaned back in her chair. "I told the officers that was a legitimate prescription."

Wheeler held up a hand. "Why aren't the pills in the bottle that the pharmacy gave you?"

"I was going to be on the boat overnight. I wanted something waterproof."

"Seems like a lot of pills for an overnight trip."

"I just poured out of the plastic bottle into the metal one. I didn't think about it."

"You understand that in the state of Connecticut it's illegal to carry narcotics in something other than the original container?"

"I just found that out this morning from the other officers. No one at the drug store said anything like that." She looked back and forth between the cops. "Am I under arrest?"

"Look," Wheeler said, "we have the pills, and we're going to be able to prove that you were selling drugs to Helena Fraser. Worse, to a couple of minors, including Taylor Fraser. That's pretty bad. No, that's very bad. But here's the thing – we don't even really care about the drugs. What we're really interested in, what you really need to be thinking about, is the two people who died. One died in your own home. So, you need to try to help us in any way that you can. If your only problem is the drugs, maybe we can help you."

"The pills had nothing to do with what happened to Helena!" Addison shook as she spoke. "Or Taylor."

"Okay," AJ said. "Then help us to understand."

"I don't know what happened to them!"

Wheeler tapped his notepad with the pencil. "Ms. Addison, no one here thinks you're a killer. I don't. Officer Bugbee doesn't. Right, AJ?" Wheeler glanced at AJ, who shook his head. "But drug dealing is a nasty business. It attracts nasty people. Violent people. Surely I'm not telling you something you don't already know."

"It's not like that. I'm not a drug dealer."

"You sell controlled substances for profit," AJ said. "I think that's the definition of a drug dealer."

"It's not like that."

"That's what you keep saying," Wheeler said. "Tells us, what is it like?"

Addison put a hand to her forehead and began to cry. For a while, the only sound in the room was an occasional sharp gasp.

"If you help us," Wheeler said, gently, "we'll do what we can to help you."

Addison looked at him. "How can I help? I have no idea what happened."

"You can start by being straight with us about last night. Why was Helena Fraser at your house?"

Addison gathered herself. "She just showed up there, late. She wanted pills."

"Oxycontin."

"Yes. I'd been selling my pills to her. I had been for a while. I guess the stress... what happened to Taylor... She was using more than usual and had gone through what she had. I didn't have any pills in the house. She begged me to get some for her. She was a mess. I gave in and went to get them. I told her to wait at my house."

"What time was that?"

"Late. Maybe one o'clock. Maybe later."

"Okay, so you left. Where did you go?"

"To my mother's."

"I don't understand. Why were the pills at your mother's house? It's your prescription, right?"

"I didn't like keeping them in the house. I just thought it was safer that way."

"Okay. What happened next?"

"I picked up some pills and went back home. Before I even turned off of Route 1, I could see color in the sky. I knew the fire was somewhere in the Borough. As I got close, I realized I was driving right toward it. I thought it might be near my house. I was worried. Then I made that last turn and saw it was *my* house. The whole place was in flames."

"What did you do?"

"I drove away."

"Your house was on fire with Helena Fraser inside and you just drove off?"

"The fire department was already there, and the police, and an ambulance. There wasn't anything I could do. I freaked out! It's all been just too much. First Taylor, then this. I was scared."

"You mean you were scared you'd get caught with drugs in your car and a dead body in your house."

Addison pulled her windbreaker close around her.

"Were you selling Oxy to Taylor Fraser?" AJ said.

"No!"

"Do you know who was?"

"No one."

"What do you mean?"

"She was stealing the pills from her mother."

"You know this?"

"Yes. Taylor had figured out that her mom was getting the pills from me. She threatened to tell the administration if I didn't meet her demands.'"

"What demands?" Wheeler said.

"It changed from week to week. Favoritism, mostly. Grades, letting her skip homework or skip class."

"Small stuff," Wheeler said.

"Not to her." Addison closed her eyes for a second.

"Can you tell us where you were the night that Taylor died?" Wheeler said.

"I was on my boat."

"All night?"

"Yes."

"Can anyone confirm that?"

Addison shifted uncomfortably in her chair. "Bob Sampson. He teaches at the high school, too."

Wheeler jotted down the name. "He was with you?"

Addison shifted again. "Yes."

"So all Taylor ever asked for from you was a few favors?"

"At first. In the last few weeks she started asking me a lot of questions."

"Questions about what?"

"Things like how I got the Oxycontin, how much I paid for it, how much her mother paid me."

"Do you think she was thinking about selling drugs herself?"

"Maybe. I know she wasn't happy with the allowance her step-father gave her. I heard her complain about that."

"So did you teach her how to become a dealer?" AJ said.

"No! I'm not a dealer. I know a doctor who will write prescriptions for me. That's it. It was only for Helena."

Wheeler lifted the water bottle again. "That's a big stash for one customer."

"I stockpile. She's gone on the wagon a few times. I have to save up for when she falls off again."

"How did it come about?" AJ said. "How did it happen that you were selling Oxy to Mrs. Fraser?"

"I've known her for a long time. She was working at the casino when I met her. I was dating someone who was into gambling and I was there a lot. I didn't enjoy gambling that much, so I was always looking for someone to talk to. Helena was friendly. We hit it off. Two lonely women looking for a better life. That's what she used to say. She was needy. She has that addictive personality. I should have known..." Addison shook her head. "She drank a lot. I found out after a while that she was doing drugs, too. Pot. Painkillers, once in a while. But she was keeping herself together. She seemed to be able to handle it."

"How'd she get you involved?"

Addison looked somewhere across the room. "I was in a fender bender. She started pushing me to take advantage of it, to get a prescription out of it. I really did have some back pain for a while. I tried a few doctors and eventually one wrote me a prescription for Oxycontin. Helena bought the pills from me. I thought it was a one-time thing. But when they were gone, she wanted more. So I went back to the doctor and he wrote another prescription. He wrote one for my mother, too. At first I thought I was really fooling him. But he knew. His office was really busy. He was writing a lot of prescriptions."

"What's his name?" Wheeler said. "The doctor?"

Addison gave the name and Wheeler wrote it down.

"Who else knew about your arrangement with Helena?" Wheeler said. "Besides you and Helena and Taylor?"

"No one."

"What about her husband?"

"He didn't know. He would have stopped it."

"Why do you say that?"

"When I first met Helena, she was Helena Burns. Then she hooked up with Fraser, this big shot at the casino. He knew she was a little wild. He liked that. But once they were together, he wanted her to clean up, settle down. So, she dropped the drinking and the pot and whatever else. The Oxy was the one thing she kept. It was her lifeline, she told me."

"So if he had found out, how would he have stopped her?"

"You mean, would he have killed her? No. He would have sent her to rehab." She paused. "I wanted her to stop. She'd stopped before, so I knew that she could. I didn't need the money anymore. I have – had – a good job. And my parents had more money put away that I realized. But then Taylor got involved. She wouldn't let me stop."

Wheeler made some more notes on his pad. "What about the stepbrother? Jonathan Fraser. Did he know about the drugs?"

"I don't think so. He wasn't around much."

"You're sure no one else knew?" AJ said. "Friends or people at school?"

"No one knew."

"Did Helena or Taylor ever mention anyone who was bothering them," AJ said. "Anyone they were afraid of?"

"No."

"You gave us that list of students – "

"Yes."

"Why did you do that? I can't help but wonder why you were so eager to stand up for a girl you think so little of."

"Think so little of? You have that wrong. I thought the world of Taylor. She may not have been sweet but she was special. Smart. Beautiful. She was destined for big things."

"She was blackmailing you. Threatening to ruin your reputation and end your career."

"That was all recent – just something she was going through. I could have guided her."

"So it was all because you really cared about her?" AJ said. "Because I have another theory. By standing up for Taylor in such a big way, you were just trying to draw suspicion away from yourself."

"No! You're wrong. I've known Taylor since she was nine years old. You have no idea what that girl had been through."

"You mean the trailer fire," AJ said.

"Yes. But before that. Helena's boyfriends, they were horrible. Especially the one who died in the fire."

"Horrible? Are you talking about abuse?" Wheeler said.

"Helena said no, but I don't know if I believe her."

"What do you know about the fire that killed the boyfriend?"

"Helena was at work when it happened. The guy fell asleep with a cigarette and burned the place to the ground. Taylor was staying with a friend, thank God, so she was safe, but they lost everything. To make matters worse, a neighbor claimed to have seen Taylor and her friend sneaking around right before the fire. People started to talk. There was a police investigation. It all worked out, eventually. But the experience scarred her."

"What about this boyfriend who died that night? Did he have a brother, a best friend, someone who harbored a grudge?"

"Not that I know of. I never heard anything like that."

The three sat for a while without speaking.

Wheeler closed his notepad. "You've been very helpful, Ms. Addison." He stood up, then followed AJ to the door. Just before he stepped out of the room, Wheeler turned around. "One more question. Do you know anything about a man with yellow eyes?"

"What?"

"Yellow eyes."

"I don't know what you're talking about."

Wheeler stood there for a second, his hand on the jamb. "Neither do I," he said.

34

They joined the chief in the observation room. "It's all but official," he said. "The body in the morgue is Helena Fraser."

On the other side of the one-way glass, Addison clasped and unclasped her hands.

"Do you believe her story about the drugs?" the chief said. "That she was selling only to Mrs. Fraser?"

Wheeler looked doubtful. "It's easy for her to deny selling drugs to Taylor when Taylor's not around to say anything different."

"Okay," AJ said, "but she admitted that Taylor knew she was supplying Mrs. Fraser, and that Taylor used that information against her."

"Which could be a motive for murder," the chief said.

"Exactly," AJ said. "So why would she volunteer any of that? Unless it was the truth. And as a teacher she'd be nuts to try to sell to kids. All it would take is one comment on social media to ruin her career."

"She accomplished that without the help of social media," Wheeler said. "We need to talk to that guy who was supposed to be with her on the boat. Sampson."

The chief faced the glass. "You get on that. I'm going to call Mr. Fraser."

"I'm surprised you haven't heard from him," Wheeler said. "His wife goes out late and doesn't come home... With what happened to his step-daughter, you'd think he'd be concerned."

The chief nodded. "I'd like to go to talk to him in person, but he may be all the way up at a lake in Massachusetts."

"What are we going to do with Nicole Addison?" AJ said. "Are we going to book her?"

"We have no choice," the chief said. "She admitted to selling a controlled substance. You want to give her the bad news?"

AJ left the room.

The chief put a hand on Wheeler's shoulder. "You've got to admit it, AJ's information checked out. He said he saw Helena Fraser in the Addison house, and it looks like it was her body there."

"Yes, but – "

"I know. Believe me, I know. Just keep an open mind."

"You can have an open mind, Chief, and you can have a mind so open that your brain falls out."

"Uh huh. So what are you saying about my brain?"

Wheeler shook his head and started for the door. "I gotta talk to Ms. Addison's alibi."

***

The two cops sat on one side of a round table. On the other side, a stocky, middle-aged man squeezed the back of his neck with one hand.

"Let's start with where you were last Friday night, Mr. Sampson." Wheeler placed his notepad in front of him.

"This past Friday night?" the man said. "I was at home."

Wheeler stared pointedly at Sampson's wedding ring. "Really? We'll have to check that with your wife."

Sampson sat back and let his hand drop to his lap. "You can talk to her. She was away, but we spoke a couple of times."

"Your wife was out of town?"

"Yes."

"Cat's away, the mice will play, huh?" Wheeler said.

"Look, what is this about?"

Wheeler leaned forward. "According to Nicole Addison, you spent Friday night on her boat."

"Wait. What? Nicole? She's alive? Thank God."

"We really need to know if you were with her on Friday night," Wheeler said. "Tell us the truth and it will go no further."

"Yes, I was with her. I thought I was just going there to look at the boat..."

"What time was that?" AJ said.

"Right after school. A little before four."

"And when did you leave for home?"

"Around nine."

"Nine p.m.?" Wheeler said.

"Nine a.m. the next morning. Look, I'm not proud of what I did. But I didn't break any laws."

"You were on the boat the whole time?" Wheeler said. "Both of you?"

"Yes."

"Could she have left at any point? Maybe while you were asleep?"

"No."

"How can you be sure?" AJ said.

"The boat was anchored out in the water. It wouldn't have been easy to sneak off." The man looked away. "Besides, we didn't sleep much."

35

As they made their way toward the chief's office, a patrolman stopped them. "He's talking to Mr. Fraser. They found his wife's car in the Borough, near the fire."

The chief's door swung open. Mr. Fraser came out, looking bewildered. The chief went with him across the room and out through the glass doors. A minute later, on the way back, Chief Brown motioned for AJ and Wheeler to follow him into the office.

"That guy really loved his wife," the chief said, when the door was closed again. "It turned out he had already come down from the lake. He was here looking for her."

"What story did she give him when she went out last night?" Wheeler said.

"She told him she was going to see her sister. He wasn't thrilled – I guess the sister's a drinker. But Helena had been so upset that he didn't argue with her."

"Mike said they found her car," AJ said.

The chief sat down behind his desk. "Yeah."

"Do we have dental records yet?" Wheeler took one of the molded chairs.

"Just got the dentist's name from Mr. Fraser. We'll have an ID by tonight. What did you find out?"

Wheeler recapped their conversations with Mr. Sampson. "What Addison told us checks out. With Sampson and what Mrs. Jones told us earlier, I think we've confirmed Addison's alibis for both murders."

"Okay," the chief said, "so if it's not her, who do we have left?"

"There's still the drugs," Wheeler said. "We need to talk to the doctor who was writing the scripts."

"There's the yellow contact lenses," AJ said.

"Right." The chief glanced at Wheeler, who turned away.

"I still want to talk to Jonathan Fraser," Wheeler said.

The chief tapped the desktop. "I've been thinking about him. Correct me if I'm wrong, AJ, but when you talked to Helena's ghost, she didn't mention Jonathan. The man she saw – all she said was he had yellow eyes. She didn't know him."

Wheeler looked at the chief. "Let's go back to Taylor's murder." He held up one hand and began ticking points off with his fingers. "Jonathan was in those pictures on Taylor's phone, with Ryan. Someone messed with his room. He showed up at the Fraser house that first night that AJ was there – just to grab a couple of shirts from the closet and a bottle of wine, he said. At two a.m."

"So why was he really there?" the chief said.

"Maybe he came back for the cell phone. Or there was something that he wanted to be destroyed by the fire, but since the fire was put out so fast, that didn't happen. He had to chance coming back for it."

"That's not a bad theory," the chief said. "We know that Taylor was using what she knew about the Oxy to control Addison. Maybe she had something on Jonathan, too. He had to destroy it and kill her to get out from under it. But still, it's got to be the same guy that killed the stepmother. And she didn't identify him."

"Sometimes they don't remember much from right around the time that they died," AJ said. "At least, Ben didn't."

"All right. But why would Jonathan kill the stepmother?"

"Same reason he killed Taylor," Wheeler said. "She found out whatever it was that Taylor knew."

"I agree, we need to talk to him," AJ said.

"Jonathan's father told me that Jonathan will be at the house tonight," the chief said. "He's going to pick up some things. They're clearing out, selling the place."

"Can't blame them," AJ said.

The others just looked at him for a second, as if they were thinking of Claire staying in her house, after everything that happened there.

"So if we're there, we can talk to both of the Fraser men,"

Wheeler said.

"It sounded like it was going to be just Jonathan," the chief said. "I don't think those two spend a lot of time together. When I asked Fraser if he wanted me to call his son to tell him about Helena, he cut me off and called someone at his office, told them to handle it."

"Jonathan definitely seems to be the odd man out in that family," AJ said.

"I like the idea of interviewing him at the scene," Wheeler said.

AJ nodded. "I'll call him and set it up."

"Okay." The chief slid forward, his hands on the desk. "You're going to talk to Jonathan tonight. What else do we have?"

AJ opened his mouth but then looked away without speaking.

"What's on your mind, AJ?" the chief said.

"I was just thinking that Maggie Strang is connected to Taylor and Helena Fraser, Nicole Addison, Ryan Hardy – all the key pieces of this puzzle. I don't see her as the killer, but..."

"Someone connected to her? Her dad?"

"I don't know, maybe. Except he was on the road when Taylor was killed."

"Do we know that for certain?"

"We'll check it out," Wheeler said.

"All right," the chief said, "let's get started."

Wheeler made the call to the trucking company. The man on the other end of the line was able to verify that Dan Strang was five hundred miles away at the time that Taylor was dying in her own house.

"Cross another one off the list," Wheeler said, when he'd hung up. "You want to grab a bite before we meet up with our friend Jonathan?"

"I'd like to run home for a while. Maybe you can drop me off?"

"Tell you what – I'll drop you off, run out and pick up dinner, then swing back by for you."

"Sure, that works. I just want to check in with Claire."

"How's she doing?" Wheeler said.

"Okay. Pretty good."

"It's tough. The trauma she went through... It's only been, what, less than a year?"

"Coming up on a year. Mostly, she's all right. But with everything that's happened in the last few days – "

"It's got to bring it all back."

"Yeah. She's trying not to show it." AJ took a slow breath. "Christ, Sam. What happened to her – how do you ever forget that?"

"I don't know," Wheeler said. "I give her a lot of credit, staying in that house. That's brave. Eventually, it'll sink in that the bastard is locked away and she's safe."

"I hope so," AJ said. He went back to his paperwork.

As he and Wheeler wrote up what had happened so far that day, the station grew quiet – measured voices, the occasional ringing of a phone, the clicking of keys. From the sounds, it could almost have been any office, where the business was finance or software or life insurance.

After a while, Wheeler switched off the monitor. He looked at his watch. "You ready to head out?"

Wheeler took the driver's side of the cruiser. They went down Route 1 as far as Flanders Road, where they turned away from the water. They passed houses tucked into the woods. There were rocks everywhere, piled up in walls, scattered under the trees. They passed the old cemetery on the left.

"This is where I found that glass in the road, the night after Taylor's murder." AJ pointed. "I still think the guy who hit the deer could have been the killer fleeing the scene."

"I checked the glass into evidence," Wheeler said. "It's tough to do much with it, unless you can physically match up the pieces." He turned onto Pequot Trail. They passed the Road Church, its back to the world. "First church in Stonington, did you know that?" he said. "Sixteen hundreds."

AJ nodded without saying anything.

Before long, Wheeler took the dirt lane that led away into the trees. As Claire's house came into view, they could see Melody's sedan parked by the garage. Wheeler stopped next to it.

"You want to come in?" AJ said.

"Thanks. Some other time?"

AJ got out.

"You want me to pick up anything for you?" Wheeler said.

"I'll grab something here. You know you eat for free at my parents' place."

"I appreciate that. Today, there's a pizza with my name on it down at Angela's."

Wheeler looked past AJ at the house, stretching away across a deep yard. "It's a nice place. No wonder she decided to stay here."

"Yeah," AJ said. "I just hope nothing happens to change her mind."

36

As she went down Route 1 toward the Bay Market she tilted the rearview mirror, took a good look. Bad idea. Even though she'd made an extra effort with her hair and her make-up, what she saw was all huge shiny forehead and out-of-control curls and spotty skin. She should have known better than to look, but it was like her reflection was a shock every time – like she expected to see cute bangs and dimples. Like she expected to see Lola. Lola probably loved the mirror.

Maggie tipped the thing back again.

At least she liked the top she'd put on and the way her jeans fit. From a little distance, she looked okay. If she could somehow get a picture of her with Parker at the market, put that online, that would give Ryan something to think about. It would make him forget about Lola for a little while.

If Parker was even working. She had no idea about his hours.

All the way down Route 1, with Parker and Ryan on her brain, she didn't think about the gray car once. Even though she'd seen it at that same market. The guy behind the wheel, looking across the parking lot at her. His smile when their eyes met.

She remembered all of that when she turned onto the access road. She drove slow, holding her breath. There were a few cars parked close to the tables. A couple on the side of the building. No gray car.

She pulled into the lot, breathed again. She turned the key, dropped it in her purse. Parker probably wouldn't be here, either. Or he'd be too busy too even notice her. She'd just get her food and go.

She didn't even check herself in the mirror before getting out of the car. She went up to the porch, through the screen door. She looked across the room. Straight into Parker's eyes.

"Hey, it's Maggie, right?" He was behind the counter.

She froze for a second, as if she wasn't sure of her own name. "Yeah. Hi."

"Hot dog, fries and a Coke?"

"Yeah, but I need a couple of other things, too."

"Okay. You might want to come a little closer. So you don't have to shout, you know?"

Like an idiot, like his gaze had turned her to stone or something, she was still standing by the door. She felt him watching as she went over to him.

"Okay, shoot," Parker said.

She read from her list. "A container of coleslaw and two large cups of clam chowder. And two more fries."

"Just two fries? We don't really sell them individually."

She laughed. "Two orders of fries."

"All right!" He sounded all enthusiastic, like this was the best thing he'd heard all day.

Beth was there, too. "Hi, Maggie." She slid a cup off of the stack.

Another customer came in, a woman in tight exercise clothes, and went past Maggie, right up to the counter until she was practically leaning on it. She asked Parker something about clams. Maggie moved to the side and pretended to read the big menu on the wall. Parker was being all helpful to the exercise woman, like clams were the most fascinating subject, like this woman's need for just the right clams – they had to be tender and sweet, but not too small – was the most important thing in the world.

"Maggie, why don't you take a seat at a picnic table?" Beth said. "I'll bring your order out in a minute."

So Maggie went back through the door. She sat down at the nearest picnic table. She could still see the counter, but she tried not to look. The clam woman came out with one of those heavy paper bags they put the steamers in. Parker didn't even glance through the window.

Maggie watched seagulls scrounge under the tables. A few just stood there, staring, like they were waiting for someone to tell them what to do.

Beth came out with Maggie's food. "Here you go! Enjoy!"

Maggie started toward her car, going slow. Maybe if she gave Parker time... Which was ridiculous, because he'd probably already forgotten she was here.

Then Parker stuck his head out the door. "Hey! Wait! I think we forgot your coleslaw!"

Beth stopped where she was. "I did not!"

"Let me check." Parker ran over to Maggie. He took her bag and carried it over to the table. He poked around inside. "Found it. Sorry. Just wanted to make sure. Why don't I help you get this in the car? We don't want another soda accident out here."

He walked with her. Might have even brushed her arm. Maybe.

"So what do you do for fun, Maggie?"

She had no idea. She couldn't think of a single thing that she did, for fun or for anything. "Hang out, I guess?"

"Eat hot dogs, we know that."

She laughed. "Yeah, sometimes."

"Do you eat other stuff, too? Like maybe ice cream?"

"Sure."

"Good. Me, too. Glad you're not one of those girls who's always on a diet – not that you need to – you don't at all. So, do you want to get ice cream sometime?"

"Sure." She could feel her smile spreading out of control. She tried to reign it in.

"Awesome! I don't have a car, so, can you meet me here tonight at, like, eight? You don't have to bring me home after – my mom's going to be in Mystic, so I'll go back with her."

"Okay, yeah."

"Cool."

Parker went to the passenger side and set the bag on the seat. He came around and took the cup from her as she got in. "See you tonight, Maggie." He handed the cup back to her.

"Thanks."

It took her two tries to get the car turned around even though there was plenty of room. Parker finally went inside, and that helped. Still, she was shaking, just like the last time she'd talked to him. For a second, she wasn't sure she could drive. Never mind drinking, she needed a designated driver when she talked to Parker.

She pulled up to the stop sign. She sat there for a second, amazed, going over it all again, to be sure it had really happened. Him coming out at the last minute, with that lame excuse about the coleslaw. Helping her into the car. Asking her to meet him, instead of coming to pick her up, which was so perfect, because he didn't have to see the trailer. She wished, when he teased her about the "soda accident," that she could have explained things – how she freaked when she saw the gray car pulling out of the lot. Maybe Parker had seen the guy before. But then, she could only describe the car, not the guy behind the wheel. Parker wouldn't know anything about the car, probably hadn't even seen it. Even if he had, he wouldn't remember it. The car was so *gray*, so ordinary, so forgettable. Unless it was following you.

She checked Route 1 both ways as far as she could see. No gray car. She looked in the mirror. No one behind her, either. She dug her cell phone out of her purse. She pressed a couple of buttons. The traffic cleared and she stepped on the gas.

Olivia answered. "Hey, Maggie."

"Hey. Guess who has a date tonight?"

37

When he stepped inside he heard laughter and got a whiff of an herby incense smell.

"Hey! You're home!" Claire peeked out from the kitchen, then retreated.

AJ followed her. He found Melody on a stool, reaching up to the window above the back door, tipping a box of salt. Claire was behind her, a wine glass in one hand and a bundle of dried leaves in the other. The leaves were on fire.

"What's going on?" AJ said.

Melody stepped down and pushed her dark bangs away from her face. "We're ghost-proofing the house." She looked at AJ like she dared him to contradict her.

"Okay..." he said.

"It was Melody's idea." Claire dropped the smoking leaves onto a plate. The feeble flame winked out. "With that angry ghost on the loose, it made sense."

"We looked it up online," Melody said. "You need salt, sage and iron." She pointed at the table, where there was a collection of dark metal objects and a half dozen boxes of salt.

"We hit a couple of junk shops." Claire lifted an old flatiron. "Isn't this cool? It's so heavy."

"What are you going to do with all of this stuff?" AJ said.

"This finial could go over a doorway." Claire picked up a black fleur-de-lis. "Some of it we'll just set on windowsills. I kind of like the way they look, anyway."

"You know how the old cemeteries always have iron fences around them?" Melody said. "When people first started doing that, it was to keep the spirits in."

"But it's too late by then, right, AJ?" Claire said. "By the time the body's in the ground, the spirit is already gone."

"I guess so," AJ said. "Sometimes."

"How's your day going?" Claire said. "Can you have some wine?"

"I pilfered something good from Jack's collection," Melody said.

"I'll have to take a rain check," AJ said. "You know, you should share your ghost-proofing techniques with DaSilva."

"Why?" Melody said.

Claire looked from AJ to Melody. "Sorry I didn't say anything. I'm never sure how much of what AJ tells me I can share."

"AJ?"

He took a glass of water that Claire had poured for him. "Dave had an encounter."

"What do you mean by an encounter?"

"I should probably let him tell you the story."

"Oh, come on."

"No, it's his story to tell." Stepping over the greyhound, who had crashed in the middle of the floor, AJ went to the fridge. "I was hoping to get something to eat."

"Actually, Jack's going to bring us grinders," Melody said. "Do you have time for that?"

"A grinder does sound good. When's he coming?"

"I don't know. Let me call him."

"Call DaSilva, too," AJ said. "Get him to come over and tell his tale."

"Claire, what do you think?" Melody had her phone out.

Claire raised her wine. "The more the merrier."

Pushing buttons on her phone, Melody went toward the living room.

"Did I do the wrong thing, by inviting Dave?" AJ said. "You don't look happy."

"It's all right. But you can't keep the house full of people, AJ. I will be alone at some point, and I will be just fine. Anyway, we have a guard dog." She looked at Buck, who lay on the floor with his feet out straight and his eyes closed.

"I just thought it would be fun. And I'd love a grinder. As soon as

Melody said the word, my mouth started watering." He reached for Claire. "I'll give you a big sloppy kiss to prove it."

She dodged his lips, laughing. Eventually, he made contact.

"I can't leave you two alone for a second," Melody said, as she came back into the room. "I caught Jack at the sub shop. The new one, Montini's."

"Great!" Claire said. "I've been planning to try them."

"And both Daves are coming. They were together, of course, so I couldn't invite just DaSilva." Melody gave Claire a sheepish look.

"No, that's good. Absolutely."

AJ's cell phone rang. "Sam," he said, the phone to his ear. He took a step toward the back yard, then paused. "Okay, good. See you then." He put the phone away.

"You still have time to eat?" Claire said.

"If Jack gets here soon."

They were all waiting on the screened-in porch, the table set, water glasses making puddles on the place mats, when the doorbell rang. Claire and Melody went to answer it. They let a strikingly handsome, gray-haired man into the front hall – Jacques Westbury, now known to them all as Jack. A plastic bag hung from each hand.

"That was quick," Melody said, kissing him.

"I drove a little fast. Don't tell AJ."

"He may figure it out. He's practically a detective these days."

"Then I'm in trouble."

"Let me take those," Claire said, reaching for the bags.

"So good to see you." Jack kissed her on each cheek and made the exchange. He and Melody went back outside, returning with soda, chips and a watermelon. The Daves arrived then, with beer and a bag of cookies the size of a bed pillow. They all converged on the porch. AJ was there, looking through the screen at the long, sloping yard.

Jack shook his hand warmly. "I'm lucky to get this chance to see you, with everything..."

"Yeah. I'm just taking a quick break."

"Well, you know, after what you did for me a year ago, I have complete and total confidence in you. You'll get to the bottom of things."

"Thanks. I hope so."

Claire came over to them. "See your violets, Jack? They're doing great."

"They are, aren't they? You know, Claire, selling this place to you has to be one of the best things I ever did. I get to enjoy you bringing life back to it, without any of the responsibility."

"I appreciate that. It is a little overwhelming sometimes."

A crinkling sound came from the table. DaSilva was unwrapping a sandwich.

"Maybe we can check out the flowers later," Claire said.

Seated, they each unwrapped a bundle. DaSilva, way ahead of them, gripped his grinder in both hands.

"So, Montini's," Claire said. "Have you tried them before, Jack?"

"When I was young, Mrs. Montini sold sandwiches out of her house. We'd buy them to take out on the boat. I remember them being delicious. She's passed away, of course, but her great grandkids have opened the shop."

Sela took a deep whiff. "They sure smell good."

"Oh, man," DaSilva said, his voice muffled by a mouthful.

Sela slapped him on the shoulder. "Don't wait for us."

Jack took his own huge bite. "Mmmmm." He half-closed his eyes. "Mmmmm. Every bit as good as I remember."

Melody touched Jack's arm. "I'm so hungry lately. Will you think I'm a pig if I eat this whole thing?"

"I promise I won't check for the curly tail," he said.

They all dug in, passing the chips around.

"So, Dave," Melody said after a while. "I hear you had some kind of ghostly encounter?"

DaSilva nodded without pausing in his assault on the grinder.

"Can you tell us about it?"

DaSilva swallowed. "I don't think I can say anything. It's part of an ongoing police investigation. Right, AJ?"

"Oh, come on," Melody said. "AJ, tell him it's okay."

"Go ahead."

DaSilva looked around the table, put his sandwich down, then took a gulp of beer. "Okay. It was at the Fraser house. Where that girl died."

"You saw her ghost?"

"Yeah, but first, I felt her."

"Excuse me?" Melody said.

Jack laughed. "You mean, like a cold touch on your shoulder?"

"Not exactly. She knocked me down. For a second, she was – "

DaSilva put a hand on his chest. "She was inside me."

"God!" Melody said. "Jack, did you know about this? You have to use it on the show!"

Jack raised one hand. "That's a life-changing experience. It's entirely up to you, Dave, whether we use it. "

"Maybe you really should ghost-proof your place," Melody said.

"What?" DaSilva said.

"We burned sage and put iron at all of the openings." Melody pointed to the screen that surrounded them. "I poured salt along the ledge."

"So, what, you're making the world's largest Margarita?" Sela said.

"Okay," Melody said. "Maybe I should have asked you. Do you guys know about this stuff? Does it work?"

"I've heard about it," DaSilva said.

"I don't know," Sela said, "but it seems to me like ghosts are more interested in getting out of houses than getting in."

Melody brought a pointed finial out from the kitchen. "We're putting these by the windows and doors."

Jack took the object and weighed it in his hand. "Can't hurt, I guess. But you wouldn't know if it was working. Unless AJ was with you."

"Dave would know," Sela said.

DaSilva glared at him.

"How would he know?" Melody looked back and forth between the two Daves, then around the table. "Does everyone know something that I don't?"

"I'm in the dark, too," Jack said.

"Dave," Melody said. "If Jack's going to help with your ghost hunting show, you can't hold out on him."

"All right," DaSilva said. "Since Taylor Fraser ran into me, I can see ghosts. I've seen a couple already."

Melody sat back. "Whoa. That's good, right? Sort of your dream."

"I guess."

"You don't sound too sure."

DaSilva took another swig of beer. "It's not as much fun as I thought it would be." He drained his bottle and got up for another one. No one chased him with a question. When he returned, the chips made another trip around the table and the conversation moved on to something else. Before long the plates were empty.

"I can't see ghosts, but I see two more grinders," Jack said. "Who wants a second?"

Everyone groaned.

There was the sound of tires in the driveway.

"That's my ride." AJ thanked Jack for the meal and said his goodbyes.

Claire led the way to the front door, then continued outside to say hello to Wheeler.

Catching up to AJ, DaSilva took him by the elbow. "Did you see her? The black-haired woman, in the house in the Borough?"

AJ paused in the doorway. "Yeah."

"I knew it." DaSilva pumped one fist. "Who is she?"

"We'll talk later."

"All right." DaSilva glanced up over AJ's head. A little iron finial sat on the frame. "Too bad Ben's not here. We could ask him if this ghost-proofing stuff works."

He looked at AJ again. "Be careful."

"That's the plan. That and catching the bad guy."

Claire came away from the police car. "You're heading over to the Fraser house."

"Yeah."

She leaned in to kiss him. When she pulled away, AJ looked down at his hand. She had slipped something into it. A small iron knob.

"What's this?"

"Ghost proofing."

"Does it work for people, too? I mean, can a person protect himself that way?"

"I don't know."

AJ dropped the thing into his pocket. "Well, let's hope I don't have to find out."

38

All afternoon Maggie had been counting down the hours and then the minutes until she'd be back at the Bay Market, but now that she was on the way there, she felt doomed. She was going to have to keep up an actual conversation with Parker – more than just jokes about dropping a cup. What could she say? There was nothing interesting in her life. Well, one thing – a guy following her a couple of times and then two people ending up dead. But there was no way she was going to talk about that.

Parker was going to get a good long look at her, too. Even though she knew better, she tilted the rearview mirror. Her mutant forehead looked even bigger than it had the last time. Her hair looked even frizzier. Perfect.

As she pulled into the lot, she realized that she didn't even know how she and Parker were going to meet up. Should she go inside, hang around the counter until he was done with work? Would that seem pushy, like she thought she was his girlfriend, like she was trying to announce it to everyone? But waiting out here in the parking lot would just be weird. Like she was a stalker. Like she was hiding something.

It turned out she didn't have to decide, because she had just shut off the car when he came out of the building and gave her a big wave. "Hi, Maggie."

She opened the door and stood up. "Hi." She didn't know what else to say, and she couldn't just watch him cross the parking lot, like he was some kind of supernatural phenomenon or something. She sat down again.

He got in the passenger side. It was scary how small the car seemed, how close together they were. She was almost afraid to look at him.

"Sorry to make you drive," he said. "I have a car – I mean, my brother and I do – but he has it today."

"No problem." She tried to take a quick look at him, but her aim was low, and all she saw was his arms as he clicked the seatbelt.

"Since you're driving," he said, "I'll pay for the ice cream. Are you into soft serve or regular?"

"I think I'm in the mood for soft serve."

"Me, too. I was thinking of that place by the train station. Is that all right? You're the local, so..."

"The Sea Shell? Yeah, I like that place." It was really a clam shack that also had ice cream – sort of competition for where he worked. But she wasn't going to say that. She started down Route 1.

"You *are* a local, right?" he said. "Lived here all your life. Never had to move."

"Pretty much. Well, one time." Because a trailer burned and someone died. Something else she wasn't going to say.

"I didn't mean that was a bad thing," Parker said. "I'm just jealous, that's all. I'm a Navy brat. Moved a gajillion times."

"Oh." She knew she should ask a question to keep things going, but she couldn't think of even one normal thing to say, so she pretended that she had to concentrate on the driving. Which consisted of going straight down a deserted road. Thank God it was like a half mile total, so it was over before he could change his mind about being with her. The Sea Shell was all lit up. It couldn't have been any brighter if it was on fire.

Picking a flavor gave them something to talk about, even though they ended up both getting large vanilla cones. Parker didn't want to sit in the car, so they walked down to a table by the water. It was starting to get dark, kind of nice with some color in the sky and lights on some boats in the cove. At the table, Parker put a big, new phone down in front of him, like he'd be getting texts the whole time they were together. Maybe he'd be on Facebook. They'd hardly talk.

But then he said, "So let me tell you all about myself in one minute or less."

"Okay."

"You can time me." He tapped the screen, then pushed the phone closer to her. "Say 'Go' and press the button. Just let me prep my cone first." He took small bites, working his way around the ice cream. "Okay, I'm ready."

"Go."

"All right. Born in Ingleside, Texas – don't remember it. Preschool in Annapolis, Maryland – been told I was happy there. Kindergarten through part of second grade in Jacksonville, Florida. Leaving there is the first move I remember – I had a crush on my teacher and was very upset. End of second through fourth grade, Norfolk, Virginia. Made my first real friends there. By the time we left they had invented email, so I tried keeping my friendships that way, which was pathetic. Then, San Diego, California. Then, Pearl Harbor, Hawaii. Yes, *the* Pearl Harbor. And yes, it is awesome to live in Hawaii. Stayed for five years, long enough to give me a false sense of security. I had my first girlfriend there. No, she didn't dance the hula or wear a grass skirt or coconuts or whatever. If she was anything, it was Swedish or something. Very pale. When we moved, I tried to keep in touch with her with emails, too, and long, rambling phone calls. Extremely pathetic. Then there was Norfolk, again. Which makes you wonder why the Navy had to break up the Norfolk years with California and Hawaii. Coming back to Norfolk was like moving there for the first time – I didn't know anybody anymore. The people who had been my friends before – some had transferred and the rest had changed too much, so it was just kind of sad. Then, just before graduation, I got yanked out of Norfolk and moved here. So now, Groton. Which I wasn't too thrilled about at first, but which is starting to seem like a good thing."

He gave Maggie a smile.

"My mom died when I was little but my dad remarried. My stepmom's cool. I have one stepbrother, Ash. Older. We're not especially close, because he's kind of...weird. There, done. How'd I do?"

She was going to ask about the stepbrother, about what made him so weird, but Parker touched the phone to stop the timer, and her hand was there, too, so they made definite contact. She almost jumped.

Maggie held the timer up for Parker to see. "Forty-eight seconds. Very good."

"I've had a lot of practice. They always say you can tell a Navy brat by how fast he can pack. But I think it's more about how fast he can tell his life story." Parker took a bunch of nibbles around the cone, catching the drips. "Okay, your turn."

"Oh, I don't... " For a terrible second she could almost hear herself, rattling it all off the way he did it – her mother having her at fourteen, her dad being much older, which made it much worse, those years living with her grandmother, then moving into the trailer with her parents, the trailer fire that killed a man and now the gray car and the houses burning down and more deaths. Thank God it was just in her head.

"So, it's all secret?" Parker bit into the ice cream. "What, are you in the witness protection program?"

Maggie laughed. "No. It's not that my life is secret, it's just that nobody ever asks me about it. Everybody already knows." Which seemed like a pretty good save.

"Townies always feel sorry for the Navy brats," Parker said, "because we have no home town, no old friends... I do feel sorry for myself sometimes. But sometimes I feel sorry for you guys."

"Yeah. We are boring."

"No, that's not what I mean. It's like, everybody knows your story. They've got you pegged. You can't reinvent yourself."

"Oh." She felt ice cream on her finger, hurried to catch a drip. "Have you done that – reinvent yourself?"

"Sure. Every time we move. Like, for the past two years I needed good grades and recommendations, so I was the nerd. I got all that checked off, we moved and now I'm a skater."

Maggie bent to get a quick look at his shoes. Skater, for sure. "What else have you been?"

"Wait – you still have to tell me something about you."

"There's nothing to tell." Maggie stayed focused on her cone.

"Okay," Parker said. "If I asked some kid in your class to tell me two things about you, what would they say?"

Maggie shrugged. "They'd say I'm quiet."

"That's not a surprise."

"Okay, here goes," Maggie said, already feeling a hot blush come over her, like her hand would turn the ice cream into a puddle in one second. "I live in a trailer park."

"My stepmom grew up in a trailer park," he said. "Do kids give you a hard time about it or something?"

"I don't know."

"They shouldn't. So what? It's where you live. Lots of people do. Half of them probably live in trailer parks. Or their parents did."

"I doubt it. There are a lot of rich people here. I don't think anyone in most families has ever been in a trailer park."

Parker just shook his head and that was the end of the conversation about her big secret. He dug deep into his cone with his tongue, then finished the thing off with a couple of big bites. "That was good. Want another one?"

"No, thanks. That's enough for me."

Parker smiled across the table at her. After a second Maggie turned away toward the water and the train tracks. Maybe he'd look away, too, and she'd be able to finish the messy bottom of the cone without being watched. But no. She ended up having to lick the last drips from her fingers while he was looking right at her.

"So tell me a couple of things kids *don't* know about you," he said.

Maggie swiped her lips with the napkin, then twisted it in her sticky hands. "Maggie isn't short for Margaret, it's short for Magdalena. My grandmother used to call me Magda. I hated that."

"Magdalena's pretty. And Magda is...different."

They both laughed at that.

"Okay, something else," he said.

"I like old movies. Black and white. Especially the scary ones."

"Yeah? Like what?"

"*Psycho*. The original. Not the remake or the sequels."

"Hitchcock is great."

She couldn't think of what else to say. He already knew about Alfred Hitchcock. Probably more than she did. When he lived in California, he probably took the movie tour and saw the Bates house and everything. She wished a loud train would go by so it would be normal to sit there without saying anything.

"You don't like talking about yourself, do you?" Parker said. "Okay, I'll tell you a family secret. Remember I said my stepbrother is kind of weird? Well, he's not just kind of weird. He actually has some certifiable emotional problems."

"Oh," was all Maggie could think of to say.

"He's had a hard time. It's been real tough for my stepmom."

"Oh," she said again.

"He's why we're here. He had some trouble in Norfolk and my dad had the chance to transfer, so he took it. He wanted to give Ash a fresh start. Again."

"Is it going better for him here?"

"It's kind of too soon to tell, but yeah, I think it is," Parker said.

"That's good."

"Yeah. I mean, it sucked for me, moving right before I graduated, don't get me wrong. But if it helps him, it'll be worth it."

"You're a good brother."

He shrugged.

This would have been another perfect time for a train, so they could just sit there.

But then Parker said, "Are you busy Friday after school? My parents are having a little backyard barbecue."

Somehow, she managed to respond with "Sure. Sounds cool."

"My parents are really nice."

"Will your stepbrother be there?" Trying to sound just curious.

"I'm not sure. He might have to work. Even if he is there – he tends to keep to himself. He gets into something, and that's all he does. He's obsessive. For a while it was naval battles, then planes. Then sharks."

"So you mean he sits in his room and watches *Jaws*?"

"Yeah, he stays in his room, but it's not sharks anymore."

"What is it now?"

"Now it's wolves."

39

AJ eased down the narrow road toward the Frasers' house.

"I hope he shows up," Wheeler said.

"He assured me he'd be here."

"Still, it seems..." Wheeler paused. "What kind of relationship does he have with his father that he doesn't want to be with him right now?"

"I know. He said his father wants the house cleared out ASAP."

The trees were tall and close on either side. Heavy clouds had come in and the sun was giving up early. Now and then, a fat drop of rain hit the windshield and AJ made the wipers swing across.

AJ said, "I hope we don't have any trouble."

"I think the two of us can handle Jonathan."

AJ just looked straight ahead.

"You weren't talking about Jonathan." Wheeler touched the bandage on his wrist. "You mean Taylor."

Without replying, AJ turned into the driveway. A white minivan was parked by the house. "That's him," AJ said.

The van had been backed up to the end of the walk. As they went around it, they saw that the cargo door was open. Inside, there was a stack of empty cardboard boxes.

"That's a lot of boxes," Wheeler said. "There wasn't that much stuff in his room."

AJ was looking off across the back yard toward the trees.

"Let's go see what he's up to," Wheeler said.

More fat raindrops pelted them as they went along the front of the

249

house. The plastic covering the missing window popped when the rain hit, making both men turn. The front door was open. Light and a sharp guitar riff came from above.

"Sounds like he's in Taylor's room," AJ said.

They climbed the staircase under the black ceiling. Jonathan, his back to the door, was pulling books from one of Taylor's shelves and loading them into a box. A big camp lantern threw a cold light, making huge shadows on the wall. A tiny speaker blared from the carpet. Next to it, a folded blanket covered the blood stain.

"Jonathan," AJ said.

Jonathan spun around, startled. "Jesus! I didn't hear you come in." He took a deep breath. Then, trying to look calm again, he slid another paperback into the box.

"Think you could turn that down?" Wheeler said.

Jonathan lifted the digital player from the floor. The music stopped.

"You said you were coming to pick up your things," AJ said.

"Yeah."

"So why are you in Taylor's room?"

Jonathan grabbed one of the last books from the shelf. He held the cover open. *Jonathan Fraser* was written there in pen. "I am getting my things." He scooped up the remaining books and fit them next to the others. "I don't know why she even had those. It's not like she ever read anything."

"Jonathan," Wheeler said, "why don't we go downstairs."

Jonathan lifted the box. "I just need to put this in the van."

"Let's go."

They went down with Jonathan between the two cops. At the bottom, AJ held the screen door open.

"You know, I can't help you," Jonathan said. "I don't know what all Taylor was mixed up in."

They crossed the yard in the same order – AJ, Jonathan, Wheeler.

Jonathan looked over his shoulder. "You guys – I'm not going to make a run for it."

Wheeler began searching his pockets for his notepad. AJ went on, Jonathan behind him. The rain had stopped, but the wind had picked up. It rattled the plastic on the window and hissed in the trees. As AJ reached the driveway, he saw something, to his right, deep in the shadow of the house. A glow that became a shape that became a shining teenage girl. Taylor.

"Wait," AJ said, reaching behind him.

But Jonathan kept walking. He cleared the house. Taylor rushed out of the dark, her hands in front of her, grasping. They collided, silently, Taylor and Jonathan, the ghost's fingers sinking into his flesh. Jonathan toppled over. The box went flying, scattering the books.

"Jesus Christ!" Jonathan picked himself up. He turned to Wheeler. "Why'd you do that?"

Wheeler stood there, several feet away, with his notepad and his pen. "Nobody touched you. You must have tripped."

Jonathan looked back and forth between Wheeler and AJ, who was staring at the van. If AJ felt Jonathan's eyes on his back, he didn't acknowledge it. He was staring ahead, intently watching what only he could see. The setting sun and the clouds had made shadows of the three men, but Taylor Fraser was plainly visible, there by the open van, bright in her own light, her skin glistening.

"Jeez." Jonathan began collecting the books and throwing them back into the box.

"I'll give you a hand." Wheeler bent toward a book.

Taylor reached into the van. There was an ice scraper inside, a wide curve of plastic. Her hand swept it up and flung it at the house. AJ saw it zip over his head. It struck a window pane dead center and smashed the glass.

Jonathan whipped his head toward the sound. "What the hell was that?"

AJ still didn't turn. "Put Jonathan in the car."

Wheeler took Jonathan by the elbow and walked to the cruiser.

"What's going on?" Jonathan said. "What are you doing?" But he went.

AJ waited for the car door to close. When he looked back at the van, the girl was gone.

"Taylor," he said, his voice nearly lost in the wind. "We're trying to help you. We're trying to find the person who hurt you."

He turned around, looked in all directions. There was a light, behind the house. It grew, began to move, took form and detail, until it was Taylor, speeding toward him. Now there was a sound, too, a wail, blending with the wind, adding an anger without words, without bottom. AJ reached into his pocket. Taylor was on him. AJ thrust this hand out, struck her where her sternum used to be. Their eyes met. Then she vanished.

AJ stood there, staring down at the iron knob in his fist.

"Where are we going?" Jonathan said from the back, as AJ got into the driver's seat. "Is there somebody out there? Do you need to call for backup or something?"

Wheeler stared at AJ, waiting for an answer.

"I called it in," AJ said. "We're going to get you away from the scene while someone else checks it out."

"Okay." Jonathan was silent as AJ drove to the end of the road. Then he leaned forward. "Was someone there? I didn't see anyone."

"Our guys will check it out," AJ said.

No one spoke the whole way down to Route 1. They sat there at a red light.

"Are you taking me to the station?"

"I thought we'd get something to drink," AJ said.

Wheeler glanced across the seat at AJ but said nothing.

The light changed and AJ pulled up to the gas station across the road. He parked in front of the building.

Wheeler looked into the back seat. "Do you want something?"

"Coke," Jonathan said.

"Make it two," AJ said.

Wheeler went in and came back a minute later with three soda cans. He passed one back to Jonathan. AJ drove another half mile or so, took a left into the trees.

"Where are we going?" Jonathan said.

AJ's only response was to take a right, then pull up to an iron fence surrounding a small cemetery. He eased through the gate, then stopped the car. The headlights lit up a row of worn headstones.

"I didn't know this was back here," Wheeler said. "Interesting choice."

"I used to come here as... Never mind." AJ was undoing his seat belt. "Trust me. No one is going to bother us back here."

Wheeler got out, then opened Jonathan's door. "Come on, Jonathan. AJ found us a nice, peaceful place for our talk."

Jonathan eyed him warily. "What the hell? A cemetery?" He stood up.

AJ had cut the headlights. There was still a faint glow in the clouds, and the warmer glow of the dome lamp inside the car. All around them, the black tops of the trees whipped back and forth in the wind.

"Why didn't you just take me to the station?" Jonathan said. He turned slowly in place, looking across the graves.

"This was closer," AJ said. "Saves gas."

"What?"

"Budget cuts," Wheeler said. "Every penny counts." He put his can on the roof of the car. "This won't take long. Then we'll get you back to your van."

AJ walked to the fence, swung the gate closed, then traced the fence with his eyes. Four unbroken sides of iron.

"So let's start with this," Wheeler said. "Where were you the night that Taylor died?"

"I was in Webster, Mass. My girlfriend's band had a gig at a bar there. I was with her."

Wheeler got the name of the girlfriend and the bar and wrote them in his notepad.

Jonathan finally opened his drink. "Like I said, I really can't help. I don't know who Taylor was involved with."

"How would you describe your relationship with Taylor?"

"Non-existant."

AJ had come around to their side of the car. "Your father was married to Taylor's mother almost five years now. He adopted Taylor. You must have spent some time with her."

"You'd think so, but not so much. I mostly stayed with my mom, when I wasn't away at school."

The wind raged for a few seconds, then quieted down again.

"We found some pictures on Taylor's cell phone," Wheeler said.

Jonathan scowled but didn't say anything.

"One of my favorites is Taylor's boyfriend smoking pot, with you in the background."

Jonathan looked at his drink. "Yeah, yeah, I remember that night. Are you going to arrest me for that? For being there? I didn't give Ryan the pot, and I didn't smoke any myself."

"What were you doing there?" Wheeler said.

"Trying to keep that poor kid out of trouble. Obviously, I failed."

"Did you hang out much with Taylor and Ryan, or her other friends?" AJ said.

"No. That one time, I was at the house to get my dad's signature on something for school. Like I already said, aside from Ryan, I don't know who Taylor was messing with."

"But she was getting into trouble with someone."

"I know this sounds cold, but bottom line, Taylor was a first class bitch who was always trying to make trouble for somebody. She always had someone on the hook."

"If you didn't hang around with her," Wheeler said, "how would you know? Did she have you on the hook?"

"No. No way." Jonathan took a few steps, then turned around. "When our parents first got together, my dad said she needed a big brother. So that's what I tried to be. But..." He stopped, as if struggling for something.

"She didn't want a big brother," AJ said.

"No. Partner in crime, is more like it."

"How did you handle that?" Wheeler said.

Jonathan was pacing back and forth, now. "Tried to avoid her. Keep her out of my business. But I couldn't completely, not without cutting my dad out." He took a few steps one way, then the other. "Anyway, she eventually stopped trying to get me involved with her shit. Still, when I'd see her, she'd brag about it."

"Yeah?" Wheeler said. "What, or who, did she brag about?"

"She never talked names. She was never specific."

"Was it about drugs?" AJ said.

Jonathan stopped. "I don't know anything about drugs. Other than the pot. I know she had pot sometimes."

"Look, Jonathan," Wheeler said. "We're only interested in finding out who killed your stepsister. We're not looking for an excuse to arrest you. So just tell us what you know."

"Okay." Jonathan took a drink. "Like I said, I don't know anything. Nobody I know was selling to her. But she did tell me that she was lining up a source for something good. She didn't say what. Only that I could get in on it if I wanted to."

"You weren't interested?"

"Do I look stupid?"

The wind kept on pawing at the trees.

AJ leaned back against the car. "The night after Taylor died you came to the house in the middle of the night, when I was there. You said you stopped by for a few things, but all you took was a few shirts and a bottle of wine. That has never made sense to me. What were you really looking for?"

Jonathan paced. "I wanted to check my room. If Taylor did have drugs it would be her style to stash them in my room."

"So you'd get blamed, if they were found."

"Yeah." Jonathan took a sip.

"What were you going to do if you found them?" AJ said.

"Flush them down the toilet, I guess. I know, I'm probably supposed to hand them over to you. Maybe I would have."

No one spoke for a while. Jonathan kept pacing. AJ scanned the cemetery, his eyes sweeping right, as if following the fence.

"Just one more thing, Jonathan," Wheeler said. "Where were you on Monday night?"

Jonathan stopped. "Monday night? The night Helena died?"

"Yes."

"I thought she died in a fire." He looked from Wheeler to AJ. "Jesus. I was with my girlfriend, at her parents' place. In Webster."

"Can anyone else confirm that?"

"My girlfriend."

"Uh huh," Wheeler said.

"So Taylor, then Helena... Is my dad in any danger? Am I?"

Wheeler folded his notepad closed. "If anything happens that makes you feel like you are, call us."

AJ took Jonathan by the elbow. "Come on, we'll take you back to the van."

"Are you going to call to be sure it's safe?"

"Yeah, get in. I'll call."

When Jonathan was in the car, AJ opened the gate. The hinges let out a birdlike cry that cut through the wind. He stood there for a while, taking one last look into the darkness.

***

AJ and Wheeler watched the van roll down the Fraser's driveway.

"Guess he lost interest in packing up his things," Wheeler said.

"Yeah."

It was quiet for a moment.

"You still think he had something to do with Taylor and Helena's murders?" Wheeler said.

"He has his dad all to himself for the first time in years. That could be a motive."

255

"I don't know," Wheeler said. "That seems like a reach. We need to make a few calls, see if his alibis check out."

"Yeah." AJ pulled his seat belt across.

"About that window..." Wheeler looked toward the pane that had been smashed by the ice scraper.

AJ reached for the keys in the ignition.

Wheeler blocked his hand. "Was she here?"

"Yeah."

"So that's why you wanted to leave?"

"I thought if we wanted to have any chance of getting to talk to him..."

"Why the cemetery? That kid thinks we're both a little nuts."

AJ reached into his pocket, then handed the iron finial across the seat. Wheeler rolled it around in his palm.

"Do you know why the old cemeteries have wrought iron fences around them?" AJ said.

Wheeler looked down at the knob in his hand. "Something tells me I don't want to know."

40

AJ dug through the dark, heavy objects – the remains of Claire and Melody's haul from the junk shop. They clanked against each other.

"AJ?" Claire's voice came from the stairs.

"In the kitchen!"

Claire appeared in the doorway, dressed for bed. "Hi. What are you doing?"

"Hey. Sorry if I woke you. I'm looking for more finials."

Claire came over to him. She gave him a squeeze with one arm, then looked into the box. "Mostly trivets, huh? I think we put all of the finials out." She looked toward the window. "There's one." She went to it and picked it up – it was a knob like the one AJ had been carrying. "Why are you looking for finials?"

"Let's go sit down for a minute."

"This sounds serious."

He led her into the living room, switched on the light. They sat down on the couch.

"What is it, AJ?"

"You know that iron finial you gave me?"

"Yeah."

"I used it tonight, on Taylor Fraser."

"You mean, carrying it kept her away?"

"No, I mean, she came at me and it stopped her."

Claire looked toward the window sill, where a trivet stood next to a miniature tea pot, both of them as black as the night behind them.

"This stuff really works."

"Yeah, it looks like it does."

"How did you use it? Did you just show it to her, or throw it at her, or what?"

AJ explained about Taylor appearing in the shadows, flinging the ice scraper, charging him, then vanishing when he pierced her with the finial.

"So she's gone," Claire said. "You got rid of her."

"I wouldn't count on it. I'm not sure it's permanent."

"Does Wheeler believe, now?" Claire said.

"I think he's getting there. It's still just my word about the ghost. Though he has seen some things that are hard to explain." AJ glanced at the window. "I gave him the finial, and he took it. That's something."

"Yeah. You should take this one, then." She tried to hand the knob to him.

"No." He closed her fingers around it. "I want you to keep it. Keep it with you all the time."

Claire looked down at her hand. "You've encountered ghosts that seemed crazy and aggressive before, right?"

"Yeah, but Taylor is different. She's particularly good at manipulating the physical world, for one thing. She's not tied to one place, either. I haven't seen that before. And the others – it seemed like their anger was a result of their death, of the way that they died. With her, I feel like it's something else."

"Don't you think this limbo they're in – it eats them alive? Some of them. That's where the anger comes from."

AJ only nodded.

"Maybe it's particularly bad for her," Claire said. "A pretty, popular girl, used to being the center of attention wherever she goes, suddenly finds herself invisible..."

"I think it's way beyond that. I think there was something seriously wrong with her before she died."

"You mean she had a personality disorder, and now that's been magnified?"

"Something like that. It's like whatever was worst in her is all that's left."

"So if she comes back, how do you get rid of her for good?"

"We need to solve this case. Both murders. I think then she'll move on."

Claire opened her hand. "You should keep this, then."

"I'll take one that you put out." AJ turned toward the window. "We may want to get more iron."

"Already on my list for tomorrow."

***

A noise downstairs – something brittle hitting the floor. AJ slips out of bed. His bare feet make no sound. Gliding down the stairs, he's swift and silent.

Ben is sitting in a chair, CDs scattered at his feet. He holds one up in front of him. *See?* Then he turns to the fireplace. Stares at it intently. "Uh oh," he says. "Melody missed a spot." He keeps looking at the fireplace. In the blackened, brick hollow, there is suddenly a pinprick of pink light.

Upstairs again, in the dark bedroom, AJ sat up quickly, tugging the sheet aside. Claire didn't stir, but Buck rose up on his long legs. AJ took a flashlight from the end table and then, with Buck behind him, followed the path of his dream, across the floor, down the hall, down the stairs. He continued on to the room at the end of the house. He flipped on the light, then went straight to the fireplace. Leaning into it, aiming the beam, he checked the flue. It was open. He reached up and grabbed the looped handle, tugged it until the door slapped shut. He straightened up again. On the hearth there were a set of old iron tools for tending the fire – a poker and a flat shovel. He placed them so that they tipped back across the opening. Then he circled around the whole downstairs. Other than himself and the greyhound, there was no one, living or dead.

***

When AJ came into the kitchen, already in his uniform, Claire was at the little table, with a mug of coffee and *The Day*. Looking up, she pushed the blonde hair away from her face. "Hey. Are you going to have something to eat?"

"No. I'm meeting Wheeler for breakfast." He stopped for a kiss, then went to the coffee maker and filled a mug. "I want to show you something."

He led Claire out of the kitchen and around the corner. Sunlight slanted across the plank floor. Buck lay sleeping at the foot of a chair in front of the hearth.

"I know it looks silly," AJ said, looking at the iron poker and shovel leaning across the fireplace, "but leave those there, okay?"

"You think Taylor might come down the chimney? Isn't that more of a Santa Clause thing?"

"Just bear with me. I'll be out all day today. Part of the time up in Massachusetts, just over the border. You may want to – "

She waved him off. "I can't go anywhere or have anyone here. I have work to do. The book has to be ready for my editor next week."

"Okay, okay. But if you have any problems, call the station."

"Well, I do have this lull in the second act..."

"Come on, Claire."

"Don't worry. I have all the members of the cavalry on speed dial."

"Okay." He kissed her, longer this time. "I have to go."

Claire reached for his coffee. AJ took a big hit before handing it over. As AJ went toward the door, Claire bent down to pat the dog. "I wondered where you were, boy. Why are you hanging out here all by yourself?"

Buck writhed in appreciation of the rub.

"Shoot," she said. "Dave forgot the CD."

AJ turned in time to see Claire pull a jewel case from between the cushions of the chair. She brought the CD to him. "DaSilva wanted to borrow this. I have most of the Beatles stuff. I tried to give him *Rubber Soul* or *Revolver*, but for some reason he wanted this one. It's definitely not their best."

"Can I see?" AJ came back to her. He took the plastic case, studied it. "Weird." He handed it to Claire.

"What do you mean?"

"Nothing. I gotta go."

Claire headed for the kitchen again. "Do you want to take some coffee with you?"

"No, thanks."

"Okay. Bye." Claire went around the corner.

AJ stopped with a hand on the doorknob. He looked back at the room. "Ben, if you've got something to say, just say it."

"What?" Claire called from the kitchen.

"Just talking to the dog!"

Buck looked up at him.

"Keep an eye on things, okay, boy?"

The dog lowered his head and let out a long groan.

41

AJ and Wheeler sat over empty plates, finishing their coffees. Outside, the traffic on Route 1 was picking up. "You ready for a long day?" Wheeler said, reaching for his wallet.

"Yep."

"How about Claire?"

"She's determined to be fine." AJ pulled out his own wallet. "Sometimes I wish she had family close by."

Wheeler smiled. "Maybe." When AJ gave him a look, Wheeler added, "My parents are a Wheeler married to a Wilbur – half the local population is some kind of relative. Sometimes it can be too much of a good thing." He seemed to think about that for a while. "So If Jonathan's alibi checks out, we can cross family off. "

A pair of older women appeared at the nearest table. They were exact copies of each other, down to the bright outfits and the silver perms.

"Sam! Our favorite little cousin!" one of the women said. "How are you!"

Wheeler slid out of the booth and kissed the woman on the cheek. He bent to kiss her companion. "Just fine, Mary. Hello, Myrtle. You two are looking sharp today."

Putting her hand on Wheeler's arm, Myrtle whispered, "Are you working on that awful business on Whitfield Road? Or the other one, in the Borough?"

AJ grabbed the check and went to the register.

"I've seen them around," AJ said, when Wheeler had caught up to him. "Twins, right?"

"There you go," Wheeler said. "You're already done some detective work today."

AJ only nodded.

Connecticut Route 2 took them north. For a while, near the huge casino owned by the Pequot tribe, it was no longer a country road but a wide, elevated highway.

"Fraser's employer," AJ said, turning toward the building that towered over the trees.

"Ever been?"

"No. Giving my money away doesn't do much for me."

Two lanes again, the road led them to 395. From there, it was a straight shot to the Massachusetts border. They got off the highway and almost immediately came across a sign welcoming them to Webster, Mass. There was the profile of an Indian in feather headress, and the words *Home of the Nipmuck Indians.* Making a long, long arc over all of that was the name of the local attraction – Lake Chargoggagoggmanchaoggagoggchaubunaguhgamaugg.

"Look at that," Wheeler said. "It's supposed to be the longest place name in the U.S."

"I heard it was spelled wrong on the sign."

"Is there a right way?" Wheeler put an address into the GPS.

They went around the lake, ending up at an old-fashioned inn buttressed on two sides by an enclosed porch. Big white letters between the second and third stories spelled *Lakeside Tavern.* The lot was still mostly empty. As AJ parked, a man carrying a box disappeared through a back door. AJ and Wheeler followed him in.

"Ron Deaver?" Wheeler said, showing his badge.

"Yes?" He was mid-forties, with an expanding forehead and a bit of a gut. He waited behind the bar as the cops came toward him.

"I'm Detective Wheeler and this is Officer Bugby. We're from the Stonington, Connecticut Police Department."

"This must be about the Frasers."

"Yes, it is. So you know about that."

"Sure. It's been in the papers. They're part-time locals, so... Come on in."

They all took stools at the bar. Up close, Deaver looked like he'd mostly divided his time between the sun and the bar and gotten the worst of both.

"Do you know the Frasers well?" Wheeler said.

"Not well, no. Martin Fraser has come in a few times a season ever since he bought the house. More with the second Mrs. Fraser than the first."

"Why is that?"

"The second Mrs. Fraser seemed more...down to earth. Fun, too. We were sorry to hear about her."

"What about the daughter, Taylor?"

"She came in with the family now and then, but you know teenagers – they're quiet when they're out with their parents."

"Did you ever hear anything about Taylor or Jonathan and drugs?"

"No," Deaver said. "I never heard anything. My daughter, Chrissy, might have a better idea – she's just a year older than Taylor. You want me to call her?"

"Sure," Wheeler said.

Deaver made the call and the introduction, then handed Wheeler his cell phone. Wheeler asked the same questions he'd just asked Deaver. He got nothing new about Taylor and drug use. The girl hadn't known Taylor well.

"It kind of felt like she didn't want to talk to us locals 'cause she thought she was better than us," Chrissy said. "And as far as I know, the summer kids didn't have anything to do with her. Some called her trailer trash. Basically, she had no friends here."

Wheeler thanked her and left his number, then handed the phone back.

"What do you know about the son?" Wheeler said, after Deaver had set the phone down. "Jonathan?"

"He wasn't around much for a few years – I guess because of the divorce. I've gotten to know him a little this year. He goes out with Sammy Schuyler. She has a band that's played here a few times. He does the sound, hauls equipment. From what I've seen, he's a good kid."

"When was the band here last?"

Deaver went to the end of the bar and thumbed through some papers. He slapped a flyer on the counter. "Last Friday. Sammy and the Sunfish. Kind of a retro thing. The customers love them."

"Was Jonathan here that night?"

"Sure."

"How late would he have been here?"

"The band, Jonathan, and a couple of other kids, stayed until I locked up around three. Why are you asking about Jonathan?"

Wheeler turned to a fresh page in the notepad. "Just routine."

Deaver put the flyer behind the bar again.

"I appreciate your help," Wheeler said. "If you think of anything later, will you call me?" He slid a business card across the bar.

"Sure thing."

When they were in the car again, AJ said, "So, Jonathan's alibi holds up. He was here with the band." He put the key in the ignition. "Where to?"

"Let's try the Frasers' house." Wheeler put the address in the GPS. "I had an idea on the way up here."

They continued around the lake, eventually turning onto a side road with smaller houses, close together. When they'd found the address they were looking for, AJ pulled onto the shoulder. They walked to a door. Wheeler knocked.

A man about Fraser's age responded. "Can I help you?"

"I'm detective Wheeler. This is Officer Bugbee. We're hoping to speak to Mr. Fraser. Martin Fraser."

"We've just come from the funeral home. I don't think now – "

"Detective, do you need to talk to me?" The voice came from somewhere inside.

"Yes. It won't take long."

The man in the doorway motioned for the police to come in. They entered a cramped mud room. Fraser hadn't shaved in a while. His eyes had a hollow look.

"You know, we'd be better off outside." Fraser led the way out a pair of French doors onto a short, curved patio, then across a sloping yard to a dock with a screened-in structure.

"Beautiful place you have here," Wheeler said.

Fraser didn't respond. When they were in the pavilion, he pointed at the padded lawn chairs. They sat facing the water.

"Thanks for talking to us." Wheeler shifted his chair so that he could look at Fraser.

"What did you need to talk to me about?"

"Chief Brown asked you about your employees and associates at the casino."

"Yeah, we covered that."

"When you met your wife, Helena, she was working at the casino, right?"

"Yes." His voice was flat and even, like it was all he could do to form the words.

"Did you go back that far with Chief Brown? Did you go back to when she was working there, before you knew her, or around the time that you met her?"

"No, we were looking at current staff. We didn't go back that far."

"It's a number of years, right? I bet there's been a lot of turnover since then."

"When Helena worked at the casino, she got along well with everyone. But if you think it could help, I'll speak to personnel, have them pull the records from that period."

"That would be good."

"Mr. Fraser," Wheeler said, "were you aware that some of the kids here at the lake referred to Taylor as trailer trash?"

Mr. Fraser looked away. "No, but I'm not surprised. My first wife was very close with some of the other families here. That would have started with her."

"Can you tell us which families?" Wheeler said.

"Yeah. It would be the Rossis, and the Wagoners, and probably the Rosenbergs."

Wheeler brought out his notepad and wrote the names.

AJ said, "Do you think there's anyone from up here who – "

"Who what?" Fraser's voice was suddenly sharp. "Who killed Taylor and Helena – strangled them and set fire to the houses where they lay dead? No. No, of course not." Fraser ran a hand across his face. The air seemed to go out of him. "Sorry."

"It's okay. I know this is difficult."

For the first time, Fraser looked the cops in the eye. "You really think it could be someone from the casino?"

"We need to check out every possibility."

"Okay. I'll contact you about those employee records."

"We'll speak to you soon." Wheeler stood up. He and AJ climbed back up the hill, went around the garage, then got in the cruiser. When they cleared the house, they could see Fraser sitting on the dock, looking out at the lake. AJ paused there for a moment.

"What is it?" Wheeler said.

"I keep thinking about the kids calling Taylor trailer trash."

"You think someone decided to take out the trash?"

"Jonathan said she always had something on somebody. Maybe that somebody was up here. I know it opens up a whole new pool of possible suspects."

"Well, our last stop is at the station here. Maybe Chief Kent can help us shrink that pool."

The Webster police station was a low building just one road over from 395, right off the lake. It housed all of the emergency services, so it had the big bay doors for the fire trucks and the ambulances, too. Inside, a uniformed officer led them to Kent's wood-paneled office.

"How's it going so far?" Kent said, after the introductions. "Anything I can do to help?" He had a friendly smile and a graying mustache. His uniform shirt was a glaring white.

"Can't say we came up with much," Wheeler said. He recounted what they'd heard at the tavern, and from Mr. Fraser.

"What were the names that Mr. Fraser gave you?" Chief Kent took a seat.

Wheeler read from his notepad.

"I'll look into it, but they don't set off any alarms." The chief was writing on his own pad.

"Any kids, teenagers, you've had trouble with? Locals, summer residents?"

"Sure, routine stuff, mostly around drinking. But if you mean, do we have any budding sociopaths, or psychopaths – I can never remember which is which..."

"Do you have anyone like that?" AJ said.

"No. And nothing that connects to the Frasers at all. After you called, I did have a chance to talk to a few officers, see if they had any information that would help you. Nothing yet. I'll talk to the rest, check on those families, let you know. "

"Thanks, I appreciate it."

The three men shook hands, and then AJ and Wheeler went back out to their car.

Lunch was fast food along 395. They sat outside at a painted metal table and ate without saying much. After a while, Wheeler threw his burger down onto the paper wrapping. "Ugh."

"Something wrong with your food?"

"No. It's this case. We keep hitting walls. We've eliminated the family, ex-family, friends. And Taylor's boyfriend, and the drug-dealing teacher. Everyone we talked to alibied out."

"Yeah," AJ said. "We have nobody from Stonington, and so far, nobody from up at the lake."

"No one from the casino."

"Unless Fraser comes up with something during that second look," AJ said. "That was a good thought."

"I'm not going to hold my breath," Wheeler said. "The Strangs had solid alibis. The guy who died in the trailer fifteen years ago – maybe we should take a second look at him. Look harder at his family." He drank from his cup. His scowl didn't change. "There's the drugs."

"There's still the yellow-eyed man."

Wheeler nodded but looked pained. "Who do you think that guy is? Some random psychopath?"

"It's not impossible."

Wheeler pushed his fries around in their salt. "Maybe Major Crimes will have some new ideas. I hate to admit it, but I'm almost ready for help. I just hope it comes before somebody else gets hurt."

42

The man at the desk told them to go straight back to the chief's office. They were barely across the threshold before they were shaking hands with Detective Mike Thompson of the Connecticut State Police Major Crimes Squad, Eastern District.

"Good timing, guys. Chief Brown just finished catching me up on the case." Thompson was an imposing man in a stiff blue shirt and tie.

"Let's head next door," the chief said. "We're a little crowded in here."

Thompson led the way, as if he'd spent his whole career in this precinct. The chief hung back, his lips pressed shut. There was a cup of coffee in his hand, but it didn't seem to be helping him any. He had the sagging face of someone who was getting about half of the sleep that he needed.

In the conference room, AJ and Wheeler sat down on one side of the table, the chief and Detective Thompson on the other. Thompson placed a sheaf of papers in front of him – everything that AJ and Wheeler had written up so far on the case.

"Good work, here." Thompson tapped the papers. "Do you have more for me, after this morning? I hear you were all the way up in Massachusetts. That lake with the long name. I'm not even going to try to say it."

"People call it Webster Lake," Wheeler said. "We verified Jonathan Fraser's alibi. Didn't really come up with anything new." He ran through their conversations at the Lakeshore Tavern, with Fraser, and with the Webster chief of police.

Thompson crossed his arms across his thick chest. "So who do you like for this? Where would you go next?"

"We have a couple of things. It's mostly going back over old ground." Wheeler ran through this list. "Probably the first thing is the drugs. See if there's more there than Addison led us to believe."

Thompson turned to AJ. "You feel the same way, Officer Bugbee?"

"Yeah, I do."

Thompson began flipping pages. Through all of this, Chief Brown hadn't said a word.

"I'm with you guys," Thompson said after a while. "That's the direction we need to go. Unfortunately, it's a little complicated." He slid a couple of sheets of paper forward. "I already talked to someone in the DEA. This doc who was writing the scripts –" Thompson pointed to the paper. "The DEA already had their eyes on him. So, they want in. It's going to be a coordinated effort – CSP, DEA and SPD. We're going to have two goals – bust up a supply of illegal prescription drugs and solve two homicides. Same time. That's never easy."

"So just to be clear, you're taking the lead?" Wheeler glanced at the chief.

"Yes." Thompson neatened his papers again. "We're going to have a good team. Resources you haven't had up til now. We're going to catch some bad guys. All right?"

"Okay."

"Chief, you want to explain about the assignments?" Thompson said.

"Detective Thompson asked for two men, as a start," the chief said. "Two detectives."

Wheeler looked at AJ, his eyebrows raised.

"So, I'm taking Detective Nardi off those burglaries to join you, Sam." The chief sank back in his chair. "AJ, you and I will talk."

"Chief," Wheeler said, "AJ's been working this case from the beginning. Knows things that – "

"Like I said, Officer Bugbee." Thompson tapped the papers again. "Excellent work. No doubt you have a future if you decide to become a detective. Let's make it official – I'm recommending it. But a case like this? Double homicide, with drugs and arson thrown in?

It's not a good first case, even if you were already a detective."

"I disagree," Wheeler said. "AJ – "

Thompson cut him off. "This isn't really open for discussion. Detective, why don't I go meet Detective Nardi while you write up the events of the morning. The team will reconvene here in an hour."

They all stood.

"AJ," the chief said. "See you in ten?"

"Sure."

"I'll treat you to a cup of coffee," Wheeler said to AJ as they went out.

With their backs against the counter, sipping the scalding drink, they could see the chief doing the introductions. Nardi and Thompson shook hands, all smiles. The chief stood behind them, his face blank.

"I'm sure that was Thompson's doing," Wheeler said. "The chief would have kept you on the case. In fact, I'm sure he fought for you."

"I know."

Thompson had put his arm around the chief's shoulder and was talking directly into his ear. It was the closeness of a judo master about to execute a throw.

"Maybe I lucked out," AJ said. "How do you feel about working with that guy?"

"He's something, isn't he? Even his smile looks like it will knock you down. Have you ever seen a shirt that stiff before? I'm thinking he ironed it after he put it on."

AJ faced the counter again, looking for a stirrer for his coffee.

"The chief wants you," Wheeler said.

"Let it go, Sam."

"No, I mean, the chief is waving you into his office."

"Oh." AJ took his coffee and went out. He found the chief behind his desk.

"Sorry, AJ," the chief said, motioning for AJ to close the door. "It all happened kind of quick. I got a call, then Thompson was here." The chief was quiet for a moment. "Listen, this thing with Thompson, it's not easy for me, either. I don't like someone telling me how to do my job. In fact, there's been a lot of that lately."

"What do you mean?"

"I'm getting hassled about the budget again. We're a week into a double homicide and they're worried about money."

"The council? It's their job, I guess."

"I know. And with Thompson putting together this team, all the new resources being brought to bear, well – " The chief frowned. "If you're not on that case, I can't have you working extra hours."

"Right. Back to part time." AJ shook his head. "You know, it's going to be tough for Wheeler to follow up on some things if he's working with Thompson."

"The yellow eyes?" The chief watched AJ for a moment. "I know it's going to be hard for you to stay out of this."

"Two women have been murdered! I can't just go back to part time patrol and forget about that."

"I'm not asking you to forget about it, I'm asking you to stay out of it. Just until I get you back on the case." A cell phone on the desk in front of him buzzed. The chief grabbed it, checked the screen, then put it down.

"Everything okay?" AJ said.

"Yeah."

"How's your granddaughter?"

"Tara's doing great. She's one tough little girl."

"Takes after her grandpa."

"She found out that this Wilms Tumor is also called nephroblastoma, so she's taken to calling it her *blast*."

AJ smiled but said nothing.

"They think they're going to take one kidney."

"Damn."

"Actually, that's what we're rooting for. That's the good result. Surgery's tomorrow morning."

"I'll be rooting for that, too, then. Hope everything goes well."

"Thanks." The chief flattened his hands in front of him. "About your schedule. I've got you off for the next couple of days."

AJ said nothing, just looked back across the desk. Then he checked his watch. "Guess I've done all I can do here."

"Sure. If Wheeler doesn't need anything, you don't have to stick around."

"How'd that go?" Wheeler said, when AJ reached his desk.

"Perfect. I'm not just off the case, I'm off. For the next two days, anyway. Then it's back to part time."

"Shit."

"Do you need anything from me?" AJ had his keys in his hand.

"You're headed out?"

"Yeah. If you're good."

"I'll walk with you," Wheeler said.

When they were standing by the Jeep, Wheeler said, "This sucks."

AJ squinted up at the indistinct sun.

"You know," Wheeler said, "I can't say anything to Thompson or Nardi about what you've seen – "

"You mean, what I think I've seen."

Wheeler didn't respond.

"Or what you've experienced."

Wheeler didn't respond to that, either.

"So you won't be following up on the yellow eyes." AJ got into the driver's seat.

Wheeler stepped close and put a hand on the door. "I like working with you, AJ. I'll try to get you back on this case, but no matter what, I want to keep you in the loop."

AJ looked out through the windshield. "I like working with you, too, Sam. I'll do anything I can to help – as much as they'll let me."

Wheeler stepped back. AJ started the engine. He got the Jeep turned around, gave Wheeler a wave, then drove off into the hazy afternoon.

43

AJ is in the back seat of a cruiser. Wheeler in the passenger seat. Nardi behind the wheel, navigating a narrow road. Black, the headlights barely denting the darkness. They stop at an intersection by a large, dilapidated sign, lit from below. Wheeler and Nardi keep looking straight ahead, but AJ turns to read the big letters on a peeling background – *Dusty Roads Trailer Park*. Tacked to one corner, *Help Wanted* in fluorescent orange. Standing next to it, in shorts and a T-shirt, just like the last time AJ saw him alive, and every time since – Ben Shortman.

He says, "Now there's something you don't see very often."

AJ looks where Ben is looking, toward the intersection. A low shape lopes across. A wolf. It turns its head and there's a flash of yellow eyes. The wolf keeps going into the trailer park. It disappears into the darkness.

"Did you see that?" AJ says.

Though they are looking at the cross road, where the wolf has just been, Wheeler and Nardi say nothing.

"Did you see that?" AJ says again.

They ignore him.

Nardi starts the engine. "Dead end," he says.

"No, it isn't," Ben says.

"See?" Nardi points. There's a yellow Dead End sign on the other road.

"He's not seeing it right," Ben says.

As Nardi pulls away from the trailer park, there is the howl of a wolf, which turns into a scream, which becomes a siren, which is finally the sound of the train whistle as AJ comes to.

Claire was asleep. AJ looked across her and out the window of the train. They had left the city behind and were heading up the Connecticut coast.

As if awakened by AJ's gaze, Claire opened her eyes. "I guess I fell asleep," she said. "When you went out like a light, it seemed to jinx me. I thought for a while I'd be awake the whole way home." She tilted her head back, stretching her neck. "The train is so relaxing, isn't it? Maybe it's the solution to your sleep problems."

"Might be cheaper than the last prescription I got."

"Which you have never taken."

AJ kept looking out the window.

"I'm so glad you came with me today." Claire squeezed his arm. "I hope you had a good time."

"I had a great time."

"You seemed to hit it off with Linda. She's a fantastic editor. I'm lucky to have her."

"I gotta believe it's the other way around."

Claire squeezed AJ's arm again. "The brunch was pretty good, right?"

"It was great. I feel funny that Linda paid for mine."

"Don't. That wasn't her money." Claire removed the sunglasses from the top of her head and dropped them into her purse. "It was nice to have an excuse to revisit some places I haven't been to in a while. We were lucky to see Chelsea Market on a Thursday. You wouldn't have liked it on a weekend."

"So that wasn't crowded?"

"Oh, no. That was dead." Claire looked out the window, too. "Are you hungry? There's a cafe car."

"I'll be all right until we get back."

AJ's cell phone buzzed in his pocket. Claire watched him anxiously as he read from it. He tilted the screen toward her. "Good timing," he said.

"*Staff pig-out*," she read. "What does that mean?"

"It means they overbought on fish, and Mom's cooking up a batch. Dad throws in fries and drinks. The staff stays and has a little party."

"That sounds like fun. Delicious fun." She checked her watch.

"We're supposed to be back by 6:35, but we're running late. It might be more like 7:00. Then we have the drive from Westerly. Too bad this train doesn't stop in Mystic."

AJ laughed and put his arm around her.

"What?"

"You seem more excited about eating surplus seafood in the back of my parents' glorified clam shack than you did about that fancy brunch we had in the city."

"Yeah, well, does that make me?"

"Perfect." He kissed her.

"Reply to Sela, make sure they save us some."

"Okay, okay. Give me my arm back."

***

They were heading down Route 1 when AJ's phone buzzed again. He pulled onto the shoulder.

"Hey, Sam." AJ undid his seat belt and stepped out of the car. "What'd I miss?"

"The Feds arrived. I don't know what you were up to today, but whatever it was – mowing the lawn, defrosting the refrigerator – you did as much to catch our killer as we did here."

AJ was walking back and forth between the car and a billboard for Buzzi's Memorials. "Great. What's next?"

"We're sending a guy to the doc undercover. He's going to complain about back pain or something, see what he gets for his troubles."

"That seems the long way around to get to our killer."

"That's how they want to do it. Build a case against the doctor, then use that as leverage to get information out of him. The idea is that he might be supplying a gang who in turn are the suppliers on the street. And it's the gang that had a run-in with Taylor and Helena."

"Possible."

"Yeah, I guess these guys know what they're doing," Wheeler said. "I put your name out there a couple of times today."

"I appreciate that." AJ passed by the billboard, then turned around. "How's the chief? His granddaughter had surgery today."

"I guess she's doing well."

"That's good news."

"Yeah. I don't think the chief could take much more of the other kind."

"Well, keep me updated if you can."

"I will," Wheeler said. "And listen, there's a lot left to go here. Before it's all over, you'll be back on this case."

"Whatever you say, Sam."

AJ got back in the car.

"Well, I kept you distracted almost the whole day," Claire said.

"So that was your plan?" AJ looked at her. "Because I'm still plenty distracted." He leaned across the seat and kissed her.

"Okay," Claire said, pulling back but laying a hand on his chest. "Now let's go eat some seafood."

It wasn't quite closing time, eight o'clock, when they rolled down the access road, but there were already orange cones across the parking lot. AJ maneuvered between two of them, then continued around behind the building, where he squeezed between two cars and shut off the engine.

Inside, the air was thick from a fryer working at capacity. AJ's dad, the two Daves, Beth and Parker were moving about the big, cluttered kitchen, each busy with a task. The one still figure was the fisherman everyone knew as Old Bacchiocchi, or just Bacchi, a lean man whose bright white hair looked like it had been styled by a gale. He stood propped up by the central table, clearing enjoying the industry that surrounded him.

"Hey, Bacchi," AJ said. He introduced Claire.

"Hope you haven't eaten," Bacchi said. "You're going to want to be real hungry."

"We are," Claire said.

AJ's mom poked her head in from the front room. "AJ, get drinks for you and Claire. The rest of us will get the food onto trays."

They ate at two picnic tables pulled together, by the light from the big front windows. Fries and fried fish, clams and cole slaw and corn on the cob. They talked and laughed and ate until they couldn't eat anymore – everyone except George, who had a single helping, then nothing but diet soda. They talked about everything but the two murders in town. The night stayed just warm enough, even without the sun.

Bacchi was the first to leave, saying that it was already past his bed time. Then Parker asked if he should stick around and clean up.

"You're the only one with a drive," George said. "Go ahead, whenever you're ready."

"Well, I should get going. Thanks for dinner. It was great."

"Of course it was." George wiped his mouth with a greasy napkin.

"Bye." Parker went around the building. A moment later, he was back. "Sorry, but, AJ, would you mind moving your car? It's a little tight. I don't want anyone to get a scratch."

"Oh, sure." AJ followed him back into the shadow of the building, then out of sight.

DaSilva stood up suddenly and went after them.

"Where are you going?" Sela said.

DaSilva ignored him.

AJ backed the Jeep out of his spot. When he was clear, he watched Parker steer the little gray sedan. Parker waved and drove off.

DaSilva waited for AJ at the back door of the building. "I heard you're off the case. Your mom told us. We weren't supposed to say anything, but..."

"Yeah."

"So what happens now?"

"Wheeler and Detective Nardi are working with the State Police and the Feds."

"Wow. Big time."

AJ didn't say anything.

"What about Taylor and her mother? Wheeler won't be able to do anything about them. And they're the best sources of information about the murders."

"Not so far, they aren't," AJ said.

"But they will be. Just like Ben. And you can't just leave Taylor out there hanging around. She's bad news."

The back door opened and June Bugbee came out carrying a box of ice cream sandwiches. "Can you believe your father? He's supposed to be watching what he eats."

"He did go easy on the fried fish tonight," AJ said.

"That's right, and he's not going to blow it all now." June came down the steps, stopped in front of AJ and DaSilva long enough for them to grab an ice cream sandwich from the box, then continued on to the dumpster. She hesitated, but tossed the whole thing. When she turned around, she was holding one of the wrapped sweets. "Don't you say a word."

"Mom, do you need me to work tomorrow?" AJ said. His ice cream was already half gone.

"I didn't want to ask, but that would be nice." June devoured her dessert as she made her way back across the lot. "Are you two coming in?"

"In a minute," AJ said.

When June was gone, DaSilva said, "I had another dream about Ben. It was really weird. He was standing on a rock at the edge of the water – I'm not sure where – and he was singing the Beatles song, *Yellow Submarine*."

"That's why you were looking at Claire's CD."

"How did you know that?"

"You left it in the chair."

"Oh yeah. She told me that when she brought it over. I thought maybe there'd be a message in the lyrics."

"Was there?"

"Not that I can figure out," DaSilva said. "Ben kept singing that phrase over and over. *We all live in a yellow submarine.* Then a sub surfaced out in the water. It wasn't the cartoon sub from the album cover, though. It was a real one. Except that it was painted all crazy, with these curling flames on the front. The rest of it was covered with eyes. Yellow eyes. They were blinking. Ben looked at me, and his eyes were yellow, too." DaSilva shuddered. "It sounds stupid, but there was something really creepy about it."

"I believe you."

"Do you think it means something?"

"Remember when you said maybe Ben was trying to connect with this world?"

The door opened and Sela appeared. "Hey, you guys are missing out on all the fun clean-up."

"We'll be right in," AJ said.

The door slapped shut again. DaSilva stood in front of it. "So, what were you going to say?"

AJ shook his head. "I don't know. But tell me if you have any more dreams."

"I will."

AJ reached past him for the door handle. He paused. "Are you doing okay?"

"Yeah."

"No more encounters?"

"No. I haven't gone looking for them, either."

"Good."

"I just hope they don't come looking for me."

44

AJ was dropping his cell phone into his jeans pocket when Claire came out into the yard. It was early. The birds were loud and the grass was drenched with dew.

"Bet I can guess who you were talking to," Claire said.

"Bet you can't."

"Oh, good. It wasn't Wheeler."

"No. Mom's optometrist."

"Really?"

"Trying to follow up on a tip."

"Shouldn't Wheeler or Detective Nardi be the ones following up on tips?"

"Not this tip." AJ stared down the long slope into the trees. "It came from Helena Fraser. After the fire."

"Oh." Claire came over to him and slipped an arm around his waist. "So did you find out anything good?"

"I didn't talk to him yet. His wife said he's walking at Barn Island. I guess he's leaving soon for a bridge tournament in Stratford, so I'm going to try to catch him now. You're still heading over to Melody's, right?"

"I made those plans when I thought you'd be working. Melody would understand if I changed them. You and I could spend the day together."

"No, you should go. That would leave me free – "

"For some off-the-books police work?"

From the kitchen came the trill of the house phone.

"Who's calling on that phone?" Claire said.

"Probably a sales call." AJ walked in behind her.

"This early in the morning?"

"Sure. For them, no time is too inconvenient."

"They're as bad as the police."

AJ lingered in the porch, looking away down the yard.

After a few minutes, Claire stuck her head out of the kitchen. "That was Melody. She's really sick."

"Sick how?"

"I'm not really sure. Jack's away and she wants me to come over right now."

"Do you want me to come with you?"

"I actually offered that already. She wants just me. I have to get dressed."

"Okay," AJ said. "I need to grab something before I go." He followed Claire in, then up the stairs, down the hall and into their bedroom. He went straight to a closet and produced a gray box of business cards. He pulled a few out – they were blank. When he turned around, Claire was at the dresser, sorting through a drawer. She had just removed her top. He took in the narrowing lines of her back, the long furrow of her spine.

"We owe ourselves more days like yesterday," AJ said.

"Yes, we do." She looked over her shoulder. "Soon, right?"

He stopped to kiss her as he went by, letting his hand linger on her hip. "I hope so."

***

In the small parking area of the Barn Island Wildlife Management Area, AJ wrote his cell number on a blank business card. He got out of the Jeep and took a trail into the marsh. A man stood looking across the grass toward Wequetequock Cove.

"Ho! Is that AJ Bugbee?" the man said as AJ approached.

"Hi, Dr. Schwartz."

"Call me Barry, please."

"Okay. I spoke to your wife. She said I might find you here."

They met on the wide path. The sun burning through the morning fog was already warm. The marsh grass and the open water that snaked through it were all washed by a soft, salty breeze.

"Is it about your mom? Is she having trouble with her eyes?"

"No, her eyes are fine. This is police stuff. I just want to ask a few questions."

"I hope you're not going to start with *Where were you on the night of...*"

AJ smiled. "No, nothing like that. It's about contact lenses. Have you ever sold contacts that look like animal eyes?"

"I haven't gotten into the novelty contacts."

"Anyone carry them locally, that you know of?"

"Maybe Greene's in Westerly? They have a lot of trendy eye wear. You used to be able to get that kind of thing at all kinds of places – costume shops, party stores, head shops. Now they're regulated – considered a medical device. You need a prescription."

"So you can only buy them through an optometrist."

"Well, you can get them on the Internet. I'm not sure the online retailers are always strict about the prescription requirement. And contacts still pop up in other places. I saw some recently at a sunglass kiosk along the interstate."

"I know you don't sell them, but has anyone asked you about novelty contacts recently?"

"No, I don't think so."

"Have any of your patients had the eye exam but didn't buy glasses or contacts from you – they only wanted the prescription?"

"Not that I can remember. But I can check with my wife. Lisa helps the patients pick out the frames. She may remember that happening."

Neither spoke for a while. Out in the green marsh, an egret waited, still and white as a chalk line.

"Here's a number where you can reach me," AJ said. He handed the man the handwritten card. "Thanks, for your time."

"No problem. Say hi to your mom for me."

"I will. Thanks again." AJ started toward the parking lot.

"You know, if you're trying to track someone down using novelty contacts, I think you're going to have a hard time."

"Yeah, sounds like it."

"Unless you catch him wearing them."

***

AJ did his research on the porch, sitting at the table with his laptop and a sweating glass of iced tea. He put together a list of local optometrists and Web sites. He added costume shops and a few odd stores that sounded promising, including one that claimed to cater to "vampires, lycanthropes and other creatures of the night." Browsing a site that sold contacts, he found a whole page of wolf eyes and sent a couple of images to the printer. Then he called Claire. "How's Melody?"

"Okay."

"You sure? You don't sound – "

"Yes. Fine."

"Should I come over? Do you need anything?"

"No."

AJ stood up from the table. "You can't talk."

"Yep."

"But everything really is all right."

"Yes. Everything's fine."

"Okay." AJ crossed the porch to the screen. "I've got some running around to do, then I'm supposed to help my parents out at the market. But if you need me, call."

"I will."

"Okay. Bye."

"Bye."

AJ went back to the computer, which was still showing the yellow eyes, garish and glaring – a gallery of insanity. He called Wheeler. "Hey, Sam. Are you somewhere you can talk?"

"I've got maybe three seconds."

"How's it going?"

"It's only been a day but I already miss you. This team, or task force, or whatever you want to call it, is getting nowhere fast. And Thompson – let's just say he's not always as warm and fuzzy as he was when you saw him."

"That was warm and fuzzy?"

"Shit," Wheeler said. "Here comes my new best friend. We're going to have to talk later."

"I'm working at the market tonight. Maybe you could come by for that dinner that I promised you."

"Good idea. I'll fill you in tonight."

A car door closed.

"Gotta go," Wheeler said.

45

Maggie sat on the front step, staring down the hill between the trailers, watching for his car. She'd been there for a while, just her and a canvas bag and a big, whole pineapple. The longer she sat there, the weirder the pineapple seemed. All prickly, all armored. Like a giant fruit hand grenade. Not exactly the perfect thing to give someone who had invited you to a family barbecue. Too late to change now, though. It was the pineapple or nothing.

She was looking for a red Subaru – his mom's car – not the one Parker shared with his weird, disturbed stepbrother. She wondered if she would meet the stepbrother today. She had to be ready for that. She remembered a middle school trip to the aquarium. There was a group of older boys with extra adults who stuck really close. One of the boys got all worked up over the penguins and yelled "Oscar!" over and over. For weeks afterward, kids would shout that randomly at school, when they were just walking down the hall, or during a test when the whole room was quiet. *"Oscar!"* What would she do if Ash was like that?

Red, at the bottom of the hill. She didn't know if that was a Subaru, but it was the right color. The car came up the road. It was close now – that was definitely him behind the wheel. He pulled over onto the grass.

"Hey, nice looking pineapple," he said, out the open window.

"Thanks." She handed the thing to him the instant he stepped out of the car, like she was trying to get rid of the pineapple-grenade before it exploded. "I got it at the fruit stand in Pawcatuck. The guy said it should be a good one."

"You can tell by the smell." Parker lifted it to his nose. "What should it smell like?"

"Like a pineapple."

Maggie laughed.

"Perfect." He put it on the back seat. "Here, want to drop your bag in, too?"

She reached past him and set it down – the bag with her towel and her suit. Which she was supposedly going to wear in front of him. Which she didn't even want to think about.

He said something about the trailer being nice, but she was already getting in the passenger side.

"Okay." He got in, too. "Let's go."

On the way, he explained that they were having a sort of a birthday party for his dad. "I didn't tell you before because I didn't want you to feel like you should get a present or card or anything. The actual party, with a whole bunch of people from the base, is tomorrow. Today it's just us. It's not really a birthday party except that this is his actual birthday. I couldn't take both days off, so I picked this one."

If she was going to be hanging out with his parents, he must have thought they'd like her, which was kind of amazing. But he could be wrong. What would she have to talk about? Her life was so boring. At least, what she could tell them about her life.

"Do you go over to Groton much?" he said.

She could have launched into it then. How she went to Groton to get nail polish, how she'd seen the guy in the gray car, and how he followed her, and... No way. She just said, "Not too much."

It was quiet for a while.

Maybe if there were too many awkward pauses, she would pull that story out. If Parker started to get that look that she'd seen on guys' faces before, that look that said they'd already moved on, even if they hadn't moved their feet yet.

But Parker filled the pauses. He gave her the rundown on the menu for today, which was standard cookout stuff, just like she'd have with her parents – meat on the grill, potato salad and soda. He asked her what her parents did, and when she told him, he said he liked the idea of being a trucker, traveling by yourself, that without truckers there'd be no barbecue, or much of anything. He asked her if she'd been to the submarine museum in Groton, so they talked about that for a while. He said there was a debate in their house over how you pronounced the name of the river – his mom wanted to say Tems, like they did in England. "The fair and lovely River Thames," Parker said, in a fake accent that made them both laugh. He never let the lulls in conversation drag on. So she wasn't even close to spilling her only beans when they were already pulling into his driveway.

He noticed her staring up at the house. "Kinda cool, huh?" he said.

"Yeah, definitely." She didn't want to seem too much like a hillbilly, so she didn't say any more. But this wasn't a regular house. It was shaped like a triangle, and tall, with glass all across the front. Like some kind of Swiss chalet or something. Pretty much the coolest house she had ever seen.

He handed the canvas bag to her, then got the pineapple. She followed him around the house. In the back yard a thin, pretty woman with a big hat was putting bowls of chips on a picnic table.

"Hello," she said.

"This is Maggie," Parker said. "Maggie, this is my wicked stepmom."

The stepmom shook Maggie's hand. "Nice to meet you, Maggie. You can call me Terry. Everyone else does." She gave Parker a look.

"Hi," Maggie said.

"Are you two going for a swim? We put the heater on, so the water should be a nice temperature."

Parker raised his eyebrows at Maggie, then looked past the little fence at the pool. There was a wide patio all around it and a little roof for lounging in the shade. It was ridiculous. Now that she'd noticed the pool, Maggie could smell the chlorine and hear the humming that must be the filter.

"This would be a good time, before we put the food on the grill," Parker's stepmom said. "Maggie, I'll show you where you can change."

So much for hoping that the swimming would never happen.

"I'm going to go skim," Parker said.

Terry led her inside to a bathroom and pushed the door open. "Here you go. It looks like you have a towel. Do you need anything?"

"No, thanks. I'm all set."

"To go out, you just go straight back that way." She pointed.

"Thanks." Maggie went into the bathroom and closed the door. She wished now that she had put her suit on at home, so she didn't have to be naked, even for a second, in this bathroom in Parker's house. She hadn't worn the suit because it would have shown, and that would have made her look too eager, like she wanted to jump right in, which was the exact opposite of the truth. Besides, if she had her suit on already, there was supposedly no reason not to just take off her shirt and shorts right by the pool. She always hated doing that on the beach. That sort of half strip tease.

She got out of her clothes and into her suit in a couple of quick motions, like some kind of stage performer between scenes. Then she tried the cover-up that her mom had insisted on getting when they bought the new suit – a flimsy thing that you tied around your waist. She looked at herself in the mirror over the sink. Weird. She undid the tie and reached back into the bag. She pulled out a big, denim shirt. *Carson Trucking* in little red script. She put the shirt on. The blue matched the flowers in her suit and actually looked okay. She stuffed everything else back in the bag.

She put her hand on the doorknob. Now she had to walk back through the house in her swimsuit. Who else might she run into? The Navy dad? The weird brother? She turned the knob and stepped out. The place, thank God, was empty.

Parker was sitting on the edge of the pool with his feet in the water, looking sort of Johnny Depp with his longish hair and super-dark shades. He was still wearing his T-shirt. He looked up at her. "Cool shirt. Your dad's?"

"Yeah."

"You might want to keep it away from the pool. The water's got a lot of chlorine. You could get spots."

"It's okay. This is old. Dad doesn't even work for this company any more." She decided Parker was being nice and not just trying to get a look at her without the shirt. If that's what he was after, he'd already have his own shirt off, already be showing off his manly perfection. Which she would kind of like to see.

They didn't say anything for a long time. The water felt cool on her legs. The sun was hot and bright and the pool was so shiny that it was almost hard to look at. Maybe they'd just sit there all afternoon, with their feet in the water and their shirts on.

"The pool's really pretty," she said.

"I'm not wearing my contacts, so everything's kind of blurry," he said. He looked around, squinting, like he wasn't sure where she was.

Maybe he was trying to make her feel more comfortable about being in her suit.

"Listen, there's one other thing that I've got to tell you," he said. "Or I guess I'll just show you." He pulled his T-shirt over his head and turned toward her. There was his slightly hairy chest. His muscles. And a giant scar.

"Oh!" she said, before she could stop herself.

It started just below his throat and went down dead center between his nipples. A thick pink line. You couldn't draw it any straighter with a ruler.

"Impressive, right?" He touched the scar with a finger.

What do you say to that? She sat there like a stump. Like a crazy, confused stump.

"Sorry," Parker said. "I hope I didn't freak you out."

"No," she said. "It's just, you didn't say anything about that when you did your one-minute-or-less life story."

"Yeah. It's medical stuff. Old guys talk about medical stuff. You know what's great about this?" He slid his finger along the pink line. "I've been excused from gym class forever. Not that I need to be – I can do just about anything. But the gym teachers don't know that."

"Cool."

"Come on, let's swim!" He slid into the pool and went all the way under.

She undid her shirt while he was doing a lap. Once she got in, they chased each other around for a while. The water was super clear and when you were under it, looking up, it was like being inside a huge blue jewel. They ended up sitting on the edge again, all goosebumps, feeling the sun, glowing in it. A man came out into the yard. He started messing with a grill.

"You have to meet my dad," Parker said.

Maggie grabbed the denim shirt on the way by, but there wasn't time to put it on. She clutched it in front of her. But then, Parker was going around with his big pink scar hanging out.

"Dad, this is Maggie."

"Nice to meet you, Maggie."

"Happy birthday, Mr. Stevens," Maggie said.

"Thank you, I appreciate that." Parker's dad talked in a quiet voice that somehow made you want to pay attention. It was the kind of voice that could tell you you were leaving your high school with just a few weeks left before graduation. "I see you brought a pineapple. I don't know if you know how appropriate that is."

"I told her about Hawaii," Parker said.

"Well, then you do know. Smart girl. I'm taking orders. Hot dogs or hamburgers for you two?"

They both asked for hot dogs. Thinking alike.

"They'll be ready in a few minutes."

"Just enough time for a quick tour of the house," Parker said. They put on their shirts and went inside. He led her upstairs, to the top floor, where they took a peek into the master bedroom – big windows, a giant bed made so neat and tight it was like the thing was gift wrapped. Then they went downstairs again to the huge living room. With the high ceiling it was like a church, except there was a bar, all set up with liquor bottles and bar stools.

Parker slid a door in the wall. "Dumb waiter. It goes down to the kitchen."

Maggie reached in with her hand. "I want one of these." Which was stupid, since she lived in a trailer, where there was nothing up or down.

Instead of calling her on it, Parker said, "Dad gives lots of parties, for his job. Otherwise, we don't really use this room. Come on, I'll show you the real living room." He took her down to where they'd started, to a kitchen and another room with a sofa and chairs and the biggest flat screen she had ever seen.

"Now the bedrooms," he said.

Back upstairs again. This part was more like a regular house – straight walls, normal ceilings. There was a bathroom and a couple of closed doors.

"Mine and my bother's rooms," Parker said. "I can't show you his, because he freaks out if anyone goes in there."

Maggie pictured the guy at the aquarium. *"Oscar!"*

"He's not around, but still – "

"Parker! Maggie!" Terry called from downstairs. "Your dogs are almost ready!"

Parker pointed to the farthest door. "I'll show you my room later."

They ate at the picnic table while the pool filter hummed,

reminding you that you could cool off anytime. The hot dogs were a little charred, the way she liked them, and the potato salad was the best she'd ever had. Terry had cut up the pineapple and everyone had some and said how good it was.

"So how's your birthday so far, Dad," Parker said.

"Almost perfect." Mr. Stevens described a walk he'd taken on Barn Island and birds that he'd checked off his life list.

"Sounds like it is perfect," Terry said.

"The only thing missing is Ash. He knew about the cook-out, right?"

"Of course," Terry said. "He wasn't sure he'd be done at work." She looked at Maggie. "He just started a job at a flower shop. In Mystic, which is good, since the boys are sharing a car. He does deliveries, mostly. They seem to give him the stops that are over this way, like the hospital in New London. He's there a lot."

For the first time, Maggie almost wished she could meet Ash. If he worked at a flower shop, and if his dad really wished he was here, then he couldn't be so bad.

When they were done eating, Parker took Maggie back inside to show her his room. Which was normal, because it was one of the only rooms she hadn't seen. Still, when she thought about being all by themselves in a separate part of the house...

He left the door open.

He hadn't really bothered to neaten up for her – or maybe this was as neat as it got. There were socks on the floor and jeans on the bed. A couple of cardboard boxes like exploded clothes bombs. She went over to some pictures tacked up on the wall – Parker's dad looking through binoculars, and a boy in a hospital bed surrounded by nurses and doctors with big smiles. In that picture the line down Parker's chest was still bright red.

She turned around. "This is a nice room."

Parker pulled a swivel chair back from the desk. He patted the seat. It was either that or the bed, so she took the chair. Parker got behind and rolled her toward a poster of Hawaii – green, pointy hills.

"That's where I'll be in fourteen months."

"It's beautiful. You're so lucky." She meant it, but she was already looking at something she had just noticed on the dresser. A plastic model of a heart.

Parker picked it up. "Watch this. It comes apart." He pulled one side away. "My one grandfather is a surgeon. He got this for me, after they discovered what was wrong. So that I could see it."

"What was wrong?"

"Okay, let's get that out of the way. It's called an atrial septal defect. It's basically a hole where there isn't supposed to be one. It lets blood go between these parts of the heart, these chambers." He pointed. "That's not good. But they closed up the hole, so I'm normal now. I mean, heartwise, anyway."

"Can I see?" She took the model from him. She put the pieces together, then pulled them apart again. It was just plastic. But it made her feel weird, like she was holding Parker's actual heart in her hands.

"Okay," he said, taking it back, "science class is over."

A door slammed downstairs. Then voices. It seemed like an argument.

"Shit." Parker listened for a second, went to his door and closed it. He pushed the little button in the center of the knob. "Just..." he said.

More voices, shouting, from downstairs. Parker's mom. Then a guy.

"That's my stepbrother." Parker stepped away from the door.

"Do they fight a lot?"

"Lately, yeah. Since they made Ash get a job. He was doing so well – I guess they figured he could handle it. But he's not too happy."

The shouting stopped, but now there were loud footsteps, coming up the stairs.

Then Terry's voice. "Don't walk away from me!"

The footsteps were at the top. They came right down the hall toward them. Maggie and Parker both watched the door knob and the little pushed-in button.

"And don't start with that noise!" Terry shouted. "We have a guest!"

A door slammed, so close by it sounded like it was in the room.

Parker gave Maggie a sort of helpless shrug.

There was a sound. Soft at first. It had to be the noise that Terry was talking about, the one she didn't want to hear. Long notes, rising and falling. Maggie couldn't quite figure out what it was, but it made her skin cold.

"Ash, for Pete's sake!" That was Terry's voice, from right outside.

She must be in the hall, standing by Ash's room.

All of a sudden, the noise got loud. Sad, wild cries. Howls. Wolves.

"Ash! Please!" Terry knocked on Ash's door. Which seemed to work. The wolf noise stopped. Then the door opened.

"Mom! Shut the door!"

"Ash, just let's talk. Don't hide out up here."

A pause.

"Ash!"

More footsteps, going away, fast. Back down the hall and down the stairs.

"Ash!" Terry was still in the hallway. "Don't leave!"

From below, a door slamming. Then more footsteps going down.

Parker let out the breath that he'd been holding in. "Well, I think the show's over." He turned the knob, opened the door a little and looked into the hallway.

Outside, an engine revved, then a car drove away.

"Sorry about all of that," Parker said. "You want to swim some more? There'll be birthday cake. You should see the cake. It's kind of a masterpiece." He talked fast, like he wanted to take her mind off what had just happened.

"Okay," Maggie said.

They went out into the hall. Just as they passed Ash's room, there was another loud wolf call. Parker rolled his eyes, like it was something he could joke about. He went into Ash's room. Maggie hung back at first, because hadn't he said that Ash freaked out if you went in his room? Then she followed him. He pushed a button on a CD player and the howling stopped.

"Welcome to my brother's world," he said.

The walls were covered with pictures of wolves. Everywhere you looked, yellow eyes looked back at you.

"Crazy, right?" Parker said.

Maggie didn't say anything. All of those eyes made her dizzy. She searched for something normal to latch onto. There. A glass shape, dark blue. It seemed so out of place in this room. Old and pretty, like something your grandmother would have. She picked it up. "I like this paperweight," she said.

Now that it was in her hand, she could feel bumps on the side. She turned it to get a better look. At first she saw just random ridges in the glass. Then all of a sudden they made sense, like they just snapped into place. It was a wolf's head, tilted back, its mouth open.

"I wonder where he got that? Can I see?" Parker took it, lifted it up, studied it. "You know what? It's not a paperweight. There's a little wheel and a wick on top." He pressed down with his thumb and a flame jumped up. "It's a lighter."

46

AJ was at the market, putting the kitchen back together after a busy dinner rush, when he heard Beth's voice from out front.

"Hi, Sam. How are you?"

"Just great. Is it too late to order?"

"Not for you. What would you gentleman like today?"

AJ moved a little closer to the plastic curtain, but stayed behind it.

"Are your fried clams bellies or strips?" That was Thompson, of Major Crimes.

"Bellies, of course," Beth said.

"You sure?" Thompson said. "I'll know the difference."

"They're bellies."

"Okay. Because this looks like the kind of place that would serve strips. No offense."

Beth didn't say anything to that. Sela, who had come over to where AJ was standing, cursed under his breath.

"I'm going to have a big plate of those bellies," Wheeler said.

"Okay," Beth said.

"I'll go with the roll, just to play it safe," Thompson said.

"You got it."

"Hey, isn't that your officer back there?" Thompson said. "What was his name, Bug something?"

"Yes, that's Officer Bugbee," Wheeler said.

AJ pushed his way through the plastic. "Hello, detectives."

"Officer Bugbee," Thompson said. "So you're what, a cop slash fry cook?"

"My parents own the place."

"Good, you have something to fall back on, if law enforcement doesn't work out." Like the last time, Thompson wore a tie with a blue shirt that looked like it had been molded onto him.

"AJ is the best officer we have," Wheeler said, sounding annoyed.

"I'm just joking around. I'm sure he is." Thompson surveyed the counter and the tables outside on the strip of grass. "You might be able to do something with this place. Of course, it would cost."

"I'll get that order started," Beth said. She slipped past AJ, who followed her.

"What was that about?" DaSilva said, looking up from a sudsy sink.

AJ just shook his head.

Once the clams were in the oil, Beth climbed on a stool and began rooting through some bottles on a high shelf. "Do we have any more of that Stonington's Finest sauce?"

"I think the last bottle we had exploded," DaSilva said.

Sela came over to Beth and watched her shift bottles around. "What are you up to?"

"Here we go." Beth droped a small bottle into the pocket of her apron. "Nothing."

When the meals were ready, Beth took them out to the picnic tables, empty except for the two cops. Thompson grabbed his roll and immediately bit into it. "Not bad. Sam, I'll give you one thing, your guy knows his way around a fryolater."

Wheeler raised a fork from his plate and said nothing.

Beth had the tiny bottle in her hand. She held it out for Thompson to see. "I thought you might like to try some special fry sauce. It was created by a Stonington police officer. It's real popular with our men in blue here."

Thompson reached for the bottle. "Stonington's Finest," he said. "I have to try it. I like a good hot sauce."

Beth started back to the building, then turned around. "Our guys really pour it on, but you may want to start slow. It's pretty strong."

"I think I can handle it."

Thompson gave the bottle a quick shake over his plate, then took a taste from his fingertip. "Nice." He poured it liberally over his fries, then held the bottle out for Wheeler, who waved it away. "More for me," Thompson said, giving his fries another dose. He popped three sauce-soaked fries into his mouth. Smiled big. Then his eyes teared up. He stifled a cough.

"You okay?" Wheeler said.

Thompson cleared his throat. "Something went down the wrong way."

Inside, Beth found Sela watching the whole thing through the front window. "Have I told you that I love you?" he said.

"Many times." She held out her hand to show a ring. "Still engaged."

June Bugbee came out from the kitchen. "What did she do to deserve a proposal this time?"

"Offered a guy some of that Stonington's Finest Sauce," Sela said. "He really went for it."

"Oh, good Lord, Beth! That stuff will take the barnacles off a boat." June went toward the front door.

"He deserved it! He insulted AJ. And this whole place."

"What do you mean?"

Beth explained.

June Bugbee took her hand off the door handle. "Well..."

Just then Wheeler came in, grinning. "Can I have some milk? And maybe a fire extinguisher? I swear I saw smoke coming from Thompson's hair."

"Sorry, we're out of milk," June said.

AJ joined them out front. "What's going on?"

Beth explained again. Shaking his head, AJ fetched a small milk carton from the glass case. "On the house," he said, handing it to Wheeler.

"We're not going to get to talk tonight," Wheeler said. "This guy's been attached to me all day. He's like a leech."

"Or a tick," Sela said. "Be sure to check for the bulls-eye rash."

"Exactly." Wheeler glanced out the window, then turned back to AJ. "Have you been enjoying your time off?"

"I started looking into the yellow contacts."

"Yeah?"

"I'd like to do a little legwork," AJ said, "but – "

"If anyone you talk to follows up with a call to the station, that could be a problem. It can't get back to Thompson, for sure."

"Yeah. So, I have some blank cards that we used to use in Bridgeport, for gang members, or anyone who couldn't be caught with a business card from the Bridgeport P.D. I'm only going to give out my cell."

"That helps. If I talk to the chief, I'll let him know what you're up to. Beyond that..." Wheeler waved to Thompson, who was looking toward the building, his face a blazing red. "You know what? He's even starting to look like a tick."

47

When Parker brought her home, there was a different car where her parents' car should be and Ryan was sitting on the front step. The day just kept getting weirder.

"Who's that?" Parker said.

"He's a friend from school. Ryan."

They parked next to Ryan's car. He was standing up now.

"Should I come with you?" Parker said.

"No, it's fine. Thanks for having me over. And for driving me."

"Sure. I'll text you later, okay?"

"Okay."

They looked at each other. More like stared into each other's eyes, something she'd only heard about before, so she wasn't prepared for it, how much it pulled you in, like it could swallow you. They were so close, in the little red Subaru. Maybe if Ryan hadn't been there, watching, they would have kissed. It really seemed possible. Parker would lean toward her, and then they would both move at once, and then their lips would touch. In her head, Maggie cursed Ryan a little. She tried to push him out of her mind and focus on Parker's eyes again. Was it the light – dim, with the streetlight already on – or was there something...

"Your eyes look different," she said. "Almost more blue." It felt scary, to admit that she'd noticed the exact color of his eyes.

"Yeah, I have the contacts in again," he said. "They're a little tinted. That's not weird, right?"

"No, it's cool."

"Okay, good." He smiled, seeming actually relieved.

She waited one more second, like he might still give her a kiss goodnight. "Bye," she said. She got out of the car, then watched it back up and start down the hill. When she walked over to the step, Ryan was standing there looking awkward. She'd never seen that before. "Hi, Ryan. What are you doing?"

"Who was that?"

"Someone I met at the Bay Market. His name's Parker." Maggie was still wearing her dad's shirt over her bathing suit top, and the shirt was unbuttoned kind of low. She pinched it closed with her hand.

"Did you get my texts?" Ryan said. "I was starting to wonder if you were okay."

"You know my phone and its sucky battery. It's probably dead."

There was a long, uncomfortable pause – only she didn't really feel that uncomfortable. Ryan looked across the yard. "Did you see that?"

"What?"

"I don't know. I thought I saw something. Over by the grill."

"What'd you see?"

"Like a candle or something."

For a while they both stared at the grill but there was nothing there.

"Can I come in for a minute?" he said.

Maggie turned to Ryan. What was he doing? Was he trying to remind her of the lighter flickering on at his house, right before all of that crazy stuff started happening – the candle crashing through the glass and then running across the street in the dark, and that feeling of something touching her back, knocking her down? Was he trying to use that to make a move on her? Get her a little scared, so she wanted to ask him in? It was too weird.

Ryan swatted at something on his arm. "It's kind of buggy out here."

Maggie went past him to the front door. She had her key out. "My parents don't want me to have boys over when they're not here." She was amazed to be saying that, to be using that excuse to turn him down. Ryan Hardy.

"So I guess you're okay," he said.

"I'm good." She didn't say that all she wanted right then was to go inside and crash on the couch and think back about the afternoon, remember every detail. Sitting on the edge of the pool with Parker. The water like a big jewel. The model heart. His warm hand when he led her out of his brother's room.

Nobody said anything for a long while.

Ryan swatted at another bug. "Hey, do you want to get something to eat? Or maybe see a movie?"

Maggie wanted to say, *What about Lola?* But she couldn't just drop that name now, because she and Ryan hadn't really talked about Lola at all. Anyway, it didn't matter. Things were way past being about Lola. "I was just at a cook-out. I think I ate enough for the whole weekend. I need to crash."

"Okay. Maybe another time."

"Yeah."

"All right. See you later, then." Ryan gave a little wave that was supposed to look casual but came off awkward. It was weird to see that being done by someone else, and especially by Ryan.

He headed toward his car. Right before he got in, he said, "Charge your phone!"

Maggie watched him drive off. Then, for a second, she looked at the grill again. "Thanks, Ryan, for creeping me out." She went over to it, looked around for the lighter. It was there in the grass. She picked it up, touched the long metal tip. It was warm, but maybe that was just from sitting in the sun all day. Maybe they shouldn't leave it out here.

Inside, she dropped the lighter on the kitchen counter, then went to her bedroom and got the charge cord for her phone. But she couldn't find her phone. She remembered it sitting on the picnic table when they were all having birthday cake. She was showing Terry pictures of Green Falls, which were lame because of the crappy camera and the tiny screen. She must have left the thing there on the table. Hopefully when Terry and Parker cleaned up they hadn't just picked the phone up with the paper plates and thrown it in the garbage. Though that was about right.

She rinsed her suit in the bathroom sink, to get rid of the chlorine, and hung it dripping off the shower head. Then she went ahead and got in the shower herself. She was drying off when the kitchen phone rang, so loud that she jumped. She almost just ignored it, because only her parents got calls on that phone. But she ran out and answered, to make the ringing stop. "Hello?"

"Hey, Maggie, it's Parker. Guess what I'm holding in my hand?"

"My phone?"

"Yep. I can't bring it over right now. But I can stop by on my way to work tomorrow."

"That would be great. Or I could just come by the market and pick it up."

"I'll bring it by, unless Ash is being a dick. I guess if you don't see me by ten, could you come pick it up at my work? I'll be there all day."

"Okay. Thanks."

"No problem. Hope you can get by without it for a night."

"It's fine."

"I had a really good time today," he said.

"Me, too."

"See you tomorrow, Maggie."

"See you." She put the phone down. Weirder and weirder, better and better. She would see Parker tomorrow. Even her mistakes were turning out good.

48

"Parker seems like a good find," AJ said, as he rinsed out one of the big steel sinks at the market.

His dad was leaning against a counter while his mom and the Daves worked cloths across metal surfaces.

"Yeah, I think so," George said. "Still, not the same as having you here."

June bumped him as she made a big circle with her hand. "Oh, stop. You're going to make AJ feel guilty."

"Well, I hope so. That was the point."

With a quick flick of her wrist, she smacked him with the cloth. He winced dramatically.

"It was nice to have you here, AJ," June said.

"I like being here. And it's going to be nice to get that paycheck."

June laughed and went back to her cleaning.

Sela looked up from the fryer. "I thought I heard you volunteer to be here tonight."

"Yeah, volunteer," DaSilva said.

"Okay, okay." AJ raised his hands in surrender. "Dad, Mom, you should take off. The Daves and I can finish up."

"You don't have to ask me twice," George said. "June, put down that rag. We're leaving." He made a beeline for the back door.

June grumbled but followed, grabbing her purse from the corner desk along the way. "Good night," she said, on the way out. "Thanks, everyone."

Beth came through the plastic divider and slid a spray bottle into a cabinet. "Front's done. I came back to do Parker's job." She began cruising around the room.

"It's okay, Beth, I got it," AJ said.

Sela shook his head. "She's not talking about cleaning counters."

"Parker cleans up the leftover food," DaSilva said.

Sure enough, Beth had found a plate of fries and was nibbling at them.

"Well, I guess someone's got to do it," AJ said. "Do you think Parker will stick around?"

"I think so," Sela said. "I just hope he doesn't ask for too many Friday's off."

"Oh, come on," DaSilva said. "It was his dad's birthday."

"And he had a date for his dad's birthday party." Beth picked up another fry. "With one of our regular customers."

"What?" DaSilva said. "He's only been here a week!"

"The sub base boys don't waste any time," Beth said. "They know how to be charming."

"I should join the Navy," DaSilva said. "So which customer is he dating?"

"Silent Maggie."

"Really? She is kind of cute."

"Who the hell is Silent Maggie?" Sela said. "How do you know her, DaSilva?"

"Unlike you," DaSilva said, "I work the front once in a while. She and her mom come in pretty often."

"What's she look like?"

"Dark, curly hair." DaSilva held his hands on either side of his head, to show the volume. "She's short. She's in high school."

"Are you talking about Maggie Strang?" AJ said.

"Yeah, that's her," Beth said.

"Why do you call her Silent Maggie?" AJ said.

"I was her camp counselor a few years ago. She hardly spoke the whole week. I felt bad for her. She'd had some kind of trauma or something. It seems like she's better now, though. She's still quiet, but much more normal."

"How long has she been seeing Parker?"

"They met here earlier this week. This is their second date."

"I don't know, he seems too cool for her," DaSilva said.

"Nah." Beth licked salt off of her fingertips. "He's faking. He's a nice guy. Straight-A student, I bet."

"Nerd in disguise," Sela said.

"I hope so," DaSilva said. "I hope the nice guy thing isn't the act."

Sela grabbed the sponge away from DaSilva. "This episode of *Real World Stonington* is fun and everything, but, can we finish up and get out of here?"

"Yeah," Beth said. "I'm off tomorrow, so I'd like to get started on my weekend."

"I think you've pretty much finished your job." Sela pointed at the plate of fries. "Why don't you take off? If that's okay with you, AJ."

AJ nodded without saying anything.

Beth went to the back desk and pulled her purse out of a drawer. Before going out, she paused in the doorway. "Hey, AJ, how do you know Maggie Strang? She hasn't been in any trouble with the police, has she?"

DaSilva looked up from the counter. "Silent Maggie? Right."

"It's always the quiet ones," Sela said.

"I don't really know her," AJ said. "Have a good weekend." He picked up the last plate and took it to the sink.

***

It was still warm enough to be comfortable on the porch behind Claire's house, though the sun had been down a while. AJ sat at the table with some papers, his laptop and his cell phone. He shifted through the papers, moving a handwritten list of local optometrists to the top. Most of the names had been crossed off. He read through some notes scribbled in the margins.

His cell phone buzzed and Claire's face appeared on the screen.

"Hey," he said. "How's it going? How's Melody?"

"Not good. She has really bad nausea. Her doctor wants her to go to Lawrence Memorial. I'm not sure I know how to get there, and anyway, I want to be free to help her on the way. Can you drive us?"

"Westerly's closer. Shouldn't we go there?"

"No. I guess it has to be the other hospital."

"Must be bad. All right. I'll leave right now." AJ was already moving into the house, the laptop under his arm. At the front door, he stopped and looked back at the stairs. "Shit, Ben. Just about a year ago I followed you to the hospital. It's going to end better this time, right?" He stood there for a moment, as if waiting for an answer.

***

They took Claire's car, AJ at the wheel and Claire and Melody in the back seat. Melody had her head bent over a wastebasket. It had been established that there was nothing he could do to help other than drive, and that Jack had been called, so AJ stayed quiet and in the left lane of I-95. They passed the signs for Groton and the sub base, then the bridge rose up over the Thames River. On the left, the Electric Boat shipyard was brightly lit, the huge green building open to the night. In front of it, in the water, you could make out the distinct shape, long and dark and low, of the newest submarine, fast closing in on its launch date. When it was finished, the sub would be all about secrecy, but for now, it was on display next to the interstate.

They crossed over to New London, took the exit for Connecticut 32. AJ circled back over the interstate and worked his way onto Montauk Avenue. A few minutes later, he drove up the loop to the hospital entrance.

"I'll help Melody," Claire said, getting out.

"Okay. I'll park the car and then meet you inside." AJ watched Melody and Claire start for the door. He drove down the hill, found a spot in a lower area, then hiked back up. Inside, he found Claire and Melody in a waiting room. Melody was already in a wheelchair, a plastic band on her wrist.

She gave him a weak smile. "Thanks for driving, AJ."

"Of course."

An orderly came around the corner. "Here's my girl," he said, smiling at Melody as if they were long-lost friends. He took the handles of the chair and began to push. "We're going to the fourth floor. So you get a bit of a ride."

Claire and AJ hung back.

"You can come along," the orderly said. "There's a little waiting room up there."

They all moved into the elevator, Claire taking up position next to Melody, touching her hand.

"We'll get you something else instead of that wastebasket," the orderly said.

Melody nodded.

They all watched the lights marking the floors. The bell chimed and the doors opened. On the wall ahead of them was a big arrow and the word *Maternity*.

"Here we are," the orderly said, heading out.

AJ hesitated. Claire tugged on his hand and they followed the wheelchair. They passed a small lounge, and the orderly tipped his head toward it.

"That's your home for now. Once we get your friend settled, someone will come for you. Okay?"

Melody waved and they were off down the hall.

"Maternity?" AJ said.

Claire took a seat. "That's why we had to come here instead of Westerly, since they closed the unit there. I'm sorry I couldn't tell you what was going on. Melody was determined to talk to Jack first."

"What is going on?"

"Well, she's pregnant."

"Yeah. I kind of guessed that."

"She's had menstrual problems most of her life, and been on and off different birth control pills. Her doctor just started her on a new pill a couple of months ago. I guess she got pregnant anyway."

"That can happen?"

"I've heard of it, but never known anyone it actually happened to."

"So this is just morning sickness? I mean, really bad morning sickness?"

"I don't know. She's not cramping or spotting, just viciously sick. She hasn't been able to keep anything down since yesterday. I guess the doctor is worried that she's getting dehydrated."

"How did she figure out that she was pregnant?"

"Something she read about the pills. That's why she called me this morning. She wanted me to bring a test kit."

"Jack still doesn't know?"

"No. Melody called him and told him to meet us here. But she didn't say anything about being pregnant."

"Jesus, he must be freaking out."

"I guess she made it clear that she wasn't in any danger."

"Is that true?"

"I hope so."

"I hate to ask, but is she happy about being pregnant?"

"Hard to tell. I think she's just shocked. Between her medical issues and relationship issues, I guess she just figured it would never happen."

"She must not know how Jack will take it."

"He is kind of old to be a first-time dad."

A nurse stuck her head into the room and said they could come to Melody's room. They found her in bed, hooked up to an IV.

"You look better already," Claire said.

"They gave me something for the nausea. It seems to be working."

"When will you see the doctor?"

"Apparently she's here, delivering a baby. So, as soon as that's done, I guess."

"Good."

"You look almost as tired as I feel," Melody said. "I'm sorry to put you through this. You, too, AJ. You guys should go. I'm in good hands. And Jack's on his way."

"We'll wait until he gets here," Claire said.

"Actually..." Melody smoothed her sheets around her belly. "I think it would be better if I'm alone when Jack gets here. I already feel funny that both of you know before he does. Visiting hours are over, anyway. The nurse is probably going to kick you out. She said she'd make an exception for Jack, but..."

Claire moved closer, touched the edge of the mattress. "You sure?"

"Yeah. Thanks. Keep the news under your hat, okay?"

"Of course," Claire said.

"If you need anything, just call," AJ said.

Claire gave Melody a peck on the cheek. Then she and AJ went back out the way they had come.

"Never a dull moment," AJ said, as they traversed the parking lot.

Claire took his hand. "At least this is something positive. Maybe things are turning around."

"That's a good thought. Let's hold onto that."

49

AJ woke up for good on the downstairs couch. He went into the kitchen, heated up a mug of coffee and sat at the little table. His laptop was there where he'd left it. While it started up, he brought the papers in from the porch and pored over them, jotting more notes in the margins. He stayed at it through a second cup of coffee, then the shower running upstairs.

Just before eight, the doorbell rang. AJ opened the door to see Jack Westbury, his shirt thoroughly wrinkled, strands of gray hair pointing up from the back of his head in an unmistakable cowlick, bags under his eyes. But when he smiled, he looked happy in a manic sort of way.

"Jack. Come in."

"I wasn't sure you'd be up."

"How's Melody?" AJ closed the door behind them.

"Much better." Jack glanced at the stairs. "Is Claire up?"

"I'll go get her." AJ climbed quickly, one hand on the wall as he rounded the turn.

She met him in the hall. "Did I hear the doorbell?"

"It's Jack."

"Oh. How's Melody?"

"Much better, he says."

Claire shot past AJ and went down. "Jack! Melody's doing okay?" She stopped with one hand on the bannister and got a good look at him. "How are *you* doing?"

Jack reached up with one hand and patted the unruly hair at the back of his head. It sprang up again. "I guess I'm a little... I don't know what I am. But yes, Melody is doing well. I just had to stop and thank you. I don't know what would have happened if you weren't there to talk some sense into her, Claire. The doctor said she was in real danger of severe dehydration."

"I'm glad I could help," Claire said. "Do you want some coffee or something to eat?"

"No, thanks. I've got to get home, shower and change. Then I'm going back to the hospital."

"How long will she have to stay?"

"They say she can probably leave after lunch."

"Maybe I should try to make it over there this morning."

"Melody thought you might say that. She said to wait and see if they let her out. She'll call you."

"Okay, great."

"I should go," Jack said.

"Make sure you call us if you need anything. I can bring you some food."

"Melody may be on a special diet," Jack said. "You'd better wait on that, too, until you talk to her."

"Okay, but you have to eat. You have to keep your strength up, too."

"I know." A big smile broke out across Jack's face. "I'm going to be a dad!" He took a step toward Claire.

Beaming, she put her arms around him. "Congratulations!"

"Thank you!" After letting Claire go, Jack gave AJ's hand a firm shake, then pulled him in for a quick slap between the shoulder blades. "Isn't it fantastic!" He stepped back, the smile holding on his face. Once he was out the door, he practically sprinted to his car.

AJ and Claire watched him drive away.

"I'm not sure, but I'm guessing he's okay with the pregnancy," AJ said.

"You think?"

50

She was out back, which was a good place to listen for Parker's car coming up the gravel road, because she could do something while she listened, so she didn't have to feel like she was just obsessing over him. Even though she was. She'd been thinking about him all night. Stuff that was unbelievable but had really happened, like sitting by the pool with him, his smile and his shoulders and his scar, and stuff that felt real even if it hadn't happened yet, like the first kiss.

Her dad was there reading the paper under the tree. He didn't know any of that.

She sat in a plastic chair with her feet on another one and put polish on her toenails. It was the polish she'd bought that Saturday when all the crazy stuff started – when she first saw the gray car and it followed her all the way to Taylor's house. She hadn't touched the little glass bottle since then, like it was cursed or something. Until today. After spending the afternoon with Parker, after swimming in his pool, after being alone with him in his bedroom, after holding his model heart, after sitting just inches from him in the car – after all of that, it seemed like all kinds of curses had been lifted.

She heard the pop of tires on gravel – a car coming up the hill. It slowed down as it got close. That had to be him. She dropped the nail brush into the bottle and jumped up. She ran around the side of the trailer.

Coming right at her was the gray car.

Maggie let out a shriek and ducked back behind the trailer.

Her dad tipped his newspaper down. "What are you doing?"

"Nothing. There was a bee."

"If you stay still they won't bother you." He raised the paper in front of his face again. Like, problem solved.

Maggie peered around the corner. The gray car should be past by now.

It wasn't going past. It was right out front, and it was pulling over next to her dad's car.

Maggie stayed where she was, practically hugging the corner of the trailer, like a kid who was really bad at hide-and-seek, the kid who was the first one to be found. She was shaking. But she was safe, right? Her dad was close by. Her mom was inside. Nothing bad could happen.

"Maggie!" Her mom was calling for her, from the kitchen.

Maggie stood there in the back yard by the corner, just trying to keep her knees from bending.

Her dad folded his paper down again. "Are you going to answer?" He waited a second. When Maggie didn't say anything, he yelled, "She's out back!"

The door opened and her mom stuck her head out. "Your friend is here. I'll send him around the side." She leaned a little further out, until she found Maggie. "He's cute."

"No, wait – " Maggie said.

But the door was already closed.

"Hey!"

Maggie started to move away, but it was too late. He'd already seen her. She stepped out into the side yard.

Parker was there holding her phone. "Here you go."

Maggie couldn't move. Like there were no muscles or joints in her body.

He came toward her. When she just stood there, he sort of shook the phone at her. "Are you going to take it?"

Maggie reached out. Her arm was stiff and slow, like it was someone else's arm stuck onto her body. "Thanks."

"I have a power cord that fit, so I tried charging it. Not sure how much that did. I think you need a new battery. Or a new phone." Parker looked at her. "Are you okay?"

"Yeah, I'm fine." She stared down at the phone. She could barely think. She couldn't see it now, but out front, parked right on the other side of the trailer, was the gray car. Parker was here and so was the gray car. What did it mean?

"I'd tell you to come meet Ash, but he's in a mood today. Some other time, I guess?"

Maggie didn't say anything. Her brain felt just as stiff as her body. Even her thoughts could barely move.

One word formed. Ash.

"All right. I have to get going, or I'll be late to work. See you." Parker went around toward the front, then yelled back to her. "I sent you a text. Check it out when you get the thing charged up."

Maggie knew that she should stay there, wait for the sound of the car driving away, but she couldn't stop herself. She had to look. Her heart was pounding. She went to the front corner, slowly leaned around. There it was, the gray car. The same one. And there he was, in the passenger seat – the guy from the dollar store, and from Route 1. The guy who had followed her to Taylor's house and Ms. Addison's.

Parker swung the car back to the right, and Maggie and the guy in the gray car were suddenly staring straight at each other, like the whole point of the maneuver was to put them face to face. Just like the first time, he gave her a tight, squinty smile. Like he knew her. Like he knew all about her. One thing was different though. Something about his eyes. They were light where they should be dark. Empty and cold. They were wolf's eyes.

51

Her mom was there at the back door. "What's the matter?"

"Nothing." Maggie waited for her to move.

"I thought you liked him."

Her mom was too skinny to really block the way, so Maggie shoved past. She ran to her room. She got into the bed and buried herself under the covers. Like that would protect her.

The guy in the gray car was Parker's stepbrother. Parker's wolf-obsessed stepbrother.

She'd been to his house, swam in his pool. Heard him shouting at Parker's mom, right on the other side of the door.

Parker's locked door, the little button pushed in.

Maggie held the pillow tight.

She'd been in his room. Wolf sounds. Wolf pictures on every wall. She'd held the lighter with the wolf's face.

He didn't just like wolves. He thought he was one.

Curled up under the covers, she couldn't breathe.

Now he'd been to her house. Whenever he wanted, he could come for her. In the middle of the night. When she was alone.

Unless he wanted the whole family.

Maggie hugged her pillow and tried to get one good breath into her lungs.

After a long time, she began to feel something – pressure, something hard, something digging into her leg. Eventually she realized that the thing was her phone. She pulled the cell from her pocket.

She had a text from Parker.

I had fun today. I knew you wouldn't get weird when you saw my scar. I think you have scars too. You shouldn't hide them. See you soon? Tomorrow? :)

Maggie read the words over and over again.

There was a knock on the door. "Are you okay?" Her mom.

"Yeah."

"Can I come in?"

Maggie climbed off the bed. She faced the window. "Okay."

The door opened. "Did something happen with that boy?"

"No." *That boy* was perfect. She'd met the perfect boy and his brother was...

"Well, if you want to talk about it, I'll listen."

Maggie stood there holding the phone and looking out the window.

Her mom waited. Finally she started to close the door.

"Mom?"

"Yeah?"

"Can I get some pepper spray?" She'd find the strongest kind, spray the whole can into those empty eyes.

Her mom stepped into the room. "Did that boy do something?"

"No. No. It's just with everything going on, I'm starting to get creeped out. It's stupid, I know. But I'd just feel safer."

"Oh, Maggie." Her mom took a breath. "I understand. Perfectly natural. But you don't have anything to worry about. Helena and Taylor got themselves mixed up in something. Who knows what. It doesn't have anything to do with you, or any of us."

Of course that's what her mother would think. How could Maggie Strang have anything to do with what happened to Taylor and Helena? It even seemed crazy to herself.

"But still," she said. "I just don't feel safe. My cell phone is dead half the time, and..."

Her mom held up her hands. "Yes. I know your phone is a problem. I'll talk to your dad about it. And the pepper spray, too, if it would make you feel safer. I have to go to the shop right now. Try not to worry."

Maggie heard the back door close, hard, like her mom was pissed off. Her mom and dad had some sort of argument in the back yard. Then the car started up and drove away.

The back door opened again, and then her dad was standing in the door to her room. "Mags?"

"Yeah?"

"You all right? You look pale."

"I'm all right."

Her dad stayed in the doorway. "What are your plans for today?"

Maggie shrugged.

"No homework? I guess it's winding down, since you're getting through."

"Yeah. I really don't have any."

"Why don't we go get you a new phone?"

"Are you kidding?"

"Nope."

"Okay, yeah. Now?"

Her dad laughed. "I have some things I have to take care of first. I was thinking this afternoon, closer to dinner time."

"Okay, great."

"And listen, Maggie, your mom is right. These murders...they've got everyone upset, but you don't have anything to worry about. They don't have anything to do with you. Still, the pepper spray isn't a bad idea, so we'll get that while we're out, too."

"Good."

Her dad still didn't leave.

"What?" Maggie said.

"Come here." Her dad went out into the hall.

She followed him into her parents' bedroom, where she never went. He pulled the mattress away from the headboard a little.

"Look down there." He held the covers back.

Maggie moved closer, leaned across the pillow. A little sling hung there. A holster. With a gun.

"Your mom wouldn't like you knowing about this, okay?"

"Is it loaded?"

Her dad nodded.

"I thought you said we were safe."

"This is basically your mom's. Just for general protection, with me being away so much. I think it's time you know about it. You know how to handle a gun. How to shoot. So, it's there. You can't tell any of your friends – not Olivia, not Ryan – about this. And not Parker, either. Okay?"

Maggie backed up. She knew how to shoot? She remembered that one time, back when her dad wasn't living with them. When he came to pick her up, he told her grandmother that they were spending the day at a farm. He didn't say that a big part of the day would be spent shooting cans and bottles off a stone wall. Her dad's friends were there with kids, but she was the youngest and the only girl. And the only one using a pistol. Did her dad really think sticking a gun in her hand years ago counted as some kind of self-defense training? When her grandmother found out, that night, she said only idiots fooled around with guns. Maybe she was right.

52

"I just can't wrap my head around it, Buck," Claire said. She was sitting at her desk, her phone and a manuscript in front of her. "A baby. Our friends are having a baby."

The greyhound, on the floor at Claire's feet, perked up his ears.

Claire patted his head. "Let's go for a walk around the yard. Maybe some fresh air will help me get my concentration back." She grabbed the phone.

The greyhound led the way downstairs. They had just stepped outside when there was the sound of a car turning in the lane. Claire reached for Buck's collar. They waited on the front step as the car raced out of the trees, then slid to a stop by the garage, leaving dust hanging in the damp air. Claire could make out the name of a florist painted on the side door, next to a bright red blossom.

The driver got out – a tall man in his twenties, wearing dark sunglasses. Without yet acknowledging Claire, as if he were all alone in this secluded front yard, he reached into the back seat. When he turned around, he was holding a large bouquet of pink and blue flowers. For the first time, he looked at her. "Flowers for Claire Connor."

"That's me." Claire didn't move except to close her fingers tighter around the dog's collar.

When the man reached the bottom step, he said, "I can bring them inside."

"That's okay." Claire let go of the dog and went down one step. She slid her phone into a pocket, then reached for the flowers with

318

both hands.

"They're heavy," the man said.

"It's fine."

"Okay, well, I guess you got them," the man said, as the weight passed to her. "Want me to open the door for you?"

"No, that's okay. Thank you."

"All right. Enjoy."

Buck remained in place at the top of the stairs, his head tilted, curious.

Claire went toward the house, then stopped. "If you wait a sec, I'll get your tip."

But the man was already on the move back to the car, and he kept moving, as if he hadn't heard. "You have a good day," he said, when his hand was on the car door. "And congratulations!"

Claire looked at the pink and blue flowers, understood the man's mistake. "No, it's – "

The delivery man was in the car, with the door closed.

Claire stood there, holding the flowers, watching the car speed away. She exhaled heavily. "You know, Buck, I have to stop being such a scardy cat."

Cradling the vase, Claire backed into the house. She had just set the flowers on the kitchen table when her phone rang. Melody's face was on the screen.

"Hey!" Claire said. "How are you?"

"So much better. I had some real food for lunch and I feel pretty good."

"That's great. You had me worried. So, everything is fine?"

"The doctor says I'm good, the baby's good, so, yeah. Jack, too. Physically, emotionally. We're shocked, but happy. Hey, did you get anything..."

"Oh, yes! The flowers! They're right in front of me." Claire plucked the card from the blossoms and read the note. "They're beautiful. Jack is so thoughtful."

"Yes, he is. I got some, too. Pink and blue. I guess I'll be seeing a lot of those colors."

"I guess you will," Claire said.

"Did you have the creepy delivery guy? With the freaky eyes?"

"Freaky eyes? I don't know. He was wearing sunglasses, I think."

"Okay. My guy had yellow eyes. You know, some kind of special contacts. It was really weird. Hey, here's Jack."

There was the sound of a kiss.

"I should go, Claire. Talk to you later."

"Tell Jack I love my flowers. Let me know when you're home. And please, call me if you guys need anything."

"Okay, thanks. Bye."

Claire went to the front hall, closed the door and turned the lock. The greyhound followed her back to the kitchen. After pouring some dog food into the big silver bowl, Claire retrieved a bag of chips from the cupboard. With that and a glass of iced tea, she sat down at the table. AJ's computer was there, along with some papers. Claire slid all of that aside, misjudged, and sent a couple of sheets to the floor.

"Damn."

She bent down, closed her fingers on the papers, and found herself staring into a pair of glowing yellow eyes.

***

Wheeler and Detective Thompson came through the door of the Stonington precinct together, but immediately veered off in separate directions. Thompson headed toward the desk he had commandeered. Wheeler went toward the coffee pot. "You want a cup, Detective?"

"Thanks, I'll wait until I can get the real stuff."

"Of course you will," Wheeler said under his breath. He had just picked up the coffee pot when a woman wearing a blue blazer approached him.

"Hey, Jen," Wheeler said. "Something going on?"

"AJ's girlfriend called a little while ago. She left a message for him. When I saw you, I thought..."

"Thought what?"

"She said she had some important information. That's all she would say, except that she had to talk to AJ. She said she couldn't get him on his cell. I guess because he's busy with an accident."

"Hmmm."

"When she said she had *information*, right away I wondered if it wasn't personal. To me, if it's personal, you say *news*. So, I was thinking it might be about police business, about a case. The Fraser case, since that's the one AJ was involved with. And since he's not on that case anymore, and, anyway, he's tied up with that accident..."

When I saw you, I thought I should tell you."

"You may be onto something," Wheeler said. "What accident?"

"By the off-ramp for 95. Taugwonk Road."

"Bad?"

"I guess one woman was hurt. Drunk drivers, apparently. Two of them."

"Sounds like a circus."

"Yeah. I was about to call AJ, anyway, when I got word that he had just called Dee for assistance, so..."

"Right," Wheeler said. "I'm glad you talked to me. I'll take it from here." He skipped the coffee and went back to his desk.

Thompson noticed Wheeler's empty hands. "I talk you out of the cheap stuff?"

Wheeler just shook his head.

"Well, I think we're done for the day. Why don't we grab a cup at that donut place, what is it, Happy Donuts?"

"Thanks. I'll take a rain check."

"Okay." Thompson put some papers into a briefcase. "See you tomorrow, then. We can make it a little later start. Say, eight-thirty." Thompson snapped the latches on his briefcase and went out the door.

"Yeah, sure," Wheeler said to himself, "Sunday's the perfect day to spin our wheels." He tried AJ's cell, got his voicemail. "Hey, it's Sam," he said. "I'm headed over to talk to Claire. Jen here seems to think you have her working on the Fraser case. We can't have that. I mean, we might actually get somewhere."

***

Claire was at the kitchen table, AJ's papers in front of her, when she heard a car in the driveway. "Hey, Buck, is that AJ? Let's go see." She stood up.

The grayhound was sitting alertly by the back door. He didn't even turn around.

"You must really want that squirrel." Claire hurried through the house and looked out a front window. Instead of AJ's Jeep, she saw a plain sedan, like the ones the SPD used, coming to a stop in the driveway. "Oh, God, now what?"

She hung by the door as Wheeler came across the yard. "Sam? Is something wrong? Is AJ all right?"

"He's fine. He's tied up with an accident. Can I come in for a minute?"

"Oh. Yeah, sure." She let him into the hall.

"I understand you left a message for AJ at the station, and that it might have something to do with the Fraser case."

Claire frowned. "I didn't say anything about the Fraser case."

"The woman who took your call did some reading between the lines. Was she wrong?"

Claire held her breath for a second. "No. I mean, I don't know. Should I have called you? I know AJ's not on the case anymore. I called him because of some pictures he has here."

"Pictures?"

"I'll show you." She led Wheeler to the kitchen. Buck was still there at the back door. Claire went to the table and pointed at the images printed from the Web site. Two left eyes, both a glaring yellow.

"The contacts," Wheeler said. "I thought he wasn't getting anywhere with this."

"All I know is, today, Jack Westbury sent flowers to me and Melody Johnson. When I talked to Melody, she asked if the creepy delivery guy had brought my flowers. She said he had yellow eyes. Then I saw this printout, and..."

Wheeler gestured toward the bouquet near the window. "The man who brought those, did he have yellow eyes?"

"I don't know. He was wearing dark sunglasses."

"But Melody said the man who delivered her flowers had yellow eyes?"

"Yes."

Wheeler took out his cell phone, punched a number. "Hey, Dee, it's Sam. I need you to get AJ on the radio. Tell him to call me ASAP."

53

"Guess what I'm holding in my hand," she said.

"I don't know, what?" Olivia said.

"I'll give you a hint. I'm using it to make this call."

"A new phone? You got a new phone?"

"A new iPhone."

"You're kidding."

"No, I'm not." Maggie dragged the lawn chair further out from under the tree, trying to catch whatever sun was left. "My dad took me to the store today and basically let me just pick out what I wanted. He's paying the monthly thing, too."

"Wow. How did that happen? I mean, not to knock your dad but – "

"No, I know."

"Jeez."

"Yeah." The phone beeped in Maggie's ear. "Wait – I just got a text." She pulled the phone away and looked at the screen. The text was from Parker. He wanted to take her to a movie, tonight – a special midnight show. He could get the car. Which meant *the gray car. She would have to ride in the gray car.* That would be way beyond weird. She wondered if she could even do it. Then she thought, it would almost be a good thing – if she and Parker were using the gray car, then Ash couldn't have it, couldn't be out doing God knows what.

She typed a reply. *Sounds cool can you come over early?*

He answered right away. *After work mom wants me and ash to stop in at the party. Maybe 11?*

ok

"Sorry," Maggie said into the phone. "I'm back."

"So who's already texting you on your new phone? Is it that boy you told me about?"

"Parker. Yeah. He wants to take me to a movie tonight." Maggie felt such a rush of energy as she said those words that she had to stand up.

"Everything's going right for you, isn't it? New phone, new boyfriend..."

Maggie laughed. It was so true.

Then there was the sound of a car out front, slowing down, the tires crunching, and for one weird dark second, everything changed. It couldn't be Parker. Maybe it was Ash, coming for her.

Maggie stepped behind the tree. Her hand dropped from her ear. The new phone didn't help her. She imagined it sealed up in some kind of evidence bag, the cop and Detective Wheeler looking at it through the plastic, shaking their heads.

Wait. Wait. Her dad was inside. Ash would never come in broad daylight when her dad was here. She was safe.

The whole evening – she'd be especially safe. Her parents would be here, Ash would be tied up with the birthday party and then she'd be with Parker. In the gray car. It was like the perfect plan.

Maggie came out from behind the tree.

"Maggie! I want to see your new phone!" Her mom opened the back door.

"Sorry, Olivia, I have to go. Talk to you soon, okay?"

"You have no excuse now, so you better call. I want to hear all about this boy."

"You will." Maggie ended the call. She did a little demo for her mom, who oohed and aahed at even the simplest thing.

Then her dad joined them outside. "Did you tell her yet, Cary?"

"Tell me what?" Maggie said.

"You know Gale," her mom said, "the woman who owns the shop?"

"Yeah."

"She has these contests for top producer – the stylist who brings in the most to the shop. And it turns out that, for the spring, that was me."

"That's great, Mom," Maggie said. "So is there a prize?"

"There is. Gale and her husband have that big boat – I pointed it out once when we were crossing the drawbridge. She's taking us out on a sort of booze cruise."

"You want me to go on a booze cruise?"

Her dad laughed. "No. That's the only thing. We can't bring you – you're underage. We'd be leaving you alone, and it could be a late night. Could you do that – stay on your own?"

"When?"

"Tonight," her mom said.

"You'd be all right," her dad said. "You have a phone that works now."

He didn't say *and the pepper spray, and the gun.* Instead he gave her a long look.

This was her opportunity, right now. She could tell them about Ash. But what a mess that would be. Her dad would freak, and her mom might call the police, which would make her dad freak even more. And forget about Parker. Her first chance to have a real boyfriend would be over before the second date. "Sure," she said. "I'm fine." She even felt like she meant it.

"It's kind of last minute," her mom said. "I mean, Gale told us about the contest a long time ago, but she just announced the winner today. I never said anything because I never thought it would be me. Never in a million years. I've never won anything before."

Her dad put an arm around her mom. "Our luck is definitely changing."

"Well, go ahead," her mom said. "Your turn."

"Okay." Her dad slouched back against the tree, a sort of cocky glad look on his face. "I'm coming off the road, Mags."

"What? What happened?"

"I got the job at the new commercial driving school. I'll be working out of Westerly."

"You mean, like, all the time?"

"That's right. I'll be home every night. And every weekend. So, tonight...it's going to be the last night I'm not around for a long time."

Maggie ran over and hugged him. He wasn't really ready for it and it took a minute for him to get his arms around her. He didn't know how good that sounded, to have him nearby every day. He didn't know what a big problem that solved. He didn't know about Ash.

Maggie let go.

"You'll get sick of seeing me so much." Her dad's smile faded and some of the cockiness, too. "I wish I could have done this sooner. I know it was hard on you and your mom, me being away sometimes two, three weeks at a time. But better late than never, right?"

"Yeah, no, that's really great, Dad."

Now her mom gave her dad a hug. They stood there under the shade tree like they were the world's happiest couple.

Things really *were* going good, Maggie thought. She couldn't screw it up. She definitely couldn't tell her parents about Ash. She couldn't tell anyone.

54

"So how do you want to handle it?" AJ said. He and Wheeler were sitting at the kitchen table. Claire leaned against the counter.

"We work it right now, on our own." Wheeler picked up the printout of the yellow contact lenses and studied it for the hundredth time. "I don't want to try to explain to Thompson how we know about the yellow eyes, do you?"

"No." AJ checked the card that had come with the flowers. "Let me see if I can catch the florist before they close for the night."

While AJ punched the numbers, Buck, who had been sitting at AJ's feet, jumped up and went to the back door. After retreating a few steps, he began to bark.

"There he goes again," Claire said. "He's been like this all afternoon. Buck!"

AJ put the phone down. "No answer. My mom is friends with the owner. Maybe I can get a home number from her."

Buck barked at the door again.

"You get that number. I'll take Buck outside," Wheeler said. "If you can give me a leash."

"There's one hanging in the porch," Claire said.

Buck kept on barking as he tugged Wheeler across the porch and then out toward the trees.

Claire stood up. "Must be a squirrel, though I don't see anything."

AJ joined her at the door while he talked to his mom. When he had ended the call, he followed Wheeler into the back yard. Buck was nosing around quietly in the grass.

"Apparently Mrs. Williams, the florist, screens her calls," AJ said. "She only answers if she recognizes the number. So, Mom's calling ahead. I'll give her another minute."

"Whatever was bothering Buck seems to be gone," Wheeler said.

AJ scanned the woods without saying anything.

"While we're waiting, why don't you call Melody, see what she can tell us about the delivery guy?"

"Okay. Let me get her number." AJ went inside. When Claire wasn't in the kitchen, he checked an address book on the counter.

Jack answered. He and AJ spoke for a few minutes. Then, with Melody on speaker, AJ left the house and joined Wheeler in the yard again. They listened as Melody described the delivery man. "His eyes were really weird – bright yellow. Some kind of special costume contact lenses, I guess? He looked right at me, like he wanted to be sure that I saw." In response to AJ's questions, she filled out the man's appearance – twenties, five nine or ten, average weight, brown hair, cut short.

AJ dropped his phone back into his pocket. "This guy's the most average man in the world."

"Except for the eyes." Wheeler looked at AJ for a second without saying anything. "This sure looks like our man, AJ. Maybe you were right with the psycho killer thing. Maybe he's picking victims from people he delivered flowers to."

"We don't know anything about flowers being delivered to Taylor or – "

"You're right. Just a thought."

They both watched Buck sniff the grass.

"I don't mean to pry, AJ, but I couldn't help noticing the pink and blue colors."

"What?"

"The flower arrangement in the kitchen? The baby colors? Is there something you're not telling me?"

AJ smiled. "Melody is pregnant. She had some really bad morning sickness, bad enough to put her in the hospital. Claire and I helped her out. Jack sent the flowers as a thank you."

"Oh." Wheeler seemed to think about all of that. "How old is Jack Westbury?"

Just then, Claire came out the back door, looking worried. "Jack booked us rooms at the Cove House. Is that necessary?"

Wheeler's eyebrows went up. "Really?"

"I wouldn't say it's necessary," AJ said, "but..."

"Why turn down a night at the Cove House," Wheeler said. "Have you seen it?"

AJ pulled his phone out of his pocket. "Let me show you."

Claire came up beside him as AJ pecked out letters into a search bar. They both watched the glowing screen. Then Claire yanked the phone from his hands.

"Haunted inns of New England?" she read. "You've got to be kidding me."

***

By the time AJ got through to the florist, Claire was already on her way to the Cove House with Melody and Jack. Buck was pressing his nose to the back door again. AJ said that he needed to ask about some deliveries that had been made that day.

"Certainly. Anything I can do to help."

"One delivery was to Melody Johnson at Lawrence Memorial. The other one was to Claire Connor, here in Stonington. We need to know who made the deliveries."

"I let Ramone divide those up. I think he made the local delivery, and Ash did the one at Lawrence Memorial. All of my records are at the shop, so I'd have to check them to be sure."

"Can you check, Mrs. Williams? This is important. We'll need the full names and home addresses for those two employees."

"Oh, well, it's Ramone Smith and Ash Beaudette."

"How to you spell Beaudette?"

She told him. "For the addresses, I'll need to go to the store. I can be there in ten minutes."

"Thanks. Could you call me at this number as soon as you're there?"

"Absolutely."

AJ ended the call, then caught Wheeler up. "Can you watch my cell for the return call from the florist?" he said. "I'm going to see how Claire's doing. I'll use the house phone."

"Sounds like a plan."

AJ was still talking with Claire when Wheeler answered the cell phone. He sat at the kitchen table, writing in his notepad, while AJ paced in another room. AJ came back into the kitchen.

"Got both addresses," Wheeler said. "How are things at the Cove House?"

"Just fine. Amazing view, I guess. Jack ordered champagne from room service. She said they might do some ghost hunting later."

Wheeler shook his head. "You people and your ghosts."

"You sure you mean that? We're about to follow a lead that – "

"I know, I know. I'm not in a position to say anything." Wheeler stood up. "Let's start with Ramone. I want to see what he can tell us about Yellow Eyes."

55

AJ pulled up to the curb.

"Lights are on," Wheeler said. "That's a good sign."

They climbed a short set of stairs and rang the bell. A twenty-something man with a patchy, two-day beard and thick-framed glasses opened the door.

"Stonington Police," Wheeler said, showing his badge. "We're looking for Ramone Smith."

"Come in." The man retreated into the hallway. "Ramone! They're here!"

Another man, blonde, thin, in jeans and a T-shirt, appeared behind him. "Hello?"

"Ramone Smith?"

"Yeah. I know I don't look like a Ramone. My mom was really into the Ramones – the band."

"I'm Detective Wheeler and this is Officer Bugbee."

Ramone came forward, hands in his pockets. "Joyce called us, said to hang around. I mean, we *were* going out." He glanced back down the hallway.

The man who had answered the door held up his phone. "I'll just take a walk. Call me."

Ramone gave him a quick wave. There was the sound of a back door opening and closing.

Wheeler took out his notepad. "Tell us what you know about Ash Beaudette."

"This is about Ash? Well, he hasn't worked with us very long, so I don't know much. Mostly, he's quiet, but once in a while, he can be a little manic."

"How do you mean?"

"Well, like, at first, he was so quiet and serious on deliveries, people didn't know what to make of him. I told him to be more friendly, or at least smile a little. But then a couple days later – Tuesday – we were taking flowers to a funeral home, and he was totally wired, laughing, joking. I had to tell him, 'Ash, what I said before, about smiling and stuff – today is not the day.'"

"Do you know why he was behaving like that?"

"Yeah. When he didn't calm down, after I talked to him, I finally said, 'What's with you?' He said he was all charged up because of some girl he met. He said something about her being a mermaid."

"A mermaid?"

Ramone scratched his head. "No, not a mermaid. The things that call you into the rocks. A siren. Right?"

Wheeler's pencil moved across the pad. "Did he mention her name? This siren?"

"Not that day. He did today, though, 'cause he saw her again. I'm trying to remember the name. It was something weird."

"Weird?"

"Yeah. Like, made-up."

Wheeler and AJ gave him a minute, but Ramone finally just shrugged.

"So he saw her today," Wheeler said. "Tell me about that."

"There isn't much to tell. It was a tense day. Joyce was freaking out because we already had a lot of orders to do, then this rich guy called and wanted his orders done like yesterday. On top of that, Ash was late. Just a few minutes, but he had Joyce thinking he was going to be a no-show, which made her even more stressed. When he came in, he said he'd had to stop at his girl's house, then drop his stepbrother at work. After that he was kind of quiet, probably because he thought Joyce would be mad at him for being late. She wasn't, though. She was just glad he showed up."

"If you think back on what he said, about stopping at the girl's house – did he say anything that would indicate where she lives?"

Ramone squinted, thinking. "No. He didn't say anything about that."

"Do you know anything else about this girl?" AJ said.

"Sorry, no. I don't think he ever said anything else about her."

"He didn't mention where he met her, what she looks like?"

"No."

"I understand you and Ash both made deliveries today?" Wheeler said.

"Yeah, we each took one of the orders for that rich guy."

"How did you divide them up?"

"Joyce said it was my call. I did the local deliveries and Ash did the hospital in New London."

Wheeler made a note.

"What color eyes does Ash have?" AJ said.

"What? Blue, I think. That's not the kind of thing I notice on a guy."

"Have you ever seen him wear colored contact lenses?"

"Like I said, I'm not sure I would have noticed."

"I'm talking about really obvious lenses. Novelty lenses, the kind that give you a very different look."

"You mean like the Halloween type?"

"Yes."

"No, definitely not. Joyce would never put up with that. Not if you're dealing with customers."

"Has Ash said anything about his family?" Wheeler said.

"Not really. Like I said, most of the time he's quiet. He only mentioned the stepbrother this morning. And his stepfather – he called him the commander once. I don't think he was thrilled with either one."

"The stepbrother – can you tell me anything about him?"

"Just that Ash dropped him off at work. I don't know where."

"You know his name?"

"I don't think Ash ever said."

"How about his mother?"

"I don't remember him saying anything about her."

"Is there anything he said or did that sticks in your mind?" Wheeler said.

"Not really. Sorry."

Wheeler handed Ramone a card. "If you remember that girlfriend's name, or anything else, give one of us a call. Don't call the station – call us directly. AJ, give him a card."

AJ passed one to Ramone, who seemed confused by the

handwritten number.

"That's my cell," AJ said.

"Officer Bugbee is the night owl," Wheeler said. "So, if it's late, why don't you try him first."

"I will."

"We'll let ourselves out." Wheeler turned toward the door.

When they were back in the patrol car, Wheeler said, "Anything strike you?"

"Ash was manic on Tuesday. That would have been just a few hours after Helena was killed."

"Right. Did you put Ash's address in the GPS?"

"Yeah," AJ said. "It's Saturday night – what are the chances he'll be home with his family?"

"Well, if he really is our guy, he's probably not going to be someone with a big social life."

"He says he has a girlfriend."

"Yeah, the siren. Let's hope he's not out right now answering her song."

56

After her parents left, Maggie locked all the doors and windows. She watched some TV and played with her phone. She took a bunch of dumb pictures of herself and put them online. Finally, she couldn't wait any longer. She texted Parker – asked him how the party was going.

His answer came back right away. *Good. Maybe I can leave a little early.*

She typed *Cool let me know when your on the way here!* She watched her phone, waiting to see the little dots that meant he was typing. No dots.

She couldn't sit still. There was too much to think about. The date with Parker. The gray car, in her yard. Ash knowing where she lived.

While she was pacing back and forth, she started to notice how big the window was in the living room. With it dark outside and the lights on, she might as well be walking around in some kind of display case. She closed the curtains.

In the kitchen, she opened the fridge. She could drink one of her dad's beers – that might help. Then she'd have to pee during the movie, though. Her dad always said you don't buy beer, you rent it – a stupid joke he told when he'd rented too many.

She wished he was home right now, making that joke. She wished he was in the living room, hogging the television, cracking open his third or fourth beer, not just making that joke, but thinking it was actually funny. She checked her phone again for Parker's reply. Nothing. It was going to be a long evening.

57

The GPS took them onto an old road, crumbling at the shoulders, squeezed by vegetation on either side.

AJ stared at the little glowing map. "This can't be it."

Wheeler tapped the device. "It's a new unit. It should be right."

A woman's voice came from the tiny speaker. "Arriving at destination."

"Yeah?" AJ peered ahead, seeing nothing.

He slowed as the trees opened up on the left, revealing a house. Charred clapboard, burned long ago. Plywood over the windows.

"You've got to be kidding." Wheeler swiveled in his seat, looking for an alternative.

AJ pointed across the dash. "You can still see a number on the mailbox. That's it. No name, though."

They sat there, looking at the wreck of a house – dark, and fading willingly into the darkness.

"All right. Let's at least take a look."

AJ turned into a driveway that was half overgrown. Weeds scraped against the bottom of the car. They got out and walked up to the front door, tried it. Locked.

AJ found a break in the wood on a side window, aimed his light inside. "No sign that anyone's been here for a while."

"Nope. So he used a burned-out house for an address. He definitely has a thing for fire."

"Right," AJ said. "He doesn't live here now, but maybe he used to live here. Or, he lives near here?"

Wheeler pointed across the road at the thick foliage, vines draped across shrubs. "Yeah? Where?"

They went back to the car. As Wheeler went around to the passenger side, AJ raised a hand to stop him. "You hear that?"

"What am I listening for?"

"Music, voices."

They stood flanking the car. Finally, as if a door had just opened somewhere, there was a sudden surge of sound – a mix of crowd noise and guitar.

"Sounds like a party," AJ said, pointing further down the road. "That way."

"It does."

"Want to see what's over there?"

"Let's go."

They got into the car. AJ steered back onto the pavement. When they rounded a bend in the road, there were a few small houses on either side, windows glowing. Just ahead the road met a curbed boulevard that led into a upscale development.

"Huh," Wheeler said.

AJ stopped at the intersection. "There's the party."

Diagonally across the street was an A-frame, its yard well lit front and back, cars filling the driveway and crowding the street. As AJ and Wheeler watched, another car drove past and pulled into a spot along the curb. A nicely dressed couple in their forties got out.

"Okay," Wheeler said. "Think that's the kind of party our guy would be invited to?"

"I don't know. But maybe this is his neighborhood."

"Let's take a drive around, look for a Beaudette."

AJ navigated a big loop. The houses were of all types, on large lots, landscaped, tended to. Spurs stretched off of the loop. AJ took each one, in turn. He drove slowly. Each time the headlights found a mailbox, AJ and Wheeler read the name there. No Beaudette. They ended up back at the intersection, near the party.

"I know someone who lives over this way somewhere," AJ said. "A kid who works at the market. His family was having a party, sometime this weekend – a birthday party for his dad." AJ stopped in front of an A-frame, found the name in gold letters on the mailbox. *Stevens*. "I think that's him. Parker Stevens."

"How about that," Wheeler said. "Small world."

"Yep. According to Beth, he's dating Maggie Strang."

"Our Maggie? *Really* small world."

"Silent Maggie," AJ said.

"What?"

AJ told Wheeler what Beth had said, about the nickname the counselors had given Maggie during summer camp. About her seeming like she'd been through something bad, and how she was a little better, now.

"Silent Maggie," Wheeler said, looking across the road at the lights.

"Parker's a good kid," AJ said. "But dating him right now might not be the best thing."

"Why?"

"If this really is Ash Beaudette's neighborhood..."

"You're thinking if she's over here visiting her boyfriend and runs into him..."

"Yeah," AJ said. "I don't want her catching Beaudette's eye. His goddamn yellow wolf eye."

58

She found the app that lets you play with the photos, tried it out on one of her face, squished her cheeks and made her eyes pop out. Her phone beeped. A text.

Will do.

That was Parker, finally, saying he'd let her know when he was on the way. Which, if he left the party early, could be soon. She should start getting ready. She was so ready to get ready.

She went to her closet, flipped through the hangers, already feeling better, more relaxed. In fact, the whole time she picked out and tried on outfits, and brushed her hair, and did her make-up, she was thinking just about Parker and what it would be like tonight. What they would talk about. When they would kiss for the first time. With all of that going through her head, she didn't think about Ash, hardly at all.

59

After a careful search for any houses that they'd missed, any side street or hidden part of the development, they circled back to the A-frame again. AJ stopped just past it. From somewhere in the well-lit yard, mixing with the music, there was an occasional splash.

"Swimming pool," Wheeler said, turning around in his seat. "Just about warm enough to use it, too."

AJ faced ahead. "Well, we've gotten exactly nowhere."

"Yeah." Wheeler faced front again.

"What do you want to do, Sam?"

"Let's go back to the road that Ash gave as his address. There were a few houses on this end. We'll check the names, knock on doors. Maybe one of the neighbors there can tell us something."

"Okay." AJ swung the car around and they drove past the party one more time.

***

"Magda!"

Ramone's voice cut through the raucous conversation of six people crowding around a table in a cramped kitchen. A ukelele that one man had been strumming fell silent.

"Jesus," the guy with the ukelele said. "What was that, Ramone?"

"Is it like sudden onset Tourette's?" a young woman suggested. She had hair the color of strawberry licorice.

Ramone was on his feet. "Magda is the name of the girl – I was

340

trying to remember it for the cops. It just came to me. I have to call them."

"Oh, shit." Another partier looked at Ramone with bleary eyes, a joint glowing in his hand. He was the same guy who earlier that night, at Ramone's apartment, had opened the door for AJ and Wheeler. "You can't call them. You're stoned."

Ramone was searching his pockets. "They gave me those cards. What did I do with them?"

"Can't you just call the police station?" the red-haired woman said.

"I was supposed to call them – those cops. They gave me their cards."

"You changed your pants," the man with the joint said. "Before we came over here, you changed your pants. The cards are probably in your other pants."

"Oh, shit. Can somebody give me a ride home?"

"I'm stoned *and* drunk," the man with the joint said, sounding it. "I'm not driving anywhere."

The others all claimed, convincingly, that they were in the same state.

"This girl, she could be in danger," Ramone said.

"Really," the man with the ukelele said. "Did they say she was in danger?"

"They said if I thought of anything, I should call right away. They kept trying to get me to remember the girl's name."

"The cops are smart," ukelele man said, strumming the strings again. "They'll figure it out without you."

"Screw you guys," Ramone said. "I'll walk."

A few members of the group yelled after him, but no one got up to stop him as he went out the door.

60

She went through three completely different outfits but still was ready by ten forty-five. She spent the next fifteen minutes mostly just checking the time, on the wall clock and on her phone and on the microwave. They each said something different, which made it seem more reasonable to keep checking all of them.

To look for his car, she had to go to the window and hold the curtains open a little with her hand. She did that about a thousand times. Every time, for a second, she held her breath.

She kept checking her phone for a text and kept seeing his last one, *Will do.*

Will do Will do Will do.

Partly to make sure that texting was still working she texted Olivia.

Waiting for parker wish he would let me know when he's coming

Which immediately made her feel better. That was a cool problem to have.

Olivia's text came back right away. *He better not be late!* They texted back and forth for a while. When Olivia texted *He's being a pain* Maggie texted back *I'm not going to complain at least I have a boyfriend.*

Olivia didn't respond to that. Maggie realized it might have sounded like *at least I have a boyfriend and you don't.* Which wasn't what she meant. But it was too hard to fix that. She tried texting Olivia again but got just silence.

She texted Parker a few times. Nothing from him, either.

It was already after eleven. To make the midnight movie he'd have to pick her up soon. Any minute.

Pacing didn't really help anymore. There was too much energy shooting through her body. She really needed to be full out running. Sprinting from room to room.

Now when she looked at the screen in her hand she sometimes wanted to throw the thing. Finally she put it down on the counter, just to keep herself from breaking it. She thought having a new phone would make everything better. But it was only making things worse.

61

After leaving the last of the square little houses, AJ and Wheeler walked back to their car.

"Well, another dead end," Wheeler said.

In the distance, there was the wail of a siren.

"That's coming this way," AJ said.

"Yeah." Wheeler got in.

The siren got louder.

"It's right behind us," AJ said. "In that development."

"Let's check it out."

AJ pulled into the road and headed back the way they had come.

An ambulance was backed up to the A-frame, a Groton P.D. car next to it. The party had spilled out into the front yard, only it wasn't a party anymore, it was a collection of stunned witnesses.

AJ found a spot on the shoulder. He and Wheeler walked to the edge of the scene and AJ approached a man standing by himself. "I'm Officer AJ Bugbee of the Stonington Police," AJ said.

"Stonington?" The man had short-cropped hair and eyes that seemed accustomed to a stern look.

"Yeah, I just happened to be in the area. Can you tell me what's happening?"

"The Stevens's son, Parker, is in the ambulance. He has some kind of heart condition."

The ambulance was moving. The crowd pulled back, letting it pass. It reached the pavement and raced away. Close to the garage, a man climbed in behind the wheel of a gray sedan. With the Groton cop directing, another car made room for him to swerve across the grass. Then he sped off down the street.

The man next to AJ said, "That was Parker's brother. If he drives like that, he's going to beat everyone to the hospital."

"Were the parents in the ambulance?" AJ said.

"His dad was. His mom drove herself."

"Come on," Wheeler said, putting his hand on AJ's shoulder. "We're not needed here."

AJ followed him back to the car. "I didn't know Parker had a heart condition. I hope he's okay."

"That's got to be the worst," Wheeler said. "Having a kid with a serious illness like that."

"Yeah. There's probably only one thing worse – having your child murdered."

Wheeler ran a hand across his face. "Let's head back. We had our shot. It's time to call Thompson."

***

Ramone touched one pocket then another. "Shit."

He tried the door again, then moved to a window. He looked up at it, pushed clumsily at the lower frame, which he could barely reach. It didn't budge. "Shit!" He tried another window. Same result. He smacked the glass. He stared at the pane for a second, as if he expected it to shatter. Then he dug out his phone.

A lit window on the second floor slid open. "Ramone, what are you doing?" A young woman leaned out.

"I'm locked out."

"That sucks."

"And I need to make a phone call. It's important."

"Your phone is in your hand."

"The number I need is inside."

"Oh, what a pain. I'll come down."

A second later, she came around the corner. "I might be able to get you in." She held up a plastic gift card.

"You know how to do that?"

"Maybe." She went to the door and set to work.

***

"Can you believe Thompson?" Wheeler said, dropping his phone onto his lap. "He's been stuck to me like glue since he got here, and now when I want him, he's incommunicado."

AJ didn't respond. They were on a side road, heading toward 95.

"You still with me, Officer Bugbee?"

AJ slowed the car and swerved into a wide spot on the shoulder. "How would you describe Parker's brother?"

"Twenties, average height, medium build, short, brownish hair." Wheeler looked across the seat. "Hmmm... Just like our delivery guy."

"Parker's father is Navy. I'm guessing from the house and the neighborhood, he's an officer."

"The Commander." Wheeler's eyebrows went up. "Ramone said Ash used that nickname for his dad."

"It's a short walk from Parker's house to Ash's fake address."

"What about the names?" Wheeler said. "It wasn't Beaudette on the mailbox."

"It was Stevens. Maybe Beaudette is a fake name. Fake address, fake name. Or maybe the brothers' names are different. Maybe Parker and Ash are stepbrothers."

Wheeler squinted into the darkness. "Maybe we just got our first look at the killer."

62

At eleven thirty she went to the bathroom and peed and then when she was washing her hands she started crying. Was he going to stand her up? Pretend until the last minute that they were going to have a date, and then not show up? The crying gave her something to do – repairing her make-up. That's what she was doing when the phone rang. She bolted out of the bathroom and grabbed the phone off of the kitchen counter. She didn't recognize the number, but it had to be Parker, using someone else's phone.

"Hello?"

"Is this Maggie?" A woman's voice.

"Yes."

"This is Terry. Parker's stepmom."

"Hi." Maggie felt a fist close inside her chest.

"I'm afraid Parker's had a problem. A medical problem. He's going to be okay, but they want to keep him in the hospital overnight. Just to be on the safe side."

"Oh. You said he's going to be okay, though?" Maggie pictured the big scar, starting to come open. "Is it his heart?"

"Yes, actually. Just an arrhythmia. Do you know what that is? A little hiccup with the rhythm. They're watching it, that's all."

"Okay."

"He said to tell you he's sorry he couldn't take you to the movie."

"Can I come see him?"

"Well, it's too late for visitors tonight. Anyway, he'll be home tomorrow. Maybe you can see him then."

"Yeah." Maggie turned around. Through the living room curtains, there were headlights. "So he's alone there?"

"I'm sorry?"

"I mean, are you guys all with him at the hospital?"

"Oh. His dad and I are with him now. Parker is very used to hospitals, I'm afraid. Don't worry. He'll call you as soon as he can, I'm sure. They won't let him use his cell phone in his room, unfortunately. That's the only thing that's really bothering him about being there, I think."

"Okay. Thanks for calling me."

"Well, Parker was very insistent. Good night, Maggie."

"Good night." She ended the call and stood there with the new phone in her hand. The trailer was dead quiet.

Parker was in the hospital

Parker was not coming.

Her parents were out on a boat, getting drunk.

She was alone.

She knew why she had asked that question, even if Parker's mom didn't – *are you guys all with him at the hospital?* And what the answer meant – *his dad and I*. Just his parents. Not Ash.

Maggie went from window to window checking all of the locks again. She peeked out through the living room curtain. The big bay window at the end of the trailer down the street was dark and you couldn't see anything inside. Maggie flipped the wall switch. Then she went through all of the rooms, turning off the lights. She only left the one over the stove on, and the nightlight in the bathroom, and the ceiling light in the hall.

She went back to the living room and sat down on the couch, holding the phone in front of her with both hands. She texted Olivia. She could go to Olivia's house, maybe stay over or just hang out until her parents came home.

No response.

Maybe Olivia really had taken things the wrong way and gotten mad. Maggie punched Olivia's number. The call went straight to voicemail. Olivia's phone was off. Maggie swore and put the phone back in her pocket. She had to figure out what to do. She could get in the car and go somewhere. Some public place that would be open, like a restaurant. That would be creepy, though. The whole time she'd be afraid he'd followed her, that he'd be waiting for her when she finally stopped the car and got out. But if she just waited here...

He'd gone right into Taylor's house for her. The trailer would be even easier to get into.

The big difference was, Taylor had no idea what was coming. She'd probably heard the front door open and thought it was Ryan. Thought it was Ryan right up until it was too late. Or maybe she even let him in. He'd showed up at the door with some story and she'd fallen for it.

If Taylor had known, she would have had a plan. Just like she had a plan all those years ago, when she was still Tiffanee. Maggie closed her eyes for a second. "Tiffanee," she whispered to herself. It was more than just needing her help. Maggie had a strong rush of *missing* her, too. It had been a long time since she'd felt that. "Tiffanee. Tiffanee."

What Tiffanee had done that night in the trailer park hadn't made things easy. There had been lots of trouble afterward, for her and for Maggie. Fights with family and friends. Nervous talks with the police. Always ducking the neighbor, the guy who said he'd seen them outside the trailer that night. He'd even put up a stenciled sign in his yard that said *Tiffanee Burns*. You couldn't complain about it, because it was just her name.

But the thing you had to admit, even with all of that? Tiffanee's plan had worked. For her, at least. She ended up with everything she wanted. She got out of the trailer and put herself on the path to her shiny new life. And she got rid of a bad man, a man almost as bad as Ash.

When she opened her eyes again, Maggie didn't have a plan. But she knew that she needed two things. She got her new pepper spray and put that in her pocket. Then she went into her parents' room, to the head of the bed on her mother's side, moved the pillow. She reached down and felt for the gun. Her hand found the grip – two things that were made for each other. For a second she stood there like that, feeling that perfect fit. Then she slipped the gun out of the holster and straightened up. The gun was much lighter than she remembered. Not cold to the touch. Some kind of super strong plastic. Black, so that there in the dark room, with only a little light coming in from the hall, she could hardly see it.

As she turned to go, she bumped into the end table. Something fell – one of her mom's lighters. Maggie slid the gun into the back of her pants, like she'd seen cops do on TV, and picked up the lighter. She spun the little ridged wheel with her thumb. Flame lit up the room. In that instant, she knew what Tiffanee would do. It was almost spooky, that she would think of Tiffanee, and now this. Like Tiffanee was sending her a message. For a second, she imagined the guy out cold on the floor while the fire raged all around him.

No. She wasn't like Tiffanee. She didn't want to destroy everything. She let the flame go out.

Maggie went to the big window and looked down the lane, then across the yard. When she saw the shed, almost invisible in the dark, she suddenly had a plan. She took the gun in her hand again, weighed it. She'd use the shed. Set a trap and wait. She opened the curtain wide.

63

Wheeler looked at AJ, the cell phone to his ear. "I"m still on hold with the main desk. We should just head over to the emergency entrance. We'll get answers faster than whoever's got me on hold."

"Okay." AJ switched on the light bar. He was just about to start the U-turn when his cell phone rang. He dug it out of his pocket. "Hello."

"Officer Bugbee?"

"Yes."

"This is Ramone Smith, from the flower shop? That girl that Ash mentioned – I remembered her name. It's Magda."

AJ's jaw stiffened.

"That's it," Ramone said. "I just thought I should call."

"Thanks, Ramone." AJ let the phone drop. "That was Ramone. The name of Ash's siren? Magda."

"Maggie Strang," Wheeler said. "Jeez." He turned away suddenly, holding the phone a little closer to his mouth. "Yes, hello. This is Detective Wheeler."

As Wheeler talked, AJ pulled back onto the road and hit the gas. Wheeler gave him a look but kept up the conversation with the hospital. After a moment, Wheeler put his cell phone down. "I spoke to a nurse. Parker's mom and dad are there – no other family. No Ash. But you must have already known that, since we're not heading that way. Where are we headed?"

"The Strangs' trailer."

"Worth a try, but it's a Saturday night. Maggie could be anywhere.

Ash could be anywhere."

"We need to go to the trailer. You've got to trust me on this."

"What is it, another hunch? Instinct?"

"More like a tip."

"A tip? From who?"

AJ kept his eyes on the road, which came at them fast. "Ben."

"Ben who?"

"Shortman."

"Shortman? When? How?" Wheeler turned as if to check the back seat.

"I had a dream a few days ago." AJ kept looking straight ahead. "Ben was in it."

"So a ghost in a dream told you to go to Maggie's trailer."

"Yeah."

Wheeler stared hard at AJ, then faced the windshield again. "Works for me."

64

It seemed like she'd been in the shed forever, with the door cracked, looking out at the yard and the trailer. Waiting. There was nothing to see – just darkness and the glow of her own windows – so she listened. She tried so hard to hear every sound that after a while it was like her ears were making things up that weren't there – clicks and squeaks and rustling. Sometimes she'd swear she heard her name – her mom, back from the booze cruise, saying her name. Sometimes it was like the gun she was holding had its own hum, its own heartbeat.

If her parents came home now, how would she explain to them about being in the shed with the gun? But there was no sign of anyone. She had a good view across the front yard and down the hill. Inside the trailer, she could see straight through her parents' window, past the kitchen, all the way into the living room. She could see the television that she'd left on. The bait.

Her parents might come home any minute. Her dad had said it could be a late night, but wasn't this already late for him? He didn't party like her mom. The next car she heard could be them.

There was a sound. A crunch of gravel. Maggie stopped breathing. The sound again. Not tires, footsteps. Someone walking carefully. She shifted to see the lane better. A man was walking up the hill. She couldn't see his face. He was just a dark shape. Moving steadily. Going straight for her trailer.

Maggie tried to stay absolutely still, even though every muscle was screaming. Her hand squeezed the gun so hard that it felt like the knuckles might pop.

The guy kept coming, right up to the edge of the porch light. He stopped, in the shadow. If you looked out from the living room, you wouldn't even know that he was there. He stood there, his hands at his sides, like he was totally relaxed, like everything was totally normal, just staring at her trailer.

Maggie's body told her *move! yell! shoot!* She had to fight it. She had to wait until the right moment. But when? How would she know the right time? She could be like the deer that waits, waits, waits in the trees and then jumps right into a car.

The guy stood there so long she thought maybe he was going to just turn around and go back down the hill. Then he took a step toward her.

She raised the gun, tried to point it. Her hand danced around in the air, wild, like she'd grabbed a snake.

He was in the light. She could see his face. The face she'd seen outside the dollar store, and at the Bay Market and then in front of her trailer, when Parker was driving. Ash.

He was coming toward her. She tried to get her hand under control. Any second now she was going to have to shift her finger to the trigger.

He was sticking close to the trailer. Not looking at the shed at all. He was headed around the corner, toward the back. And that's what he did – he went right on past, never noticing that the shed door was cracked, never even looking her way. When he was out of sight she took a deep breath. She tried to make her hand obey, to act like a normal hand. But the gun bounced in front of her.

She looked into the trailer again, waiting for him to find the back door. Suddenly he was in the living room. Walking around, careful. She could tell from the way he moved that he wasn't making any noise, that even if she was in the room with him, she wouldn't hear a thing. He picked something up from the sofa – a stuffed animal. She could see the oversized tag on the ear. He was holding the thing close to his face, like he was smelling it. He crossed in front of the TV, went partway into the hall. Far enough to see the rest of her trap – the door to the bathroom closed, the light coming from underneath, so he'd know she was home alone and just had to pee.

He went back into the kitchen, crouched down behind the counter. Waiting for her to come out, settle down in front of the TV again. Waiting to jump.

Maybe she should just let him wait. Forget the plan. Stay here, stay safe. Let him do whatever he wanted to do in the empty trailer.

No. After a while, when she didn't come out of the bathroom, he'd go looking for her. If not tonight, tomorrow. Anyway, her plan was working. She just needed to finish it. Get into position. When he came out, shoot him.

She pushed the door, told herself that the squeal only seemed loud, that really it was just a whisper. She checked the yard, then ran, crouching down the whole time, first to the one tree, then to her car. She peeked over the hood. Her heart was beating so hard it hurt, like it was suddenly stiff and sharp. She held the gun in front of her. It had seemed light, when she first lifted it from behind the mattress, but now the thing was like lead.

From here, she could see through the big picture window into the living room. No sign of him. He was still hiding behind the kitchen counter.

Something was different about the light. There was the flicker from the television, but now there was yellow, too. It was fire! The curtains were on fire! Jesus, he was going to burn the place, like he did Taylor's and Ms. Addison's!

He was at the window, swinging a pillow at the flames. Then a ball of it – a round, orange burning ball, flew past him, and he came bursting out the front door.

She'd been so focused on what she saw through the window that she'd forgotten to stay down behind the car, had forgotten to keep the gun up. She was just standing there.

Ash stared across the yard at her. "What the hell was that?" He glanced behind him.

Maggie raised the gun.

All of a sudden Ash looked calm again, like seeing her with the gun did the opposite of what it was supposed to do – it made him relax. "Really, Maggie? A gun?" He moved toward her.

Maggie tried to steady her aim. She was going to shoot him in the chest. The chest was the best target. The head – too easy to miss. This was going just like her plan. If she could only keep the gun steady enough for one goddamn second.

He was already at the car, already coming around it.

"Stop." She shouldn't be talking, she should be shooting. *Shoot*

355

him!

He kept coming.

She took a step back, stumbled a little.

He lunged. Grabbed the gun by the barrel. Took it out of her hands like it was a baton in a relay race, like what she wanted more than anything was to hand it over. Then he smacked her across the face. She fell back against the car and ended up on the ground, on her back looking up at him. There was no breath anywhere in her chest.

He looked down at her. "When I first saw you, I thought you were different, Maggie. Special. There was something hurt, wounded, about you. I saw it that very first time outside the dollar store. I couldn't resist." He shook his head. "Then you led me to the others, and I thought that you were like me. We were a team. We were a pack." He leaned close with those yellow eyes. "But then you had to get involved with my brother. Poor, sweet, Parker."

Her lungs suddenly sucked in air. She kicked hard, hit his shin. She tried to slide under the car. His foot came down on her leg. She screamed.

"No more of that, Maggie. No more leading. It's time to be submissive." He bent down and put a hand over her mouth, then touched the gun to her chin. "Understand?"

Ash yanked her to her feet. Maggie let herself dangle, made him hold her weight. She heard the sound of a car. Maybe it was coming up the hill. Her parents, coming home, coming to save her. But when she looked down the lane there were no headlights. No one was coming.

65

As AJ made the turn into the trailer park, he cut the headlights. "Go slow," Wheeler said.

They crept up the hill, AJ barely touching the gas. Still the gravel crackled under the treads. The glow of a quarter moon was enough for AJ to stay on the narrow lane. The side streets and the compact yards were still. Lamps glowed in a few windows, but their car was the only thing moving.

Their destination was at the top, the far end, as close to private as you could get in this place. They rolled upward. They were almost to the Strang's trailer before they saw the flame in the big living room window. Then, something moving. Outside. A figure in the yard. AJ reached for the switch, threw it.

The high beams found Maggie, to one side of the trailer. She was struggling, her feet kicking in the air. Behind her was a man, his arm across her chest, dragging her backward into darkness.

AJ and Wheeler threw the doors open. Their guns were on target the instant their soles hit the ground.

"Stop!" AJ yelled.

With Maggie as his shield, the man was safe and he knew it. He looked straight at AJ, then Wheeler, and went on dragging the girl away.

A muffled explosion came from inside the trailer, then a flash, like an aerosol can going up. The man hesitated but kept his grip on his captive. For the first time, he showed the weapon in his hand.

"Ash," Wheeler said, "put the gun down."

Ash wrapped his arm tighter across Maggie's chest, lifted her higher. He touched the gun to her ear.

Boom! Something else went up inside. The screen door flew open, violently, banging against the wall. They all turned to the sound, saw the rush of flame that followed it. AJ saw something more. Gliding through the blaze was Taylor Fraser. The fire roared and snapped all around her but could not touch her.

"You need to let Maggie go," Wheeler said. "Drop the gun. Now."

"You drop your gun, or I'll put a bullet in her head." Ash tapped Maggie's ear with the barrel.

The fire was throwing heat now. Acrid and angry, it scampered up the wall, licked at the roof.

Taylor glided across the yard. She stayed close to the house, taking a direct line, paying no attention to the two cops with their pistols drawn and ready. When she reached the glare of the headlights, her glow was overwhelmed, so that she almost could have been a girl, an ordinary if beautiful living girl, dressed for an ordinary summer night. She kept moving.

AJ let one hand fall from his gun. He pulled the iron finial from his pocket, weighed the thing, as if considering his aim.

"AJ," Wheeler said, softly. "Focus."

AJ slipped the finial back into his pocket and raised his hand to the gun again. "Don't make things worse, Ash," he said. "You already have Taylor and Helena Fraser's murders on your head. Let Maggie go."

"Yeah? Or what?" Ash laughed.

Taylor closed in. There was ferocity in her eyes, and something new. Determination. Purpose.

"Just let her go," AJ said.

As if released by AJ's voice, Taylor shot forward.

"Maggie!" AJ yelled. "Move! Now!"

Taylor crashed into her target. Staggering backward, Ash lost his grip on Maggie. She fell, scrambled to Wheeler and got behind him. Taylor was nowhere in sight. Ash stood alone in the glare of the fire and the headlights, not looking at the cops, not looking at Maggie. Instead, he stared at the gun in his hand. The gun turned.

"Ash!" AJ said. "No!"

"Drop the weapon," Wheeler said.

Ash's hand curled, his arm bending slowly, as if it were a fight.

"Stop!" AJ said.

The gun came to rest at Ash's temple.

"No," Wheeler said. "Don't do it, Ash."

"It's not Ash," AJ said. "He's not in control."

Wheeler glanced at AJ, then faced forward again.

Ash's eyes were wide open. Yellow. Terrified.

The pistol fired. Ash fell.

Where he had been, Taylor now stood, as if Ash had dropped from her like a heavy coat. She looked at AJ, triumphant, radiant. Then she drifted back into the shadows. She flickered, faded and was gone.

A siren howled in the distance.

Wheeler reached for Maggie. "It's okay. It's over."

She only nodded, clenching her fists.

As Wheeler put his arm around the girl, as the siren closed in, AJ stayed there, staring into the darkness.

66

AJ sat at a picnic table in the little patch of grass outside the Bay Market. It was the dead middle of the afternoon – only one other table was occupied. Even the seagulls had somewhere else to be. Dressed in jeans and a T-shirt, AJ nursed a tall cup of ice tea and looked across the scratchy ground, his eyes focusing nowhere in particular. A car took a spot near the building. As the chief got out, Wheeler's sedan pulled in next to him. AJ waved the men over.

Chief Brown let out a slight groan as he slid onto the bench.

"Lunch is on the house," AJ said. "What would you guys like?"

"Just an ice tea for me," the chief said. "I ate at my desk."

"I could have a clam roll," Wheeler said. "And ice tea sounds good."

AJ went inside. A few minutes later, he was back with the drinks. "So Thompson is gone?"

"Yeah," Wheeler said, "finally. Now that they got a break on the drugs, all the fun's going to be elsewhere. Closer to Hartford, mostly, but Rhode Island, too. He won't be back here."

The chief squeaked his straw through the lid. "I *hope* he's gone for good. He knows we weren't completely straight with him."

"With all due respect, Chief," Wheeler said. "If you want to use AJ's...insights on the job, you can't complain about a patched-up report."

The chief gave him a look, then faced Route 1. They were all silent for a moment.

June Bugbee came out from the building with a tray. "Here you go, Sam," she said. "And some extra fries for you two." She set a bowl between AJ and the chief. "AJ, what night did you want the food? Saturday?"

"Yeah. Around six, six-thirty?"

"That would be fine." June watched a single gull swoop over the tables and land on the far side. "I just can't believe it's already been a year since we lost Ben." She clasped her hands. "Well, let me know if you need anything else."

"Thanks, Mom."

"Delicious, as always," Wheeler said, finishing his first bite.

June smiled and went back across the grass.

"That year did go quickly," the chief said.

"Saturday is the anniversary," AJ said. "We're having a little get-together. We thought it would help us all get through. DaSilva especially."

The chief nodded without saying anything.

"You know," AJ said after a while, "everything in that report was true."

"That's right," Wheeler said. "Melody Johnson called attention to Ash Beaudette. In the process of checking him out, we got a solid lead from Ramone Smith that connected Beaudette to Maggie Strang. So, we went directly to her trailer. It just happened that we got there in the nick of time. All in all, it was a typical combination of police work, good instincts and dumb luck."

"Yeah, I read the report." The chief grabbed a couple of fries. "Don't think Thompson doesn't have his own instinct. Don't think something isn't tingling on his radar. And I don't like being on Thompson's radar."

The chief focused on the fries for a while. "At least all of our follow-up confirmed Baudette as the guy. His little collection of trophies from the victims – the antique lighter from the Fraser house and the old-fashioned sextant that belonged to Addison."

"Don't forget the broken headlight," AJ said. "His parents said he came home with that the night Taylor was killed. It's circumstantial, but it fits with the headlight glass I found, and suggests that he was in the vicinity of the Fraser house that night. He probably hit the deer heading to 95 after the murder."

Wheeler dipped a clam in the tarter sauce on his plate. "Maggie Strang saying she remembers seeing Beaudette parked near the school a couple of weeks ago. That's where he saw Taylor and Addison – maybe even saw them together. Picked them out as his first targets."

"That still bothers me," the chief said. "Maggie didn't mention seeing Beaudette when you interviewed her that first time."

"It doesn't surprise me," Wheeler said. "The questions we asked were focused on her relationship with Taylor." He wiped batter from his fingers. "With Beaudette dead, we won't be involved with a murder trial. Thompson will be chasing the drugs. He won't have time to give us a second thought."

The chief nodded, looking unconvinced. "You saved Maggie Strang and whoever would have come next. That's what's important."

They talked for a minute about the two murder victims, and then about the other lives that had been turned upside-down – whole families, the high school, even the navy base.

The chief reached into the bowl one last time, took the two remaining fries. "We made short work of those, didn't we?"

"What do you mean *we?*" AJ said.

Wheeler laughed. "You know, Chief, I think I'll accept your offer to take the rest of the afternoon off."

"Sure. Put your feet up. I've got one more interview with *The Day*. Then I hope that's done."

"Okay, then," Wheeler said. "I'll leave you guys to talk about AJ making detective."

The chief let that go. He watched Wheeler get into his car, then looked down at the table, silent.

"Something else bothering you, Chief?" AJ said.

"Maggie Strang. Her story about that night – seeing a stranger coming through the front door, getting the gun from her parents' bedroom, chasing Ash out of the trailer, then him getting the drop on her. I don't know, I feel like there's something... It's probably just the way she comes across. A little off."

"I know what you mean about her. She's odd, for sure. But I buy the story. She was sick of being the victim, I guess."

The chief rubbed his smooth scalp. "Do you know how Parker's doing?"

"I guess health-wise, he's fine. He's been out of the hospital for a while. The other part of it – emotionally – I don't know."

"Is he coming back to work here?"

"Mom says he'll be back next week. She took some food to the family yesterday. I guess Parker's mom still seemed like she was in shock."

"There's got to be an awful lot of guilt there. The stepfather, when he said that he took a transfer partly because of Ash, because of the trouble with the neighbors – their fight over whether Ash killed their dog... I could see what was going through the man's head." The chief let out a breath. "He didn't want to believe it. But now..."

"No one wants to see evil in someone they care about."

"Yeah." The chief sipped at his ice tea, then removed the lid and probed the ice with his straw. "You and Wheeler did okay together."

"Yeah, we did."

"He didn't bat an eye when you told us what really happened to Ash. I think I had a harder time believing Taylor took control of his body than Wheeler did."

"Wheeler was there, Chief. He couldn't see Taylor, but he could see Ash. The look on Ash's face... Wheeler was great. He kept me focused."

"I told you, he just needed to see some results from what you do."

"What I do." AJ let that sit for a while.

The chief raised his cup and drained it. He stood. "Todesco is going to hold down the fort for a few days. I want some uninterrupted time with my granddaughter. She came home yesterday."

"She's doing okay?"

"She's doing great. I told you, she's tough." The chief was halfway to his car when he turned around. "You know, no one else on the force would have arrived at that trailer in time to save Maggie Strang. Thanks to you, not only is that girl alive, she has a future worth looking forward to."

AJ watched the chief walk away, moving slowly, weariness in his every step. Then he tipped his head back and shut his eyes, let the sun warm his face for a second. "Thanks to you, Ben," he said. "Thanks to you, too."

67

"Hello!" AJ backed through the door carrying a foil-covered dish. A plastic bag hung from his arm. Sela followed right behind, a six-pack in each hand and a third balanced on one cocked elbow.

"Here, Dave, let me help you with that," Claire said, coming out from the kitchen. She took a six-pack and led the way down the hall.

AJ set the dish on the stove. As he turned on the oven, Claire lifted a corner of the foil. "So this is June Bugbee's famous lobster mac and cheese?" she said.

"Yep," Sela said. "Ben's favorite."

AJ began unpacking the plastic bag. "Drop biscuits and baked beans. Also my mom's, also Ben's favorites."

"Let me get a pot for the beans," Claire said. "Where's DaSilva?"

AJ slid the casserole into the oven. "He's getting the dessert."

"I thought you were bringing him."

Sela raised his eyebrows but said nothing.

"He'll be here," AJ said.

There was the chime of the doorbell, then the swish of the front door swinging open, and Melody's voice. "Hi!"

"Come on back!" Claire said.

Melody and Jack joined the others. Melody put two bottles on the counter. "Something from the Westbury cellar."

Jack placed a bottle of sparkling water next to the wine. "And something for Melody."

"That doesn't seem fair," Claire said.

"It's okay," Melody said. "You can drink my share of the wine and

I'll eat your share of dessert."

"We were just talking about dessert," Claire said. "DaSilva is supposed to be getting it." She gave AJ a look.

"Is something wrong?" Melody said.

"I'm afraid he won't show," Claire said.

"Why wouldn't he?" Melody said. "Never mind the dessert – Dave needs to be here. Of all of us, he has to be here tonight, to celebrate Ben."

"He's been kinda down," Sela said. "He only made it to work one day this week."

"So the anniversary is hitting him hard," Melody said.

"I don't think the anniversary is the whole story," Sela said, "but I don't know. He's not talking. AJ, you need to talk to him. You're the only one who understands it all."

"I'll try," AJ said.

The doorbell chimed again.

"That's got to be him," Claire said, moving toward the door. She let DaSilva, carrying a large cake box, into the front hall, then planted a kiss on his cheek.

He grinned. "I'll have to bring cake more often."

They got drinks and moved to the porch. Melody took a seat by the screen. Next to her, on a small table, was a wooden box. She reached into it and took out a heavy, rough nail. "So you'll be putting all of the iron away?"

"AJ said it was safe," Claire said "I vacuumed up the salt already. Before you leave, you should pick out any pieces that you want. I've got enough here to decorate a dozen houses."

"Maybe a flatiron. A souvenir of our latest adventure."

Inside, the oven timer went off. They all filed into the kitchen and filled their plates.

When they were seated at the table, Sela raised his beer. "Ben, wherever you are, we miss you."

"To Ben," Melody said.

They clinked bottles and glasses.

"I can't believe it's been a year," Claire said.

"To the day," DaSilva said. He checked his watch. "Almost to the hour."

"A lot has happened since that night," Jack said. "AJ, I'm sure you never expected to solve two multiple murder cases in your first twelve months back in Stonington."

"You're right about that." AJ looked into his beer. "I couldn't have done any of it without Ben."

"Did I miss something?" Jack said. "How did Ben help with the most recent case?"

AJ took a long drink before answering. "I had a couple of dreams about him. They helped me make some important connections."

"Tell us about the dreams," Melody said, leaning across the table.

AJ gave a quick rundown – the deer by the cemetery, the spider in the jar, the fireplace, Ben pointing out the wolf running past the trailer park.

"Wow," Melody said. "So he's still out there? Watching us, communicating with us? With you, anyway."

"Not just him," DaSilva said. "He's been in my dreams, too."

"Of course, it doesn't have to be anything paranormal," Jack said. "You both were close to Ben. It's natural that you would be thinking about him, and dreaming about him, as we got close to this date. Whatever clues you picked up, AJ – couldn't they just be intuition?"

"That's what it says in the police report," AJ said. "Maybe it's even true."

***

"Dave brought this from the Honey B Dairy," Melody said, as a slice of cake was placed in front of her. "I miss their food so much – it almost makes me want to take my old job back."

"We could just eat there once in a while," Jack said.

"Yeah, maybe that's a better plan."

Sela sat down with his piece. "If Ben was here, we'd need a second cake."

"He could eat," AJ said.

"He loved his Honey B milkshakes," Melody said. "He was the only customer I ever had who ordered two at a time."

More stories followed – Ben's epic consumption at the Bay Market's staff pig-outs, unsuccessful ghost hunts with Mystic Afterlife, his unending pursuit of Melody.

"He certainly had good taste in women," Jack said, putting an arm around Melody. "I'm sorry I never got to know him."

"Me, too," Claire said. "Especially since I owe him so much."

"I guess in some way we all do," Jack said.

"That definitely includes me," AJ said. "I owe him for the other one-year anniversary we're celebrating." He turned to Claire. "To Ben, the matchmaker."

There was applause. Buck, the big greyhound, as if he had his own story to tell, approached the table and squeezed in next to AJ, his dark eyes looking across the table.

"You remember Ben, don't you boy," DaSilva said. "You knew about him coming back before any of us. Except AJ."

AJ scratched the dog on the flank and Buck leaned into him, yawning.

When the cake was gone, the glasses and coffee cups empty, Claire stood up and offered more.

"I think I need to get ready to head home," Melody said. "I get tired easily these days."

"Let's get that flatiron for you, then. Or whatever you want." Claire picked up the box. "I'll collect as we go."

They worked their way toward the front of the house. In the living room, Claire retrieved a short section of heavy chain from the windowsill. Melody stood nearby, weighing a flatiron in her hand. "That was pretty nice, what AJ said."

"It was."

"I don't think he gives a lot of toasts, so... Do you feel the same way? I mean, even with all the..." Melody hesitated. "With everything that you've been through in the past year."

Claire's looked at the links in her palm. From the kitchen, there was Sela's voice, then AJ's, then laughter. Claire smiled. "Yeah, I feel the same." She closed her hand. "It has been quite an exciting year."

Melody touched her belly. "And there's more excitement on the way."

"That is for sure."

After Jack and Melody left for home, AJ and Claire returned to the kitchen. AJ stuck his head out into the porch, where the Daves sat in silence.

"You guys want another beer?" AJ said.

"Yeah, that'd be great."

"Sure."

AJ looked back at Claire and smiled sheepishly. She came to him and gave him a hug. He held her, feeling her warmth, breathing deep.

"Do you want some wine?" he said, pulling back.

"I might take a glass upstairs, do a little reading. Would you mind? It would give the three of you some time." Claire poured her drink, then headed upstairs, taking the dog with her. A chill in the air sent AJ and the Daves into the living room

Sela settled into the couch. "I think we'd left the hospital by now."

DaSilva checked his watch. "I'm not sure. That night is kind of a blur for me."

"Sorry," Sela said. "We don't need to relive that."

"Remember when we first discovered that you could see ghosts, AJ?" DaSilva said.

AJ smiled. "That pitcher."

"And we were so pissed at you for not telling us sooner."

"Yes, you were."

"Not half as mad as Claire was," Sela said. He sank back into the cushion, his eyes half closed.

"Claire's okay about it now, right?" DaSilva said. "All this ghost stuff?"

"She's getting there," AJ said.

It was quiet for a long time.

"You think that was him," DaSilva said. "Those dreams we had? That was him, communicating with us, right?"

"Yeah, I think it was," AJ said.

"How did he know all of that? About the deer and the submarine and the wolf?"

"I have no idea. I don't know if I even want to know."

"It's kind of freaky." DaSilva looked down at the floor for a while. "You think he'll come back someday?"

"I wondered that, too." AJ turned the bottle in his hands. "I sort of think if he could come back he would have already. I mean, he had something important to tell us. Why communicate through dreams if you can just have a conversation?"

"I guess you're right. You could just talk to him, before? Just like we're talking."

AJ nodded.

A snuffling sound came from the end of the couch. Sela's head tipped back.

"He's out," AJ said.

He and DaSilva finished their beers.

"How about you, Dave?" AJ said. "Are you okay with it? This

ability you have now?"

"Yeah. No. Not really."

"I can't say you ever get used to it, but you will learn to live with it."

DaSilva shook his head. "Honestly, AJ, I'm not sure I still have the ability. For a while after Taylor hit me, I felt different. Weird. Now, I don't. I feel..."

"Normal."

"Not even normal. More like, closed off."

"Do you want to test it? We could go back to the cemetery."

"No. Not tonight, anyway."

There was a faint, metallic clatter from the back of the house.

"Did you hear that?" AJ said.

"I didn't hear anything."

They sat listening for a second.

"Could I have some coffee?" DaSilva said. "Then I'll take Sleeping Beauty home."

"Okay, sure. I'll get it for you."

"That's all right. I know where everything is."

DaSilva took the empty bottles and headed for the kitchen. AJ stayed seated, his eyelids heavy. The microwave beeped, and DaSilva returned with a mug. He snapped the fingers of his other hand, sending a bottle cap zipping across the room. AJ bent to pick it up.

"Sorry," DaSilva said. "It was on the floor in the kitchen."

AJ studied the bottle cap, then glanced toward the back of the house.

DaSilva sat down with his coffee. They talked about plans for the summer, including the Alaska cruise that AJ's parents had announced they were taking.

"That doesn't sound like fun to me," DaSilva said. "We just got rid of the snow. I don't need to visit it."

When the coffee was gone, DaSilva woke Sela and they took off for the little cottage by the water that had been AJ's home, before Claire. Back in the living room, AJ grabbed the empty coffee mug. He picked up the bottle cap, then went into the kitchen.

Ben Shortman, tattooed and T-shirted, glowing dimly, was there by the table.

Head down, AJ got as far as the counter without seeing. He put the mug in the sink. He turned around, flipping the bottle cap in his hand. At last he looked up.

"Hey, AJ!" Ben said.

AJ flinched and the bottle cap fell. It spun noisily across the tile.

With his foot, Ben reached out and slapped it still. "Nice party," he said. "Sorry I couldn't join you, but with all that ghost-proofing, I couldn't find a way in. I have to thank Claire for picking that stuff up."

Ben waited there with a big smile. Upstairs, the greyhound barked behind a closed door. AJ still hadn't said a word.

Janis Bogue, a native of Stonington, and William Keller, are married and have two daughters. They live in Woodstock, New York, where they are hard at work on the third AJ Bugbee mystery. You can see what else they are up to on Facebook at
https://www.facebook.com/authorJanisBogueandWilliamKeller

64945399R00215

Made
Mic
02